*The Waiting Sands*

AND

*The Devil on Lammas Night*

# SUSAN HOWATCH

---

## *The Waiting Sands*
### AND
## *The Devil*
## *on Lammas Night*

STEIN AND DAY / *Publishers* / New York

THE WAITING SANDS

THE DEVIL ON LAMMAS NIGHT

# The Waiting Sands

# *Prologue*

There were still times when Rachel thought of Daniel. She would think of him at the height of summer when the city sweltered beneath the hazy summer skies to bring back memories of another land where the sun was cool and the sea breathed white mist over remote shores. She would think of him sometimes at night when she awoke for no reason and sat up listening to the restless city around her, the city so many thousand miles from the past she had no wish to remember. She would think of him when the other girls in the apartment talked of love and romance and happy endings, and she would say to herself how strange it was that she should think of him so often when she knew for certain now that she had never loved him.

She had not always lived in New York, but now she had been there nearly five years. Her home was in England, in Surrey not far from London; she was the only child of an elderly Anglican parson and his wife, and for the first twenty-two years of her life she had moved in the orderly, old-fashioned circles of the world of the country vicarage. She had gone to a local day school, pro-

gressed from there to secretarial college where she had acquired
the necessary skills without undue difficulty, and then had gone
abroad to Geneva for six months. On her return, she had begun
to earn her living in London.

It had all been typical, a career duplicated by a great many other
girls. She had several good friends, was happy at home, enjoyed
tennis on weekends during the summer, and in general was perfectly content with her life; certainly if anyone had ever suggested
to her then that she would alter her entire circumstances radically
by emigrating to a foreign country she would have been astonished
and then indignant that anyone could suggest such a thing.

The only extraordinary and unusual element in her otherwise
normal existence was her relationship with her friend Rohan
Quist.

It seemed to her often that Rohan had been the most consistent
thread in her life, his presence flickering across the pattern of the
years like quicksilver darting over shifting sands. For Rohan had
always been there. He had shared her past and she shared his. She
could remember clinging to the bars of her playpen while he had
ridden his tricycle up and down the driveway to show off to her
that he was free and mobile while she was still behind the bars of
infancy. But later he had taught her to ride the tricycle, led her
hand in hand to kindergarten, drawn her into all the intricate
games of childhood, the societies, the sworn oaths, the pacts which
led to adventure. "And nobody's to say Rachel's too young," he
had shouted to his adherents in the pack he led. "Because she's
my friend!" She could see him now, eight years old, thin and wiry
with thick straw-colored hair and enormous blazing gray eyes.

Rachel's my friend. . . .

And Rohan was good to his friends. Long afterward when they
were grown up it was he who would provide an escort whenever
she wanted to go out, he who had the little red Volkswagen to take
her on weekend drives into the country, he who had invited her
to the May Ball at Cambridge where she had met a whole host of
eligible young men. "We'll say we're cousins," he had ordered au-
thoritatively. "Then no one will get the idea that I have any pos-

sessive rights over you." And no one had. She had danced the night away and drunk a little too much Heidsieck '59, and after breakfast at dawn in Grantchester when she was quite exhausted, Rohan had materialized from a punt on the river and had ferried her safely back to town.

There had been quarrels, of course, times when they were not on speaking terms. Rohan was an emotional extrovert who preferred to give vent to his grievances in a splendid display of rhetoric, and Rachel, who had more of an Anglo-Saxon temperament, found such exhibitions annoying. But the moods passed; the words were forgotten, and soon they were picking up the threads of their friendship as if nothing had happened and life continued as usual.

But they were getting older, and Rohan's grievances in a certain direction were becoming more acute.

"It's all very well," he had said crossly, "but I'm always the one who makes the effort. I'm the one who takes you around and introduces you to all the good-looking men. What do you ever do for me? When have you ever introduced me to a pretty girl? When? Just answer me that!"

"That's not fair!" Rachel had retorted, rising to an argument with spirit. "What about all my school friends? I constantly introduced them to you!"

"Hardly my type, were they? I mean, seriously—"

"Helen's very pretty!"

"But poor Helen," Rohan had said in the tired voice he used when he wanted to annoy her. "Absolutely no sex appeal."

"How the hell am I to know how you define the term sex appeal?"

"No swearing, please. I always hate to hear women swear."

"You're impossible!" Rachel had blazed. "Quite impossible!" But she had felt guilty all the same. And then when she had gone abroad to study French for six months she had met Decima in Geneva, and Decima was very different from the kinds of girls Rachel had known at school.

When the six months had come to an end, Rachel and Decima

had returned to England together and Rachel had introduced her new friend to Rohan at the earliest opportunity. Decima was staying with Rachel for a few days before returning to her home in Scotland; the three of them had planned an exciting weekend together before her departure. "We'll have a grand time," Rohan had said, jaw stuck out to show his aggressive determination to enjoy life to the full. "My cousin Charles is coming down from Oxford and we'll make up a foursome. You remember Charles, the professor in medieval history, don't you, Rachel? He would do very nicely for you—you're always saying how you like older men. . . . Yes, that would be a good foursome. You and Charles, Decima and me. . . ."

Decima and Charles had married less than four months later. After the engagement was announced, all Rohan had said was: "It's just as well. She wasn't really my type—much more suitable for Charles, and I'm sure they'll be very happy. . . . I wonder if they'll live at Oxford all year round? Charles used to spend the university vacations in Edinburgh."

And Rachel had said: "Maybe they'll stay at Roshven."

Roshven . . . Rachel had never been there, but Decima had talked so often of her home that Rachel had evolved a clear picture in her mind of the house to which no road led, its gray walls imprisoned between the mountains and the sea, the savage coast of western Scotland, remote, vast, and unmarked by time. She had thought on more than one occasion how nice it would be to visit Decima there.

But Decima and Charles had been married well over two years before an invitation came, and long before then Rachel had resigned herself to the fact that she would never be invited, since Decima had not bothered to keep in touch with her and their correspondence had soon lapsed. Rohan thought nothing of inviting himself to Roshven now and then for a few days of fishing and shooting with his cousin Charles, and couldn't understand why Rachel did not merely arrive on Decima's doorstep, but Rachel was proud; if Decima wanted to see her, then Decima should write and ask her to come. Until then Rachel had no intention of turning up where she was apparently not wanted.

Then, finally, after two years, the invitation arrived out of the blue, and the chance came for Rachel to visit Roshven at last. It was late summer; Rachel had just come back from a holiday in Florence and happened to be between jobs, so the invitation could hardly have come at a better time.

The postmark was Kyle of Lochalsh, the handwriting unquestionably Decima's. Rachel ripped open the envelope with a pleasant feeling of anticipation and eagerly began to read the letter inside, but a second later bewilderment had displaced her eagerness, and presently even the bewilderment had vanished, leaving her feeling both uneasy and disturbed.

"Dearest Raye," Decima had written, "I'm so terribly sorry I've been such a hopeless correspondent, and please don't think just because I've not written much that I never think of you. I have thought of you so much, especially when it's seemed that there's no one I can turn to, and I'm writing to ask if you can possibly come up to Roshven for a few days. My twenty-first birthday falls next Sunday, and it would be such a relief if you could stay until after the celebration dinner party which Charles is giving for me on Saturday night. Please come, Raye. I may be behaving very stupidly by panicking like this, but I would feel so much less frightened if I knew you were beside me at Roshven till after midnight on Saturday. I can't say any more than this now as I'm just about to leave for Kyle of Lochalsh to meet Rohan, but please, please come as soon as possible. I'll explain everything when I see you and meanwhile much love, Decima."

# 1
*Roshven*

# Chapter One

*i*

Shortly before the long-awaited invitation was sent, or even
thought of, Decima Mannering was sitting on the window seat of
her bedroom overlooking the ocean and thinking of her friend
Rachel. Rohan Quist was due to arrive that day at Roshven to begin two weeks' holiday, and Decima always thought of Rachel
whenever Rohan was due. The two seemed to be inseparable in
her mind; it was as if they were husband and wife, she thought,
or, to describe the relationship more accurately, brother and sister.
It was odd how an unrelated man and woman could know one
another since infancy and yet never become sexually involved with
each other. It was not even as if it were a casual childhood friendship long since outgrown. They were nearly always together, almost inseparable, and yet it was quite evident there was no sexual
attachment of any kind uniting them. It was really most curious.
But then, remembering Rachel, one might perhaps conclude that
the situation was only to be expected. Rachel had such an un-

fortunate attitude where men were concerned; she either frightened them right away or else she desexed any possible relationship
by being apparently cold and withdrawn. There was some basic
inferiority complex, of course; she had to be constantly reassured
that a man was interested in her, and the need for reassurance
led her to set up impossibly high standards which any admirer
could not conceivably hope to attain. Or maybe there was no
inferiority complex and Rachel was simply old-fashioned, desiring
her various beaux to be pure knights in shining armor riding to
court her on spotless white chargers.

Poor Rachel. . . .

She could remember when she had first met Rachel in Geneva.
Rachel had worn a very English tweed suit which was a little too
big for her, and still wore her dark hair in braids coiled around the
top of her head. Quaint, Decima had thought. Pretty in a way. If
one liked that kind of thing.

It was odd how they had become such friends when they had
nothing whatsoever in common, but Decima had been lonely
and unhappy away from her father, and Rachel, separated from
her parents for the first time, was kinder and more sympathetic
than anyone else. Rachel's peaceful world of vicarage tea parties
and lawn tennis on weekends was such a different world from any
Decima had ever known. For Decima was a child of high society,
the daughter of a Scottish aristocrat and an Italian princess long
since divorced, and until the age of fourteen Decima, in the cus-
tody of her erratic, volatile mother, had been shuttled to and fro
across the continent and twice around the world while her mother
took part in the endless social whirl of the current international
set. And then her mother had died of an overdose of sleeping pills
taken incontinently after a surfeit of alcohol, and Decima had
been extricated from her cosmopolitan whirlpool and withdrawn
by her father to the west coast of Scotland.

Decima had loved Roshven from the first moment she had seen
it. Her father had worried in case she might hate to come to such
a backwater after the glamour of a dozen different cities, but to
Decima, saturated with the sophistication of city life, Roshven

was a fairy tale, a miraculous escape from that other world where she had been a forced onlooker at her mother's feverish pursuit of gaiety. She had loved it better than any place on earth.

Her father had been delighted by her marriage to Charles Mannering, an Oxford professor and author of two books on medieval history. He had liked Charles from the first, and had even added a clause to his will to specify that Charles should assist the trustees in administering Roshven for Decima if she inherited the estate while still underage. He even inserted a clause to say that if Decima died before her twenty-first birthday the estate should pass to her children, and if there were no children then title to the land should pass to Charles outright. But this was only to happen if Decima were to die before attaining her majority. Once she was twenty-one the trust ceased and the property became hers entirely to dispose of or retain as she wished. The house itself, being so remote, was in fact of little financial value, but the timber forests on the land were worth a small fortune and were leased to the Forestry Commission at an extremely profitable annual rate.

When her father died six months after her marriage, Decima found herself a wealthy heiress. She was nineteen at the time.

And now she was nearly twenty-one.

She sat for a long time on the window seat that morning and stared out over the dark sea as she considered her problems. The difficulties were quite clear in her mind. It was the task of solving them that was so hard. Surely there must be some perfectly simple solution which was staring her in the face. It was a pity Rohan could not help her, but he was after all Charles's cousin. Rohan. . . .

Rachel.

Decima was very still. If Rachel came, it might be the solution. Conventional, solid, dependable Rachel. It would be perfect. She had to come.

Moving swiftly over to the small secretary in one corner of the room, she found pen and paper and began to write in a small, neat, flowing hand.

*ii*

Charles Mannering was sitting in his study, which faced east to the mountains, and thinking of his wife. On his desk in front of him was a portrait of Decima on her wedding day, and after a while he took the frame in his hands and stared at the picture for a long time. It was hard to believe it was a mere two and a half years since he had first seen her. But then, it had been a very eventful two and a half years.

Leaning back in his chair he closed his eyes for a moment. He saw himself at thirty-six, a scholar highly regarded in intellectual circles, a  bachelor snugly ensconced in his rooms at Oxford. He had almost everything he wanted by then, success in his work, personal freedom, and a large circle of friends. It would have been entirely perfect, he had thought at the time, if he had had enough money to retire from teaching, which took up a good deal of his life, and to give him complete personal independence. He could have traveled, spent more time on research, had more time for writing books. But then, one could not expect life to be entirely perfect, and he had on the whole been very fortunate. It would have been wrong to complain.

And then he had gone down to London one weekend to stay with his cousins the Quists, and Rohan, with the air of a conjurer producing two white rabbits out of a top hat, had appeared triumphantly with two girls. He could remember vaguely seeing Rachel on a previous visit several years ago, but the other girl with her slanting blue eyes and silky black hair was unknown to him.

Of course she was absurdly young. It went without saying that a man of thirty-six would necessarily find a girl of eighteen a mere child. But after a few words with her he was struck with her sophistication and the knowledge that lay hidden in those slanting, watchful eyes. This girl was not as young as her years implied. There was something about her which was as old as time itself, and she knew it all too well.

Charles was fascinated, intrigued. He had always been attracted to older women before, and this was the first time he had felt even a remote interest in a woman so young.

When he was sure he had not the slightest chance of being refused, he asked her to sleep with him.

Never had he more badly miscalculated. For one most unpleasant moment he thought he had ruined all his chances with her, but presently she forgave him and seemed anxious to see more of him. But any deviation from conventional morality was quite out of the question. If that was all he was interested in, he could forget about her.

Charles, like most clever men, fancied himself as being irresistible to women when he put his mind to it, and his amour propre had suffered a severe blow. In fact it was so badly bruised that on his return to Oxford he found it difficult to concentrate on his work and was completely unable to write any more of his book on Richard *Coeur de Lion*. Presently he sent a letter to Roshven and received a charming reply inviting him up for the weekend. Charles was on the next plane to Inverness almost quicker than he could escape from his lecturing schedule.

He had liked Roshven. Hopelessly primitive, of course, and completely impracticable (imagine having no road connecting it to the nearest town!) but a good place for a holiday and ideal for working quietly on a book or doing concentrated research. Decima's father, only a few years older than he, seemed a nice chap. He was pleased because he had just renewed the lease of part of his land to the Forestry Commission and thus ensured a comfortable income for himself for the next few years. Useful things, trees. Timber was valuable these days. Since the coming of the Forestry Commission Roshven's value had increased from barely two thousand to well over one hundred thousand pounds. . . .

"I'm surprised you don't sell out," Charles had said, thinking that so much money could be much more sensibly invested—a villa on the Costa Brava, perhaps, or a house in the Canary Islands. "But then, of course," he had added adroitly, "it's your home and of great sentimental value to you."

"Exactly!" said Decima's father, pleased that his guest should have understood his sentiments so well. "Decima and I both feel the same way about that."

"I quite understand," said Charles, not understanding at all. "I agree with you absolutely."

Surely Decima could not really feel so attached to such a rambling, remote, ramshackle old house miles from anywhere! Decima with her background of international society, her education in Paris, Rome, and Geneva—it was inconceivable that she could ever want to cling to this little corner of western Scotland for any length of time. When she inherited the land she would no doubt change her mind about retaining it. . . .

But she hadn't. That was what was so extraordinary. He replaced the photograph of her carefully on his desk and looked out of the window again at the bleak mountainside and moor which stretched to the forestry plantation. "I'll never sell this," she had told him bluntly, "so you may as well forget about it. This is my home now and for all time."

"But it's so remote, Decima!" he had protested. "So cut off! A young woman like you should travel and meet interesting people and—"

"I had enough travel when I was a child to last me a lifetime," she had said, "and I'm tired of meeting so-called interesting people. God, I have enough boring social life stuck down at Oxford with you in termtime, don't I? After a few weeks of that it's a relief to get back here."

"I know you dislike the life at Oxford," he had said carefully. "God knows I'd be much happier if I didn't have to teach to supplement our income. But if I—you—were to sell Roshven we could have enough money to invest to enable me to retire and we could easily settle in another part of Scotland near here—"

And she had said in contempt: "I'm not selling Roshven just so that you can live on my money for the rest of your life."

It hurt even now to remember the tone of her voice. *I'm not selling Roshven so that you can live on my money.* As if he were a gigolo or an opportunist instead of a self-respecting Englishman with a great deal of pride.

Things had been very bad after that. They had gone for a whole week without speaking to one another, and he had been miserable, unable to write or read, unwilling even to go fishing up the burn. But she hadn't cared. She had gone riding every day over the moors, or taken brief swims in the icy sea when the sun shone a little warmer than usual, and when the time had come to order the month's provisions she had taken the boat alone into Kyle of Lochalsh to do the shopping.

He could remember her very clearly coming back from the town. She wore a dark blue sweater which reflected the blue of her eyes, and her dark hair was streaming behind her in the wind. He had never seen her look so beautiful or more hopelessly beyond his reach.

And then as he came down to the jetty to help her unload the provisions she spoke to him for the first time since their quarrel a week ago and said: "There's a letter for you. It's addressed in an exquisite Gothic handwriting and the postmark is Cambridge."

There was only one person who could be writing to him from Cambridge in a Gothic script. In the midst of his depression Charles was aware of pleasure, a quick pang of anticipation.

"Who is it from?" said Decima. "I've never seen such a remarkable handwriting."

"It's from a former student of mine," he said mechanically. "He went from Oxford on a scholarship to Cambridge to do post-graduate work; he's now making a study of the economic and social position of the monastic orders in England in the thirteenth century." And even as he spoke he was ripping open the envelope and unfolding the single sheet of paper within.

"My dear Charles," someone had written with elegant strokes of a pen dipped in black ink. "My sister and I will shortly be in Edinburgh for the Festival, and I wondered if there was any possibility of meeting you there? Alternatively, if you do not intend to go to the Festival this year, I would very much like to visit you; Rebecca and I plan to hire a car after the Festival and see a little of Scotland so it would be easy enough to drive up to Kyle of Lochalsh. If such a visit would inconvenience either you or your wife in any way, please don't hesitate to say so, but I would very much like to see you again and you always wrote such enthusiastic letters in praise of Roshven that I find myself more than anxious to go there. Hoping, therefore, to see you again in the near future, I remain etc. . . ."

Charles folded the letter and put it away in his wallet.

"What's his name?" said Decima casually. "Have I ever met him?"

"No," said Charles. "He left Oxford before I met you. His name is Daniel Carey."

That had been two months ago. The Careys had now been six weeks at Roshven and showed no sign of leaving.

Charles was still sitting in his study and thinking of the past when there was a soft knock on the door, and the next moment a young woman of about twenty-four was slipping into the room. She hesitated as she saw he was deep in thought, and then, as he looked across at her and smiled, she stepped forward toward him.

"Am I interrupting anything?"

"No," he said, still smiling. "Sit down and talk to me for a while. I was just wondering how I could write of King John's obsession with the young Isabella of Angoulême without giving the impression I was writing a medieval version of 'Lolita.' "

Rebecca laughed. "You're teasing me as usual!"

"Why do you say that?"

"Historians of your caliber aren't concerned with the sexual obsessions of middle-aged potentates."

Now it was his turn to laugh. "Yet this particular infatuation had widespread consequences. . . ." Really, he thought, looking at her, she was a most unusual girl. Possibly too intelligent for most men's tastes, but nonetheless attractive in a dark, fine-drawn, unusual way. . . . And it was pleasant for once to talk to a woman who was well aware that Isabella of Castile and Isabella of Angoulême were very far from being the same person.

For some reason he thought of his cousin. Perhaps Rohan would take a fancy to her. On the whole he hoped not. Rohan was much too much of an extroverted young philistine to appreciate the fine qualities of a woman such as Rebecca Carey.

"Have you seen Decima this morning?" he inquired. "I hope she hasn't forgotten that my cousin Rohan is arriving today."

"No, she was talking of going into Kyle of Lochalsh to meet him this afternoon. I understand she has some shopping to do."

"I see. And Daniel?"

"I believe he volunteered to go with her."

"I see," said Charles and idly began to picture how he would spend the long, peaceful afternoon at Roshven. . . .

### iii

When Rebecca left Charles she went upstairs to her room and flung herself face downward on the bed, her hands crushing the pillow fiercely and pulling it against her breast. Her whole body was trembling, alive with a million vibrations, and after a while she could lie still no longer but ran from her room and out of the house to the sea. The sun was warm; there was no one about, and if she had not seen the boat moored to the jetty she would have assumed Decima and Daniel had already set off for Kyle of Lochalsh. Charles was no doubt still in his study, which faced east over the mountains.

When she was about two hundred yards from the house she sank down behind a rock out of the wind and paused to regain her breath. For a moment she wondered whether to go swimming; the cold would be acute at first, she knew, but after a moment it would become more tolerable, and she loved fighting the high waves which pounded into surf on the deserted beach. She was just considering going back to the house for a towel and a bathing suit when she saw Daniel coming toward her across the sands.

Daniel was her only brother, and there were no sisters. Her parents had died soon after she was born; she could remember neither of them, only the cousins who had brought her up in Suffolk near Bury St. Edmunds. Consequently, because Daniel was the only close member of her family she had ever known, it was not surprising that she should have relied so much upon his companionship and derived such a sense of security from sharing his interests. As she had grown older she had conscientiously modeled herself on him, straining to keep up with all his interests and follow the development of his thoughts and philosophies. He liked to talk to her, and all she wanted was to be a worthy companion to him on such occasions. She admired his mind so much that she felt it a compliment when he tried to share it with her. She was, after all, only his young sister. A lesser man would have ignored her or else merely talked to her in a patronizing manner, but when Daniel talked to her it was as if she were his equal.

She felt the most important person in the world on those occasions; she could even forget she was merely a thin, sallow girl with plain features and a moderate intellectual capacity which would always fall short of brilliance.

Her looks had improved as she entered her twenties and she found men were beginning to take an interest in her, but she had no patience with anyone less clever than herself and so her friendships never lasted long. Charles Mannering, however, was very different from the young men she was accustomed to discarding in impatient disappointment; she soon realized not only that Charles was exceptionally clever but also that he was the first man she had ever honestly admired—apart from Daniel, of course, but Daniel was only her brother. She wondered idly why Daniel had not yet married; there had been plenty of opportunities, she knew, but no woman ever seemed to interest him for long.

As he came within earshot she called a greeting and he raised his hand in response, his footsteps soundless on the soft sand, the wind whipping the words from his mouth as he tried to reply. She saw him smile, shrug his shoulders in resignation; his dark eyes were narrowed against the sun, his hands thrust casually into the pockets of his trousers to confirm his air of nonchalance, and when he reached her a moment later his voice was low and cool and unhurried.

"Are you coming into Kyle of Lochalsh with us?" he asked. "We're going in ten minutes."

"No," she said. "There's nothing I want there."

He looked at her for a moment and she had the feeling he could see right into her mind and knew exactly why she had no interest in going. Presently he said: "You like it here, don't you? It's a pity you can't marry Charles and live here with him."

"Roshven doesn't belong to Charles."

"It would if Decima died before she was twenty-one."

"I hardly think she's likely to die within the next eight days!" Then, suddenly: "How did you find that out?"

"She told me." He turned aside. "Are you sure there's nothing you want in Kyle of Lochalsh?"

"Quite sure, thanks, Danny."

"I'll see you later, then," he said and moved away from her on his way across the shore to the jetty. As she watched him, she saw Decima leave the house with a basket over her arm and step into the waiting motorboat.

Decima always looked so smart. This afternoon she was wearing dark slacks and a pale blue sweater with a turtleneck. Daniel too would think she looked smart. Rebecca always knew how Daniel would feel about women.

After a while she moved slowly back to the house. The sun was already overcast, and she knew the best of the day was gone. For the first time she wondered vaguely what Charles's young cousin would be like, and then when she entered the house a moment later she forgot about Rohan Quist until his arrival at Roshven several hours later.

*iv*

Rohan was drinking Scotch and water in a pub overlooking the harbor when they arrived. He had reached the town an hour earlier after an uneventful journey from Inverness in the red Volkswagen, and after garaging the car had decided to have a drink to pass the time. He recognized the motorboat at once as it nosed its way through the fishing boats to the quay, and he recognized Decima at the wheel almost as soon as he saw the boat, but the dark man in the black windbreaker was a stranger to him, someone whom he had not expected to see.

He was conscious instantly and inexplicably of jealousy.

They moored the boat and stepped onto the quay. The man was not as tall as he had at first anticipated, but he had a broad, powerful build. Rohan's slight frame tautened. Instinctively his scalp started to prickle; if he had been a dog the hackles would have risen on the back of his neck, and yet there was no logic in his reaction, no reason for his distrust.

The man touched Decima's arm without taking it and they walked along the quay side by side. They were talking. Rohan saw Decima laugh.

Who was this man?

They came nearer and nearer. Within minutes they had reached the door of the pub and were walking inside to look for him, but he was still so absorbed with the force of his reaction that he made no move from his chair. He felt cold suddenly, chilled by a series of emotions he had never experienced before. It was as if he had felt someone walking over his grave.

"Why, there you are!" cried Decima. "Silly thing, why didn't you call out when you saw us come in? How are you? It's such a long time since you've been up here."

"Yes," he said. "It is." But he wasn't looking at her. He

was looking right past her over her shoulder, but even as she turned to make the introductions the stranger stepped forward of his own accord and held out his hand.

"My name is Daniel Carey," he said with an unexpectedly charming smile. "Welcome back to Roshven, Mr. Quist."

# Chapter Two

*i*

It was Thursday when Rachel arrived at Roshven. She reached Kyle of Lochalsh in the early evening and found Rohan waiting for her at the little station. He wore two sweaters, a jacket, and a pair of heavy tweed trousers, and still contrived to look cold.

"Decima's in the boat to avoid the current breeze from the Arctic," he told her. "I hope you brought your winter clothes with you, because if you haven't you'll freeze to death in twenty-four hours. The weather changed yesterday, and I've never been so cold in all my life. . . . Is this your luggage? Okay, let's go. . . . Yes, it was quite warm till yesterday and then the mist started to blow in from the sea and the thermometer dropped twenty degrees or so. I think it's more the damp than the actual cold that's so chilling—it seems to get right into your bones and stay there till you shiver it out again. . . . Did you have a good journey?"

"Fair." She followed him as he left the station, a suitcase in either hand, and as they walked out into the street the damp chill of the wind blew across the sea from Skye toward them. "I can hardly believe Decima really lives right out here," she said to Rohan, drawing up the collar of her raincoat. "Decima of all people! I can only visualize her in town against sophisticated backgrounds. I can picture Charles playing the role of country gentleman but the very idea of Decima playing the outdoor country-tweeds type is too much for me altogether."

"Yes?" said Rohan with vague interest. "And yet, curiously enough, it's Charles who seems ill at ease in his role and Decima who seems perfectly relaxed and content at Roshven. . . . There's the boat across the harbor—can you make it out? And there's Decima in the wheelhouse—you can just see her blue jacket."

They walked on and were soon at the jetty by the water's edge. There were fishermen attending to their nets, white gulls soaring aloft on the wind currents, the sounds of water and Gaelic voices, and the occasional throbbing of an engine. Rachel was aware of strangeness, as if she were a traveler in a foreign land. This remote corner of Britain might have been a thousand miles from the Britain she knew, the soft, verdant slopes of the Surrey Hills with their tall, swaying beech trees and blazes of gorse and rhododendron. A world removed from the graceful houses and shining roads and half-hour train service to the throbbing metropolis of London. Perhaps, she thought, it was not so strange that Decima should feel at home here while Charles did not; Decima, with her cosmopolitan upbringing, would see nothing strange and hostile about this land, while Charles would always be conscious that he was an Englishman in foreign territory, an intellectual far removed from Oxford's spires, a product of civilization adrift among barbarous surroundings.

"Is Charles really so ill at ease here?" she asked Rohan curiously.

"Well, perhaps that's a slight exaggeration, because I know he enjoys fishing and the opportunity to work in peace, but I think he's always anxious to get back to Oxford after a while. I can see his point of view, God knows. This place is all very fine for a holiday but to remain here for any length of time would be too much

of a good thing. That's why I'm surprised the Careys have stayed
so long. They've been six weeks at Roshven now."

A gull screamed overhead and dipped toward the sea. The sun
shone briefly through the clouds for a moment; the gray landscape
seemed to glow in response, and then harden as the sun disappeared again.

"Who are the Careys?" said Rachel.

"Didn't Decima mention them in her letter? How odd! I would
have thought she'd have been sure to mention them."

"But who are they? Some friends of Charles's?"

"My dear R., they're the most extraordinary couple—I can't
imagine what on earth you'll make of them. Rebecca Carey is one
of those frighteningly intellectual women with a curious dramatic
intensity which I find rather unnerving. Everything she does, she
does with a passionate zeal which quite takes one's breath away.
Rather tiring, actually."

"Not your type, from the sound of her!"

"Well, she could be if she had a sense of humor, but unfortunately she's too busy taking everything—including herself—much
too seriously."

"You mean," said Rachel, "she doesn't find your jokes amusing."

"I mean nothing of the kind! All I was saying was—"

"Yes, I see. And what about her husband? Is he full of passionate, humorless zeal too?"

"He's her brother, not her husband, and a former pupil of
Charles's now doing research at Cambridge." Rohan was watching the boat. They were two minutes away from it now. Decima
had caught sight of them, he noticed, and was waving to them.

"How dull," said Rachel, waving back with a smile. "Whatever
made Charles invite them to Roshven? Ah, here comes Decima!
Lord, she looks prettier than ever and I feel so untidy and travel-
stained. . . ."

Decima was already stepping off the boat and moving swiftly
toward them. The wind tore for a moment at her black hair and
she swept it out of her eyes with a laugh. She wore no makeup,
and as the result of many weeks spent in the damp, moist climate

of the Highlands, her complexion was flawless, her skin pale but not pallid, her cheeks faintly glowing with a mere trace of rose. She wore loose-fitting slacks and a bulky windbreaker and still contrived to look beautiful.

"Raye! How lovely to see you!" She had a low, soft voice with a slight, indefinable hint of a foreign accent. It was a voice that needed few words to convey whatever emotion she chose to put in it. "I'm so glad you could come."

There was no sign of nervousness, none of the anxiety which had shown itself so clearly in the hurried letter. She was composed, effortlessly poised. She might have been a mature woman nearly thirty instead of a girl not yet twenty-one.

"It's most exciting to be here," said Rachel politely, suddenly smitten with the full force of her inferiority complex. "I've never been to the Highlands before."

"All aboard!" sang out Rohan, detecting the stiltedness in her voice and at once rushing to the rescue. "Next stop Roshven! Do you want to take the wheel, Decima?"

"We'd soon be aground if *you* took it!" the girl retorted, and they laughed, the moment of awkwardness forgotten. "Are you cold, Rachel? Do you want to go below to the cabin out of the wind? You must be so tired after your journey."

And as Rachel hesitated, not wishing to appear unsociable but dreading the chill of the wind, Rohan said: "I'll call you just before Roshven comes into sight—go and sit in the cabin and peer through the portholes and sip some of Decima's best Scotch."

"Yes," said Decima, "get her a drink, Rohan. I can manage up here once you've helped me cast off."

"I'm sure you can," said Rohan, and added to Rachel: "Decima handles a boat as well as she drives a car—better than most men."

Decima laughed. "Only the British can say a woman's masculine and mean it as a compliment!"

"My dear Decima," said Rohan, "only a man who was blind, deaf, and dumb could ever doubt your femininity. . . . I'll be with you in a moment, Rachel. Go on down to the cabin and make yourself at home."

Rachel did as she was told. The cabin was warm and snug and had two bunks, one on either side of the gangway. As she sat down on the nearest one she was suddenly conscious of weariness, and leaning back against the wall of the cabin she closed her eyes for a moment as the engines roared into life. She could hear Rohan's voice shouting something, then a thud from somewhere on deck, and gradually she could feel the boat moving, swaying away from the jetty and out to sea.

She sat up and glanced out of the porthole. The harbor was already receding and Kyle of Lochalsh a mere huddled collection of gray stone buildings below the bare gray mountains inland.

Footsteps clattered above her. "Found the whiskey yet?" said Rohan, entering the cabin amidst a draft of cool air. "No? You will have some, won't you?"

"Please." She watched him take a bottle from a cupboard above the bunk and then go aft into the tiny galley for a glass and some drinking water. A minute later the liquid was fire in her throat and she was beginning to feel better.

She glanced out of the cabin again. There was nothing to be seen at all now except the rocky coast and the bleakness of the moors and hills inland. Once more the sun shone for a moment, and its light flickered fitfully over the dark landscape.

"How odd," she said, "to see no houses, no trees, no roads. It's almost unnerving. I must be more overcivilized than I thought I was."

"I don't know about being overcivilized," said Rohan. "Even the Highlanders themselves find it oppressive—aren't they always drifting south to the Lowlands and the towns? And you can understand why. Imagine trying to make a living from land like that! Even the crofters around Roshven drifted south in the end with their sheep."

"And yet in a way it's very beautiful."

"Certainly," said Rohan, "for a little while." He went back into the galley to mix himself a drink. When he returned she moved up on the bunk so that he could sit down beside her, and she thought how curious it was that she, who was so often shy with men, should always be perfectly at ease when she was with him.

"Well," she said with a smile, "tell me all the details. What's been happening?"

He shrugged. "Not too much. I've been fishing a few times on my own. Charles came with me once, but he's very involved in his book at the moment and I think he decided to fish more out of politeness than anything else."

"And have you been riding with Decima?"

"No," he said, taking a gulp of his Scotch. "But I've been out a couple of times alone—and nearly galloped into Cluny Sands without realizing I'd come so far. For God's sake don't go riding on your own, Rachel—if you ride inland you'll probably get lost on the moors and if you ride along the seashore you'll go straight into dangerous quicksands. You won't even know they're quicksands till your horse starts to flounder. They look so white and beautiful and inviting, just like any other stretch of deserted seashore around here."

"Why didn't Decima go with you? I'm sure she'd have kept you out of dangerous territory."

"She seems to have lost interest in riding lately."

"So you've been having a solitary sort of holiday!" she teased. "Charles won't fish with you and Decima won't go riding! What about the Careys?"

"They don't ride or fish."

"No? What on earth have they been doing with themselves for six weeks, then?"

"Rebecca swims."

"*Swims?* In this climate?"

"It was warmer a little while ago. And she spends the rest of the time reading Jean-Paul Sartre and imagining herself to be a second Simone de Beauvoir."

"And her brother?"

"Daniel? I really don't know. I never seem to see much of him." He offered her a cigarette and gave her a light. "I think I'll just see how Decima's managing on deck," he said suddenly, standing up. "We can't be too far from Roshven by now. I'll be back in a minute."

She was just closing her eyes in a moment of drowsiness a short while later when he called down the hatch to her. Rousing herself with an effort, she left the cabin and went up on deck.

The wind struck the side of her face as soon as she stepped outside the deckhouse, and she felt her body tighten in an attempt to lock out the cold. The sea was a swaying gray shot with white flecks, and the sky was a pale, ragged blue streaked with banks of stormy clouds. At the wheel Decima's face was glowing, her long hair streaming behind her, her eyes bright, and beside her Rohan, hunched in his coat, called out something which was lost in the hum of the engine and the roar of the wind.

Rachel turned to face the wind, and as she did so, the boat rounded the peninsula and she saw Roshven.

The wind whipped at the foam; there was salt on her lips, spray in her eyes, a mist of water billowing from the prow of the boat. And through it all there were the turrets and towers of Roshven, gray walls clearly etched against the vast background of the moors, while beyond the walls, seemingly encroaching almost to the water's edge to the north and south of the bay, were the mountains wreathed in billowing mist.

Decima was at her elbow suddenly; Rohan had taken the wheel.

"Isn't it beautiful?" she said, and her eyes blazed with a passion that Rachel had never seen her show for any man. "Isn't it the most perfect place in all the world?" And as she laid her hand on Rachel's arm, Rachel could feel the nervous strength flowing through those slim fingers, the vibrant tremor of joy.

"It's unique, Decima," she heard herself say. "I've never seen anything like it before."

The landscape was so powerful that it was almost overwhelming. She wondered if she had ever felt as far from civilization as she felt at that moment, and the pang of fear, unexpected and ridiculous, made her stiffen for a moment before she pulled herself together.

Decima had returned to the wheel; as they approached the shore, Rachel could see the house more clearly, the rugged stone, the blank, dark windows, the partially cultivated garden. There was a jetty with a boathouse, stables, and outbuildings beyond the house. A cow nibbled tranquilly in a grassy field to the right, and six little pigs frolicked in an enclosure beyond the cow. Hens wandered near the front door, and an enormous St. Bernard who was snoozing on the porch with lofty disregard for fowls, opened his eyes at the sound of the motorboat and began to pad down toward the jetty.

The domesticity of the scene in close-up was oddly reassuring after the wildness of the long-distance view.

The boat curved toward the jetty, nudged it neatly, and swayed to a halt as the motors died. The enormous dog put out a paw and patted it vaguely.

"Careful, George," said Decima, jumping down onto the jetty and turning to help Rachel. "Rohan, can you manage those suit-cases? I can see Charles coming, so he'll be able to give you a hand with them."

Rachel scrambled onto the jetty. The damp air felt deliciously cool and fresh now that they were out of the wind. She took a deep breath, half closing her eyes, and when she looked up again she saw Decima's husband crossing the sands toward them.

There was a girl with him, a dark young woman in a thick green sweater and a tweed skirt.

"That's Rebecca Carey," said Decima's voice carelessly. "I don't think I mentioned to you that we had guests at Roshven, did I, Raye?"

"Rohan told me."

The St. Bernard rose with vast dignity and advanced toward Charles. His bulk filled the jetty.

"Out of the way, George," Rachel heard Charles say good-naturedly. "That's better. . . . Why, Rachel, how very nice to see you again! Did you have a good journey? You did? Splendid. . . . May I introduce you to one of our guests? Rebecca, this is Rachel Lord. Rachel—Rebecca Carey."

The girl's hand was limp. Rachel took it but soon let it go. "How do you do?" she said politely.

Something else had caught the attention of the St. Bernard. He was plodding majestically over the sands and his long tail was waving with unhurried grace.

"Can I give you a hand with those suitcases, Rohan?"

". . . come up to the house. All right?"

". . . sea's a bit choppy. . . ."

"Not so good for swimming, Rebecca! Decima, why don't you. . . ."

A man had come out of the house and was walking down toward them to the beach. When he reached the St. Bernard he paused to put a finger lightly on the dog's head, and the dog looked up at him as if that one caress signified immeasurable honor.

"This way, Rachel," said Decima, walking along the jetty away from the boat.

The man and the dog reached the edge of the sands together. The St. Bernard was moving surprisingly fast without giving the appearance of making any extra effort. The man, too, was moving slowly yet gave the impression of speed. He wore a dark pullover and dark trousers, and his hair was as dark as his eyes.

"Ah, there you are!" said Decima, and her voice rang out across the sands. "I was wondering where you'd gone to!" She turned to Rachel, and her eyes were as vivid as a southern sky in high summer. "This is Rebecca's brother, Raye," she said. "This is Daniel Carey."

## ii

Daniel saw a tall, slim girl with soft, brown hair, shy eyes, and a wide, beautiful mouth. Because he was an observant man he also noticed that she was badly dressed in a raincoat that did

not suit her, and wore ugly shoes in a style that might just possibly have been fashionable some years previously. Her smile was
hesitant but full of warmth, and he knew at once that she
was honest and would find any insincerity distasteful. Beside her,
Decima's poised brilliance seemed strangely artificial and cold, an
exercise in perfection which was as empty as it was unarousing.

"Have you much luggage, Miss Lord?" he asked her, scrupulously polite. "Can I help bring it up to the house?"

"Charles and Rohan are seeing to that," said Decima before
Rachel could speak. "Come on up to the house with us, Daniel."

Perhaps it was her tone of voice which made him at once want
to do exactly the reverse of any suggestion she happened to make,
or perhaps he was too conscious of the knowledge that she did
not attract him at that moment and that he wanted to escape from her. Whichever it was, he stepped past them toward the
jetty and called back over his shoulder: "I'll just see if there's anything I can do."

The St. Bernard lumbered after him placidly, brushing Rachel's
raincoat with his waving tail.

"George!" called Decima sharply.

But the dog pretended not to hear her.

"I can't think why George likes you so much, Daniel," observed
Charles, descending from the jetty with one of Rachel's suitcases.
"You never pay any attention to him."

"You sound almost jealous, Charles!" said Rohan from behind
him. He was smiling, but the smile never reached his eyes. "I
thought you were above feeling jealous of things in your possession."

My God, thought Daniel. This is a stupid man.

He felt himself go ice cold with rage.

But Charles was laughing, deaf to all insinuations, happily
oblivious of any emotional undercurrents in the atmosphere. "I
wouldn't grudge anyone a dog's affection! But I've never known
George to be so friendly toward a stranger before—Daniel must
have a way with animals, I suppose."

"Daniel has a way with all kinds of things," said Rohan Quist, but Charles had moved on down the jetty and wasn't listening to him.

Rebecca spun around. "What's that supposed to mean?"

"He's merely paying tribute to my many talents," said Daniel very quickly before Quist could open his mouth. "Let's go back to the house."

As they stepped off the jetty, Rebecca began to say something to him but he cut her off abruptly with a single movement of his hand and she was silent at once. Really, he thought in irritation, Rebecca was unusually sensitive these days. Dangerously sensitive, in fact. He must have a word with her later.

When they reached the house he went into the living room while the others took the luggage upstairs, and moved over to the sideboard to mix himself a drink. He had just gone over to the window with his drink in his hand when his sister came into the room.

"Shut the door, please."

She shut it. "Danny—"

"What's the matter with you?" he said angrily. "Why couldn't you have ignored Quist altogether? You played right into his hands!"

"But Danny, when he said—"

"Ignore it. Forget it. Can't you get into the habit of ignoring anything Quist says which might conceivably be a double en-tendre?"

"But—"

"He's out to make trouble, that man—you know that as well as I do. Why give him the satisfaction of knowing he's succeeding?"

"But Danny, supposing Charles—"

"The hell with Charles!" said Daniel, and then stopped dead as Charles walked into the room.

Quist was right behind him.

"Can I get either of you a drink?" he heard himself offer, giving them his most charming smile.

"Thank you," said Rohan, "but no."

"Charles? Will you drink some Scotch on the rocks with me?"

"'Thanks," said Charles cheerfully. "That's exactly what I need."
He sat down in a chair and stretched out his legs before the
hearth in a picture of relaxed ease. "What about you, Rebecca?"
he added. "Will you have a drink?"

"Not at present, thank you, Charles." Her voice was taut and
uneasy.

There was a silence. Daniel served cubes from the ice bucket
into the glass, and stirred the whiskey carefully without any apparent trace of tension.

"Here you are, Charles," he said at last, turning to face his host,
and even as he spoke he wondered if Charles was really unaware
of Rohan's attitude, of Rebecca's nervousness, of his own mixed
emotions of disillusionment, scorn, and contempt. Daniel had a
sudden painful memory of those days not so long ago when he
had been a freshman at Oxford and had waited eagerly to gain
admission to the hall where the celebrated historian Charles Mannering was lecturing. It was hard to believe it was such a short
time since he had admired and respected Charles. No doubt,
Daniel thought, it would have been different if he and Rebecca
had never come to Roshven.

Roshven had changed everything.

The silence was threatening to become prolonged again when
the door opened and Decima came into the room.

"Why, how quiet it is in here!" She was so poised, so apparently
unaware that anyone was ill at ease in that plain, cheerful room
that her very presence seemed to mock the tension among them.
Rohan said: "I think I will have a drink after all," and Charles was
already reaching for his pipe; over by the window Rebecca picked
up an old magazine to take over to the armchair in the corner,
while Daniel sat down opposite Charles by the hearth, with the
massive St. Bernard at his feet.

"Dinner will be in about an hour," said Decima. "I thought that
would give Rachel sufficient time to have a bath and change and
recover a little after her long journey."

The talk became desultory; after a while Decima departed to
see if the cook was coping satisfactorily with the meal, and soon

after she returned Rachel came downstairs from her room to join them. She was wearing a gray dress in a style that was too old for her, and a plain, elegant brooch which even the best-dressed woman in the world would have been pleased to wear. Her short hair had been carefully brushed and shone in the ray of sunlight which slanted into the room. She still looked shy.

Everyone made a great fuss over her, Daniel thought. Charles immediately offered her a drink. Rohan insisted that she sit next to him on the couch. Decima immediately assumed the role of perfect hostess, anxious, solicitous, exerting every surreptitious means to make her guest perfectly relaxed and at ease.

He still couldn't understand why Decima had suddenly invited her to Roshven.

". . . haven't really had the chance to talk to you about the cele- brations for my twenty-first," Decima was saying with animation. "It's all rather exciting—I'm so glad you could come, Raye—I do hope you'll enjoy it. . . ."

The birthday party seemed to have given Decima an excellent excuse for issuing her unexpected invitation. But an excuse for what?

". . . Charles is giving a dinner party for me on Saturday. There'll be sixteen guests and we'll light the fires in the hall and get out the long dining table and if Willie—that's the gamekeeper —and the men have luck shooting, we'll be able to roast venison on the spit. . . ."

Daniel thought of his own twenty-first birthday five years ear- lier on the eve of his last term at Oxford. There had been a party which had made the dean blanch and the townsfolk complain, and he had almost decided to get married. Luckily, even in spite of a surfeit of champagne, he had avoided committing himself. The next morning a letter had arrived from his parents' lawyers to the effect that he was now fully entitled to the money which had been held in trust for him since childhood.

Decima would come into money, too, of course. And once she was twenty-one she could do as she pleased with Roshven.

"Who will the sixteen guests be?" the girl was asking.

"Oh, Rebecca and Daniel, of course, you and Rohan, Charles and I—and the MacDonalds and Camerons from Kyle of Lochalsh, and the Kincaids from Skye, and my father's lawyer, old Mr. Douglas of Cluny Gualach, and his daughter Rosalind; we had to ask Mr. Douglas, as he wrote me an enormously long legal letter the other day, all about my father's will and inheriting all the money and all the sordid little details about that. . . ."

"You would hardly describe the ownership of Roshven as a sordid little detail, would you, Decima?" Daniel could not resist saying.

"Well, no, I agree!" She laughed carelessly, took a sip from her glass. "But lawyers somehow succeed in taking the romance out of becoming twenty-one and reduce it to such mundane levels. . . . May I have some more wine, Charles?"

Daniel wondered idly if Decima was aware that she drank too much. The preliminary glasses hardly seemed to affect her, and even after that the effect was barely noticeable.

In contrast, the other girl scarcely seemed to touch her wine at all. Yet she appeared to enjoy the meal, for she smiled often and seemed to lose much of her reserve. Once or twice she glanced at him and caught him watching her, and he saw her blush faintly after she had looked away and pretended to interest herself in something else.

He wondered what kind of relationship she had with Rohan Quist, but decided it was probably true that there was nothing between them except ordinary friendship. Quist, even though only a year younger than Daniel himself, seemed a mere child still, excitable, overemotional, and immature and those qualities were hardly sufficient to attract any woman, let alone a woman with such unusual simplicity of manner as Rachel Lord.

When she and Decima rose at last to leave the men alone with their liqueurs, he realized to his astonishment that he had been thinking about her continually throughout the meal, and as he watched her leave the room, he was aware of wondering curiously whether she too had been thinking of him.

## *iii*

Rachel excused herself early, saying that she was tired after the long journey, and with a lamp in her hand found her way up the curving staircase to her room. Someone, presumably the housekeeper, had lit the fire in the grate and the flames had already taken the chill from the air, but outside the rain hurtled in from the Atlantic and dashed itself against the windowpane, and as she knelt on the hearth to warm her hands she could hear the wind rasping against the outer walls.

It was strange to remember that it was only September and that far away in the south people would be wearing summer clothes and perhaps taking a stroll in the evening sunlight.

The wind hummed through the eaves again; she shivered and drew closer to the warmth of the fire.

The flames were flickering, spiraling columns of light, distorted patterns, fragments of vitality. She stared at them for a long time, and as she watched she thought of Daniel Carey and wondered why it was that she was so shy with men and lacked all trace of her usual self-confidence. With any man whom she did not know she was always painfully ill at ease.

Carey had no doubt thought her very gauche.

She was just recalling Decima's perfect poise and maturity of manner, and thinking that self-confidence was undoubtedly easy if one happened to be beautiful, when there was a knock on the door. At first she thought she was imagining it or confusing it with the soughing of the rain and wind outside, but even as she started and turned her head uncertainly toward the door, the knock came again.

"Rachel?" said a soft voice urgently, and the next moment the door was opening and Decima was slipping into the room. "Ah, there you are." She shut the door behind her and moved swiftly

over to the hearth where Rachel was still sitting. "Thank God I've
at last got a chance to talk to you alone."

Rachel looked blank, and then realized she had been so
absorbed in remembering the conversations at dinner that she
had temporarily forgotten the letter which had brought her to
Roshven.

"I've been waiting for a chance to talk to *you* alone," she said
lightly to Decima. "What on earth were you hinting at in your
letter? I couldn't make head or tail of it except that you seemed
to be in a rather panic-stricken state—and yet here you are as cool
as a cucumber and just as balanced as you always were! Just what
exactly's going on?"

Decima had a fur stole over the midnight blue dress she had
worn at dinner, and as she sat down on the floor beside Rachel
she drew the stole more closely around her shoulders. Her face
looked white and pinched suddenly; the firelight flickered across
the violet circles beneath her eyes and glinted on an expression
which made a mockery of Rachel's light, amused remarks.

Rachel suddenly felt her heart beating uncertainly, and the
shock of recognition prickled beneath her scalp. "Something's
very wrong," she heard herself say. "That's it, isn't it, Decima? Something's very wrong."

Decima didn't answer.

"Tell me what it is."

There was a silence. And then as the wind sighed again in the
eaves and the rain hissed in the darkness beyond, she heard Decima whisper: "I think Charles is planning to kill me."

# Chapter Three

*i*

The fire was still dancing, wrapping greedy tongues of red and yellow around the logs. And the light danced on Decima's face so that the fear shone in her eyes and her knuckles gleamed white as she clasped her hands tightly together.

Rachel said: "Charles?"

"I've suspected it for some while."

Rachel's mind at that moment seemed incapable of anything except recalling odd random memories. She thought of Geneva where she had first met Decima and how little she had suspected at the time that the meeting would lead to this moment at Roshven years later; she thought of the spires of Oxford and an adolescent Rohan boasting of his celebrated cousin Charles; she thought of her first meeting with Charles Mannering, the occasion when he had first seen Decima; she thought of his charm and erudition, his wisdom and wit, his vanity and conceit and pride.

It came as a shock to realize fully, for the first time, how much she had always disliked him!

"You can't believe it, can you," Decima was saying. "You can't believe that it could ever be true. You've only seen Charles in his role of academic celebrity, respected and admired by countless intellectuals, the pillar of Oxford society, the perfect English gentleman. You don't believe, do you, that he could ever be otherwise than charming and good-natured and generous."

"I—"

"Well, I didn't believe it either! When I married him he seemed everything I could ever want, an older man whom I could trust and lean upon, a clever man whom I could respect, the kind, considerate husband I felt sure could make me happy. But I was wrong. He never loved me! He married me because of my looks, because I would cause a stir wherever I went in Oxford and he could bask in my reflected glory and listen to other men congratulate him on his wife! I soon discovered how selfish and vain he was, soon realized that the only person *he* cared about was himself! However, I too was proud and I didn't want to run to my father and admit that I'd made a terrible mistake in marrying this man, so I said nothing and pretended all was well when all the time disillusionment followed disillusionment and I wished to God I'd never met him."

There was a silence. The warmth of the firelight seemed strangely incongruous in contrast to the stormy darkness without and Decima's low, unsteady voice close at hand.

"But it wasn't until after my father died that I realized the main reason why Charles married me. I can't think why I never saw it before—I must have been blind, but it wasn't until Father was dead and the lawyers were trying to decide what his will meant, that I realized Charles had married me for my money.

"Charles is basically very lazy. He's not interested in teaching students—or in doing any formal work! He pretends he likes free time to write and do research, but he doesn't write much! He just enjoys being a gentleman of leisure, and if I sold Roshven and invested the proceeds he'd never have to teach again. When he married me he thought I'd sell it as soon as I reached twenty-one—he couldn't conceive that I could ever really *like* living here, that I

wouldn't sell it for all the money in the world. He didn't understand what it meant to me to have a home I loved after so many
years of traipsing from one hotel to the next with my mother
throughout my childhood. He made no pretense of even trying to
understand. He was angry because he wanted the money and I
was quite determined that it should never get into his hands.

"I don't suppose you have any idea of the terms of my father's
will. My father, like everyone else, was deceived by Charles's
superficial charm and thought he would be the ideal person to
look after my interests if I was left an orphan before I was twenty-
one; so in his will, my father made Mr. Douglas the lawyer and his
partner trustees of his estate if he died leaving me a minor, and
recommended they should work in close conjunction with Charles
in matters relating to the estate. And he inserted a clause to say
that if I died before I was twenty-one the estate should pass to my
children, and if I had no children, then it should pass to Charles.
That's why he never actually made Charles a trustee—because
Charles was a beneficiary under the will, and beneficiaries can't
be trustees. If I died after I was twenty-one, and had left no will
disposing of the estate as I wished, Roshven would still pass to
Charles as my next of kin."

"And have you made a will?"

"It's all drafted and ready to be signed as soon as I'm twenty-
one. I have to be twenty-one before I can make a valid will, as I
expect you know. But if I die before I'm twenty-one, the terms of
the trust will come into effect and Roshven will pass to Charles.
There's nothing I can do to alter that."

"Has he already tried to force you to sell it?"

"Soon after my father died Charles tried to urge the trustees
to sell on my behalf, but they wouldn't when they knew I was very
much opposed to the idea of the sale. As trustees they have
a power of sale, but in practice they would never force a sale without my consent. Mr. Douglas was an old friend of my father's."

"So—"

"Charles wants Roshven—or rather the money that the sale of
Roshven would bring him. He knows damn well that I would

never leave him a square inch of it in any will I might make after I'm twenty-one, and so his only chance to acquire it would be if I were to die before my twenty-first birthday."

"But Decima, your birthday's Saturday and this is Thursday evening—"

"My birthday's on Sunday. The dinner party is on Saturday so that everyone can drink my health as the clock strikes twelve and my birthday officially begins. The idea was Charles's, not mine."

"But that means he has only forty-eight hours left—"

"That's why I invited you to Roshven—because I couldn't face it any longer on my own. My nerves weren't strong enough, and there was no one I could trust—"

"Not even Rohan?"

"Charles's cousin?" said Decima ironically. "No, I wouldn't trust Rohan."

"And the Careys?"

"I don't trust the Careys," said Decima.

"Why? Because they're Charles's friends?"

"Because they've outstayed their welcome without any apparent reason and are both determined to stay until after my twenty-first birthday party. . . . Because Charles likes them and begged them to stay. Because . . . of many things." She looked into the flames, and her eyes were bright and hard. "Rebecca is the kind of woman I despise, and Daniel—"

She stopped.

"Daniel?"

"Daniel isn't interested in women," said Decima. "History and learning and books are all he cares about. Do you think he would listen even if I did tell him my suspicions about Charles? Of course not! He would smile politely but think me a mere neurotic female highly unworthy of any attention he could spare me. . . . And anyway, I could never confide in Daniel."

"But Decima, has Charles made any move, given you any hint that he might try to—"

"He hasn't mentioned selling Roshven since the Careys came," Decima interrupted. "That in itself is unusual. And his behavior in general has been strange. He's been so extraordinarily nice to me! He really has taken trouble over the dinner party arrangements, and he's promised to give me a beautiful diamond necklace for my birthday (which he can't afford, incidentally), and he's even suggested—" She bit her lip and glanced at Rachel from beneath her lashes. "We haven't lived together for over a year," she said after a moment, glancing back into the flames. "Recently I've been locking my door at night when I go to bed. Charles suggested that I start sleeping in his room again as I did when we were first married."

"But—"

"And he has debts," she said suddenly, as if rushing away from a subject she had no wish to discuss. "I—I looked among his papers once when he was out fishing. . . . We lived far beyond our income after we were first married—I think he was relying on the money from Roshven's sale to help him with the bills. . . . He has even borrowed money to pay his earlier debts. And yet he talks of buying me a diamond necklace as if he had all the money in the world! Besides, we're always quarreling over money. Before the Careys came we used to quarrel almost every other day and the subject of Roshven's sale was always cropping up."

"Why should the Careys' arrival make him drop the subject, I wonder?"

"I don't know, but I think he has some scheme and the Careys have some leading part in it. I don't know why else he would drop the subject entirely unless he had decided that reasoning with me was useless and it was necessary to make other plans."

"Have you never thought of leaving Roshven? You must have been very frightened these last few days."

"Of course I've thought of it! But there are two things which have always deterred me. The first is simply that I've no proof that Charles is planning violence and it *is* possible that I may be mistaken about his intentions—this doesn't reverse anything I've just said against him, because I'm still convinced he married me for my money and would love to get his hands on it. But I've no tangible proof that he plans to kill me. Supposing I was wrong? If I left him now when he may well be genuinely eager to be generous toward me and to organize such a lavish celebration for my birthday, I don't think a judge would be very sympathetic if I tried to get a divorce; Charles won't divorce me. It would reflect too badly on his ego and pride—to have to confess that he, the great success, had made a failure of marriage and couldn't hold on to his much-displayed wife! And with his job and background he's not going to smear himself by providing the evidence for any adultery petition of mine. My one hope of a divorce is being able to prove he drove me into desertion. Besides, who knows? If he is innocent and I've misjudged him, perhaps the situation may improve once I'm twenty-one and he no longer has a hope of getting his hands on my money . . . but perhaps I'm expecting too much. Certainly, as things stand at the moment that's a hopelessly optimistic view."

"I see. . . ."

"My other reason for staying is minor in comparison but not unimportant. Ironic though it may seem, at present I've no money of my own and couldn't afford to go away—all my income from the Forestry Commission is used by the trustees in seeing to Roshven's upkeep and giving me a ridiculously small allowance; the balance is put into the trust fund for me to inherit when I'm twenty-one."

"So Charles can't even borrow money from you?"

"He can get nothing whatsoever unless I die before midnight on Saturday."

Rachel stared at her. "But Decima—" She paused, trying to marshal her thoughts into a sensible pattern and ignore the knowledge that she was far from the protective shields of civilization, but the howl of the wind and the hammering of the rain outside seemed to undermine her reserves of strength with horrifying thoroughness. She could only think that she was ten miles by sea from the nearest town, imprisoned between the vast mountains and the stormy sea, and that the danger in that still house suddenly seemed immensely alive and vital. This was no half-imagined illusion conjured up by any neurosis of Decima's; this was a reality in which she herself was personally involved. "But what can I do?" she whispered to Decima. "Tell me what I can do."

"Stay with me. Don't leave me alone with Charles. And be on your guard for me."

"Why, yes . . . of course. It'll only be till Sunday, won't it? Once you're twenty-one you're no longer in danger because Charles would have nothing to gain from your death."

There was a silence. At last Decima glanced at her watch. "I must go back before they start wondering why I'm staying here so long. . . . I shall go down and tell them I feel tired and have decided to follow your example in going to bed early. Then I'll go to my room and lock my door and try and get some sleep."

"Would you like to sleep in here? One of us could sleep on the couch. . . . But no, I suppose that would cause suspicion if we were found out."

"Yes, I think so, and I want to avoid letting Charles know I'm afraid and suspect him of anything. . . . Once he thinks I suspect something he'll be on his guard."

"Didn't he think it suspicious that you'd asked me to stay when we'd more or less lost touch with each other?"

"No, you were a friend of Rohan's and he thought inviting you was a clever idea on my part to make the numbers even for the dinner party. . . . Oh, and he was probably glad you could come because he would feel you would divert Rohan's attention from me." She stood up, automatically straightening her dress, her fingers working nervously over the material. "Charles is convinced that Rohan and I are having an affair," she said with a laugh which held no trace of mirth. "Amusing, isn't it? As if I would! Anyway, I'd be more than glad if you could occupy Rohan for me, if only to allay Charles's ridiculous suspicions. . . . Now I really must go—I'll see you tomorrow morning, of course. Perhaps you'd like to have breakfast with me in my room at nine thirty? Mrs. Willie, the housekeeper, always brings breakfast up to me in the mornings. . . . And thank you for listening to me so well, Raye—I feel better already, just through talking about all my fears and worries to someone. . . . Till tomorrow, then—I hope you sleep well, by the way. Do you have everything you want here?"

"Yes, I think so, thanks. Good night, Decima—and try not to worry too much."

Decima smiled faintly; there was a draft as she opened the door, and the next moment her footsteps were receding down the passage and Rachel was alone once more by the fire in the darkened room.

She threw another log into the flames. Sparks flew up the chimney. She sat for a long while watching the wood burn and then very slowly she began to get undressed. But even as she got into bed some time later and drew the blankets tightly around her, she found she was still wondering what part Daniel Carey played in any plans Charles might have for Decima's future.

*ii*

When she awoke the sun was shining through the curtains, and on moving to the window she saw that the sea was a rich, dark, swaying blue which stretched to the clear line of the horizon. The sky was pale and cloudless, bearing no trace of the stormy evening before, and the white sands shone invitingly in the light of early morning.

It was eight o'clock, long before the time for the promised breakfast with Decima at nine thirty. The memory of Decima and the conversation of the previous evening made her pause motionless by the window for several long seconds, and then, on realizing she was cold, she retreated to the warmth of her bed once more.

But she was uneasy, restless. After a time she recognized the impossibility of falling asleep again, and she got up, found a pair of slacks and a thick sweater, and started to get dressed. Within ten minutes she was slipping out into the corridor. At the head of the stairs she paused to listen but the house was quiet and she supposed everyone else was still sleeping. She reached the hall. She could hear faint sounds now, but they came from the kitchens far away where the housekeeper was already at work. Moving in the other direction, Rachel opened the front door and stepped into the clear, cool air outside.

The landscape seemed different in sunshine. As she walked downhill toward the jetty she could see that the mountains beyond the house were shimmering in green and purple shades, and now that there was no mist covering the scene she could see the dark line of the trees forming the edge of the forestry plantation far away across the moors. Above the jetty she paused to look around her; to the left the sands stretched south along the black cliffs which rose abruptly from the harbor of Roshven, and to the right the sands were curtained by the rocky arm of a peninsula thrusting out into the ocean.

Rachel turned south.

The breeze was cool, but no longer damp and chill. The sunlight, though pallid, was faintly warm. Gulls swooped above the roar of the surf and soared high over the black cliffs and their screams carried shrilly on the air currents to echo among the rocks.

Rachel was conscious suddenly of loneliness. She glanced back over her shoulder at the house, but Roshven was gone, hidden by a jutting corner of the cliffs, and there was no sign of civilization. She hesitated uneasily and then pulled herself together with a smile at her city dweller's reactions and walked on.

The cliffs were taller now, great scarred walls of granite with rocks piled at their base and embedded in the sand. There were caves, too, some enormous caverns the size of a church, some mere holes barely high enough for upright stance. Rachel, venturing nearer the cliff face, found deep pools left behind by the tide and an assortment of shellfish and seaweed clustered in the water among the rocks.

She was just stooping to examine a large shell when she suddenly felt she was being watched. She swung around abruptly, but there was nothing there, only the roar of the surf and the screaming of the gulls. Her heart was pounding in her lungs so hard that even her movements away from the cliff were stiff and awkward, but once she was close to the breaking waves and away from the dark gaping mouths of the caves she felt better. She started walking again and soon she had rounded another rocky peninsula and was standing before another expanse of wide white sands, unmarked, untouched, effortlessly beautiful. She stepped out toward them quickly, forgetting her absurd nervousness of a few minutes before and feeling unexpectedly lighthearted.

There was a howl from behind her. An enormous throaty baying echoed among the cliffs and as she spun around in shock she saw the vast St. Bernard pounding toward her, his jaws gaping as he bared his teeth.

Like most people unaccustomed to even small dogs, Rachel was too frightened to move. And then as the dog reached her and she stepped back automatically in self-defense, she felt her heels sinking and realized in a flash of understanding that she had wandered right to the very edge of the quicksands of Cluny.

She froze in her tracks, and the dog stopped too, still baying in warning. Then, very delicately, he stepped forward, tail swaying, and took the cuff of her jacket between his teeth to lead her away from the sands to safety. Rachel automatically wrenched her shoes free to follow him, and presently the dog released his hold on her jacket and looked up at her sadly, as if incredulous that anyone could be so stupid and careless.

She was just stroking the top of the dog's head when she saw Daniel.

He was standing at the entrance to one of the caves, but as she saw him he began to walk over to her. He walked slowly, not hurrying, his hands in the pockets of his old dark corduroys, and when he drew nearer she saw that his eyes were watchful and his mouth was unsmiling.

"Did no one tell you," he said, "about Cluny Sands?"

"Why, yes," she said, stumbling over the words just as she had

always done at school. "Yes, Rohan told me. But I didn't think—
I didn't remember—"

"I see." He whistled to the dog. "Here, George."

The St. Bernard lumbered over to him obediently and sat down
on the sand, his tail still swaying.

"Why didn't you call out to me sooner?" Rachel heard herself
demand. "Why did you let me get right to the edge before you
sent the dog after me?"

"I thought you were certain to know about the sands and would
stop before you reached the edge. Besides, the tide's out and the
sands are less dangerous; the danger comes when the tide is on
the turn." He was still motionless and there was something about
his eyes which brought her back to the rawness of adolescent emotions, a world she thought she had outgrown long ago.

She glanced away out to sea. "I still think you might have called
out sooner," she said abruptly.

Some indefinable element in his manner was at once erased; he
smiled, and his voice when he spoke was full of charm and warmth.

"I do apologize," he said. "It was wrong of me, I see that now,
and you must have had a bad shock. Let me take you back to the
house and brew you some coffee to make amends."

She glanced at him briefly but lowered her eyes even before she
smiled in return. "Thank you," she murmured. "But I'm quite
all right."

"But you'll accept my offer of coffee all the same, I hope."

"I—I've promised to have breakfast with Decima."

"Decima never looks at a breakfast tray before nine thirty," said
Daniel, "and we'll be back at the house long before that. However,
it's as you wish, of course." His shoe knocked against a pebble and
he stooped to pick it up and fling it out to sea. "How do you find
Decima, by the way? Has she changed much since you last saw
her?"

"No, she doesn't seem to have changed. But then, I've hardly
seen her yet."

"You never actually knew her very well, did you?"

"Why, yes," said Rachel, astonished enough to glance up into his eyes. "I knew her very well indeed! We were at school in Geneva together for six months and were the closest of friends."

"Oh?" said Daniel. "You surprise me."

She couldn't help asking him why.

"You seem very dissimilar types."

"You hardly know me," she heard herself say, "and you've known Decima little more than six weeks, I understand."

"I see I've expressed myself badly," he said. "Let me put it this way: I've seen enough of Decima to enable me to form an opinion of her, and it wouldn't take five minutes' conversation with you to determine that you could never in a thousand years be placed in the category in which I should place Decima."

"And what category is that? Or aren't I supposed to ask?"

"It would be better if you didn't, certainly. If I told you, you might feel bound to tell Decima as she's such a close friend."

"And as you seem to think this would be a bad thing," said Rachel, "I assume your opinion of her can't be very high."

"I didn't intend to imply that. Decima is very beautiful and very charming and an admirable hostess. I don't think anyone would quarrel with that."

"No, indeed. . . . She must have caused quite a stir in Oxford circles after she married Charles."

"Yes, I believe she did. I'd left Oxford by that time so I never met her, although I continued to keep in touch with Charles after I left." He was watching the St. Bernard paddling at the water's edge. "You knew Charles before he married Decima, I suppose."

"Yes, Rohan introduced me to Charles when we—Rohan and I —were quite young. But we only saw him occasionally. He didn't come down to visit Rohan's family very often."

"Charles is a remarkable man," said Daniel, still watching the dog. "Academically he's one of the most gifted men I've ever met."

Rachel said nothing.

"Strange, isn't it," said Daniel, "how a very clever man could be quite so foolish?"

The waves crashed on the beach in a roar of surf, but she did not hear them.

"He should never have married Decima, of course. I'm only surprised he didn't see at the time how unsuited they were. Lord knows it must have been obvious enough."

After a moment Rachel said: "He—regrets the marriage?"

"Didn't Decima tell you their marriage was a mere formality?"

"Yes, but—"

"That is the main reason why my sister and I have stayed so long —the Mannerings begged us not to leave! They were both so bored with each other's company that they welcomed us with open arms. Didn't Decima tell you that? I'm sorry if I've said too much but I was under the impression you were in her confidence."

It was only then that she realized he was trying to discover how much she knew and why she had come to Roshven.

"There's been so little time," she said, suddenly confused. "Decima hardly touched on the subject of either why you were here or why you had stayed so long."

"Well, it's easy enough to explain." He gestured toward a flat slab of rock near the cliffs. "Shall we sit down for a moment? Rebecca and I had decided to visit the Edinburgh Festival together —she'd just taken her postgraduate Diploma of Education exams and had planned to have a long holiday before looking around for a job, and my time is my own during the long vacation. Remembering that Charles had written to tell me of Roshven during the years we had corresponded, I thought it might be interesting to rent a car after the Festival and drive up to the Highlands and over to the west coast. I wrote to Charles, telling him the plans, and he wrote back by return mail to ask us to stay.

"I was intrigued by this place as soon as I saw it. I suppose every civilized man dreams from time to time of finding somewhere completely isolated and free from all the trappings of city and suburban life, but most of the time he never comes within a thousand miles of such a place. But Roshven for me was the place of my dreams." He stooped to run his index finger softly down the back of the dog at his feet. The wind from the sea flicked unseen fingers through his dark hair. "But something happens to people," he said after a while. "Something happens to them when they're imprisoned between the mountains and the sea, cut off from other human beings and forced through necessity and circumstance to have much more contact with each other than would otherwise be the case. One finds oneself being sucked into a vortex; personality grates on personality in an ever-shifting pattern; everyone gets to know everyone else much too well for comfort.

"Rebecca and I should have left long ago, but we did not. For one thing, Decima begged us to stay for her birthday, and for another . . . well, Charles too was anxious that we should stay, and I suppose the wish to leave wasn't strong enough." He stopped. There was a pause.

"I don't quite understand your remarks about a vortex," Rachel said slowly. "But surely Rohan's arrival—and now mine—must have eased matters if things were getting strained."

"It would have been better if Quist had never set foot in this place," said Daniel abruptly. "And as for you . . . I can only advise you to leave as soon as you can. There are things going on here which I couldn't even begin to explain to you. Leave before you too get drawn into the vortex and find yourself unable to escape."

Spray flew from the crashing surf. The tide was creeping further toward them, and from the south she could hear the roar of the undertow sucking over Cluny Sands.

"I don't understand you," she said woodenly. "What are you trying to say?"

A voice sounded above the roar of the surf. As they both swung around abruptly, they saw Rebecca Carey walking toward them, and when she saw that they had noticed her she raised her hand in greeting.

"But for God's sake," said Daniel to Rachel, "don't go repeating what I've said to Charles or Decima or Quist. I spoke for you and you alone."

"Of course," she said sharply, annoyed that he even considered it necessary to give her such a warning, and then she realized that her mouth was dry and her limbs stiff with tension.

Rebecca was already within earshot.

"This is the best morning we've had for days," she called out, as she came up to them. "You've brought good weather with you, Rachel." The wind blew her short hair into her eyes, and she pushed it back impatiently. She wore a tweed skirt and an olive green sweater, and the plain clothes were the perfect foil for the strong lines of her face and the glow of her eyes. It was a good-looking face, neither pretty nor beautiful, but Rachel thought her good looks were marred by a trace of aggression which seemed to hint that Rebecca had been accustomed all her life to reach out to grasp things she wanted, as they never came to her of their own accord. Rachel, who had gone to a large girls' day school before being exported to Geneva, had met a great many girls during her life and had no difficulty at all in placing Rebecca in the appropriate category. Rebecca was the one who sat in the front of the class and always knew all the answers, the girl whose tongue was as sharp as her brain and made enemies as fast as she tried to make friends, a lonely person in spite of her militant air of self-sufficiency.

With Rachel pity always outweighed dislike.

"You're up early," she said pleasantly to Rebecca. "Do you always go for a walk before breakfast?"

"I certainly don't wallow around in bed till ten with a breakfast tray, if that's what you mean. Danny, Charles is talking of going into Kyle of Lochalsh this morning to arrange for food for the dinner party. Didn't you say you wanted to go into town before Saturday evening to get Decima a present?"

"I'd thought of it." He turned to Rachel. "Do you have a present for Decima?"

"Yes, I brought a small present up from London."

"In that case, since you've had the experience of choosing a present for her, perhaps you'd care to come with us into town and help me select something? I've no idea what to buy for her and I'd appreciate some advice."

"It will hardly be as difficult to choose as all that," Rebecca said sharply before Rachel could reply. "And I don't suppose Rachel wants to go back into Kyle of Lochalsh today."

"I—I'm sure Rebecca could advise you just as well, Daniel—"

"As you wish." He turned abruptly and set off at a brisk pace across the sands, the St. Bernard padding in his wake.

"You'll probably find some very good Gaelic jewelry in town," Rachel heard herself say in an instinctive attempt to gloss over the moment of awkwardness. "It shouldn't be too difficult to find something suitable."

"Exactly what I thought," said Rebecca crisply. "I'm surprised he asked you to come. He should have realized you would be too tired after your journey to want to do much today. How are you feeling, by the way? You look tired."

"I—"

"As you're up so early, I suppose you didn't sleep well?"

"Well, actually, I—"

"It's always difficult getting used to a strange place, isn't it? And Roshven must seem so primitive after the London suburbs. . . . Tell me, how did you come to meet Daniel this morning? I was looking for him everywhere."

Rachel wondered for a fleeting moment why she always felt so irritated with people who prefaced all their questions with the words "Tell me." "I just met him down here on the beach," she said shortly, and noticed in surprise that her feeling of irritation was growing with every second that passed; she very seldom allowed herself to be ruffled by a person's manner, but Rebecca seemed to have the most unfortunate effect on her.

"But why did you walk so far south? Cluny Sands—"

"Yes," said Rachel politely. "I've heard all about Cluny Sands."

"You have? That's just as well. . . . They remind me of that novel by Sir Walter Scott—which was the one where the hero had trouble with quicksands? *Bride of Lammermoor*, was it? Or *Redgauntlet*? But of course, those quicksands were by the Firth of Forth."

"Of course," said Rachel, who had never read either novel. "So they were."

"You read Scott? Charles has a complete collection. What a wonderful library he has! It seems such a pity that Decima never reads anything except those ghastly women's magazines. . . . But then I believe she only had a very superficial education."

"I expect she finds it adequate enough."

"You think so? But then she's not really too clever, is she? And of course, she's not too well either, I'm convinced of it."

The cool, hard drift of the conversation was suddenly crystallized into the ice of innuendo.

"What do you mean?" said Rachel sharply. "Decima's as well as you or I!"

"Oh, but you haven't been living here these past few weeks as I have! She's really been acting in such a strange way—that's why we all encouraged her to have you to stay. Charles especially thought you would be good for her, a stabilizing influence. . . . She was getting rather—well, rather neurotic, although I hate to use a word with such unfortunate connotations. She's been giving poor Charles such a very difficult time."

"I don't quite—"

"I can say all this to you, you see, because I really feel you should know the truth of the situation in order to be able to cope with Decima as you think best. . . . Ah, there's Roshven! How fast Daniel's been walking! He's nearly by the jetty already. . . . And there's Rohan in the doorway—look, he's waving to you! What a strange man he is, so foreign, somehow, so unusual. Tell me, he's not entirely English, is he?"

"His father came from Sweden. But about Decima—"

"Sweden? Oh well, of course, everyone knows the Swedes are a very strange race. . . . Yes, it's really a great pity about Decima. I've made countless efforts to be sociable and friendly toward her, but she simply refuses to make any effort at all. Ever since we came here she's been hostile and trying to make things difficult for Charles—it's really been a constant source of embarrassment."

"I'm surprised you stayed so long, then," said Rachel, "if you were unpopular with your hostess."

"But my dear, there was no reason for her attitude! It was quite without motivation! Charles has confided to me once or twice that Decima is convinced that she's being persecuted in some way or other. . . . As soon as they go back to Oxford he's arranging for her to see a doctor—you understand? I mean, it's not normal, is it? All she wants to do is hide from the world here in the back of beyond—she doesn't even want to go back to Oxford. Imagine that! Imagine not wanting to see Oxford again! I think she's afraid of meeting people, of showing herself. It's quite a common nervous complaint, I believe."

"Decima seems eminently sane to me," said Rachel, "and I also disagree with your earlier remark about her intelligence. She was very clever indeed at school. Just because she's not intellectual doesn't mean to say she's not clever."

"Well, of course," said Rebecca, exactly as if Rachel hadn't spoken, "the longer you stay here the more apparent her state of mind will become to you. All I can say is that she's been acting very strangely lately."

There was a small, uncomfortable silence. Then: "Rohan seems to want to talk to you," Rebecca said as they watched him reach the beach and again wave to attract their attention. "Will you excuse me? I want to find out what time Daniel plans to go into Kyle of Lochalsh." And she was gone, her footsteps quickening across the sands.

Daniel was aboard the boat moored to the jetty, and as Rachel watched he came up from belowdecks and waited by the wheelhouse as he saw his sister coming. He seemed far away and remote, a minute part of the vast landscape of sea, sky, and mountains.

"Ah, *there* you are!" said Rohan, stating what must have been obvious to him for at least five minutes. "What's the matter with you, getting up so early?" He was still some way away from her, but his voice carried clearly on the still morning air. "And why the secret rendezvous with Daniel?" he added as he came closer. "I saw him follow you out of the house and across the sands! Rebecca looked most insulted when she came outside later and saw her beloved brother had walked off without her—usually they go together for their early morning stroll. What did Carey say to you, anyway? What did he want?"

"It was nothing," said Rachel automatically, her thoughts still on her conversation with Rebecca, and then as she thought of Daniel, she added, a shade too positively, "Absolutely nothing at all."

"Ah-*ha!*" said Rohan at once. "Ah-ha! My dear girl, don't tell me you find Carey irresistibly attractive! Don't tell me—"

"No, of course I shan't tell you, because it isn't true! Shut up, Rohan, for God's sake. It's too early in the morning for such nonsense. . . . Listen, I want to talk to you—let's sit down here for a moment before we go on up to the house."

"All right," said Rohan agreeably, moving over to a long rock and subsiding onto it without argument. "What's the matter? Did Carey—"

"Forget Daniel for a moment, would you? I want to talk about Rebecca."

"Really? Do we have to? All right, all right, all right! Don't get huffy and walk off with your nose in the air! I was only joking. What's all this about Rebecca?"

"We've just had the most extraordinary conversation. She was saying such fantastic things that I was quite speechless."

"Such as?"

"That—that Decima had a persecution complex—"

"Oh God!"

"—and was mentally ill—"

"What did you say?"

"What do you think I said? I told her as politely as possible that I thought she was the one who needed the psychiatrist, not Decima."

"You didn't!"

"Well, no, to be honest, but I did deny it and say that Decima was as sane as we were."

"Hm."

"Well, isn't she? Don't be silly, Rohan! Look, what's been going on? Why should Rebecca say a thing like that? What happened here before I arrived yesterday?"

Rohan was silent. As she watched him she saw the amused lines

about his mouth smooth themselves away, and his gray eyes
seemed to darken with his change of mood. "There are several
reasons why Rebecca should say a thing like that," he said at last.
"First of all, Decima dislikes Rebecca and makes no effort to hide
it. Secondly, Rebecca dislikes Decima for a good many reasons,
the first and foremost of which is probably because Rebecca would
always despise a woman less intellectual than herself. And thirdly,
Decima really has been behaving very oddly."

"I hadn't noticed. She seemed very normal to me."

"Well, yes, naturally," said Rohan. "She was most successful at
creating an atmosphere of normalcy when you arrived last night."

After a moment Rachel said: "I don't understand."

"Things have been very far from normal, Rachel, and it all stems
from Decima. I wouldn't say this to you if I hadn't known you all
my life, because I know you and she were close friends for a while
and as far as you're concerned you're still friends even though
perhaps not such close friends as you were once. But I know you
too damn well, Rachel, for insincerities, and I would be insincere
if I didn't tell you that Decima's the last person who should ever
be a friend of yours."

"But I thought you liked Decima! When you first met her—"

"I didn't know her then, just as you don't know her now, but
she's no good, Rachel. She's given Charles one hell of a time, and
I can tell you here and now he's at his wits' end with her. I keep
telling him to divorce her, but they haven't been married three
years yet, and it's not easy to get a divorce before then. Besides,
he's against a divorce purely from a social point of view; divorce
today hasn't the stigma it used to have, but he moves among elderly circles governed by a strict morality, and a divorce would certainly do him no good. However, it must obviously come to that in
the end. I don't think she'll leave Roshven to return to Oxford
with him this time when term begins, and that'll mean a public
acknowledgment of the rift between them."

"He'll miss Decima's money if they're divorced, won't he?"

"Charles has enough money! He doesn't have to worry about
that!"

"Nobody ever has enough money," said Rachel ironically. "No matter how much you have, it's never quite enough."

"But Charles didn't marry Decima for her money, Rachel! He married her because he was infatuated with her looks, personality, sex appeal—call it whatever you like! Perhaps you didn't see much of him before they were married and while they were engaged, but he was up to his eyes in his infatuation—and when a man's in love with a bank account instead of a pretty woman he hardly goes around with a moonstruck look in his eyes, unable to eat or sleep."

"But when did the disillusionment begin? Wasn't it when he found she wouldn't consent to Roshven's sale?"

"Is that what she says? Didn't she tell you anything about her marriage?"

"She mentioned that she'd been unhappy."

"*She'd* been unhappy! My God! What about Charles? I don't know why she married him, but it certainly wasn't for love. Maybe she was attracted by the fact that he was an older man and a well-known name in academic life. Or maybe she was impressed by his charm and found the idea of marriage appealing. But she didn't love him! She may be beautiful and exotic and seductive but she's as cold as that northern sea out there, as empty and sterile as these desolate mountains around us. As far as any form of physical intimacy is concerned, she simply isn't interested. Whose idea was it, do you think, that they should have separate bedrooms? Certainly not Charles's! Charles is a man, just like any other, when it comes to sex. He would even like children now, I think. But is Decima interested in children? Of course not! She doesn't care about anything except herself. Charles was a novelty to begin with, but she was soon bored. She yawned at the social occasions she had to attend with him, embarrassed him by her extravagances, humiliated him by making no attempt to fit into his world. She even flirted with the undergraduates in an effort to annoy him—but then she'd flirt with any man! Decima thrives on admiration."

There was a long moment of silence. Then: "There are two sides to everything," said Rachel slowly at last, "so I'm not surprised to hear there are two sides when it comes to the Mannerings' marriage. But here there are such wide discrepancies that one or the other party must be lying! According to Decima—"

"Yes, what on earth's Decima been saying? I didn't realize you'd already had the chance to speak to her."

"We talked for a little while after dinner last night, and she implied she wasn't happy and that Charles had married her for her money. She also said that *he* had been acting strangely, and that—"

"Charles? But that's nonsense!"

"Is it? Anyway, she said she was glad I had come because I would act as a diversion by keeping *you* occupied. Then Charles wouldn't go on suspecting that you and Decima were having an affair."

Rohan was suddenly white. "Decima and I—but that's preposterous! Ridiculous! Absurd!" He stared at her, his gray eyes wide and dark, and for the first time since her arrival she saw through the mask of his light-hearted manner to the tension and fear which lay beneath. So Rohan too had somehow been drawn into the vortex which existed at Roshven. Daniel's warning of the vortex rang once more in her ears, but before she could speak again Rohan was saying in a tight, controlled voice which she scarcely recognized: "Decima was lying to you. Why should Charles suspect me of trying to have an affair with her when it's perfectly obvious that she's much more interested in Daniel Carey?"

# Chapter Four

*i*

Daniel was watching Rohan and Rachel from the wheelhouse of the boat. They had been sitting on the rock together for ten minutes and still appeared to be deep in conversation.

"I don't like that girl," Rebecca said from beside him.

"So I observed." He lit a cigarette and the flame of the match was reflected for a moment in his eyes. He was thinking of Quist, wondering what game the man was playing, what he was saying to Rachel Lord a hundred yards away across the beach.

"Why on earth did you ask her to help you choose a present for Decima?"

He felt annoyed suddenly. "Why not?" he said, wishing she would go back to the house and leave him alone for a while with his thoughts. "I like her."

"I wouldn't have thought she was your type."

"Then I must be tired of my type—whatever that may be." He went out on deck, but she followed him. He was reminded sud-

denly of the times when they had been children and Rebecca had
always followed him faithfully wherever they had gone. It occurred
to him vaguely that he was becoming a little tired of this childhood
echo shadowing him wherever he went.

"I'm going back to the house," he said shortly.

"I'll come with you."

They returned in silence, not speaking till they reached the hall.
Then: "I'll call for you when I'm ready to leave," he said over his
shoulder and moved swiftly up the stairs to his room. On reaching
the door he flung it shut behind him thankfully and did not at first
notice that someone was waiting for him in the chair by the fireplace.

"Danny—"

He swung around. She stood up, graceful and poised as ever, and
the folds of her pale blue peignoir seemed to float for a second in
the draft of movement. "Danny, I had to see you—"

"There's nothing to say."

But she wasn't as meek as Rebecca, not as willing to accept the
finality of his retorts. "Listen, Daniel, I've changed my mind—"

"Then you've changed it too late, Decima. I'm sorry." She was
very close to him now; he noticed how she took a deliberate step
nearer to him so that he could see how thin her peignoir was and
how much excitement lay just beneath the lace surface. "Please,
Danny," she said, and her blue eyes were misty. "Please. . . ." It
was cleverly done, he thought. In her own way she was an artist.
And much to his anger and disgust he felt his pulses quicken as he
allowed himself to look at her for a long moment. He would have
turned away but she put a hand on his arm and halted him. "I've
treated you badly, I know, Danny; it was wrong of me and I realize
that now. But I was frightened, anxious, scared. . . ." She paused,
searching his face for some glimmer of capitulation.

"You were none of those things," he heard himself say. "You
were amused, flattered, and diverted. Diverted because my attention provided a variation from the normal course of events at
Roshven, flattered because any woman likes being paid the kind

of attention that I paid you, and amused because you're too cold to find anything except amusement in your power to interest a man when you yourself feel nothing at all."

"That's not true!" she stormed, passionate and tempestuous now as if in a full demonstration of her emotional range. "Just because I said no, just because I allowed myself one instant of loyalty to Charles, just because for a moment I was frightened by the depth of my feelings for you—"

"You didn't care, Decima, and no matter how hard you try now to play the role of the loyal young wife beset with temptations, you'll never make the part convincing. You refused because you didn't care, and once I realized that and saw your masquerade for what it was, I didn't care either."

"But I do care, I do! I'll do whatever you want, Danny, I swear it—just say what you want me to do and I'll do it!"

"You don't understand," he said coldly as the hot sweat moistened the palms of his hands. "You're making the situation much more complex than it really is. The position was simply this: I saw you, wanted you, just as I'd want any other attractive woman. After you'd played around and successfully kept me at arm's length while you amused yourself watching my growing frustration, it eventually dawned on me that you were never going to be interested enough to say yes, and even if you did you probably wouldn't have much to offer in the end. I'm not interested in cold women. And as soon as I lost interest in you sexually, I'm afraid that was the end of your power over me. Next time I'd advise you to play your cards a little differently if you want your fun to last longer."

She was very white. For a moment he had the unnerving impression that he had misjudged her and that she was, after all, capable of caring, and so strong was the impression that he instinctively drew closer to her.

The next thing he knew was that she was in his arms and her mouth was beneath his own.

Her lips were very far from being cold.

After a long moment she said, "Take me away from Charles."

He looked at her. It did not seem preposterous at all, merely the most natural thing in the world. He was still looking at her when there was a soft knock on the door and they both spun around.

"Daniel?" called Charles softly. "May I come in?"

## ii

Daniel took several seconds to answer the door. It vaguely occurred to Charles to wonder why he was taking so long, and then before he could question it further the door was opening and Daniel was on the threshold.

"I'm sorry, Charles, I wasn't sure whether I heard you. . . . Won't you come in?"

"No, I was only going to tell you that I plan to leave for Kyle of Lochalsh at ten thirty—will that be convenient for you?"

"Fine. I'll tell Rebecca."

"I've already told her," said Charles, moving on down the corridor. "I'll see you later, Daniel." He was gone.

Daniel closed the door just as Decima emerged from her hiding place behind the long curtains.

"I keep thinking he suspects something," she said. "Supposing he knows. Or supposing he suspects—"

"How can he when there's nothing to suspect?" He had himself tightly in control now. He knew exactly which course he was going to take and exactly how he was going to manage the situation. It was as if the brief interval with Charles had sharpened his sensibilities and frozen the heat in his body to ice. "There's nothing between us now, Decima, and as far as I'm concerned there never will be."

"But just now—" Her eyes were brilliant with anger, her face white with fury. "Just now—"

"Just now I was a fool, Decima, but I'm not such a fool as to make the same mistake twice. If you want to escape from your marriage you must find someone else to help you, for the help won't be coming from me."

She still stood looking at him. "But why?" she said at last. "Why? I thought a few days ago that you felt quite differently."

"I'm sorry if I misled you," he said, turning abruptly as if to terminate the conversation, "but I'm afraid there's nothing more to be said."

He waited for her to speak again, to demand a further explanation or even to lose her temper, but she was silent. And then very slowly she said: "You're sure you won't regret that, aren't you?"

He swung around. Her face was still white but her mouth was smiling.

"Regret what?" His voice was cool and casual in his ears.

"You don't want to get a bad reputation in academic circles, do you?" she said, turning from him to open the door. "They're really so fussy about professors nowadays, I've heard."

And she was gone, closing the door lightly behind her and leaving him alone at last in the solitude of his room.

### iii

Decima was not in her room when Rachel went for breakfast at nine thirty. The large, light room was neat, the bed already made, and from the window Rachel had an uninterrupted view southeast to the moors and mountains and southwest to the sea. She was just wondering whether to seek Decima downstairs when the door opened and Decima herself came quickly into the room.

"Ah, there you are!" Her cheeks were flushed and her eyes very bright, as if she were very excited. Or very angry. "I'll call for Mrs. Willie to bring up the breakfast tray. Did you sleep well?"

"Fine, thanks. I awoke early and went for a walk along the beach. . . . Is anything the matter, Decima? You look a little uneasy."

"No, it's nothing. Just nervousness. . . . I think we'll all be going into town this morning, by the way, so I hope you'll come
with me and keep me company. Daniel and Rebecca have to do
some personal shopping and I have to go with Charles to order
the food for the dinner party. As there's been no shooting party
I'm afraid we'll have to buy the venison. You wouldn't mind coming, would you?"

"Not in the least. It's a beautiful morning for a boat trip. . . .
What time is Charles planning to go?"

"About ten thirty—if I can be ready by then. I'm so bad at getting up in the mornings."

This turned out to be perfectly true. In the end it was after
eleven o'clock by the time everyone was aboard the boat and
Charles was starting up the motor.

The sun was pleasantly warm; Rachel, sitting near the stern
with the soft wind caressing her skin, found it hard in the light
of day to recall her fears of the previous evening after dark, or
even her fears of that same morning during her conversation
with Daniel by Cluny Sands. Everyone seemed perfectly normal.
Charles and Rohan were in the wheelhouse, Decima was beside
her on the seat, and the Careys were in the prow of the boat, near
enough to talk to each other but each appearing to maintain silence. She watched the back of Daniel's head for a long moment,
and then Rohan came out of the wheelhouse to join them and she
glanced out to sea abruptly.

"Are you all right, Decima? You look a little chilled."

"No, I'm fine."

Something was definitely wrong with Decima. Rohan and Rebecca had been right after all. Glancing at her friend, Rachel noticed the nervous workings of her fingers on the material of her
skirt, the restlessness of her eyes, the tenseness in every line of her
slim body. She had had nothing for breakfast except a cup of coffee, and had talked rapidly in fits and starts on any random topic
which came to her mind. It had been an uncomfortable meal and
Rachel had been glad when it was over.

Rebecca was moving. As Rachel watched, she left Daniel in the prow and went into the wheelhouse for a word with Charles before slipping belowdecks and out of sight.

Rachel began to watch Daniel again.

"Let's go below," Rohan was saying. "I'll make you some coffee, Decima."

"No, thanks."

"Sure? How about you, Rachel?"

"What?"

"Would you like some coffee?"

"Oh . . . no thanks, Rohan." Daniel had turned around and was coming toward them. The breeze was suddenly icy cool against her hot cheeks.

"Wait, Rohan," said Decima clearly. "I think I will come below with you."

"You will? Fine. Sure you won't change your mind, Raye?"

She hardly heard him. Daniel was smiling at her, sitting down in the seat Decima had just left. "I'm sorry I was rather abrupt with you this morning," he was saying, "I'm afraid I left you very suddenly with my sister."

He was sitting next to her in a casual, relaxed position, his legs stretched out and crossed at the ankles, one elbow on the back of the seat to ease the pressure on his spine, so that his body was turned slightly toward her. She felt stiff and awkward suddenly, wanting to relax and yet afraid of betraying her taut muscles by one careless movement, wanting to look at him, yet not trusting herself to meet his eyes. Her awareness of him was so immense that she thought that even if he held her in his arms it would be impossible for her to feel more at the mercy of her own emotions. And for Rachel, who had always prided herself on the level-headed advice she had given, when requested, to her lovelorn friends, such a complete reversal of her self-possession seemed to strip her of all vestiges of confidence.

She looked at him suddenly, determined that he should never know the effect he had on her, and said with candor, "Decima doesn't seem herself at all this morning. I was wondering what was the matter with her, but she says nothing is wrong."

He shrugged. "She's easily upset, it seems. . . . How calm the sea is today! The landscape looks almost at peace. Have you been to Scotland before, by the way, or is this your first visit?"

She answered him readily enough, but she had noticed how deftly he had avoided a discussion of Decima. He asked her more questions about her life in London, even about her recent visit to Florence, and while she answered she was wondering if he had had an affair with Decima and abused Charles's hospitality in the most shameful of all possible ways. Yet Rohan had not said positively that Daniel and Decima were having an affair, only that Decima was much too interested in her guest. . . . And Decima had said the previous evening that she disliked Daniel Carey and that she didn't trust him.

Either Rohan was mistaken, thought Rachel, or Decima was lying. Probably Decima was lying because she wanted Rachel's support against Charles and feared Rachel might disapprove of a confession of infidelity; she wouldn't have wanted to risk losing Rachel's sympathy at that particular moment.

Probably, too, they were having an affair. She doubted very much whether Decima would be cold and remote if she were strongly attracted to a man, and surely Daniel would have left Roshven days ago if he had failed from the outset to get what he wanted. A man like Daniel Carey would probably always get what he wanted from women with very little trouble.

"I often go down to London from Cambridge for a weekend," he was saying. "We must arrange to meet sometime. Did you say you enjoyed the theater?"

And then she was lost again, lost to the cool, clear voice of her reason appraising the situation, lost to all her sensible powers of judgment. Yes, she loved the theater, she went as often as possible, as often as she could afford it. . . .

"Afford it?" said Daniel, his fine eyes alive with surprise. "Are your escorts so mean they allow you to pay your own way?"

Normally she would have been too proud to admit that she seldom had the opportunity of an escorted visit to the theater, but some strange instinct made her be honest with him just when she most wanted to be dishonest.

"It's only girls like Decima who have a string of escorts lining up to take them out every night of the week!" she said lightly. "The rest of us aren't so fortunate. If I had to wait for a generous escort every time I wanted to see a play, I wouldn't go to the theater nearly as often as I like."

He was so astonished that she almost laughed. "You mean you go on your own?"

"Yes, of course—why not? Or perhaps I may go with a girl friend. But I don't sit around at home like a modern Cinderella if I haven't got someone to take me out."

He stared at her.

This time she did laugh. "You look as if I've just destroyed all your conventional ideas about young single women!"

He laughed too. "No, it's hardly as drastic as that, but nonetheless. . . ." He glanced away, and she did not at first realize that he was checking that no one else was within earshot. "Nonetheless, it confirms my original impression of you."

"And what was that?"

"That you're a most unusual and interesting woman." He was on his feet, not looking at her, and the breeze tore at his dark hair for a moment as he stepped over to the wheelhouse.

"May I borrow a cigarette from you, Charles? I seem to have used my last one. . . . Thanks."

She was watching him, noticing every movement, her mind teeming with every echo of their conversation and recalling every inflection of his voice. Charles gave him a cigarette and he paused in the shelter of the wheelhouse to light it. And then before he could return to her, Rebecca emerged from belowdecks and the chance to renew the conversation was gone.

Rachel turned away and stared across the sea at the inland mountains.

It was after one when they reached Kyle of Lochalsh. After they had found a place for the boat in the harbor, Charles suggested they have lunch before doing anything further, but Daniel had little enthusiasm for the idea and in the end he and Rebecca separated from the others and walked off into the town on their own. Daniel again asked Rachel to come with them, but Decima at once said that Rachel had agreed to help her buy food for the dinner party. Daniel had shrugged and said nothing further.

It was curious, Rachel thought, how everyone seemed to relax once the Careys had gone. Charles became more jovial, Rohan more loquacious, and Decima less painfully ill at ease. Rachel could even feel her own tenseness evaporate once Daniel had gone, but her thoughts were still in such turmoil that it was hard for her to concentrate afresh on Decima's troubles and the situation surrounding her. Making a great effort she managed to answer the remarks that were addressed to her, but all the time she was thinking of Daniel and remembering how he had already suggested traveling from Cambridge to London to see her.

And suddenly she didn't care what his relationship with Decima was or had been, didn't even care whether in fact it had ever existed. With something of a shock she realized she didn't care about Decima any more either. In a moment of honesty with herself she saw vividly that her world had assumed new and frightening dimensions; it was as if quite without warning she had been swept off her feet by a strong current, borne turbulently along on the crest of a huge, silent tide over which she had no control. *I'm no longer an outsider looking in at the scene being played before me,* she thought, *but part of the scene itself.*

And she felt not only a strange sense of exuberance but also a sharp pang of dread.

She had been drawn into the vortex.

## iv

Daniel said to his sister: "Things are getting dangerous."

"With Decima?"

"The situation's getting out of hand. I was a fool ever to get involved with her."

Rebecca was shocked. Daniel never made a fool of himself over a woman. "What do you mean, Danny? Why do you say that?"

He told her. They were walking up the high street past the shops selling tweeds and tartans, past the butcher, the baker, the green-grocer, but by the time they reached the little shop selling Gaelic silverware and jewelry, Rebecca had long since ceased to be conscious of her surroundings.

"My God, Danny—"

"So you can see how dangerous it is."

"But she'll have to be stopped! Something will have to be done!"

"That's my worry, not yours."

"But of course it's my worry too! She could ruin you, Danny—do you think I would stand by and see that happen? How can you say it's not my worry!"

"You've problems of your own without involving yourself in mine."

"But I'm already involved! Danny, the associate professorship you were hoping to get—supposing Decima should—"

"Precisely."

"But what shall we do?"

"You will do nothing at all," said Daniel quietly. "What I shall do remains to be seen."

*v*

They had bought all that was necessary for the dinner party after lunching at one of the inns near the harbor; Rachel had gone with Decima to buy the venison and the rest of the food while Rohan had gone with Charles to attend to buying the champagne and an assortment of other bottles that were considered necessary. By the time all the purchases were safely on board it was after three thirty and there was still no sign of the Careys.

"I think I'll stroll over to the pub at the jetty, and coax the landlord to serve me a pint of beer outside licensing hours," said Rohan. "Then I'll see the Careys when they arrive back at the boat. Will anyone come with me?"

"Perhaps I will," Charles said. "Decima?"

"No, I'm too tired. I'll wait here."

"I'll stay with Decima," said Rachel, before she could be asked. "You two go off and have your beer."

When they had gone Decima complained of a headache and went aft to make herself coffee in the tiny galley. "Do you want some, Raye?"

"No, thanks. I'm going up on deck, I think. Will you be all right down there?"

"Yes, I'll have some coffee and then lie down for a minute. I hope the Careys won't be too long. I feel like going home now."

"I'll give you a call when I see them." She went up on the deck and moved into the wheelhouse to escape the increasing chill of the sea breeze. It was cloudier now, the best part of the day already over, and the sea was swaying restlessly as if in anticipation of rain to come.

She began to wonder where Daniel was and what he was doing. She had scarcely been five minutes in the wheelhouse before she saw him. He was walking toward the jetty with Rebecca, and as they passed the pub Rohan and Charles must have attracted their attention for they stopped and looked at one of the downstairs windows. Presently Rebecca went inside the pub, but Daniel remained outside, and as Rachel watched he started walking away from the building toward the jetty and the boat.

There was a tightness suddenly beneath her heart, a hollow in the pit of her stomach. She sat perfectly still, watching him walk the length of the jetty, and as she watched it seemed to her that she had been waiting for many years without knowing what she was waiting for, knowing only that she would recognize the moment when it came.

He reached the boat, saw her, smiled. The hull shifted in the water as he climbed aboard.

"I thought I'd find you here," he said. "Where's Decima?"

"Down in the cabin resting."

"I see." He stepped into the wheelhouse beside her and glanced down the jetty toward the pub, but no one was in sight. "The others should be here in a minute."

"Yes, I saw Rebecca go in to fetch them."

There was silence.

Rachel was steadfastly watching the gray stone walls of the pub with its swaying sign above the doorway. Presently she felt Daniel's hand on her arm, and as she glanced around at him instinctively, he began to speak. "Don't believe—" But he stopped.

The sentence was never completed.

Afterward all Rachel could remember was the grip of his fingers on her wrists and the harsh warmth of his lips on her mouth. There was heat, a blaze of power, the pressure of hard muscles taut in a hard, strong body, and then suddenly it was over and the dark dizziness was ebbing before her eyes so that she could see at last past Daniel to the deck where Decima stood frozen in immobility as she watched them.

Rachel felt his lips move.

Daniel spun around.

"Well, well," said Decima politely in her softest, sweetest voice. "It seems as if I underestimated you, Raye. You certainly don't waste much time, do you? So sorry to interrupt you both at such a terribly awkward moment but I thought I'd just tell you that the others have left the pub and are on their way over here. . . ."

## vi

It was raining by the time they reached Roshven. Heavy clouds had sunk over the mountain summits and laid dark fingers across the moors behind the sands. After making her escape as quickly as possible to her room, Rachel found that the fire was already lit and the housekeeper had just put a pitcher of hot water on the washstand for her.

She undressed thankfully, stripping off the clothes which had become sodden in the short journey from the jetty to the house, and huddled herself in the quilt from the bed for a moment before taking advantage of the warm water.

She was just putting on her wool dress some minutes later when there was a soft tap at the door.

"Who's that?"

"Decima."

Oh God, thought Rachel. She could already feel the crimson of embarrassment suffusing her neck and creeping upward to her face. Decima was the last person she wanted to talk to.

"I'm just dressing for dinner, Decima—can it wait?"

"No, I want to talk to you."

The zipper at the side of the dress jammed in her hot fingers. "Just a moment."

The zipper refused to go either up or down. "Oh hell!" muttered Rachel at last, abandoning it, and wrenched open the door much more violently than she had intended.

Decima was dressed for dinner. She wore black, a plain, simple dress, and above her left breast was a diamond brooch which glittered in the dim glow of the lamp and firelight.

"Yes?" said Rachel abruptly.

Decima moved into the room without speaking. Then, as Rachel closed the door: "I just wanted to warn you about Daniel."

Rachel suddenly felt very angry indeed. After all, what right did Decima have to act so possessively where Daniel was concerned? Decima, a married woman, had much less right to Daniel than she had, and certainly no right at all to criticize Rachel's behavior with him. "I've nothing to say about Daniel," she heard herself say coolly. "I'm only surprised that you should want to talk about him."

Decima raised her eyebrows slightly. "You're very quick to take offense all of a sudden, aren't you? Why should you feel so guilty just because I saw you kissing Daniel this afternoon at Kyle of

Lochalsh? Is a kiss such a novel experience for you that you're overcome with remorse and shame for days afterward?"

"I—"

"I only wanted to warn you that Daniel has a very accomplished way with women. Charles tells me that when Daniel was an undergraduate at Oxford—"

"I'm not interested," said Rachel furiously, "in past gossip. I don't care how many affairs Daniel has had, and even if I did care, it's certainly none of my business. But what I *am* interested in is why you deliberately misled me last night when you came here to tell me about Charles! Why did you lie and say that Daniel wasn't interested in women and that you didn't trust him when you'd been secretly having an affair with him for the past few weeks?"

The light was uncertain but she thought she saw Decima turn very pale. "I—I was too ashamed . . . I thought if I could avoid telling you—"

"How much else have you avoided telling me, Decima?"

There was a long silence. "What do you mean?"

"I couldn't help wondering how much the failure of your marriage was Charles's fault and how much was yours."

Another silence. Then, "I—" She hesitated. "I suppose we were both to blame in some ways . . . I was so angry when I saw Charles had married me for my money that I didn't behave very well at Oxford. . . . There was nothing wrong, you understand, but once or twice I drank too much at the sedate cocktail parties, and embarrassed Charles. And I flirted now and again with a couple of students, just out of boredom. . . . But I was never unfaithful! Even now, with Daniel, even though he begged me and begged me to be unfaithful to Charles, I always somehow managed to keep my head and refuse him. Rachel, you've no idea what a strain I've had to endure these past few weeks! I was genuinely attracted to Daniel but was terrified in case Charles should find out. Then I began to wonder if Charles was secretly encouraging Daniel so that once I was proved unfaithful he would have the excuse for any kind of revenge. I could hardly believe, you see, that Daniel would behave so shamefully to Charles, whom I knew he respected and liked."

"That certainly seems hard to believe, but how much encouragement did you give him?"

"None at all, I swear it! But I did find him attractive, I admit it, and sometimes it was very hard—in fact impossible—to keep aloof from him. Perhaps it's hard for you to understand, but—"

Rachel found it all too easy to understand. She was beginning to feel slightly sick; her head ached dully. "I'm surprised Charles didn't realize what was happening."

"That's why I began to think he was secretly conniving at Daniel's behavior. He even encouraged the Careys to stay at Roshven as long as possible! And then I began to think—imagine—all kinds of things; I thought they might all be in a plot against me, maneuvering me into some terrible position from which there was no retreat. . . . I—I've been so frightened, Raye, it's all been such a nightmare. . . ." She was trembling; she had to sit down. "I'm sorry if I behaved badly to you this afternoon when I saw you with Daniel, but my nerves were in such shreds that I couldn't even think clearly. It just seemed to me that you, the only person I could trust, were being gradually prized away and turned against me, and the thought was so shattering and frightful that I lost control of myself altogether. You do believe me, don't you, Raye? You're not against me, are you?"

"Of course not," said Rachel shortly. "Don't be silly." But beneath her reassuring manner, she was badly shaken, her mind a mass of conflicts and doubts.

It was undeniably true that everyone she had spoken to that day had tried to turn her against Decima. It was probably also true that Daniel was so accustomed to getting his own way with women that he couldn't resist amusing himself with her. No doubt he had thought her quaint and old-fashioned and had enjoyed seeing how much he could disconcert her and disrupt her conventional behavior.

The headache had become a tight pain behind the eyes.

"Have you got some aspirin by any chance, Decima?"

"Aspirin? Yes, of course. . . . Listen, why don't we have dinner together in my room? I don't want to face the others again to-night. We could have a quiet dinner and talk for a while and then have an early night."

"Wouldn't that look rather suspicious? Anyway, I'm well enough —it's just a slight headache. I really think I'd better dine with every-one else."

In spite of everything, she still had no wish to miss an opportu-nity to see Daniel. As she returned from Decima's room with the aspirin bottle five minutes later she wondered how she could still find him attractive when she knew beyond any doubt that he could not care for her.

Daniel cared only for Decima; the entire scene in the wheel-house that afternoon had probably been enacted with the specific intent of making Decima jealous in the hope of increasing her in-terest in him.

Twenty minutes later, her headache eased, she went down to the dining room for dinner.

Decima made no appearance at dinner, but Charles and Rohan were talkative enough and spent most of the meal discussing plans for the dinner party on the following evening while recalling their own twenty-first birthday celebrations years earlier; in contrast, Rebecca said little and Rachel, too, found she had less than usual to say. Daniel did not look at her once throughout the entire meal and said no word to anyone. At the earliest opportunity he ex-cused himself and withdrew from the room.

Rebecca at length went off to the library to read; Charles retired to his study to look at his manuscript for a while, and Rachel and Rohan were left facing each other across the table.

Rohan leaned forward to move the candelabra. "Why didn't Decima come down tonight?"

"She said she was tired."

"And what do you say she was?"

"She certainly looked tired. She really is in a very nervous state, Rohan. I feel quite worried about her."

"If her nerves are in a bad way," said Rohan, "she has only herself to blame."

"Oh? And what's that remark supposed to mean?"

"She could leave tomorrow if she wanted to."

"Don't be a fool! How could she possibly walk out on this celebration dinner party which has been so carefully arranged and planned? She's committed to staying here at least until the morning of her birthday. And she tells me she hasn't the cash in hand to leave before then anyway."

"Daniel has."

"I don't think Daniel would be such a fool as to take her away with him."

"You mean you don't like to think Daniel would be such a fool."

"Look here, Rohan—"

"You're attracted to Daniel, aren't you? No, don't try and tell me that's nonsense! I know you too well, Rachel—I know when you like a man and when you don't. But you can forget Daniel. He's totally absorbed in Decima."

"I—" Rachel began, but Rohan wasn't listening.

"Do you think I didn't notice as soon as I came to Roshven how things were between them?" he interrupted. "Do you think it wasn't obvious to me that he wanted her and was trying every trick he knew to get her to go away with him?" His voice was a little unsteady. As if to cover up his lack of self-possession he reached for the carafe of wine and clumsily poured some more into his glass. But his hand was trembling; the wine spilled into dark red pools on the white cloth. "I told Charles," he said. "But he didn't believe me. Can you imagine that? This morning after I left you I saw Decima slip into Daniel's room to wait for him to come back from the boat, and I knew damn well what she was waiting for. I went to Charles and said—"

"You had no right to do that, Rohan. It's no concern of yours," Rachel interrupted sharply.

"Charles is my cousin, isn't he?"

"That's got nothing to do with it. You had no right to interfere."

"Christ Almighty!" shouted Rohan, setting down his glass with such a crash that the frail stem seemed to shiver. "Don't preach to me! Don't get up into your little Victorian pulpit and preach sermons to me about what to do and what not to do! What do you know about life anyway? You've never been in love, never gone to bed with anyone, never—"

"What on earth's that got to do with you sneaking to Charles to tell him that his guest's trying to seduce his wife? Good God, if Charles hasn't the perception to see when a guest of his is behaving disgracefully, he deserves to have his wife seduced! I'm not surprised he didn't welcome you interfering in his affairs!"

"But if he knew Daniel was trying to seduce Decima, why the hell didn't he throw Daniel out of Roshven? And besides, he didn't believe me when I told him about them! He was so vain, so incredibly pompous and conceited that he thought it was impossible that Decima should ever think of being unfaithful to him! And all along he's insisted that the Careys stay at Roshven!"

"Then either he's a fool or else he has special reasons of his own for keeping the Careys here."

"What reasons?" demanded Rohan. "Give me one good reason why he should continue to keep his wife's lover in his house!"

"According to Decima, they're not lovers."

"If they're not, it's not for want of trying on Daniel's part!"

"How do you know?"

He stared at her. "I've been watching them."

"Spying on them, you mean, don't you?"

"I—"

"For God's sake, Rohan, what on earth are you trying to do? Are you Charles's self-appointed private eye, or something? To be quite blunt, what is it to you whether Decima goes to bed with Daniel or not?"

Rohan pulled back his chair and stood up so abruptly that the chair fell over backward. "It's quite obvious," he said, striding over to the door, "that you haven't the slightest grasp of the situation at all."

She allowed him thirty seconds for his rage to cool and then followed him into the little drawing room off the great hall. He was standing by the blazing log fire, and in his hands was a carved ivory paper knife which he had apparently picked up from the desk in his agitation. The ivory was curved like a tusk, and the upper half of the tusk was the sheath into which the blade of the knife could be inserted, while the lower half of the tusk was the handle in which the blade was embedded. Rachel could not remember seeing it before.

"Where did that come from?"

"It's Rebecca's. She bought it in Edinburgh just before she came to Roshven." He put it down abruptly, and she saw that the carvings on the ivory surface were of Chinese figures, each perfectly executed and designed.

She picked it up idly.

"There are two questions I should like to see answered," said Rohan suddenly. "First, why should Charles tolerate Daniel's behavior and in fact actively encourage the Careys to stay, and second, why should Decima have chosen to stay here when she had the means and opportunity to escape earlier?"

"Roshven *is* her home, Rohan. Why should she allow herself to be driven away?" She pulled the tusk apart absentmindedly and ran her index finger along the edge of the blade. "Goodness, this knife's sharp! You could dissect an Aberdeen Angus with it." She sucked her finger where a faint line of red was already showing, and put the knife back on the table.

"But surely," Rohan was saying, "if Decima was really in such a state of nerves as the result of her relationship with Daniel or Charles or both of them, would she care much about leaving Roshven for a while? Wouldn't she be merely glad to escape?"

"But what chance has there been for her to escape?"

"Daniel—"

"I'm quite sure that Daniel wouldn't have been so foolish as to commit himself in that way."

"How do you know?" said Rohan. "He's little more than a stranger to you. How do you know what he might or might not do?"

The knife was a mere white blur on the polished surface of the table. Rachel picked it up again blindly, her fingers working over the cool surface. Everything Rohan said was true. What did she know of Daniel? How did she know that Daniel hadn't asked Decima to go away with him, and then on her refusal had paid Rachel attention to make Decima jealous? Wasn't it obvious that the scene in the wheelhouse had merely been to incite Decima to reexamine her feelings for him? It had clearly been a successful maneuver, for that same evening at Roshven Decima had come to her to try to turn her against Daniel so that she might have him for herself once more.

Decima, with her money and beauty and her effortless, graceful poise. . . . It was so easy to picture her with Daniel, much easier to picture her with him than with Charles. It seemed that Decima was playing some game of her own, planning all the time to go away with Daniel eventually.

"Is anything the matter, Rachel? You look very white."

Decima had always had what she wanted. Life was very easy for people like Decima who were constantly beset with favors and attentions, admiration and compliments. Daniel would seem just like any other man to her, another name to add to the long list of men who had stopped to look at her more than once. Decima didn't need Daniel except to use him in obtaining whatever it was she wanted. Decima didn't care.

But Rachel cared. "No," she said. "Nothing's the matter."

"Has Daniel—"

"I don't want to talk about Daniel any more." The knife slipped from her hands and fell loudly on the table. "I think I'll go to bed early. My headache seems to be getting worse."

"If you want some aspirin—"

"No, Decima gave me some already, thanks. Good night, Rohan."

"Good night," he said slowly, and she knew even though she did not glance back at him that his gray eyes were sharp and watchful as he noted her withdrawal and drew his own conclusions from her behavior. Rohan always saw too much.

Moving swiftly, hardly knowing where she was going, she found her way across the hall and stumbled upstairs to the comforting privacy of her room.

## *vii*

She awoke very suddenly just after midnight. The wind was whispering at the window again and humming in the eaves, and the rain was a light, stealthy patter against the pane. It was pitch dark. All she could see was the luminous dial of her little traveling clock and the white strip of the sheet turned down over the quilt.

She sat up listening.

The house was still, yet something had waked her. Maybe she had been dreaming and on awakening had confused the dream with consciousness.

She went on listening but heard nothing, and presently she slipped out of bed and moved across to the door without lighting the lamp. She was just about to ease the door open when she heard the creak of a floorboard in the corridor outside. Unreasonably, her scalp tingled. Her limbs froze, and movement was impossible. She was suddenly and uncontrollably frightened.

It was hard to judge how long she stood there in the darkness waiting, but after a minute of complete silence she managed to edge noiselessly back to her bedside table and find the matches to light the lamp. The glow of light was reassuring. With the lamp in her hand she turned back to the door. No doubt she was being foolish and would laugh at herself in the clear light of morning, but she knew she would be unable to fall asleep easily again unless the door was locked.

It was not until she reached the door that she discovered that there was no key in the lock.

Perhaps it was on the other side.

It was at least two minutes before she could bring herself to turn

the handle and pull the door slowly inward toward herself. There
was no one outside. Stepping into the corridor quickly, she saw it
was empty.

There was still no sign of a key. She paused, uncertain of what
she should do, and as she hesitated she saw that there was a faint
glow at the far end of the corridor, as if a large lamp was still burning downstairs in the hall. Suddenly making up her mind, she
blew out her lamp, leaving it in her room, and returned to the
passage.

Decima's door, further down on the right of the corridor, was
closed and although Rachel knocked lightly on the panels and
called out softly to ask if she were asleep, there was no reply. She
tried the handle but the door was locked. Decima at least had a
key for her room.

Rachel moved on. The gallery when she reached it was in darkness but as she glanced over the banisters she saw that one of the
large lamps was indeed burning on the table in the hall below.
Again she paused. Her knowledge of the house was still slight, but
she knew that her room was in the south wing of the house and
that Decima's room was in the southeast turret with windows
which overlooked both the mountains and moors in the east and
the sands and cliffs to the south. Charles apparently had rooms in
the west wing which faced the sea, and she could remember Rohan
mentioning that his room also faced the ocean. The north wing
was no longer used, the gamekeeper and his wife now preferring
to live in the small croft a hundred yards from the house. This
meant that the Careys had probably been given rooms in the east
wing which faced the mountains and moors, and it was in the
east wing that Rachel now stood. Unlike the other wings of the
house, the corridor was open on one side so that it was possible to
look over the banisters into the great hall below, and halfway
down the corridor the twin staircases linking the two floors curved
to meet in a wide landing. At the far end of the corridor, a more
insignificant staircase spiraled upward in the northeast turret to
lead to empty rooms on higher, deserted floors, but the main
staircase, beginning as it did in the great hall itself, had more style

and elegance. On the side of the corridor which did not face the hall and stairs, six doors led into the six rooms of the east wing. As she moved toward the landing and the head of the stairs, she saw that one of the doors was ajar.

She stopped.

The room was in darkness. After a moment's hesitation she tapped on the panels, but when no one responded she pushed the door open wider and glanced into the room.

The bed was unslept-in, the curtains of the windows still undrawn, but the embers of a fire burned in the grate, and from their glow there was sufficient light for her to see without the aid of a lamp.

Daniel kept his room neat. A pair of masculine slippers stood near the bed; a dressing gown lay precisely across one of the high-backed armchairs where it had been placed, not thrown, by its owner. There was a pair of silver clothes brushes on the high dresser, a large plain comb beside them, and by the washstand was an old-fashioned razor set incongruously beside a modern tube of shaving cream.

Not wanting to pry among his belongings, she withdrew quickly to the corridor again, but not before she was aware of her curiosity to explore further, to strain to discover more about him than the facts she already knew. After the scene in the wheelhouse that afternoon, she was conscious of an immense desire to find other evidence of his personality, other clues to his past. How had his life been spent when he was away from his books and his research? What had his childhood been like, his adolescence? Had there been disappointments and disillusionment, or had the path of his success been so clearly marked from the beginning that he had never known the pain of failure or the pangs of frustration? Had he many friends at Cambridge? Did he live alone there, or—

But she decided not to pursue this line of thought. She had already told Rohan in indignation that she was not concerned with Daniel's past relations with the opposite sex, and to dwell upon the subject now would make her earlier remark seem hypocritical.

Moving quickly, as if to shake off all thought of Daniel's possible associations, she left the room and went out onto the landing again.

There was still no one in sight.

Then where was Daniel? And who had left the light burning in the hall?

It was not until she was halfway down the stairs that it occurred to her to wonder if Decima really had been sleeping so soundly behind her locked door. She stopped, her hand on the banister as she glanced back over her shoulder at the silent gallery she had just left.

It was then that she heard the sound of voices. They seemed far away, a mere murmur sighing through the vast silence of the hall, but on reaching the last stair she found that the sound was coming from one of the rooms leading off the hall to the left of the staircase. She stepped over to the library, and then realized that the voices came from Charles's study next door, the ground floor of the southeast turret.

She drew nearer. The door was almost shut and the occupants of the room obviously believed that it was completely closed; having been about to knock and enter to find out who was up so late, Rachel instinctively hesitated as the first snatches of conversation reached her ears.

"No," Charles Mannering was saying strongly. "That would be out of the question. My dear, you've attended University. You know how things are. Of course if I were free it would be a different matter."

A woman spoke—Rebecca's strong, resonant voice, hushed now and low. "But Charles, supposing Decima—"

"Decima knows nothing, suspects nothing."

"Then why did she invite that girl here?"

"A mere foil to divert attention from herself."

"But supposing Decima should suspect—"

"My dear, Decima is totally absorbed in herself and always will be. Do you suppose she has any time for suspicions?"

"Charles. . . ."

And then a silence broken only by a sharp intake of breath, a stifled exclamation, and seconds later a small, spent sigh.

Rachel took a step backward in retreat. Her limbs were stiff and awkward as if suddenly released from a long paralysis, her thoughts spinning in shocked staccato patterns. Her first coherent reaction was that whatever happened they must not find her in the hall, must never guess that she had overheard Charles talking of a time when he might be "free," speculating on Decima's suspicions, referring to her with such casual contempt.

She must hide. She had to think. Her mind was whirling dizzily and all she was aware of was that Charles cared nothing about his wife's activities and would not risk losing Rebecca by making any move which might result in Daniel taking her away.

She opened the door of the drawing room where she had talked to Rohan earlier and stumbled inside. Something moved on the hearth. As she jumped and stifled a cry of shock, a draft from the chimney made the dying fire throw out a shaft of light and she saw that the St. Bernard had been stretched out on the hearthrug in slumber and that she had waked him.

He gave a deep growl.

"It's all right, George," she whispered. "It's only me."

He still growled, but now his tail was swaying from side to side. The firelight glinted in his eyes and made them look glazed and fierce.

She sank down in an armchair. Presently the dog relaxed too, still watching her, and they faced each other across the hearth. Beyond the dog stood the desk, its polished surface smooth, the red leather blotter glowing, the small calendar showing a date which was already three days old, the glass paperweight reflecting odd beams of the firelight.

Presently she stood up, moved restlessly over to the desk, and altered the date on the calendar. It was now the morning of Saturday, the twelfth of September. Tonight at eight the dinner would begin to celebrate Decima's coming of age, and the next time the clocks struck midnight it would be to herald the beginning of Decima's twenty-first birthday. If anything were to happen to her, it would have to happen within the next twenty-four hours.

She replaced the calendar and then stopped to look at the desk. Surely something was missing. The top of the desk looked different in some way. She recalled her talk with Rohan in that same room a few hours before, and as the scene came back into her mind she glanced at the smooth, empty surface of the table by the chair on the other side of the hearth.

Memory returned; the white ivory paper knife with the razor-sharp edge was gone.

There was a void suddenly in the pit of her stomach; her hands were clammy. Steady, she told herself. Don't jump to conclusions. Rohan probably moved it absentmindedly after I was gone.

She thought again of her conversation with him, the memory running through her mind like a strip of film. The knife had been on the desk by the paperweight and then Rohan had picked it up in his agitation, only to put it down again on the table a moment later. Then Rachel herself had picked it up and handled it for a short time. But she could clearly remember replacing it on the table by the chair.

She looked around, checking the mantelpiece, opening the drawers of the desk, even going over to the window seat on the far side of the room. She was just pausing to examine the bric-a-brac in a small cabinet by the window when she suddenly knew beyond any doubt that she was no longer alone in the room.

She whirled around, her hand flying to her mouth as she saw the dark shadow watching her.

"Looking for something, Rachel?" inquired Daniel's cool voice from the doorway.

# Chapter Five

*i*

He came into the room, his feet soundless on the soft carpet, and closed the door behind him. The dog's tail thumped on the hearth in recognition, but Daniel ignored him.

"What are you doing down here at this hour?" His voice was still polite but the hard edge to it was unmistakable. Rachel was aware suddenly of the power of his presence, his ability to take command of a scene merely by entering a room.

"I couldn't sleep." Her fingers were automatically drawing her dressing gown closer around her. "I came downstairs to look for a book I thought I'd left here."

"I see," he said, and she knew he disbelieved her. "And have you found it?"

"No. No, I—"

"What was it called?"

There was a small, deadly pause. She was completely unable to think of any title whatsoever.

"It was just a novel," she stammered. "I don't remember the title. It had a dark green cover with black lettering."

"I'll help you look for it."

"No, please . . . I'm not even sure that I left it in here." Her self-possession was ebbing so fast that she almost felt she might turn and run from the room if he persisted in questioning her about the book. Emotional claustrophobia overwhelmed her; she began to move swiftly over to the door, but he was nearer the doorway than she was and in three strides he was there before her.

She stopped.

"What's the matter?" he said. "You look very shaken. What's been happening?"

The impossibility of telling him that she had eavesdropped on Charles and Rebecca made her say the first thing that came into her head. "What are *you* doing down here?" she demanded. "Why are you still up?"

"I never go to bed before midnight," he said shortly. "I've been in the library reading and when I left to go upstairs just now I thought I heard sounds from this room."

She found to her horror that she had nothing to say. She felt the color suffuse her neck and creep upward to her face, and it seemed as if all the self-consciousness of the past had combined in one enormous moment of embarrassment and diffidence. The brass handle of the door was cool against her hot palm. She tried to turn it but he put his hand over hers and stopped her.

"I want to talk to you."

This was no scene played for Decima's benefit. Decima was upstairs behind her locked door. No matter how ambiguous his attitude might have seemed that afternoon in the wheelhouse, there could be no ambiguity this time in the drawing room with the door closed to the world beyond and the fire dying in the grate.

"Perhaps it could wait till tomorrow," she said, the old mixture of pride and fear and a dozen other muddled emotions making her withdraw from him although she longed for him to contradict her and force her to stay. "I'm very tired."

During past encounters with other men this had always been the point at which her involuntary coolness had resulted in her being left alone to regret her words. The man would have been either offended or disheartened; either he had never cared sufficiently to persist in overriding her request, or else he had never had the perspicacity to see that the apparent rejection was not a rejection at all but merely a craving for reassurance. Every man she had ever known well before had always chosen this moment to turn and walk away.

"Tired?" said Daniel. "I thought you said you were so restless you had to come downstairs for a book? Come and sit down for a moment and tell me why you look as if you'd seen a ghost."

"I—it was nothing." But she allowed herself to turn from the door and sink down on the sofa beside the hearth. "The house was so still that I became foolish and started imagining I heard noises and saw shapes in the shadows."

He sat down on the sofa beside her; the springs creaked softly beneath his weight and then were still.

"Did Decima say anything?" he said at last.

"About the scene in the wheelhouse? No, nothing."

"Nothing at all?"

"Nothing."

So perhaps after all he was merely interested in Decima, curious to find out her reaction to the scene in the wheelhouse. Standing up blindly, she moved back to the door. "You'll excuse me, but I really mustn't stay. . . . I'll find my book in the morning."

But he was already standing up to follow her. Wanting only to escape from him now, she stepped quickly into the hall and was already past the threshold when she saw to her horror that Charles and Rebecca were just leaving the library.

She stopped.

Behind her Daniel too was motionless and she heard his sharp intake of breath. Across the hall Charles hesitated, his fingers still on the door handle as he drew it shut, and Rebecca, her cheeks hot, stared at Rachel.

There was a silence. Then: "So you two are up late as well," said Charles. "Or did something bring you downstairs, Rachel?" He had noticed her shabby dressing gown.

She suddenly realized that her face was still flushed from the encounter with Daniel. No doubt both Charles and Rebecca would think that she and Daniel had had some kind of rendezvous in the drawing room. . . . She could feel the color deepening in her cheeks and then Daniel was stepping past her toward his sister, his movements easy and relaxed.

"Rachel was looking for a book she'd left behind earlier this evening." He was composed and untroubled. Once again he had entered a scene and blandly assumed control of the situation. "Are you coming upstairs, now, Rebecca? Or shall I see you tomorrow morning?"

The words drew an innuendo which was a mere nuance as thin as a razor's edge but the tone of his voice gave the implication an uncomfortable depth.

"I don't know what that remark's supposed to mean," said Charles much too quickly. "What are you trying to imply, Daniel?"

"Why, merely that I'm going to bed myself and wondered if she intended to do likewise! What else could I mean?" He was mocking Charles, entangling him in verbal snares. "Good night."

"Wait!"

"Yes?"

Charles suddenly became aware of Rachel's presence and stopped. There was another awkward pause.

"If you'll excuse me . . ." Rachel muttered, and hurried past the group with her eyes on the ground. She could feel their eyes watching her as she ran upstairs and stumbled along the corridor to her room, and then as she reached the sanctuary she wrenched open the door and slammed it shut after her in her relief.

She sat down, still breathing unevenly, but presently, when she had recovered her breath, she opened her door again and went back into the passage. Decima must be told of the overheard conversation between Charles and Rebecca. Moving cautiously back down the passage Rachel hesitated outside the door of Decima's room and then, hearing the sound of voices, she moved on to the gallery. There was no one in the hall, but she could hear an argument. They must have gone back to the study, or perhaps to the library, for although she could hear the voices she was still too far away to distinguish what was being said.

She hesitated and then, realizing that this was a good opportunity to see Decima without danger of discovery, she went back to the locked door.

"Decima! Decima, are you awake?" She knocked swiftly on the panels. "Decima, wake up!"

There was movement within, the flare of a match, the flickering of light beneath the door.

"Rachel?" called Decima nervously.

"Yes—can you let me in?"

"Just a moment."

More noises, the soft padding of slippers, the turning of the key in the lock, and then Decima was facing her across the threshold.

"What is it?" Her voice was almost hostile. "What do you want?"

This was not the welcome Rachel had expected. "Can I come in for a moment?" she said uneasily. "It's difficult to talk out here."

Decima opened the door without a word.

"Has something happened, Decima?"

"Nothing." She turned aside and went back to the bed. "I've just decided to open the door to no one either tonight or tomorrow evening before the party."

"Not even to me?"

"Not even to you."

"You mean you no longer trust me?" Rachel was both astonished and angry. "Oh come, Decima! Just because Daniel—"

"Deny you're attracted to him, then!" Decima flared, whirling around to face her. "Deny it! But you won't deny it, because it's true. And if it's true then I no longer trust you."

"You're being absurd," said Rachel coolly. "For goodness' sake, Decima, pull yourself together! You're being both melodramatic and hysterical."

"Who are you to talk of melodrama?" Decima exclaimed furiously. "You with your adolescent infatuation, your schoolgirl's crush—"

Rachel turned aside abruptly. "There's nothing more to be said."

"I'm beginning to think Rohan's the only one I can trust," Decima blazed, still trembling, her blue eyes narrow and hard. "He at least hates Daniel."

Rachel didn't listen. She was so angry that she went out and slammed the door violently behind her, and it was not until she was back in her room again that she realized she had mentioned not one word to Decima of the conversation she had overheard between Charles and Rebecca.

And as she thought of Charles and Rebecca she remembered the sounds of argument she had heard a few minutes ago, and it occurred to her to wonder what was happening in the library where Charles had gone with his guests.

*ii*

Rachel awoke early again and lay listening for a long while to the still house. At last, unable to bear her immobility a moment longer, she got up and went over to draw the curtains. The morning was pale and cool, the sun visible but remote. Soon the clouds would creep in from the Atlantic and form a gray world of sky and sea, but at present the sunlight was strong enough to give a greenish tinge to the moors and a blue darkness to the swaying sea.

Rachel dressed and went downstairs. The housekeeper was busy in the scullery, and after taking some hot water Rachel withdrew to one of the rooms near the kitchen to wash. There was a supply of running water on the ground floor of the house and two bathrooms near the kitchen, but hot water still had to be heated in the kitchen and transported gallon by gallon to the nearest bathroom. It occurred to Rachel as she staggered beneath the weight of two enormous jugs of steaming water that people who deprecated the modern comforts of the twentieth century should try living for a time in a house with no hot running water and no electricity. When she had finished dressing it was still early, too early for Decima to have stirred from her bed. Rachel wondered if anyone else was up. After hesitating for a while she went downstairs again to the kitchen. No one was about. The housekeeper had disappeared. Rachel found some porridge simmering on the range, helped herself to a bowlful, and put the kettle on for tea, but even by the time she had finished her meal no one had come to interrupt her. She was just about to take the dirty dishes out to the scullery to wash them when there was the sound of footsteps in the hall and the next moment Charles walked into the room.

He stopped abruptly when he saw her. He looked tired, she thought. His mouth was drawn and there were lines of exhaustion about his eyes so that he looked closer to fifty than a man not yet forty years old.

"Oh, it's you," he said. "Is Mrs. Willie about? I want to talk to her about the arrangements for the dinner party tonight."

"No, she seems to have disappeared."

"Perhaps she went back to her croft to cook Willie his breakfast." He went through into the scullery and looked at the saucepan of porridge without enthusiasm. Presently he came back into the kitchen and stared out of the window at the backyard beyond.

Rachel waited awkwardly, wanting to escape yet not knowing how to do so without appearing rude. She was just rising to her feet a moment later when Charles said suddenly: "I'd like to talk to you. Would you have any objection if we walked out a little way over the moors?"

Rachel was astonished. "Why, yes—yes, if you like, Charles," she managed to say. "Do you want to go now?"

"If you don't mind."

"No, of course not. I'll just run upstairs and get my coat."

There was still no one about, no sign of movement from upstairs. In her room once more, she found her coat and slipped it over her shoulders. Then, still wondering what Charles could intend to say to her, she went downstairs to the kitchen to rejoin him.

He was still standing by the window, his hands in his pockets. As she came in he turned to face her. "All right?"

She nodded.

"Good." He led the way outside, and the cool, soft air of the Highland seas fanned her cheek as she stepped into the sunlight. She drew a deep breath, savoring the breeze's freshness, and then followed Charles across the yard and up the hillside to the north of the house, past a cow nibbling at the short grass and a sow with six piglets in the meadow beyond. There was a potato patch and a row of cabbages by the small croft where Willie the game-keeper lived with his wife, and then Charles was leading the way out to the moors and up onto the cliff which rose above the sands.

"I wanted to get out of the house," he said. "Then there's no chance of anyone eavesdropping."

Remembering how she herself had eavesdropped yesterday evening, Rachel immediately felt herself blush scarlet, but fortunately he was ahead of her and did not notice. They walked on until the ground no longer tilted uphill but ran evenly along the top of the cliffs. To their left came the roar of the sea as the surf thundered on the beach, and to the right loomed the nearest of the mountains, its bare slopes arid and rocky in the clear light.

There was a ragged stone circle ahead, the relic of some ancient tribe. Charles selected one of the stones that had fallen to the ground and sat down on it.

"Cigarette, Rachel?"

"No, thanks."

She watched him light the cigarette and then toss the match away onto the damp ground. The flame smoldered, flared for a minute, and then died in a thin curl of smoke.

After a long moment, he said: "Why did Decima invite you here?"

Rachel searched desperately for a plausible explanation. "I—I was an old friend . . . I suppose—as it was her twenty-first birth-day she felt she would like to see me again—"

"I don't believe that," said Charles. "I don't mean to say that you're lying, but I think you've been misled. You're so utterly dissimilar from Decima that I can't visualize her wanting to resurrect a schoolgirl friendship."

"But—"

"Decima hadn't contacted you since her marriage, had she? Why would she suddenly decide to do so?"

"I'm sorry, Charles, but I just don't understand what you're driving at. As far as I know—"

"But you know so little, don't you," he said. "You don't know anything at all." His fingers were unsteady, she noticed with a shock; the hand which held the cigarette was shaking. There was a long pause. Then: "I've been very foolish," he said at last. "I must have been quite mad. But it's not always easy to be as clever and wise as one always imagines oneself to be, is it? Sometimes you don't even realize how foolish you've been until it's too late to draw back."

She could think of nothing to say. Below them the ocean roared far away beneath the cliffs, and the clouds were billowing toward them from the horizon.

"I've been having an affair with Rebecca," he said suddenly. "I know you're aware of that because Daniel told me last night that he had seen you outside the library listening to the conversation I was having with her."

"I—" Guilt and horror made speech impossible. She could only stare at him with burning eyes while rage against Daniel throbbed through her mind.

"Daniel was angry," said Charles as if this explained everything. "We were all angry. We had an exhausting, abortive, endless quarrel which left us all drained of any vestige of emotion." He drew on his cigarette. "After it was all over I felt as if I'd been shaken to my senses after six weeks of foolish illusions. And then I began to wonder what Decima had said to you and why you were here, and I resolved to speak to you as soon as I could to tell you the truth and find out how far the situation had been misrepresented to you."

His sincerity was almost painful. Rachel could hardly bear to look at him.

"I love Decima," he said. "I always have. I think it would be true to say that I loved her even more after we were married than before. Perhaps you find it hard to understand why I love her so much when we really have very little in common; we share no interests, come from different backgrounds, even different generations. But that makes no difference. After that terrible quarrel with the Careys last night I realized that in spite of all that had happened nothing had changed. I would never consent to losing her. How could I? Our marriage at the moment is a mockery, but I would rather have her on those terms than not have her at all." He was staring down at his cigarette, his shoulders hunched, his limbs tensed and motionless. "Besides," he said after a moment, "the situation as it exists now between us could hardly get any worse. After thinking about it all night, I came to the conclusion that if I made a great effort and did all I could, things might still work out. If I could take Decima abroad for a while—if we could get away from this place, this prison, this enforced confinement far from any normal civilized way of life, then I think there might be some hope for us. Shut away up here one tends to forget what a normal life under normal conditions is like. If we could go abroad for a while and come to know one another again, then perhaps there could be children. We could settle in the country near Oxford, perhaps. There are some beautiful houses north of Banbury."

"Decima will never leave Roshven," Rachel heard herself say.

"No, she doesn't want to leave—she doesn't want to face the normal world, can't you see? She had such an appalling childhood and adolescence trailing around the world in the wake of her promiscuous mother that she wants nothing but to retreat from anything that remotely resembles that way of life. But if only she could be shown that life in the outside world is nothing to be feared, then I think she would be happy to settle somewhere away from Roshven. At the moment she is rejecting all the values of a normal world and burying herself in this tomb—she's destroying herself, destroying me, destroying everything I've ever wanted."

"But Charles, you talk as if Decima was mentally unhinged! Surely—"

"Not mentally unhinged, but there's something definitely wrong in her psychological makeup, can't you understand?" His eyes were wide and dark, his face strained. "What girl of twenty-one, who could have the world at her feet, would choose to seclude herself in a place like this? Why should any normal girl refuse to live with her husband barely six months after they were married? I wanted her to consult a doctor, but she refused and seemed to withdraw from me still further until it seemed she was building up a store of mythical grievances against me in her mind. And yet I loved her! I tried and tried to reason with her, but there was nothing I could do. I gave her everything she wanted, spent much more money than I should have done, and still all she did was complain about our brief termtime life at Oxford and criticize my Oxonian friends. She seemed to take pleasure in embarrassing me, in making me as unhappy as possible. Last winter I let her go home to Roshven early to prepare for Christmas before I arrived, but I missed her so much while she was away that I couldn't bear to be separated from her again. I can't begin to describe to you the misery and frustration and hopelessness of it all. I didn't know it was possible to be so unhappy.

"But we went on from day to day, still together. Some days were better than others. And then this summer, when Daniel wrote to say he and Rebecca were in Scotland, I asked them to Roshven in the hope that a glimpse of the outside world which they might present would in some way help Decima. And so the Careys came to Roshven.

"I suppose it wasn't surprising that I should be attracted to Rebecca. She was everything that Decima was not, intellectual, passionate, and intense. She was interested in my work, enjoyed my company, and—it was obvious—admired me. You can imagine the effect this would have on me after the life I had been living with Decima. No doubt I shouldn't offer excuses for myself, but Rebecca gave me all that I had lacked for the past two years. I lost all hold on my restraint, my common sense, my self-control. I lost sight of everything. I never noticed that Daniel found Decima attractive or that she had decided to play around with him. I was well accustomed to ignore all her empty gestures of flirtation at Oxford, and well used to the fact that most men found my wife attractive. Even if I had noticed, I might not have taken it seriously, and as it was I was too absorbed with Rebecca to notice anyone else.

"So Decima became involved with Daniel—and found she had taken on more than she bargained for. Daniel wasn't one of the fresh-faced students she'd been so accustomed to dazzling at Oxford! And Daniel was the last man to allow her to call the tune and set the pace of their relationship. Daniel knew what he wanted and if Decima wasn't interested in playing the game by his rules, then he certainly wasn't going to bend over backward to do as *she* wished!"

"So Daniel never had an affair with Decima." She was dizzy suddenly, faint with the vastness of relief. "He never had an affair with her."

Charles raised his eyebrows. "No, you misunderstand—I see I explained myself badly. Decima wanted a flirtation with Daniel for her own satisfaction and amusement—in other words, an attachment which would never get as far as the bedroom. But Daniel wasn't interested in getting involved merely to gratify Decima's ego. So he took control of the situation and dictated his own terms, and Decima, caught off balance, no doubt, and taken by surprise, allowed herself to be dictated to."

"But you said Decima was cold—cold and withdrawn! I don't believe she would ever have had an affair with Daniel! I just don't believe it!"

"My dear, he told me last night that they were lovers. He told me himself."

The roar of the surf suddenly seemed much too close. The oppressiveness of that welling of sound made the sea blur before her eyes and she turned away instinctively to stare inland over the barren moors and the harsh lines of the mountains.

"Last night after you'd left us in the hall we went back into the study. Daniel had made it clear that he knew all about Rebecca's affair with me, but I had been so blind as to imagine he had no idea what was going on. I was angry with him for implying as much in your presence and once we were in the library I told him so. It was then that Daniel said you knew anyway as he had seen you listening at the door—he said it was perfectly obvious to anyone what was going on. That, of course, made me even angrier and we started to quarrel. Rebecca tried to speak up for me from time to time, but he wouldn't let her and she would rather argue with God than argue with Daniel. So Daniel began to speak as if he were the prosecuting counsel at a trial and I the prisoner at the bar.

"To begin with I was so furious that I could hardly listen to a word he said. Then gradually I began to realize that much of what he said was true, and I began to feel sick and ill. He told me that I was to blame for the situation at Roshven, that it was my fault that Decima had behaved the way she had, that I had behaved like a middle-aged fool over his sister. 'You moan to my sister of how your wife misunderstands you,' he said, 'but how much effort have you made to correct the situation? Aren't you just too content to sit back and let Decima go her own way while you go yours? You weep that you loved your wife and got nothing in return, but how far did you go to offer her anything apart from the honor of bearing your name and the dubious pleasures of your narrow academic social circles? Did you protest at Decima's flirtations at Oxford? Oh no, you were too busy sitting back and getting a vicarious sense of enjoyment by watching her play with her admirers and eventually send them packing! You were so smug and so self-satisfied with your beautiful wife, so damned sure she was too cold ever to be actually unfaithful to you! You basked in the reflected glory of other men's admiration for her! You were too vain to care that she was driven to amuse herself with others because you couldn't keep her fully amused yourself!'

"I couldn't contain myself any longer. I shouted at him: 'Who are you to preach to me, Daniel Carey? You come here at my express invitation and yet think nothing of abusing my hospitality in the most shameful way imaginable! Do you think I hadn't noticed that Decima has been flirting with you?' To be honest, I hadn't noticed this until Rohan pointed it out to me yesterday morning, but even then I assumed it was a mere casual flirtation and I was far too involved with Rebecca to ask Daniel to leave. 'Just deny that you haven't tried to persuade Decima to have an affair with you!' I shouted at him. 'Just try to deny it!'

"And he said coolly, with such scorn as I could never put into words, 'Of course I don't deny it. Why should I? I decided to teach you both a lesson, Charles! I thought it was high time someone showed Decima what it was like to be used as a pawn, a means of amusement—I thought it was high time she had a dose of her own medicine! And I thought it was high time someone knocked down the walls of egoism and vanity you've built around yourself, time someone showed you that your wife wasn't as cold as you liked to think she was!'

"I couldn't quite grasp what he was saying at first. I said: 'What do you mean?'

"And he said, 'You don't think I'd let any woman use *me* as a plaything, do you? I dictate my own terms, and Decima hardly paused to question them. She became my mistress some time ago.'

"I stared at him. I couldn't even think coherently. And suddenly all I knew was that this man had taken my wife and I had stood by and let it happen because of a temporary infatuation with another woman. I felt ill and dizzy, as if someone had taken an ax and smashed my world to smithereens. After a while I managed to say to them both, 'You will leave this house on Sunday morning and I never want to see either of you again.' And I left them together in the library and somehow managed to find my way upstairs to my room.

"I tried to sleep, but all the time I kept thinking of what Daniel had said and every time I went over his words again, the more truth I seemed to see in them. I resolved that once the Careys were gone I would take Decima away and try to start all over again. I realized that I loved her and wanted her still, and in the light of this realization my attraction to Rebecca seemed very shallow and meaningless."

He stopped. The world was still. The clouds had blotted out the sun now and were wreathing the mountaintops with soft, ghostly fingers.

"But what was Rebecca's reaction when you told them both to leave?" Rachel heard herself ask. "Wasn't she very upset?"

"I didn't stay to see her reaction. All I knew was that I never wanted to see either of them again." He buried his head in his hands for a moment. "Rohan was right," he said after a while. "He distrusted them from the first. There are some people like that, I suppose. They're destructive, dangerous people, leaving a trail of disaster behind them. Once they're out of our lives perhaps we'll at last be able to return to normal."

It was raining, the light sea mist fresh against Rachel's skin. The damp moistness was somehow soothing, and she faced toward the sea to meet it.

Charles stood up. "We'd better go back."

They left the stone circle and started back along the cliffs. For a time neither of them spoke.

"I'm sorry to have burdened you with all this," Charles said at last, "but I didn't know what you were thinking or what conclusions you had drawn from the knowledge that you had, and I felt it important that you should know the truth."

"Yes," said Rachel. "Yes, I quite understand. Thank you."

"I seem to be totally unable to communicate with Decima at the moment. She refuses to talk to me. I was wondering if she'd said anything to you."

"No, she was very reluctant to talk to me last night. I only noticed that she seemed very upset over Daniel."

"Well, yes," said Charles. "I've no doubt she is. . . . I'm hoping to God everything will be better after the Careys have gone. I wish now we could put off this damned dinner party tonight, but we've invited too many people from outside and it's too late now to get in touch with them."

"Couldn't you phone them and cancel it?"

"Roshven has no phone."

"Oh no, how stupid of me. I forgot."

They walked on for a few yards. Then: "You asked me in the beginning why Decima invited me to Roshven," Rachel said. "Why do *you* think she invited me, Charles?"

"I think possibly she may have fancied the notion of leaving me and marrying Daniel. She would have assumed I'd be most reluctant to divorce her and so she wanted a witness that I was committing adultery with Rebecca. Rohan, being my cousin, would naturally be averse to being a witness against me, so she found herself in need of inviting an outsider to Roshven."

"But did she know about you and Rebecca? I always had the impression she had no idea of this."

"No, she knew all the time. Daniel said last night that she had known almost from the beginning—and found my infatuation amusing," he added bitterly. "Yes, she knew, all right. I suppose I was so wrapped up in my feelings for Rebecca that it must have been obvious to everyone, even to Decima who's usually too absorbed in her own affairs to notice the affairs of others."

In Decima's eyes, Rachel thought, this would give Charles yet another motive for wanting to kill her, for he would then inherit her money and marry Rebecca. It was only surprising that she had never once mentioned it to Rachel. Perhaps she had been held back by some obscure pride; the fact that her husband was being unfaithful to her must have been a blow to her ego, no matter how amused she might have pretended to be to Daniel about the situation.

Yet it was almost impossible now for Rachel to imagine Charles planning to kill Decima. Perhaps it had all been some terrible figment of Decima's imagination. Perhaps Decima really was mentally disturbed.

They'll turn you against me, Decima had said. They'll try to prize you away from me, because you're the one person I can trust. . . .

"I don't know what to think," Rachel said aloud in despair. "I simply don't know what to do."

Charles swung around, startled. Was it her imagination or did she really see a flash of suspicion in his eyes? Perhaps the whole scene had been played for calculated effect, to deceive her. Perhaps it was all a masquerade.

"It's nothing," she said. "I suddenly felt so confused."

"I understand—I'm sorry. I almost forgot you would be fond of Decima. It must be very upsetting for you to hear bad reports of her."

Rachel said nothing.

They were in sight of the house now, following the path down the hillside past the croft, the pigsty, and the cow. The housekeeper was in the yard taking in some washing. As they approached she caught sight of them and withdrew to the shelter of the back porch to wait till they were nearer.

"Mrs. Willie looks worried," said Charles. "I hope nothing's wrong."

They reached the yard and crossed it to the porch. The housekeeper started to speak almost as soon as they were within earshot. "I was never so glad to see you, Professor," she was saying, and anxiety made her soft Highland accent broader so that it sounded Irish. "What should I be doing about preparing the dinner for tonight? Mrs. Mannering's just taken the boat and gone off to sea without telling me what arrangements she wanted me to make, and—"

"Gone off to sea?" cried Charles in amazement. "When was this, for God's sake?"

"Maybe ten minutes ago, sir. I heard the engine of the boat and saw her at the wheel heading away from the shore."

"Was she alone?"

"No, sir. She went with your cousin, Mr. Quist."

*iii*

Charles was quick to pull himself together. Moving forward into the kitchen with the housekeeper he surveyed the food in the pantry and then embarked on a discussion of how the venison should be cooked. After a moment's hesitation Rachel went outside again and walked around to the front of the house, but the motorboat was nowhere to be seen and the vast expanse of the ocean stretched uninterrupted to the horizon. She stood still, undecided what she should do, and as she paused she wondered in astonishment where Decima and Rohan had gone and why they had chosen to walk out of the house on the very morning of the party, when their help would be needed in making the necessary preparations. If she were Charles, Rachel thought, she would be very angry indeed.

Someone was calling her name. Turning abruptly, she saw Charles coming toward her from the back of the house and she retraced her steps to meet him.

"There's no sign of them, is there?" he demanded, and when she shook her head he said tightly: "I don't know what the hell they think they're doing but I can only assume they've just gone for a short spin and will be back before long. I think the best we can do is merely to carry on with the preparations and do as much as we can."

"Yes—yes, of course. . . . What would you like me to do?"

"Well, I hate to ask one of my own guests to do anything at all, but I wonder if you could possibly pick some flowers and arrange them in the hall? We'll be dining in the hall tonight, of course. I must find Daniel and ask him to help me set up the long banquet table. . . . Do you think you can manage the flowers?"

"Yes, don't worry, Charles. And if there's anything else I can do, just let me know."

After he had gone, she walked down into the overgrown garden and examined the selection of flowers, but it was late in the year and summer had already left the Highlands, so there were few flowers to choose from. There were some hardy blue-petaled shrubs beneath the shelter of the stone wall at one end of the garden, but the stems were tough beneath her fingers and in the end she decided to go back into the house for a pair of scissors. It was already beginning to rain again; the sky was heavy with billowing clouds blowing in from the sea, and the few streaks of blue which remained were pale and cold and far away.

Charles and the housekeeper were still in the pantry; Rachel found a pair of heavy shears in one of the drawers of the kitchen table and wandered back into the hall. She felt curiously abstracted from reality, as if she were moving in a dream and was powerless to control her own fate. It was as if forces around her were manipulating her at will, pulling her this way and that, and finally tossing her adrift on the strong current of a swift-flowing river which was rushing her headlong toward some destination as terrible as it was unknown. She could feel her own helplessness as clearly as she could feel that dreadful propulsion toward the hidden future which lay waiting for them all. She paused again in the huge hall and listened to the silence, and even as she realized at last how frightened she was she heard the sound of weeping coming from the drawing room close at hand.

The door was ajar. With her fingers pressing against the panels she opened it still wider and glanced into the room.

"Danny?" said Rebecca sharply as she saw the door open, and then as she realized it was Rachel she turned aside without a word and buried her face in her arms again.

Rachel did not know whether to move forward or to retreat. In the end she remained where she was, one hand still on the door handle, and said hesitantly: "If there's anything I can do—shall I find Daniel for you?"

Rebecca lifted her head so fiercely that Rachel had a stab of shock. Her eyes, brilliant with tears, were suddenly blazing with anger, and her limbs were trembling. "You!" she cried. "You! You've caused enough trouble! You leave Daniel alone! Why did you come to this place anyway except to spy and cause trouble? That's why Decima asked you to come, wasn't it? To spy on me and Charles so that she could drag Charles's name through the mud in a divorce petition? And now you've turned Charles against me and toward Decima again because you want to keep Decima from Daniel—because you want Daniel for yourself! Why, you silly, stupid fool! Do you think Daniel cares a damn for either of you? Do you think he cares for Decima's shallowness, her coldness, her boring, trivial, feminine mind? And do you think he cares any more for you with your dreary old clothes and your spinsterish mannerisms, your gaucheness and your pseudointellectualism? And now because of you and what you've done, Charles has told us to leave and my whole world is over and finished—"

Rachel at last found her tongue. The rage was so vast within her that it impaired her speech, and her voice was low and harsh and uneven. "You're being melodramatic, overemotional, and utterly absurd, only you're so in love with your role as rejected heroine that you can't bear to look at the situation as it really is!" Her hands were clenched so tightly that they hurt; her nails dug into her palms. "I've never spied on you and Charles! I don't care how much of a fool you care to make of yourself over a married man in the name of free love or whatever quasi-intellectual line of philosophy you happen to believe in—why should I care? It's nothing to do with me! And if you think Decima asked me up here to spy on you two, you must be mad! Decima was far too engrossed in Daniel to care what you did with her husband when her back was turned—she merely invited me here to keep Rohan out of her way. And if you think I would ever be interested in a man who sleeps with his host's wife—or any other woman who happens to be available—you couldn't be more wrong! You can keep your precious brother! Let him take you as far away from Roshven as it's possible to go, for I don't care if I never see either of you again!"

Rebecca was on her feet, her face white, her movements unsteady, her eyes wide and dark and hard. "That's what Charles said." Her voice was little more than a whisper. And then suddenly she was screaming, her face distorted, her eyes narrow slits of rage: "I hate you all, do you hear? I hate every one of you! I hate Decima and I hate you and I hate that fool Quist and I hate Charles—Charles more than any of you! Charles Mannering, the noble, distinguished, celebrated professor, the lying, weak, cowardly bastard who tells me that he's so sorry—yes, *so sorry*, but he's made a mistake and he doesn't want to divorce Decima after all and marry me—he's *so sorry*, but actually he doesn't want to see me again because I've served my purpose, just as if I were some tart or some harebrained little student who had a crush on him at Oxford! 'I'm so sorry,' he says! My God, I'll make him sorry! I'll teach him what it is to be sorry. I'll—"

She stopped.

Behind Rachel the door was softly closed.

"You'd better go to your room, Rebecca," said Daniel without emotional inflection. "You forget that we're not leaving till tomorrow."

There was a long silence. Rebecca was staring at him, and Rachel suddenly found she had to sit down. Daniel was motionless. Presently he held out his hand to his sister.

"I'll take you upstairs."

"It's all right." She was crying again, pushing past Rachel and stumbling toward Daniel.

He opened the door for her. "I'll come upstairs presently."

She made no reply. They could hear the harshness of her sobs as she moved across the hall to the stairs, and then Daniel closed the door and there was silence.

After a while he said: "It seems I was mistaken."

She stared at him, not understanding, and outside the squall broke and the rain hurled itself against the windowpane in an ecstasy of violence.

"I misjudged the kind of person you were." He crossed to the fireplace and was still again, looking at her. "You told Charles about Decima and myself, didn't you?"

She was wild-eyed, mesmerized by his stillness, appalled by his controlled anger. "No," she heard herself say, "Rohan told Charles. I had nothing to do with it. It was Rohan."

"Rohan or you—it's the same thing, isn't it? For a long time I was puzzled about why you had been asked to Roshven, and then at last I realized that Quist had maneuvered it. He thought you could be useful to him—and of course you were."

"Useful?" She felt dizzy, confused. "I don't understand."

"Don't tell me you hadn't realized that Quist is infatuated with Decima and would do anything to drive a wedge between her and any man she happened to be interested in?"

"I—"

"He hated me from the first but was powerless to do anything about the situation. To make matters worse, Charles was so absorbed in Rebecca that he didn't care what his wife was doing with me! So Quist conceived the idea of inviting an outsider here whom he could use and manipulate to play the four of us off against each other with the result that Decima and Charles would be reconciled and Rebecca and I would be sent away. Which is exactly what has happened."

"But what you say isn't true!" said Rachel loudly, struggling with the tangled web in which she found herself. "It was Decima who invited me here—Rohan had nothing to do with it! Nothing! It was Decima, Decima, Decima! Can't you understand? And Rohan isn't infatuated with her anyway—you're the one who's so infatuated with her that you're driven to imagine these preposterous schemes and ideas!"

"So you *are* jealous," he said, "I thought you were. You told Charles that Decima had been having an affair with me and Quist backed you up to the hilt. And Charles is so weak and so easily swayed that the two of you managed to convince him that he'd have no peace of mind till Rebecca and I left this house."

"It's not true—not true—"

"You hate Decima's guts, don't you? You'd see her dead, if you could!"

"No, no—I'm not like that—"

"Well, you've been wasting your energy being jealous! Decima's not my mistress and never has been. I told Charles last night that she was but it was a lie because I wanted to shake him. . . . He was so damned smug, so damned self-righteous, so bloody satisfied in the belief that his wife would never be unfaithful to him! I saw that he had made up his mind to be rid of us, so I didn't care what I said or how much I hurt him so long as I dragged him down from the pompous little pedestal he had built for himself. I was tired of the way he was using my sister, tired of his affectations and complacency!"

"You hate him because he's Decima's husband!"

"Decima! I care nothing for Decima! All I ask is to be rid of her —she's a danger to me, a menace to my future plans. If she gets Charles to use his influence in revenge—"

"I don't believe you," Rachel heard herself say, and her voice was no longer steady. "You had an affair with Decima, and now you suspect her of preferring Rohan—or even Charles. You're so unaccustomed to a woman losing interest in you before you lose interest in her, that you have to resort to wild flights of imagination—"

"You don't know what you're talking about."

"I just don't believe you never had an affair with Decima!"

"I don't care what you believe! Why should I? What are you to me? I thought at first you were different, but now I see you're the same as a thousand other women, petty, jealous, and mundane. The hell with you! Go on back to your so-called platonic friend Rohan Quist and vent your stupid small-minded jealousy on his obsession with Decima Mannering, for God knows I've no further use for you."

And he was gone as quietly as he had come, leaving nothing behind him but the squalling of the rain on the windows and the howl of the sea wind far away.

*iv*

She went to her room and stayed there. She shut the door and pushed a chair against it to hold it fast in lieu of a key, and she drew the curtains to shut out the tortured convulsions of the weather and the appalling bleakness of the barren landscape. And then she lay down on her bed in the cool twilight and cried till her throat ached and her eyes were too swollen to see. Her face became hot and flushed with her tears, but after a while she became aware of how cold she was and how much she longed for the heat of a fire.

She got up, stooped to examine the grate, but there was nothing there but ashes. The scuttle by the hearth had only a few small pieces of wood in it. Shivering, she drew back the curtains and stared dry-eyed at the scene before her. It had stopped raining. The squall had died, but there was mist clinging to the mountains and she could hear the hum of the strong wind as it swept in from the sea.

She shivered again. Perhaps there would be more fuel in Decima's room, and some matches, too, to set the fire alight. She started to wonder if Decima and Rohan had come back from their trip to sea, but that only made her think of Daniel again and her eyes filled with tears. She tried to dash them away, but they only fell the faster and she was still crying as she pulled aside the barricade, opened her door, and stepped out into the corridor.

It was very quiet. Stifling her sobs, she went down the corridor to Decima's room at the far end and fumbled with the latch.

There were glowing embers in the grate; evidently Decima had lit the fire that morning, and the room was still warm and comfortable. Rachel closed the door behind her and locked it before sinking down on the hearthrug to build the fire to a warmer blaze, and within minutes the flames were leaping up the chimney and the cold was slowly ebbing from her limbs.

She sat there for a long while. There was a curious burning in her mind, as if some rich and valuable vein of thought had been hacked off and obliterated by some frenzied act of destruction. Her other thoughts were dim and unresponsive, her other emotions dulled by pain and anesthetized by shock. All she was conscious of was this great searing sense of loss for which there was no cure, no solution. "I never loved him," she said to herself again and again. "It was an infatuation. He was right and I was jealous and foolish and stupid. He despises me."

But she had loved him. She had timidly reached out toward him, her longing overcoming all her shyness and reserve and fear, and her love had been wrenched from her, twisted by cruel hands, and flung back, a crippled, shameful, distorted thing, into her face. She felt too crushed, too humiliated, and too full of pain even to acknowledge that the love she had felt had been as deep as any of which she was capable. She could only acknowledge the twisted distortion which had been flung back at her, and could only tell herself numbly that she had been deluded and absurd.

"It was an infatuation," she said aloud to the hard tongues of flame in the grate. "I was foolish. I never loved him."

And the pain of loss was a raw, gaping wound from which it seemed the throbbing would never die, and the grief was a great barren waste which stretched as far as the eye could see.

"I wasn't in love," she said. "I was infatuated. I was mistaken. It was all a mistake."

And it seemed to her even as she listened to the words that the house around her and the landscape beyond the window perfectly represented the desolation of her mind, the negation of all warmth and light, and the presence only of arid starkness and a waste of isolation.

She got up and went to the window, as if by gazing out on that bleak landscape she could somehow gaze into her own mind, and as she moved she brushed the cushion from the window seat to the floor. She stooped automatically to pick it up and then she no-

ticed that on the window seat there was a slim leather-bound
volume which the cushion had concealed.

It was a diary.

She picked it up, but her fingers were still unsteady and it
slithered through them to the floor and fell open at her feet. She
stooped, and as she picked up the book she saw that the writing
was not Decima's at all but a stormy, tempestuous scrawl forming
emotional, uneven sentences.

Her eyes read isolated words even before her mind could stop
them. "Charles said . . . I told Charles I felt . . . Charles and I
made love . . . Charles promised . . . Charles. . . ."

There were intimate descriptions, passages of avowed love, ec-
static words of praise.

Rachel shut the book tightly and put it back beneath the cushion. It was only when she turned away once more toward the fire
that it occurred to her numbed brain to wonder why Rebecca Carey's diary should be so carefully concealed in Decima's room.

# Chapter Six

## i

Rohan and Decima didn't come back. The long morning drifted into a cold, gray afternoon, and still there was no sign of them. At some time after three Rachel slipped into an exhausted sleep on the hearthrug in Decima's room but no one interrupted her and no one came to see where she was.

When she awoke it was dark and the fire was dying in the grate. For one long moment she lay still, too stiff and cramped to move, and then memory flooded back into her mind with a stab of pain and she sat up, ignoring the ache in her limbs and the dry burning of her eyes. Tonight was the night of the dinner party, the night when at eight thirty sixteen guests would be arriving at Roshven to dine in the great hall below. Tonight was the eve of Decima's twenty-first birthday, the last night of the Careys' stay at Roshven, the last time that Rachel would see Daniel. Tonight was the night of masquerade, of playing a part, of letting no one know that her mind was still in the grip of that great, aching sense of loss that cast out all other thought and emotion.

No one must ever know, was all she could tell herself. No one must ever find out.

She stood up painfully, and moved to the door. It was so dark in the corridor that she had to pause for a moment to get her bearings, and then she set off in the direction of her room with one hand against the wall so that she would know when she reached the door. A minute later she was sitting on her own bed and struggling to light the lamp.

Mrs. Willie had obviously been much too busy cooking to go around lighting fires in the bedrooms; the ashes were still gray in the grate and the room seemed bitterly cold and damp. Rachel drew on her overcoat and looked at herself in the mirror.

She saw a stranger with disheveled hair and bloodshot eyes swollen with weeping. Her skin seemed blotched, her expression empty of all feeling. She stared at herself for a long time and then, lamp in hand, went back to Decima's room for a box of matches and a log for the fire.

It was six o'clock when she managed to get the fire alight. She desperately wanted hot water to bathe her face but she was afraid of meeting the housekeeper in the kitchen, afraid of anyone seeing her before she had had a chance to mend her appearance a little. Presently she used some of the cold water in the pitcher to wash her face, and then she spent some time combing and rearranging her hair before venturing downstairs to fetch hot water.

The hall looked beautiful, the long banquet table aglow with white linen and silver cutlery and red candles waiting to be lit. Someone had completed the task Charles had allotted to her, for there were flowers in tall vases on the chest and tables at the side of the hall and a small arrangement on the banquet table between the two epergnes. Four lamps were burning and huge fires were blazing in the enormous twin fireplaces on either side of the hall.

Charles came out of the library just as she stepped into the hall and paused to look at the scene. There was no escaping him.

"Hullo," he said. "Where have you been? I tried to find you a little while ago and had no success."

"I'm so sorry, Charles—I—I didn't feel too well. . . . Please forgive me for not doing the flowers—"

"No, that doesn't matter. I picked them later and Mrs. Willie arranged them when she had a spare minute. I say, are you all right? You look very pale."

"Yes, I'm much better now, thank you. I was just going to get some hot water to wash with before I change. Are Decima and Rohan back yet?"

"No, they're not. I don't know where the hell they've got to. I can only suppose that the storm caught them at sea and forced them to head for Kyle of Lochalsh for shelter. The storm's stopped here but it may still be strong over at Kyle and forcing them to stay in harbor there. I hope to God they get back before the guests start to arrive. It was a damn fool thing to do, today of all days, anyway—Decima at least, if not Rohan, ought to have been here to help with all the preparations. . . . Rachel, are you sure you're all right? You certainly don't look well."

"Yes, really, Charles, I'm quite all right now. . . ." She made her escape, obtained her supply of hot water and set off back to her bedroom again before she should meet anyone else. There was a glow of light beneath Daniel's door as she passed it, but Rebecca's room was in darkness.

Perhaps Rebecca intended to spend the evening on her own.

It was only when Rachel reached her room again that she became aware of panic. How could she possibly face all those people whom she did not know and act as if nothing had happened? How could she be sociable and friendly and hospitable just as if nothing was wrong? And how could she even begin to think of facing Daniel again after all that had been said between them that morning?

Because no one must ever know, she thought. No one is ever going to know unless I'm weak and give myself away. And I'm not going to be weak and give in and hide myself in my room because I haven't enough courage to face the world at this particular time.

No one must ever know.

The evening loomed before her, an enormous obstacle which had to be surmounted before the tranquillity and relief of the day ahead. All she had to do was to get through this evening somehow. Once the evening was over, she would be able to relax and recover herself.

She didn't know then how wrong she was. Afterward, looking back, she decided that this was just as well, for if she had known then what was going to happen that evening she would never have left her room.

## *ii*

"But where are they?" cried Charles in exasperation. "Why aren't they here? What's happened to them?"

The clock chimed half past seven. Rachel, seated tensely before the hearth of one of the big fires in the hall, made no reply, and presently Charles in an agony of suspense paced to the front door and opened it to stare out to sea.

"There's a boat coming in now. . . ." He stepped outside, shutting the door behind him, and Rachel was left alone before the hearth in the silent hall.

A door closed somewhere far away upstairs; there were voices, a murmur of conversation, the sound of footsteps on the stairs.

Rachel did not turn around. At last, when they were behind her, she glanced up and tried to force out a stiff "good evening," but Daniel moved past her without a glance in her direction and Rebecca went over to the table on a pretense of examining the silverware.

Rachel stared back into the flames.

"Someone's arriving," said Daniel to his sister. "There's a boat down by the quay."

"Rohan and Decima?"

"I don't know. There's another boat out at sea heading in this direction. The guests are starting to arrive."

"Supposing Decima doesn't come back?"

"Then Charles will look like a bloody fool, won't he?" said

Daniel and opened the front door to stand outside on the porch.

The St. Bernard, which had been closeted in the kitchen out of the way until he had escaped through the back door, lumbered solemnly into the room and settled himself comfortably at Rachel's feet before the fire. Mrs. Willie, scurrying into the hall at the same moment with two large ashtrays, caught sight of him and gave an exclamation of annoyance.

"George, what are you doing in the hall? Come here at once, you bad dog!" And she stooped to smack his head and lay a firm hand on his collar.

The St. Bernard growled.

"Let him be," called Daniel from the door. "He's no trouble. I'll see he's not a nuisance."

"Just as you like, Mr. Carey," said the housekeeper with a shrug and disappeared again in the direction of the kitchen while the dog returned to his slumbers on the hearthrug.

"It's neither Decima nor Rohan," said Rebecca who had been watching from the window. "It must be the first contingent of guests."

And the next moment Charles had entered the room with the MacDonalds and Camerons from Kyle of Lochalsh, and the party had begun.

Afterward, Rachel's memories of that last dinner at Roshven were blurred and she could remember only isolated scenes which seemed to have little or no connection with each other. She could remember Charles saying—how many times? Three? Four?—that Decima had gone into Kyle of Lochalsh to do some last-minute shopping and had apparently been delayed there with Rohan. She could remember Robert Cameron saying that he had noticed the Roshven boat moored in the harbor at Kyle, and the look of relief on Charles's face changing to one of anger as he began to wonder why Decima was deliberately delaying her return.

The Kincaids arrived from Skye soon after eight, and finally Decima's lawyer, old Conor Douglas from Cluny Gualach with his daughter, but still there was no sign of Decima and Rohan. Half past eight struck. Then a quarter to nine.

118 THE WAITING SANDS

"We'd better dine, I think," said Charles abruptly. "There's no use in spoiling the dinner, and I've no doubt you're all hungry from your journey."

Rachel could remember the glow of candles in silver candlesticks and the sparkle of champagne in the elegant glasses, but not the taste of the food, nor the order of the menu. She was sitting between one of the MacDonalds, a young man of about twenty-seven, and old Mr. Douglas the lawyer, and all the time she was conscious of Decima's empty chair at one end of the long table and Rohan's vacant place directly opposite her. Daniel was far away, hidden from her almost entirely by one of the epergnes and a candelabra of red candles, but sometimes during a lull in the conversation she could hear his voice traveling toward her from the other end of the table.

The dinner was finished at last, the speeches left unsaid. The guests lingered at the table over coffee and liqueurs, and the conversation rippled on inconsequentially, the guests mellow with good food and drink and almost forgetting that the guest of honor had never appeared to receive them. To Rachel, longing for the solitude of her room and an escape from the torture of making sociable conversation, it seemed as if the party would never end.

It was some time after ten when Decima and Rohan came back. They came laughing together up the garden path from the jetty, and it was not until Rohan flung wide the front door and strode into the room that Rachel realized they were both dead drunk.

## iii

"Good evening, everyone," said Decima, mocking them all. "How kind of you to come. Please excuse my not being here to greet you but Rohan wanted to make love to me and I had to explain that I can't be unfaithful to my husband, even though he's been sleeping with Rebecca Carey for the last few weeks, because he wants a reconciliation with me and he's promised to send the Careys away tomorrow. Why, Charles darling, how beautiful the hall looks! So sorry I wasn't here to help. . . . Rachel, you look awful! What's the matter? Hasn't Daniel bothered to give you his best smile today? Daniel, you really should be more considerate!"

"Charles," said Daniel to his host, "your wife's as drunk as a barmaid. You'd better take her upstairs."

"Why, listen, Charles!" jeered Rohan. "Listen to who's giving you advice! It's the guest who tried to seduce your wife under your own roof, Charles! Why don't you ask him to put Decima to bed for you? I'll tell you why you don't ask him, Charles. It's because you're so goddamned proud, Charles, that you can't admit you could ever be in the position of the fooled husband! You think you're God, don't you, Charles, God's gift to culture, to academic life, to women, to the whole world, but hell to all that, Charles, you're not God's gift to your wife!"

Charles was white to the lips, shocked speechless.

Daniel was on his feet, his hand gripping Rohan's arm as he tried to lead him away. Around the table the guests were frozen with shock, as silent and motionless as if they had been carved out of stone.

"Let go of me, you—" Rohan was fighting, but he was no match for Daniel's strength.

Over on the hearth the St. Bernard began to bark.

"Charles darling," said Decima, "did you give George any champagne?"

The noise of the barking seemed to send great shafts through Rachel's consciousness until she began to feel that she was waking at last to reality after a long hypnotized sleep. She stood up suddenly, her feet carrying her around the table to where Rohan was shouting abuse at Daniel, and suddenly it seemed that Daniel didn't exist at all and Rohan was the only one who was real.

"Rohan, you idiot, stop making such a fool of yourself!" Her voice was curt and cold. "Stop it, do you hear? Stop it!" And when he took no notice of her, she slapped him hard across the mouth.

The crack of the impact of hand against flesh seemed to echo throughout the length of the hall. There was a hideous silence. No one moved. No one spoke. And then Decima yawned and said idly to no one in particular: "Lord, how tired I am! Good night, everyone," and curled herself up on the hearthrug before one of the fireplaces and went immediately to sleep, her head resting on the St. Bernard's massive body as he lay beside her.

"Well," said old Conor Douglas, the lawyer of Cluny Gualach, rising briskly from the table as if nothing had happened, "I think we should be on our way, Rosalind."

"Yes, we too must be going," said Robert MacDonald, for all the world as if the dinner party had ended with perfect normalcy. "Thank you so much, Charles, for a most excellent meal."

"Most delightful. . . ."

"We did enjoy ourselves. . . ."

"Thank you again for your hospitality. . . ."

The endless stream of conversation trickled on with a remorseless inevitability until finally the last good-bye had been said, the front door closed and bolted after the last guest, and Roshven was alone at last with those who lived within its walls.

Without a word Charles went straight to the library and slammed the door shut behind him.

"Exit Charles," said Rohan, "thinly disguised as an insulted English gentleman." And he laughed.

"Exit Rohan," said Rachel unsmiling, "appearing undisguised as a very drunk, very foolish overgrown schoolboy. This way."

"Which way? Here, take your hand off my arm, Raye! What do you think you're doing?"

"We're going upstairs."

"But—"

"Don't argue."

"Yes, but look here—"

"Shut up."

"What about Decima?"

"She's passed out. Daniel and Rebecca will see to her."

"Oh no," said Rohan forlornly, "no, don't leave her with the Careys. Don't leave her with them."

"Don't be silly."

Halfway up the stairs he said: "I'm crazy about her, Raye. I always have been. I never told you."

"No," she said. "You never told me."

"I'd do anything for her," he said. "Anything at all."

"Yes."

"I'd marry her but Charles won't give her a divorce."

"No, I understand he's set on a reconciliation."

"But at least I made her leave Daniel. She saw that she could trust me more than she could trust him."

"Yes."

"Daniel doesn't give a damn for her. I'm the one who really loves her. She knows that now."

"Yes."

"She's going to come away with me. She's promised. She's going to be mine for ever and ever and ever. . . ."

"Mind the corner. It's dark down here."

". . . ever and ever and ever. . . ."

They walked on down the south wing past the southwest turret room to the west wing that faced the sea.

"Which is your room, Rohan?"

"This one. No, this one. I can't remember."

It was the second room. Rachel found the lamp, but he had fallen across the bed in a stupor even before she had managed to light the wick. After pulling off his shoes and arranging the quilt on top of him as best she could, she blew out the lamp again and went back past the southwest turret room to her own room in the south wing. She shut the door in exhaustion, lit the lamp on the table, and sank down in the chair before the hearth.

After ten minutes or so she remembered she had left Decima sleeping downstairs. Perhaps she should go and see if she were all right. No, let someone else look after Decima for a change! Decima with her sneering tongue and cool, hateful remarks. . . . What was it she had said? *Rachel, you look awful! What's the matter? Hasn't Daniel bothered to give you his best smile today?*

It was an unforgivable taunt to be made in front of a gathering of strangers, and Rachel had no intention of forgiving. Decima could go to the devil as far as she was concerned.

"Don't leave Decima with the Careys!" Rohan had said, maudlin with his surfeit of liquor. "Don't leave her alone with them. . . ."

"I don't trust the Careys," Decima had said. "They're against me—everyone's against me—don't let them turn you against me, too, Rachel. . . ."

All that nonsense about Charles wanting to kill her so that he might inherit Roshven . . . absurd. Charles wouldn't kill anyone, although God knows he certainly must have felt like killing Decima when she humiliated him before all his friends. . . .

Decima must have drunk a great deal. Normally, as Rachel well knew, she could drink a fair share of Scotch and still show no trace of having drunk more than a glass of ice water. Rohan too was accustomed to liquor. His bachelor life in London had ensured that.

I wonder, thought Rachel, why they both got so drunk. I wonder what made them drink so much.

She wanted desperately to relax and find peace in sleep, but her mind was vibrantly alive, the thoughts milling through her brain, and after a while she stood up and moved restlessly out into the corridor. There was a light glowing beneath Decima's door, and as she drew nearer she could hear the faint sound of a man's voice and a woman's murmur from within.

She knocked softly on the panels. The murmuring ceased at once.

"Who is it?" called Decima sleepily.

"Rachel. I just wondered if you were all right."

"Yes, thanks. Daniel brought me upstairs a little while ago. There's no need for you to worry."

Rachel wanted to ask who was with her but was so convinced that it was Daniel that her courage failed her. "I'll see you tomorrow, then," she said, turning away. "Good night, Decima."

"'Night." Decima sounded a long way off, barely conscious.

Rachel waited for the murmuring to begin again but it did not.

At last, not wanting to risk being found listening outside the door, she walked on to the head of the stairs and glanced down into the hall. The remains of the dinner party lay haphazardly on the long banquet table below, and although the candles had been snuffed the lamps still burned on the chest and side tables around the room. The twin fires were now mere glowing embers in the great fireplaces, and Rachel noticed that the St. Bernard had left his favorite place on the hearth and was stretched out in slumber before the door of the small drawing room across the hall.

Rachel went over to the library door and knocked softly. "Charles?"

There was no reply.

She tried again. "Charles, it's Rachel. May I come in?"

There was still no reply, but she could see the light shining beneath the door. Perhaps he had fallen asleep. Cautiously she turned the handle, pushed open the door a little way, and began to walk into the room.

Her feet stopped just after she had crossed the threshold. Paralysis flickered through her body with lightning speed, taking from her even the power to draw a breath, and then suddenly the gasp of shock was tearing at her lungs and her throat was dry as she tried to scream. For Charles lay slumped back in his chair with Rebecca's ivory dagger in his chest and she knew at once, even before she moved forward again toward him, that he was quite dead.

*iv*

She could not bring herself to touch him. He lay there, still and silent in death, his face tilted downward, his arms hanging over the arms of the chair behind the desk, and all she could do was look down at him in horror and try to think what she could do. The white ivory of the dagger gleamed in the lamplight. The carved sheath lay neatly on the window seat close at hand, where the murderer had discarded it.

The murderer. Charles had been murdered.

There was a fire in the grate, the flames flickering so feebly that they were almost moribund. There were papers burning, the trace of scorched dark leather. When she knelt down on the hearth a second later she saw that someone had tried to burn Rebecca's diary in the dying fire a short while ago.

A door slammed somewhere. There were footsteps crossing the hall, getting louder and louder as they drew nearer to the library. Propelled by fears and instincts which she didn't even begin to analyze, Rachel sprang to her feet and stepped swiftly behind the long red curtains that stretched from the floor to the ceiling in front of the french windows.

She was just in time.

She heard the door open even though she didn't dare look to see who had entered, heard the abrupt silence which came the next moment, heard the click of the latch as the door was shut quietly again.

The silence after that seemed to go on and on and on. The only thing she could see was the red velvet of the curtains before her, but she knew just as surely as if she could have seen him face to face that it was Daniel who had entered the room. She could imagine him beside the body, noticing the dagger, seeing the sheath, catching sight of the scorched diary, just as she had done.

He was very silent, she thought; it was almost as if he had known what he was going to find. . . . But that was impossible, of course.

Or was it?

She heard a small noise then, the crackling of scorched papers, and guessed he must be pulling the diary from the grate. She heard him throw on another log and use the bellows to work up the flames to a blaze which would effectively destroy everything he had been unable to remove.

After that there was another silence. What would he be doing now? Hardly daring to breathe, she found the chink in the curtains and glanced through them into the room beyond.

He was wiping the handle of the dagger with his handkerchief. As she watched he picked up the sheath from the table and wiped that too before replacing it again where he had found it. Then, very carefully, he wrapped Charles's fingers around the hilt of the dagger and rearranged the body so that Charles's weight was thrust forward still further onto the blade in his chest.

She edged further to the right of the chink in the curtains for safety, and as she shifted her position the curtain rings far above gave a small, almost inaudible squeak of movement as she touched the material in front of her by accident.

She froze.

There was nothing then, nothing at all. She tried to hear his breathing, but the room was as silent as a tomb and she could only hear the thump of her heart and the roar of the blood in her ears.

She went on waiting, hardly able to breathe. And then, just as she began to think she was safe after all, he flung back the curtains with a quick flick of his wrists and she was staring up into his eyes.

## *v*

"What are you doing here?"

"I wanted to talk to Charles. I came here about a minute ago and then I heard you coming so I hid here."

"Why?"

"I don't know."

He stared at her, his eyes wide and dark, and she leaned back against the french windows as her strength deserted her and her limbs began to tremble.

"You'd better make up a better story than that to tell the police," he said after a while. "It doesn't sound very convincing."

"Perhaps it would be more convincing," she heard herself say in a shaking voice, "if I told them I saw you take your sister's diary from the grate where it lay burning, wipe her fingerprints from the dagger, and rearrange the body to make it seem as if Charles had committed suicide."

"Rebecca didn't kill him," he said flatly.

"Then who did?"

He turned from her abruptly and moved across the room. "Why, Decima, of course," he said. "Who else?" He wrenched open the door. "You'd better come and help me find her."

"Decima didn't kill him," said Rachel.

"Why do you say that?"

Instinct made her say nothing.

"Why do you say that?" repeated Daniel, but she would not answer him.

The St. Bernard was at the foot of the staircase, his tail swaying gently, as he followed Daniel up the stairs to the gallery above.

"Shouldn't we get the police?" Rachel said suddenly.

"Yes, we'll have to take the boat into Kyle of Lochalsh. Or maybe Quist can go if we can wake him up. Did you put him to bed?"

"More or less. Shall I go and try to wake him?"

"No, we must find Decima first."

"Why not Rebecca?"

"Because Decima was Charles's wife," said Daniel, "and whether she killed him or not she has the right to be told first of his death."

Rachel's mind was spinning. The shock made her thoughts jumbled and confused so that all she was aware of thinking was that Charles had been killed and that one of his guests had killed him. It must be Rebecca, she thought. Decima was in her room. Rohan was drunk in his bed. Daniel. . . . But where had Daniel been? With Decima in her room? Had she been confessing to him that she had killed Charles and framed Rebecca, and had Daniel then immediately come downstairs to rearrange the scene of the crime so that Rebecca would be cleared? But Decima had been drunk. Decima had been carried upstairs to her room . . . by Daniel.

They were outside the door.

"Decima," said Daniel in a low voice and knocked on the panels.

There was no answer.

"Decima?" He opened the door slightly and glanced inside. The next moment he was crossing the room swiftly and Rachel was following him across the threshold.

The bed was empty, as empty as the room itself. It was bitterly cold and the lamp was smoking in the draft from the huge window, which was flung open as wide as it would go.

Understanding came to Rachel so quickly that she was conscious of neither shock nor horror, only of a dim, unreal surprise. "My God—"

"Keep back," said Daniel suddenly, but she was already beside him at the window and staring down through the darkness at Decima's lifeless body on the stone terrace below.

Somewhere far away in the hall, the grandfather clock began to strike midnight.

Decima had died before her twenty-first birthday.

# 2
*Cluny Sands*

# Chapter One

*i*

Afterward, all Rachel had wanted to do was to bury herself in the midst of some teeming civilization. She was obsessed with the desire for traffic and huge buildings and throngs of people, some foreign city far south of Roshven where the sun would scorch the concrete pavements and burn out the memory of silky mists and soft sea breezes. Even London, six hundred miles from those gray stone walls, eventually seemed too close, and even though Daniel was by that time far away in Africa, the memory of him lingered with each memory of Roshven.

She thought of Roshven often. She knew she would never forget that moment at midnight when she had faced Daniel in Decima's room.

"Can't you see?" he had said to her by that open window with the damp night air chilling the room. "I've just rearranged Charles's body to look as if he deliberately pressed forward on that dagger and killed himself. The police are going to think he murdered Decima—God knows he had enough provocation after the way she behaved tonight—and then committed suicide. If they think that, there'll be no repercussions for the rest of us. They've got to think that Charles killed Decima and then himself."

She had stared at him, trying to read his mind and decipher the meaning that lay behind what he had said. After a while she had said, shaken: "But how can we say that? I spoke to Decima on my way down to the library to find Charles. Her door was closed but I called out from the passage to ask if she was all right and she said she was. Charles died before she did."

"But no one else knows that," he had said. "Just you and I. We know that Decima killed Charles and framed it to look as if Rebecca had killed him, but nobody knows that except you and me."

She had hesitated a long time. She thought of Charles, the evidence that Rebecca had killed him, the proof that Daniel had been so quick to destroy. Daniel must have killed Decima, too, unless Daniel himself. . . . Every muscle in Rachel's body tightened in an agony of nervousness and suspense.

"Don't you understand?" he had said very deliberately. "It's the easiest way out. All you would have to do would be to omit any mention of the fact that you spoke to Decima before you found Charles dead, and omit all mention of the fact that you saw me rearrange the body. Then once the police accept that explanation the rest of us won't come under suspicion."

And still she had hesitated, torn between fear and doubt, knowing what she should do, yet not knowing whether she had the strength to do it. At last he had said without emphasis: "The police could suspect you, you know. If they thought that you were jealous of Decima, that you hated her because she humiliated you, they might think you killed her. They might think Decima had killed Charles and then you killed Decima."

He had wanted to ensure her silence, her acquiescence in his desire to suppress the truth. She wondered if he had ever realized that even after their quarrel and his rejection of her she would still have done anything to protect him.

"I think I understand," she had heard herself say at last, her voice seeming strained and distant in her ears. "Yes, we'd better do as you suggest."

So she had committed herself and after that there could be no turning back. He had not seemed grateful, she noticed, but only infinitely relieved, as if he had somehow managed to overcome some insuperable obstacle threatening his own security.

The local police had been slow and rustic; when the CID men from Scotland Yard arrived later, they had found the trail cold and the case a formality. At the ensuing inquest the coroner had been a retired doctor from Fort Williams, the jury mostly fishermen from Kyle of Lochalsh, and it had seemed obvious to all of them after hearing evidence from the dinner party guests that Charles had killed his wife and then in despair committed suicide. The papers had made a great splash of it for a couple of days on the front pages, and Charles had had his obituary in the *Times*, but after that the case had been soon forgotten, dismissed as one of the more newsworthy tragedies of the year, and the press had passed to other matters to feed to their voracious readers.

As Decima had died before attaining twenty-one, Charles should have inherited Roshven under the terms of her father's will, but since by law a murderer cannot profit from his crime, it was held that the estate would revert to Decima's next of kin. Since Decima was an orphan with no relatives, this in fact meant that the house and estate of Roshven passed into the hands of the Crown. The profitable forestry estates were sold to the Forestry Commission, and the house, which no estate agent had been able to sell, was in the end left to fall gradually into decay. As for Willie the gamekeeper and his wife, they had accepted a post on a large estate further south near Lochaber, and when they moved from Roshven some two months after the inquest they had taken George, the St. Bernard, with them.

The incident was closed; the nightmare was over. Rohan, Rachel, Rebecca, and Daniel went their separate ways.

For a short time Rachel had stayed in London, not really wanting to leave it, for she loved the city better than any other, and
then one day she had met Rebecca by chance in Mayfair. She was
teaching, Rachel discovered, lecturing in economics. And Daniel?
Yes, he was happy. He had gone out to Africa to teach English
and English history in one of the new African states. He seemed
to have found his vocation, for apparently he wanted nothing except to remain in the new life he had chosen for himself.

It was then that Rachel realized how empty England was, how
unbearably dreary her life had become. The longing to escape became an obsession. She felt she could only begin to live again if
she were in a new country, in new surroundings, and among new
people, and finally she made the decision to go to America where,
she had heard, English secretaries were in great demand. She arrived in New York three months later, found a job without difficulty, and quickly made friends at the women's hotel where she
was staying. Soon she was sharing a luxury apartment with three
other girls in midtown Manhattan just west of Fifth Avenue, and
four years later was surprised to look back and find how quickly
the time had passed.

It was then that Rohan arrived. He had been working in England for an automobile concern, and now wrote to say that he was
to be transferred to his firm's New York branch. He had, he disclosed, requested the transfer.

She met him at the airport. It was rather absurd because she
felt like crying at the sight of someone from home, and he, emotional as ever, was obviously overcome with pleasure at seeing her
again. He looked tired after the journey, but his gray eyes were as
brilliant as ever and his hair, still straw-colored, rose up in a tuft
above his forehead where he had pulled it in his excitement.

In the cab on the way back into the city she said: "But I still
don't understand why you requested the transfer."

"Maybe for the same reasons as the ones which persuaded you
to leave England," he answered, staring out of the window at the
approaching skyline of Manhattan. "And I'm not as English as

most Englishmen. There's a lot of foreign blood in me. I didn't
think I would find it hard to live abroad for a while."

"It's funny," she said. "I don't know why, but I half-thought
you might be getting interested in Rebecca. When you wrote to
tell me you were coming to the States I thought you were writing
to tell me you were engaged. You mentioned her quite often in
your letters."

"I saw a little of her now and then," he said, very casual, almost
uninterested. "It was nice, but . . . she wasn't really my type. And
besides—" He stopped.

"Besides?"

He turned toward her and she saw that his face, usually so mobile and expressive, was very still.

"There were too many memories," he said. "For both of us. It
was better to go our separate ways."

She nodded silently, making no comment. It was the one and
only reference that either of them made to Roshven, and it was
never mentioned between them again.

Yet still she thought of Daniel.

Daniel in Africa, Daniel abandoning career and home and
country to teach African children in a gesture which was as out of
character as it was striking. She could never understand what had
taken him to Africa, for Daniel was not the kind of man who offered his services to welfare organizations for a nominal salary,
and still less the kind of man who would feel any desire to teach
children in a new country with poor facilities. With his background of scholarship he might have ultimately attained all the
academic honors he could have wished for; she could see him so
clearly at Cambridge with its ancient, beautiful buildings, visualize him so easily accepting a good academic post and lecturing to
brilliant, gifted students; there would have been a professorship
waiting in the future, a successful business and social life, a life
in England among English people in an English university town.

But he had turned his back on all that. The absoluteness of the
gesture with its sweeping implications was something she could
understand, even if she did not understand the gesture itself.

Daniel had always seemed so vivid and positive to her that she could easily imagine him reaching a decision to change his entire life and then having the courage to keep to his decision and follow it through to its conclusion. That at least was in character. But to go to Africa, to seek the steamy, torrid climate of the Equator, to bury himself as an obscure teacher far from home, was a decision which seemed both bewildering and bizarre.

She wanted to talk to Rohan about it, but Rohan was always so scrupulously careful never to mention the subject of Roshven now that they were so far from the past, that she never managed to broach the subject with him. Rohan quickly settled down in the city, soon gathered a host of friends around him, and before long he was again the leader of the crowd, just as he had been long ago, as far back as she could remember, and after a while she began to feel that her life had swung back to normal again after some nightmare deviation from its appointed course.

But all she was aware of thinking whenever she met another man was: he is nothing compared to Daniel.

Her mother wrote to her from England: "So glad you're meeting such a lot of people, dear. It must be lovely to have Rohan there with you. Is there anyone special at the moment? It's so amazing to think that next September you'll be twenty-eight. . . ."

Her mother was thinking of tomorrow, and tomorrow for Rachel did not exist. Tomorrow was a great emptiness, a desert stretching into nothingness before the oasis of today, and the landscape was so desolate that she did not even dare to look at it.

I shall never marry, she thought. Not while Daniel's image is still so strong in my mind.

But Daniel had preferred his life to take a different course. He had never loved her, just as she had never really loved him, and she could see now that her whole attitude to him was a romantic attachment, a young girl's infatuation which she had never fully outgrown; it was surely best to pretend even to herself that the whole episode was already forgotten, and then perhaps she would find it easier to obliterate him from her mind for all time.

It was evening. She was going out to dinner and had just had a bath. There was a long mirror in the living room next to the desk, and she always sat in front of it to put on her makeup because the light from the desk lamp was perfect for applying cosmetics. As she began to put on her makeup the phone on the desk started to ring.

She picked up the receiver without interest. "Hullo?"

"Rachel," said Rohan, and his voice sounded thin and far away as if he were speaking from a great distance. "I had to call you."

Rohan was always dramatic. His reason for calling was probably trivial.

"I'm just going out," she said. "Can I call you back later?"

"No," he said, "no, I have to tell you. I had a letter from England today."

She thought she heard his voice tremble. Her fingers suddenly tightened on the receiver. "From England?"

"From Rebecca, Rachel. From Rebecca Carey."

She could see her expression in the long mirror, watch the color ebb from her face. It was as if she were watching a film, seeing a stranger whom she did not know.

"I got the letter this morning," he was saying. "I couldn't think why she was writing, as we only exchanged addresses as a formality."

"What did she say?"

"Can't you guess? It's Daniel, Rachel—Daniel's returning from Africa, coming back into our lives. . . ."

## ii

Daniel had often asked himself why he had gone abroad. He, who had always lived his life in the most English of environments, who had lived in the oldest and most English parts of England, who had worked in such a peculiarly English world of academic research—why should he of all people have suddenly decided to turn his back on it all and try instead to teach in a hostile foreign land for little money and little prestige? He had gone back to Cambridge after Roshven fully prepared to resume his life where he had left it, to pick up the threads as if he had never been away and to slip back with ease into the intellectual satisfaction of his work and his life among those ancient, beautiful surroundings. He had never anticipated what had happened when he went back. He had never once thought that the world he loved would have changed so that it seemed to him yet another Roshven in its arid, desolate sterility; he could never once have imagined that he would ever pause on the Bridge of Sighs and look at the smooth waters of the Cam below and think to himself: "I have no place here any more. I'm a stranger knocking on the door and trying to gain entrance, but I've come to the wrong door. There's nothing here for me."

His work suddenly seemed a mere mechanical exercise of his brain, and even his ambition had died. He had waited, hoping his apathy was some form of reaction to the events at Roshven, but the state of mind persisted and at last he realized clearly that he had to get away—away from Cambridge, away from England, and most of all away from Rebecca. It was true they had never spoken of Roshven, and Rebecca had shied away from all mention of Charles and Decima, but Daniel, convinced as he was that she had killed them both in a burst of frenzied rage and revenge, found it impossible to be at ease with her. Several times he tried to force himself to speak of it to her, but each time he had failed. She must know, he thought, that he had covered up for her; she must realize that he knew. . . . But if she did, she seemed determined not to speak of it, and the awkwardness between them became more pronounced. When he had decided to go abroad she was very distressed and for a time tried to persuade him to stay, but when she saw he was determined she gave up her attempts at persuasion and appeared resigned to the situation.

A voluntary educational organization had seized on the opportunity to enlist a graduate capable of teaching English; within three months he had a class of forty African children in Accra and was learning to live in the country which had once been called the White Man's Grave.

He found he enjoyed teaching more than he had thought he would, and contrary to what he had always imagined, the younger his pupils were the more he enjoyed teaching them. *When I eventually return to England,* he thought, *this is what I shall do. I'll get a school of my own and teach young children, not vegetate in some great university lecturing to pseudo-adults who think they're God's gift to society.*

The decision pleased him; he was happy. Perhaps he would even have stayed longer in Accra if he had not begun to think more and more of Rachel Lord.

He didn't know why he thought of her so often. Perhaps it was because he had never really been able to make up his mind about her. She had seemed so full of candor and sincerity, so honest and unspoiled and unsophisticated, that it had sickened him to discover she had stooped to spying and telling tales in the violence of her jealousy of him. And then later. . . . It was Rohan, Rachel had said, I never told Charles. It was Rohan. . . .

But Decima had said Rachel was the one who had told Charles. "Can't you see she's beside herself with jealousy?" she had blazed to Daniel. "Can't you see she has this schoolgirl crush on you and is as jealous as hell?"

He had never even considered that it might be Quist, and yet it was much more likely that Quist would have been the one to cause trouble. But why had Decima lied? Because it was *she* who was jealous, *she* who was spiteful enough to want to hurt Rachel and pay her back for capturing Daniel's attention? Perhaps after all Rachel had been speaking the truth, and if so perhaps she was still everything he had first imagined her to be. The more he considered the situation, the more convinced he became that he had misjudged her, and the more he became convinced that he had judged her wrongly the more he wanted to see her. Now, five years after he had left England, he found he was thinking of her all the time. He thought of her when his students asked him questions about English places and English people; he thought of her whenever he received his three-week-old copy of the Sunday *Times* and saw the theater news and the book reviews; he thought of her when he was introduced to other women, and above all he thought of her each year on the anniversary of those terrible days at Roshven when he relived the memories he would carry with him to the end of his life. Sometimes it seemed to him that he would only have to close his eyes to be back again at Roshven and facing her beside the open window of Decima's room.

He was not sure when it first became clear to him that he would have to see her again. Perhaps the turning point came when he received a letter from his sister mentioning that she had met Rohan Quist again by chance in London and that he was about to leave England to work in New York.

"Apparently Rachel is working in New York already," Rebecca had written, "so I suppose this will give them the opportunity to revive their platonic friendship again."

It was then that he had started to wonder whether Quist and Rachel would ever discuss Roshven when they met. Unless Rachel was very careful, such a discussion could be extremely dangerous.

He thought about it for a long time, remembering every detail of those last hours at Roshven, but the more he thought about it the less convinced he was that everything was perfectly safe. Suppose Rachel betrayed to Quist that she knew the coroner's verdict had been wrong. . . . Quist had loved Decima. Suppose he got it into his head to resurrect the entire business. . . .

It was then that Daniel first conceived the idea of seeing Rachel again to warn her not to talk, and once the idea of seeing her was in his mind there was no putting it aside.

Several of Rebecca's letters had referred to Quist after that first meeting when he had told her he was planning to join Rachel in New York.

"Rohan rang up," she had written in the next letter, "and asked me out to dinner. I nearly refused and then I thought—hell, why not? So I went. We went to an extremely good restaurant, and much to my surprise I rather enjoyed myself. He seems to have matured a great deal and it was hard to believe he was the same person as the Rohan Quist we knew at Roshven. . . . He didn't refer to Roshven at all, or to Charles or Decima, but for me at any rate, if not for him, the memories were there like a great wall between us. . . ."

Rohan had taken her out several times after that. Then later she had written: "Saw Rohan again last night. It was his birthday and he said he wanted to go out and have a few drinks somewhere, so we went to Dorchester and got rather tight on vodka martinis. After the fourth he started to talk about Rachel, and by the time he had finished the fifth he was talking of Roshven. 'It's a funny thing,' he said, 'but I'm sure Rachel knows something.' And I said: 'Knows what?'

"'About Roshven,' he said. 'She won't talk about it, though. She never talks of Roshven. But I'm sure she knows something.'

"I said: 'Why do you say that?'

"And he said: 'Because I've known Rachel over twenty-five years and I know her better than most men know their own sisters. I know when she's keeping her mouth shut and when she isn't.'

"Well, I couldn't resist it—I just had to ask him if he hadn't always been a little in love with her. And he said: 'A little, perhaps.' I thought he was going to say more but when he didn't I asked him why he didn't marry her.

"He just laughed. He was very drunk. Then he said suddenly: 'Maybe I will! It's about time I got married.' And he laughed again suddenly, as if he'd been very clever, and he went on laughing until he knocked over his glass. . . . We went soon after that. He said he'd phone me before he left for New York next week, but somehow I doubt if he will."

Rebecca had been correct. Rohan had never phoned.

It was soon after that letter that Daniel had begun to make arrangements for his departure. It was impossible to leave at once, for the summer term was just beginning and he was bound to stay until it was finished, but just over three months later he said good-bye to his students in Accra, boarded the plane for London, and began his long, dangerous journey back into the past.

### iii

All Rachel could think of was that Daniel was coming. After Rohan had told her the news and had said he would come over to her apartment right away, she hadn't moved from her position in front of the mirror for a long time, and then at last she picked up the receiver of the phone again and canceled her date for the evening.

Daniel was coming. It had been five years since Roshven but now the five years were as if they had never existed at all. Daniel had left Africa and was already in London on his way back into their lives.

"Rebecca said in her letter that he wanted to see you," Rohan had said to her over the phone. "I don't understand it at all. You haven't been in touch with him, have you?"

And she had said blankly: "Of course not."

"Then why does he want to see you?"

"I—don't know."

There was a long silence. Then: "I'll come around right away," Rohan had said abruptly, and hung up.

Daniel was coming. He wanted to see her. Why else would he want to see her unless it was because of Roshven?

She saw the house then so clearly in her mind that it seemed to her that she would only have to close her eyes to be back there again, breathing the damp, pure air and feeling the soft sea breeze moist against her cheek. She saw the bare stretches of the moors ending in the dark lines of the Forestry Plantation, the desolate mountains, the swaying sea, and there before her eyes were the turrets and towers of Roshven with their gray walls and blank windows.

Her thoughts, as if liberated at last after five years of constant suppression, went on and on and on. She was recalling each detail of her stay five years ago, reliving the horror of those last hours, the discovery of Charles's body, the realization of Decima's death, the agreement she had reached with Daniel. . . .

Daniel. Daniel wanted to see her. Daniel was coming to New York.

When Rohan arrived a few minutes later she could hardly reach the door fast enough to answer the bell.

"We'd better go out, hadn't we?" he said as she let him in. "There's no privacy here."

"The others are out. They won't be back for hours yet."

"Okay, then we'll stay here. Let me get you a drink."

She asked for a Tom Collins and went into the kitchen to fetch the soda from the refrigerator. Later, when he had mixed the drinks, they sat down together on the couch and he gave her a cigarette.

After a moment he said with wry cynicism: "Perhaps he's coming to propose."

"Oh, for God's sake, Rohan!" She was too tense to laugh at such a preposterous suggestion. "You know as well as I do that whatever relationship existed between Daniel and me certainly wasn't on that plane. I don't know why he can possibly want to see me, least of all now, five years after Roshven."

There was a silence. Rohan leaned forward to flick ash into the tray on the table and the light glinted for a moment on the gold of his cuff links and the crisp white cuff of his shirt below the sleeve of his suit. He looked well dressed and elegant, and the years had smoothed out the angular thinness of his face and body so that all impression of immaturity had been eliminated from his appearance. His fair hair, which had never lost the shining brightness of childhood, was neat and well cut, his fine eyes reflecting the thoughts in his mind like an opaque mirror. She wondered again why he had never married. Perhaps he had always been too conscious of Decima's memory, just as she herself had always been too quick to remember Daniel. . . .

"Raye?"

She suddenly realized he had asked her a question. "I'm sorry," she said, confused. "I was thinking of something else. What did you say?"

"I was just asking," said Rohan, "if you were quite sure you had no idea why Daniel should be looking for you?"

"What do you mean?"

"It's about Roshven, isn't it?"

"Honestly, Rohan, I—"

"You shielded him, didn't you?"

There was a dead silence. They looked at one another. Then: "Shielded him?" said Rachel.

"I always suspected you were keeping something back at the inquest. It had to do with Daniel, didn't it? There was no one else you would have shielded."

She didn't answer.

"Was Daniel involved?"

She still didn't answer.

"Raye—"

"It was as they said at the inquest," she interrupted quickly, a spot of color flaming in each cheek. "Charles killed Decima and then committed suicide."

"Yes," said Rohan. "Very convenient." He watched his cigarette burn for a moment. Then suddenly his eyes were looking straight into hers and she knew at once what he was going to say. "Did Daniel kill Decima?"

"Rohan—"

"He had a good enough motive. She told me on the eve of her birthday that she had originally wanted him to take her away with him, but he had lost interest in her and refused. She was furious with him and determined to pay him back. 'I'll make trouble for him,' she said to me, 'I'll see he doesn't get that post he wants at Cambridge.' She was full of plans to ruin him. Did he kill her?"

"I—" The horror of those last hours at Roshven made speech difficult. "I—don't know," she said desperately at last. "I just don't know, Rohan. He had the opportunity. He was in Decima's room talking to her before I went down to the library to find Charles."

"He was *where?*"

"In Decima's room. I knocked on her door to ask her if she was all right and she said she was. Someone else was with her at the time because I could hear the murmur of voices—"

"You mean," said Rohan slowly, "that Decima was alive then?"

"Yes. Yes, she was alive."

"But that means—"

"I know. Charles didn't kill Decima. He was the one who died first."

"But my God, Raye, why on earth didn't you tell the police?"

"It was the easiest way out, Rohan. . . ." She told him about Charles then, described how Daniel had destroyed the evidence that Rebecca had committed the murder. "He said it was obvious that Decima had killed Charles—"

"Obvious?" said Rohan, amazed. "Obvious? Why the hell should Decima have killed Charles? I talked to her that evening! She was full of plans for getting a divorce—I had offered to take her away with me for a while—we had planned to leave Roshven together the next day. That was why we both got drunk—we were drunk with exhilaration and pleasure! Why should she have murdered Charles? She didn't need to! Isn't it much more obvious that Rebecca killed him? She was out of her mind with frustration and rage. She could easily have killed him in a fit of fury and left Daniel to clear up after her! That to me is much more plausible than to suggest that Decima was the murderess."

"Daniel said Rebecca had been framed."

"Well, of course he'd say that! Of course!"

"But Decima—who pushed her from the window?"

"Why, Daniel, of course! Who else? When Rebecca came and told him what had happened, he suddenly saw how he could use the situation to his best advantage. If he were to silence Decima he could make it seem that Charles had killed his wife and then committed suicide. In that way he would extricate Rebecca from a very unpleasant situation and also eliminate the threat Decima presented to his future and prospects. So he went back to Decima's room—which he must have left shortly after you spoke to Decima on your way down to the library—killed her, and then returned to the library to rearrange the body and obliterate all trace of Rebecca from the scene of the crime. Imagine how he must have felt when he found you there! His one chance lay in the fact that you were sufficiently—that you cared for him enough to agree to shield him, so he told you what to tell the police, and gambled on the likelihood that you would do as he said."

Rachel ground her cigarette to ashes, stood up, and moved restlessly over to the window.

There was another long silence.

"Why on earth didn't you tell me this before, Raye?"

What was there to say? That she had never been able to acknowledge to herself the probability of Daniel's guilt? That even after five years she was still in love with the memory of a man who had never loved her in return? There was no logical answer, no easy explanation. "It seemed the simplest way out at the time," she heard herself say at last. "I know it was weak and stupid of me, but it was such a temptation to do as he suggested and make the inquest a simple, uncomplicated affair. I'd reached the end of the road by that time—I couldn't have endured more police investigations or the possibility of being detained at Roshven any longer. I just wanted to leave, to forget, to escape."

"It might have seemed the simplest way out at the time," Rohan said, "but I doubt if it's going to be quite so simple now. You realize, of course, why Daniel's coming to look for you."

She stared at him blankly.

"He's heard through Rebecca that I'm in New York. He realizes that I'll be seeing you constantly. He thinks you're going to talk, Rachel—he thinks that in the end you'll tell me the truth. You're a menace to his security."

The silence then was so acute that it seemed almost audible. The large, softly lit room seemed poised and waiting, and as Rachel stood beside the long mirror and caught sight of her reflection it was as if she saw a stranger with whom she had no connection, a girl with wide, blank gray eyes in a white, frozen face.

"What shall I do?" she said, and suddenly the years fell away and she was a child again, turning to Rohan for comfort and advice. "What shall I do?"

He got up, crossed the room, and paused very close to her so that they were a mere few inches apart. "You don't have to worry," he said softly. "You don't have to worry about anything. I'll look after you." And he took her in his arms.

At first she was so surprised that she had no reaction at all, and then she felt a surge of gratitude and a wave of overwhelming relief. Tears pricked her eyes. She slipped her arms around his waist and pressed her face against his shoulder, and presently she felt his lips brush her hair and touch her forehead. She raised her face to his. "What shall we do?"

"We'll leave New York. I'll say I have to go home for a few days for family reasons—I'm more or less my own boss at work, so no one's going to ask any questions. You'll have to leave your job— or take some unpaid leave. One or the other. Is your passport in order? We'll leave New York tomorrow evening."

"Supposing Daniel should arrive before then?"

"He doesn't know where you live—he only knows my address through Rebecca. His only way of contacting you will be by first contacting me, and I can stall him off. You're safe for a time, any-way. Have you got enough money for your fare?"

"Yes, I think so."

"I'll ring up and make the reservations." His hand was already on the phone. "We'll try and get on a flight tomorrow evening."

"Rohan—"

"Yes?"

"Suppose he follows us? Where shall we go when we get to England?"

"Somewhere remote and isolated, where we can set a trap for him. Of course! The obvious place! Why didn't I think of it be-fore? We'll go back to Roshven. . . ."

*iv*

Rebecca was at the airport to meet him as the plane from Accra finally touched down on British soil. After the long, tedious min-utes spent in Customs and Immigration, he passed through the barrier to join her, and she was running into his arms.

"Danny . . . oh, Danny. . . ." She was hugging him fiercely as if to make up for the five years he had spent away from her, and he pressed her to him tightly in response. Presently she looked up at him with shining eyes and they laughed together in happiness.

"How tanned you are!" she exclaimed. "You look so well. . . . Oh Danny, how wonderful to see you again. . . ."

She had her car parked outside the building and after they had all his luggage safely stowed away they set off for her tiny flat in Bayswater. They were just turning off the main road into Hammersmith some time later when she asked him the inevitable question.

"What are you going to do now, Danny? Have you any ideas?"

"Yes," he said without hesitation, his eyes on the road ahead. "I have a flight to New York booked on Monday. I'm going to spend a week or two in America."

He heard her gasp, saw her hands swerve on the wheel. "America?" she said incredulously, as if she could hardly believe her ears. "New York?"

"I plan to go to the Embassy tomorrow to get a visa."

After a moment she said: "Why?"

He made no reply.

"It's not because of Rachel and Rohan, is it?"

He stared straight ahead of him, vaguely aware of all the changes in the Hammersmith he remembered, savoring the English roads and the English houses and the signposts bearing English names.

"If it is," she said, "you can save yourself a plane fare. They're back in England."

The landscape froze before his eyes. He whirled to face her. "They're back?"

"I was going to tell you—"

"Where are they?"

"Rohan called me yesterday morning, soon after they'd arrived. He said they were over here for two weeks' holiday and were on their way north to Scotland."

He stared at her incredulously. "You didn't tell him, did you, that I was coming home?"

The car swerved again; she drew into the side of the road and switched off the engine. The traffic roared past.

"Well, yes," she said. "I did. I wrote and told him last week soon after you'd told me your decision." She hesitated uneasily. Then: "I'm sorry, Danny. I didn't realize—"

"It doesn't matter. It's done now. It was my fault for not anticipating that you'd tell him." He switched on the engine again for her and pressed the starter. "Don't let's stop here."

"But I don't understand," said Rebecca, bewildered, slipping the car into gear and easing out the clutch. "What do you want with them, Danny? Why do you want to see them now after all this time?"

"It's just something I have to straighten out with Rachel," he said, and his mouth was dry as he spoke. "I'd rather not go into details. Whereabouts in Scotland are they going?"

"To Kyle of Lochalsh," said Rebecca. "Rohan said they were planning to visit Roshven."

## v

They had taken the night train from London to Edinburgh and had just had lunch on Princes Street by a window which faced the castle. They had already rented a car for a week at one of the local garages and were planning to set off after lunch on the journey north into the Highlands toward Fort William, Inverness, and Kyle of Lochalsh. The sun was shining. Outside, the gardens at the foot of the castle were immensely green and the gray castle walls, standing aloft on the black upthrust of volcanic rock, shimmered in the heat haze.

"I still don't see how meeting Daniel at Roshven will ever induce him to admit anything," Rachel was saying as the waitress brought them coffee.

"He'll have to admit something," Rohan said dryly. "He won't follow us all the way to Roshven for the purpose of keeping his mouth shut."

"But why couldn't we have met him in London?"

"Because he's more likely to take risks and give himself away in a remote place. In London he'd be too much on his guard."

"Do you think so? I still can't help wishing we didn't have to go back."

"Look," said Rohan, "who's in charge of this plan—you or me? Right. Well, sooner or later Daniel's going to catch up with you and if he's going to catch up with you, it's best for me to be there too, isn't it? Right. Well, assuming that I'll have to face a potentially dangerous man and deal with him in whatever way the situation demands, I think I have the right to choose a location. And I choose Roshven."

"Yes," said Rachel. "All right."

He capitulated at once. "Look, Raye, I'm sorry—I didn't mean to upset you—I know it's all the most awful strain for you—"

"No," she said. "It's all right. Really, Rohan, it's all right."

They drank their coffee. Then: "Rohan."

"Yes?"

"You're not going to kill him, are you?"

"Not unless I have to," said Rohan, "but if he tries to harm you I'll break every bone in his body without any hesitation at all."

"Is that why you bought the gun?"

"Well, I have to have some protection, don't I? Besides, he may well be armed himself."

"Yes," said Rachel. "I suppose he might."

Rohan's hand slid across the table and closed on hers. "You're not still in love with him, are you?"

"No, of course not. That's all over and done with and has been for five years."

He went on holding her hand beneath his own. After a while he said: "How much longer do we have to go on pretending to ourselves that we're just good friends?"

She looked up. The sun was slanting right through the window into her eyes and he saw her expression of astonishment before she leaned forward out of the shaft of light and put her face in shadow. "I'm not sure," she said at last, "that I quite understand you."

"No?" he said. "It's very simple. Now that I know for certain that you've got over this feeling you had for Daniel, I was wondering if you'd marry me."

She was silent for a long time, looking into his eyes. In the end she looked away. Her face was grave and still, and it was impossible to tell what she was thinking, but he knew instinctively that she was going to refuse.

"Do you intend to remain unmarried all your life?" he heard himself say quickly. "We know each other so well, Rachel—we can relax and feel at ease with each other, we suit each other so well. Why go on as we have been doing in an endless attempt to find someone else? I would have asked you before if I hadn't thought you were still emotionally involved with Daniel. I've known for a long while that you're the woman I want to marry."

"No," she said. "I'm just the *kind* of woman you want to marry. It's not the same thing."

"You don't understand—"

"You don't love me, Rohan! Well, yes, perhaps you do in your own way, but not in the way a husband loves his wife."

"You're a perfectionist," he said. "You're waiting for a glamorized, unreal brand of love which doesn't really exist. You'll wait forever, Rachel, can't you see? You'll wait forever for the kind of love that doesn't exist outside the pages of romantic fiction!"

"I'd rather wait forever," she said deliberately, "than marry a man I only half loved." And then instantly: "Rohan, it's not because I care nothing for you—I do care a great deal, you know I do—but surely you must see that we wouldn't be suited, that marriage wouldn't really work . . . I'm sorry." She fumbled with her handbag, almost knocked over her coffee cup. "Shall we go? There are people over there waiting for tables. . . ."

He rose without a word, helped her on with her coat, and then went to the cashier's desk to pay the bill.

"I'm sorry, Rohan," she said again as they went out into the street. "Please forgive me—"

"There's nothing to forgive." He smiled at her. "If you have such qualms about the subject, we'd do much better not to marry.

But in case you should change your mind, the offer still stands."

They walked down Princes Street, turned up the road where they had left the car. Rachel's mind was in such turmoil that she scarcely knew where she was going. Rohan's proposal had caught her completely unawares and her thoughts, already confused over Daniel, were whirled into greater bewilderment and chaos than ever before. She had answered Rohan instinctively, but even now her logic was beginning to question her instinct. Every reason Rohan had put forward for marriage was sound; there was every likelihood that they would be as happily married as most couples; he cared for her enough to be with her now when she needed him most of all, and he was always the first person she turned to; she was nearly twenty-eight years old and could certainly do far worse than marry Rohan, who at thirty-one was successful in his work, popular with his friends, and good-looking in his own unusual way.

Why, then, had she refused his offer so quickly that her reaction was almost an automatic reflex of her mind?

The answer came straightaway, flashing across her thoughts before she could even struggle to suppress it, and she knew well enough why she had rejected Rohan.

He was nothing compared to Daniel.

*vi*

Daniel and Rebecca had discussed Roshven in great detail for some time. The subject, unmentioned between them for so long, proved to be so enlightening to both of them that they had recalled with meticulous precision each incident and scene which had preceded the murders. Afterward Daniel felt so exhausted that he had a bath and slept for a couple of hours before shaving and getting dressed. It was evening, and from the noises in the kitchen he guessed that Rebecca was cooking a meal for them. He picked up the receiver and phoned London Airport.

"When's the next flight to Inverness, please?"

"One moment, sir."

His call was switched to another extension. There was a click, another voice, and he had to repeat his question.

"The night flight leaves at ten o'clock tonight, sir."

"Is there a vacancy on it?"

"For how many?"

"Just one."

"One moment." Another click, a buzz, a few seconds of empty silence. Then: "Yes, we have a cancellation so there's a seat available. Would you—"

"Yes," said Daniel. "I'll take it. My name is Carey. What time should I be at the airport and where can I pick up my ticket?"

Rebecca had come out of the kitchen but he scarcely noticed her. Then: "Thank you," he said, and hung up the receiver.

"Danny—"

"I'm sorry," he said to her. "But I really have to go. I shan't be away long, only for a couple of days or so. I'll explain all about it when I get back."

"Do you want me to come with you?" She was fighting to overcome her disappointment at the thought of losing him so soon. "Can I help at all?"

"No," he said, "this is something that has to be settled between Quist, Rachel, and myself. You stay here. I'll be all right—I know exactly what I'm doing. . . ."

*vii*

Rachel and Rohan did not know that while they were spending the night at Kyle of Lochalsh Daniel was sleeping in a hotel at Inverness. They had arrived after dark and had found rooms in one of the small hotels near the harbor. After a late supper they had gone to bed and slept until it was time for breakfast at nine o'clock the next morning.

The weather was as unexpectedly fine as it had been in Edinburgh the previous day. Rachel woke to find the sun sparkling on the harbor and glittering on the array of boats moored along the quay. Across the sea loomed the distant heights of Skye, and the gulls wheeled and mewed over the stone houses of the town around her. Once she was dressed she paused by the window again to survey the scene, and then Rohan was knocking on her door and they went downstairs to breakfast together.

"How did you sleep?" said Rohan over the toast and marmalade.

"Surprisingly well. I suppose I was very tired after the journey."

"Yes, I was too."

They ate for a moment in silence. Then: "I'll ask the landlord where we can hire a boat from," Rohan said. "There shouldn't be any difficulty in getting one."

"No, I shouldn't think so," said Rachel, and felt a small core of fear harden noticeably inside her.

She was dreading the return to Roshven. It had been bad enough returning to Kyle of Lochalsh with its memories of shopping with Decima and the meeting with Daniel in the wheelhouse, but the very idea of seeing Roshven again was almost more than she could bear. Closing her mind against it resolutely, she poured herself another cup of tea and helped herself to an additional slice of toast, but her nervousness was soon so immense that she had to leave both unfinished.

"Ready?" said Rohan at last. "Then let's go."

It took them about an hour to find the type of boat they wanted. Then, after they had stocked the small galley with provisions of all kinds, they cast off from the quay and headed out to sea.

They lost sight of the town less than twenty minutes later.

The wave of isolation that hit Rachel then was so immense that she scarcely knew how to control it. She left the deck and shut herself in the galley below, in the hope that she would be able to block out her fear if she didn't see the increasing bleakness of the landscape and the appalling loneliness of those barren shores, but the fear persisted and in the end she drank a double Scotch to steady her nerves. After that she felt better. She had another, to be quite safe, and then went back on deck to join Rohan in the wheelhouse.

"How are we doing?"

"Pretty well. It's a beautiful day, isn't it? I've never seen the sea so calm here before."

The boat sped on through the dark blue waters, and the landscape, basking in the unaccustomed sunshine, seemed to have lost its quality of overwhelming desolation and become breathtaking in its stark magnificence. Rachel found she could look at it now without feeling fear or dread, but when, at last, she saw the promontory which would bring them to Roshven, she felt her nerves sharpen again in anticipation.

"Isn't it odd?" said Rohan, and she knew then that he too was uneasy. "It's just as if nothing had changed. It's hard to realize that Charles and Decima aren't waiting to meet us and that Mrs. Willie isn't baking bread in the kitchen and that George isn't snoozing before the fire in the hall."

They rounded the promontory. There was a shower of spray as the boat met a complex of currents, and then they were heading directly inland and Roshven lay before them across the water. The sun shone on the gray walls and made the background of mountains and moors shimmer in a green-purple haze.

"I've never seen it look so beautiful," said Rohan. "Perhaps now at last I can see why Decima loved it so much."

The blank windows stared at them unseeingly. As they drew nearer they saw that the garden was more wild and untended than ever and that the gamekeeper's little croft was already falling into ruins.

They reached the jetty. Rohan maneuvered the boat into position and jumped ashore to fasten the painter to the bollard.

"The boards of the jetty aren't too secure," he warned her. "Careful how you go."

"Thanks." She scrambled ashore and stood still for a moment.

The sea breeze fanned her cheek; a gull screamed above her. Everywhere was very still.

"I'm going up to the house," said Rohan. "You needn't come if you don't want to, but I'm curious to see what's happened and what it looks like now."

She was glad he gave her the chance to refuse. "I'll stay here," she said. "I don't particularly want to go back."

"Okay. I won't be long."

She watched him move quickly up the path to the house. When he reached the front door he discovered it was locked, and she saw him go around to the back and disappear from sight.

She waited some time in the sunshine, and then slowly the curiosity began to seep through her until she wished she had gone with him. After dreading the return to Roshven so violently, it now seemed that the reality of return was not nearly as disturbing as she had feared it might be, and in the relief of realizing this she wanted to go into the house and try to blunt the edge of her worst memories by revisiting the scenes under different circumstances.

Presently she left the deck and stepped ashore onto the creaking jetty again. It took her about five minutes to reach the house. Rohan, she discovered, had climbed in through the kitchen window, which might or might not have been broken before his arrival. As she was wearing slacks it was easy enough for her to clamber in after him, and soon she was walking through the huge deserted rooms and making her way into the massive emptiness of the great hall.

"Rohan?" she called uncertainly as she reached the foot of the stairs, but there was no reply.

Presently she mounted the staircase and then paused to listen. It was very quiet, very still. The sunshine streamed through the long windows of the hall, but the house was eerie in its deserted emptiness and Rachel was conscious of the smell of damp and decay.

She moved down the corridor and paused for a time outside the door of Decima's room, but suddenly her courage ebbed and she hadn't enough left to turn the handle and walk in. She went back down the passage to the head of the stairs and all at once it seemed to her as if she were reenacting her movements on the night of the murders and she had just stopped outside Decima's door to ask her if she were all right. She reached the landing and paused to look down into the hall.

She could see the scene then as if it were yesterday, the long banquet table, the red candles snuffed and guttered, the remains of the dinner still strewn over the white tablecloth, the twin silver epergnes, the drooping flowers. Around the hall were the lamps, still burning, and the red embers in the two fireplaces. George the St. Bernard had been asleep before the hearth. Or had he? No, that had been earlier. When she had returned to the hall to find Charles, George had been asleep outside the door of the small drawing room. She could remember wondering why he had chosen to lie in that drafty corner when both fires were still glowing in the grates.

As she began to descend the stairs it suddenly occurred to her to wonder again why the dog had been lying there. If Daniel had been in the drawing room, then it would have explained the dog's presence, for George had followed Daniel everywhere, but Daniel had been upstairs talking to Decima in her room.

Or had he?

She stopped dead.

She was recalling the scene in the library when she had found Charles. There had been the closing of a door far away, the sound of footsteps crossing the hall, and then Daniel had entered the room just after she had managed to hide behind the curtains. He had come from across the hall, from the drawing room. She would never have heard the door of Decima's room close. It had been the door of the drawing room where the dog was waiting for him.

Daniel hadn't been in Decima's room at all.

Then who had been with her as Rachel passed the door? Rebecca? But it had been a man's low murmur she had heard. Not Daniel. And not Charles, who was already dead. That left Rohan. Rohan had been with Decima just before she died.

But Rohan had been blind drunk. She had had to put him to bed.

Or had he been shamming? She had thought at the time that for two persons accustomed to liquor they had managed to get surprisingly drunk. Supposing it had all been an act, a plan to set the stage—for what?

For Charles's murder. . . .

Rebecca had been framed. Rohan, thanks to Rachel's testimony, would be found to be much too drunk to commit a crime. And Decima . . . Daniel had carried Decima upstairs to her room. He would also testify that she had been too drunk to commit murder. But Daniel hadn't stayed in Decima's room, because when Rachel reached the hall on her way to find Charles, George was already outside the drawing room door waiting for Daniel to come out. And Decima, Rachel knew, had at that time been alive and well.

Daniel hadn't killed Decima. Rebecca? No, because the voice talking to Decima had belonged to a man. And Charles was already dead.

Rohan had killed Decima. And either he or Decima had first killed Charles.

*Rohan was a murderer*, was all she was conscious of thinking, her frightened thoughts repeating themselves over and over again in a paralysis of horror. *Rohan was a murderer*.

And then the full impact of the situation struck her and she was so unnerved that she could neither move nor breathe.

Rohan was a murderer and she was alone with him at Roshven.

# Chapter Two

*i*

Daniel rose early, had rented a car by eight thirty, and by nine
o'clock had left Inverness behind and was driving west over the
Highlands to Kyle of Lochalsh. It was raining. Clouds obscured
the mountains, and mist trailed over the vast expanses of sodden
moors. There were few other cars on the road. The rain slewed
remorselessly onto the windshield to make driving difficult, and
as he drove on over that storm-torn landscape it seemed to him
that the five hot, steamy years in Accra had been a dream and that
he had never left this beautiful, appalling remoteness with its
rains and mists and pale, shrouded northern light.

This is the real Scotland, he thought. Glasgow is for the busi-
nessmen; Edinburgh is for the tourists. But up here north of the
Highland Line is the Scotland that is for no one, least of all for
intruders, the Scotland that made even the Romans turn back unnerved in retreat. No wonder they believed it was the very
edge of the world, the remotest corner of land known to man. The

mountains are crowded together as if waiting to entomb all tres-
passers in the valleys, and the moors rise up from the road like the
sides of a grave.

The heavy rain continued for some time. He was just wondering if there was any possibility at all of a break in the weather,
when the road surmounted a pass and suddenly the clouds lifted
from the mountain slopes, the rain lessened, and the sky seemed
brighter. Within twenty minutes the highest of the inland mountains were behind him and he had traveled into a different world;
the sun shone, the sky was blue, and as he descended from the
hills to Kyle of Lochalsh he could see that the horizon of the Atlantic was hazy with the promise of good weather.

He drove into the town.

Outside the small inn where he and Charles had often stopped
for a beer after a shopping expedition, he parked the car and went
inside. The landlord's wife was industriously sweeping out the
bar with a long broom.

"Good morning," she began brightly, and then stopped in stu-
pefaction as she recognized him.

"Good morning," he said, and waited for her to give him the
information he wanted.

"Well!" she said, amazed. "Well!" And when he was silent, she
added: "It *is* Mr. Carey, isn't it?"

"It is. You've got a good memory, Mrs. MacCleod."

She was pleased that he remembered her name. "Well, now,"
she said sympathetically. "What a shame! You've just missed them
—they were staying down the road at the Stuart Arms. My husband was over there talking to Ian Black, the landlord, when they
arrived last night, and he said—"

"They've already gone?"

"Hired a boat this morning from Duncan Robertson—I saw
them walk along the quay just a little while ago—"

"How long ago?"

She looked vaguely surprised by the abruptness of his questions. "Why, two or three hours ago, perhaps. I'd just lit the fire
in the kitchen and then I came in here to listen to the weather

forecast on the wireless, and lo and behold, who should I see when I looked out of the window but Mr. Quist and the young lady walking past to the quay. . . . How long will you all be staying here, Mr. Carey? Such a surprise to see you again. I said to my husband—"

"Not long," said Daniel. "Thank you, Mrs. MacCleod." And before the woman could even draw breath to say good-bye he was moving swiftly out of the house and down to the quayside and the harbor.

## *ii*

Rachel's first thought was to find the gun. Blindly, almost without thinking, she went out of the hall and back through the kitchen again to the broken window. As if in a nightmare her movements seemed curiously slow and clumsy; the window through which she had climbed with such ease earlier now seemed a difficult and dangerous obstacle in her path, and she cut her hand slightly on a piece of broken glass as she scrambled over the sill.

*I must get back to the boat,* she thought. *I must find that gun.*

There was no other thought in her mind at all. Her eyes saw the brilliant sparkle of the sun on the sea and clear sky, but it made no impression on her. She ran down toward the jetty, pushing her way through the overgrown garden, and soon she was gasping for breath and her heart was pounding in her lungs.

*I must get to the boat,* said the voice in her mind over and over again. *I must find the gun.*

She went on running. It seemed a long way to the jetty, and again she was reminded of some hideous nightmare in which one ran and ran yet never reached one's destination. Brambles tore at her slacks; giant bushes and unwieldy shrubs leered in her face;

and then suddenly she was out of the garden and running along the path down to the jetty.

*I must get to the boat,* she kept thinking. *I have to find the gun.*

Her foot stumbled against a rock; she nearly fell, and then at last she reached the rotting boards of the jetty and scrambled aboard the boat. She went to the wheelhouse. No gun. He must have left it below. She was beside the hatch suddenly, almost falling down the gangway to the lower deck. She could picture the gun lying on the top of Rohan's suitcase, and the suitcase was tossed across one of the bunks. . . .

She flung open the cabin door with a gasp of relief and then felt the gasp freeze in her throat.

"Hullo," said Rohan, "I thought I'd lost you. Where did you go?"

Instinct made her brain miraculously clear; her reactions were suddenly as sharp as a razor's edge.

"I went to the house and couldn't find you." She made no effort to hide the fact that she had been running, and sank down on the bunk opposite him to regain her breath. "Then suddenly I had an awful panic and saw ghosts in every corner. I ran all the way back here."

"So it seems!" He smiled at her reassuringly. He had the gun in his hands and was checking to see that it was loaded correctly. He looked calm and untroubled, and the very familiarity of his expression and attitude gave Rachel a strange confidence. This was the Rohan she had known all her life, her friend of nearly all her life, the man whom she knew better than anyone else.

Rohan wouldn't harm her.

He stood up. "Daniel won't be here for a while yet," he said, tucking the gun into his belt. "Let's make some of the food we bought in Kyle and walk along the beach away from the house. I don't want to sit on deck and look at Roshven. I'm not surprised you felt panic-stricken when you went inside! I felt much the same myself."

"Where were you?" she said. "I couldn't find you anywhere."

He moved to the door. "I went to Decima's room," he said abruptly, and for a moment she thought he wasn't going to add any more. Then: "I shouldn't have gone. It was horrible."

He went up on deck and she followed him.

"Why did you go?" she said.

"I don't know," he said, and his eyes as he turned to look at her were dark and blank. "I don't know. It was as if she were up there waiting for me, challenging me to come back." He stepped onto the jetty, and then hesitated. "We forgot the food."

"We can always come back," she said, "and I'm not hungry."

"All right." He walked down the jetty and led the way onto the beach.

The sun was warm; the surf roared in their ears; beneath their feet the sand was firm and smooth. They walked for a long time in silence, and beside them towered the cliffs with their gaping caves and litter of black rocks embedded in the white sand. The tide was still going out. Rohan seemed engrossed in his private thoughts, and Rachel, her initial panic overcome, felt ice-cool and alert. It was not until they rounded the promontory that she was aware of the ache of tension in her body and the fear crawling up and down her spine.

"We're at the quicksands." Her voice was harsh and abrupt.

"So we are," said Rohan. He stood still, gazing out over the miles of white beach ahead, shining deceptively in the bright light. "Cluny Sands. Just lying there peacefully in the sun. Waiting." He turned to face her. "It's odd," he said. "But I feel so strongly as if everything here was waiting. The house was waiting, the shore was waiting, and now these sands are waiting too."

Rachel turned aside sharply. "That's melodramatic, Rohan, and you know it. Don't be absurd."

"But don't you feel it?" he said. "Don't you? Don't you feel that everything is poised and waiting?"

"I could imagine all kinds of things if I wanted to," she heard herself answer tersely. "If one stays in these surroundings long enough one could imagine anything. It's that kind of place."

She hoped he couldn't hear the thumping of her heart, nor see the trembling of her clenched hands.

"Let's sit down," he said. "Let's sit down for a while."

"Why?"

"Why?" he said. "Why, to wait for Daniel, of course. We're waiting too, now, just like everything else. Everything's waiting for Daniel."

### iii

Daniel took the boat far out to sea before heading north to Roshven. He had no wish to be blatantly visible from the beach and he was already trying to decide where to land. If he went to the jetty he would immediately announce his arrival. Perhaps if he were to try and anchor near the beach between Roshven and Cluny Sands he would run less risk of Rohan seeing him immediately. It might be worth trying, although he was unaccustomed to boats after five years away from them, and did not want to risk running aground in shallow waters.

The boat sped on over the calm sea and left a wake trailing in the dark blue water. The air was full of warmth and peace, and the gulls soared aloft on the soft breeze, their wings white arcs against the sky.

He lit a cigarette.

He was thinking of Rachel again, visualizing her with Quist, unknowing and unsuspecting, being carried deeper and deeper into dangerous waters, maneuvered into a position from which she could not escape. He was conscious of how his attitude toward her had changed. He had left Accra to protect his sister, to warn Rachel to say nothing to Quist about the false verdict at the inquest, and had instead discovered that his sister was entirely innocent. She had insisted on her innocence and he had believed her;

her protests were too genuine to be disbelieved. And then even before he had time to feel ashamed of his suspicions he had realized the extreme danger of Rachel's position. If Rachel once revealed the full extent of her knowledge to Quist, she would always be a potential source of danger to him. The number of suspects was so small; she had no doubt left Roshven believing Rebecca to be guilty, probably even suspecting Daniel himself to be in some way involved, but if she once thought them innocent there was only Rohan Quist left to suspect. . . .

And Quist was a murderer who had killed before and would kill again. Daniel could remember thinking how ironic it was that Decima, who had been without passion herself, should in the end have been the victim of a *crime passionel.*

And now Rachel was alone with Quist at Roshven. Perhaps by this time she had guessed the truth. If she were to hint for one moment to Quist that she suspected him. . . .

Daniel threw away his cigarette.

There was no time to lose.

## iv

She was almost sure that Rohan was asleep. He was lying face downward on the sands, his head pillowed in his forearms, his breathing quiet and even. The gun, which he had taken out of his belt for greater comfort, lay peacefully beside him, its barrel glinting in the sunlight.

She picked it up.

Rohan didn't stir.

How did one remove the bullets from guns? If she could somehow take out the bullets, then Daniel would be safe, and she could return the gun to Rohan so that he would never know she had tampered with it.

She stood up very slowly, gun in hand. The tide had turned, she noticed; the waves were creeping back over the sands and the thunder of the surf seemed more powerful in her ears. She moved nearer the cliffs, and then all of a sudden she was among the rocks and Rohan could no longer see her.

She looked down at the gun in her hands and examined it.

It was unnerving not to be able to see Rohan, not to know whether he was still asleep. In a sudden moment of panic she moved back to the shore, but he was still sleeping, his position unchanged, and she felt her body relax slightly in relief.

It was then that she heard the suck of the undertow as the tide crept in over the quicksands.

Withdrawing behind a rock again she struggled with the gun, and at last, just as she was giving up hope, the metal broke open and the bullets spilled into her hands.

She went back to Rohan, stopped just long enough to put the gun down beside him, and then went as close as she dared to the sands.

The bullets were soon gone. She had thrown them into the sands in the path of the incoming tide and they only took a few seconds to vanish from sight. She was just wiping the sweat from her forehead and pushing back her hair when his voice said softly from behind her: "Why the hell did you do that?" Whirling around she found herself face to face with him and her back to Cluny Sands.

*v*

"So you know," he said. "I wondered if you did."

He stood watching her, his blue shirt brilliant against the background of sand and rock, his fair hair shining in the sun, his eyes dark, opaque, expressionless. After a moment he said: "How did you know?"

And she said: "I realized just now in the hall that Daniel hadn't been with Decima just before she died. The scene jogged my memory and I realized then that Daniel had been downstairs in the drawing room when I had gone to the library to find Charles. He wasn't in Decima's room, and yet I'd heard a man's voice there. And then I knew that you had pretended to be drunk earlier and that after I'd left you, you'd slipped out to the library."

"I went to Decima's room first to get Rebecca's diary and the knife." He half turned so that he faced the sea, and she saw that his hands were clenched as he thrust them into his pockets. Presently he said: "It's hard for me to explain my feelings for Decima. How can a woman ever understand? I was infatuated with her. She was an obsession with me. For a long time after she married Charles I tried to pretend that there was no infatuation and no obsession, but you can't pretend forever that black is white and white is black. And every time I went back to Roshven my hatred for Charles grew and the pretense of not caring for Decima grew harder.

"Do you remember how I used to admire Charles—almost hero-worshiped him—when we were young? My distinguished cousin! My respected, esteemed, learned cousin who taught at Oxford and was one of the great scholars of his day! Charles was everything I knew I could never be. No wonder I admired him so much. And then gradually the beginnings of the long disillusionment set in, and I saw everything I had believed in was a myth, a self-deception. Charles was a brilliant scholar, but he was weak, opinionated, vain and pompous. And worst of all, he had won Decima, the greatest prize for any man to win, and then he had estranged and antagonized her so that she wanted only to be rid of him. Can you imagine how I felt? Can't you see? The more I allowed myself to admit my obsession for Decima the more I hated Charles, and all the while I had to conceal my feelings, to pretend and pretend and pretend. . . . Something happens to a man when all the most violent passions are twisted together within him and suppressed again and again. You live in an unreal world and only your thoughts and wishes are reality. I wished Charles dead and that Decima were mine—that was my reality. I lived with that wish for a long time until it was more real to me than anything else in the world. It was a reality even before I began my last visit to Roshven. . . .

"I remember very well the first time I saw Daniel Carey. I had just arrived at Kyle of Lochalsh and was drinking beer in the pub overlooking the harbor when I saw Charles's boat draw up to the quay. Daniel was with Decima. I knew as soon as I saw him that nothing would ever be the same again, and even as I watched them laughing together while they walked down the quay I was convinced that she loved him."

The tide crept nearer; a huge wave broke and rushed greedily toward them as it ate into virgin sand.

"And then you came," he said. "And miraculously, almost unbelievably, Daniel seemed to tire of Decima and turn to you. It was then, and not till then, that Decima turned to me and it seemed at last that I was going to get everything I'd ever wanted.

"I suppose Decima guessed from the beginning how I felt for her. You remember she told you—to confuse you—that Charles was glad you'd come to Roshven because it would divert her attention from me, and that Charles suspected us of having an affair? That was untrue, for Charles knew nothing about how I felt, but I got a bad shock when you repeated the story to me! I then realized that Decima had merely told you that to throw you off the scent and conceal from you her involvement with Daniel. At that time, of course, there was nothing between us, but I think she sensed my feelings nonetheless. Women have an instinct for divining how a man cares, I think, no matter how much he may lie and pretend to the contrary out of pride, and so when she realized at last that she could no longer rely on Daniel she came at once to me for help.

"It was the day of the dinner party. She said she wanted the opportunity to talk to me alone, so we took the boat and went out to sea, intending just to cruise around in open waters for a while, but then, as you know, a storm blew up and we had to head for Kyle for shelter. We spent quite a long time at sea before we had to seek shelter. She let me do exactly as I wished. Later when we were in Kyle waiting for the storm to die she told me she would marry me if she were free but that Charles had now quite made up his mind not to divorce her, and it seemed that she was tied to him indefinitely.

"We were drinking by that time. Alcohol seemed to clarify the situation and make everything so obvious.

"'I would kill Charles,' she said, 'but I'd be too afraid, too frightened. . . . And how could I kill him? I haven't the strength or the knowledge.' She seemed so powerless, so vulnerable, so young. . . .

"I said: 'I'd kill him for you, if I could.'

"I should have guessed then what was happening, because she had the whole scheme ready and planned—she must have worked it out as soon as she had discarded her plans for using Daniel the day before, and she already had Rebecca's knife and the diary hidden in readiness. I should have realized that she was only using me, just as she had tried to use Daniel, but I was long past sane, sensible reasoning, far beyond all sanity and logic.

"'It would be so easy,' she said. 'Can't you see? Everything is already set perfectly. Rebecca has the ideal motive for murdering Charles. We can use her knife to kill him and set the scene to make it look as if she killed him in a fit of rage—he has, after all, just ended their affair against her will. I saw her this morning weeping and red-eyed, and Charles had told me by that time that he was sending the Careys away. Rebecca is the perfect scapegoat—but we must take care no suspicion falls on us. We'll go back tonight at the end of the dinner party and pretend to be drunk out of our minds. The dinner party will collapse in chaos, and someone will see us to our rooms. As soon as you're sure the coast's clear, you can come back to my room, and I'll give you the dagger and Rebecca's diary which I stole from her earlier. Then after it's done you can go back to your room and no one will ever know that we weren't really drunk at all, and then after it's all over we can go away together.'"

A gull wheeled and soared high over the sea. Behind them the tide was still sucking over the quicksands but they no longer heard it.

"So it wasn't Decima who killed Charles," Rachel heard herself say. "It was you."

"Yes," he said. "I killed him. After you'd led me to bed I waited and then went to Decima's room. Daniel carried her upstairs a few minutes later and I hid in the cupboard till he'd gone. Decima asked him where Charles was and he said that Charles had gone to the library.

"I took the knife and the diary and went down the back stairs to the kitchen. Mrs. Willie had gone back to her croft so there was no one about, and when I reached the hall I saw that that too was empty—apart from the dog sleeping outside the drawing room door.

"I went to the library. Charles was just sitting with his head in his hands. He didn't even see the dagger until I was much too close for him to avoid it, and he died almost at once. No one saw me leave the library afterward. I retraced my steps up the back stairs and went to Decima's room to tell her that all was well, and that was when you passed by in the corridor and heard us talking.

"It was after you'd gone that my whole world collapsed. I started to talk to Decima of when we would go away together, but she wasn't interested. I tried to kiss her, but she was lifeless, cold as a statue, remoter from me than she'd ever been.

" 'What's the matter?' I said frantically. 'What have I done?' And then suddenly, hideously, I saw the truth.

"She cared for me no more than she cared for anyone else. She was completely egocentric, a Narcissus in love with herself, withdrawn from other beings and beyond their reach in her own private world. Charles was an obstacle in her path so he had to be removed. How could she remove him without getting hurt herself? Why, get someone else to murder him for her! Why not? Men were always falling over themselves to do as she wished. At first she thought Daniel would probably be just like all the others. He would do as well as anyone. But first of all she must plan very carefully so that no suspicion could possibly fall on her.

"She was aware that Charles was having an affair with Rebecca, but she didn't plan then, as she did later, to frame Rebecca for Charles's murder. She had planned a scheme long before she knew about Charles and Rebecca, and it was this scheme which she intended to put into operation. She was to act the part of the terrified young wife in fear of her husband but much too nervous and weak ever to attempt to remove him. Then after Charles was dead she could sob on the Chief Detective-Inspector's shoulder and confess that Daniel Carey had been so in love with her that he had killed Charles to prevent her suffering any further and to remove her from all danger.

"But first of all she had to create the impression of the terrified young wife, and to do that she needed an audience.

"So she invited you to Roshven and spun you the story about Charles wanting to kill her. You were to be her audience, the witness who would later back up her story to the police. That was why you were invited to Roshven.

"And then everything went wrong with that scheme and got out of hand so that she was forced to reshape her plans. You fell in love with Daniel and she knew she could never trust you to give evidence for her against him. At the same time she realized that Daniel wasn't so infatuated with her that he would kill for her. In fact, he wasn't infatuated at all.

"So she used me. She tore down the facade I had presented to everyone since her marriage and destroyed all my defenses and then gathered together all my love and hate and twisted them into her own distorted pattern. And it wasn't until afterward in her room that I realized what she had done.

"I have no memory after that. I remember staring at her as I recognized the truth, and then nothing at all except isolated things—pulling open the window, the rush of cold air, my hand on her mouth as she tried to scream. I flung her from me as if I would smash every ounce of bone and blood in her evil rotten body, and after that there was just a dreadful blankness until

I reached my room again and locked the door against the nightmare of what had happened. . . . I've been trying to keep my mind locked against it ever since. The last five years have been one long struggle to shut out all the dreadful memories and submerge myself in something new and far away in another world, but there are some things you can't shut out, no matter how much you want to, and when I came back here today and went to her room I knew I would never get rid of them, never, no matter how long I lived and no matter where I went."

The surf broke down the beach and sped swiftly across the sands to their feet. It touched Rohan's shoes but he seemed not to notice, for he made no effort to step back.

"I'm glad I've told you," he said after a while. "I've wanted to tell you for a long time. Perhaps that's why I asked you to marry me. I'd have been safe if we were married, because a wife can't give evidence against her husband."

He was still looking out to sea, and suddenly she saw him stiffen. "There's a boat out there," he said, pointing behind her over her shoulder. "A small boat a long way out—can you see it?"

Rachel spun around.

At the same moment a huge wave broke and streaked up to her, knocking her off her balance, and even as she stumbled backward before falling, she heard the roar of the undertow and the greedy sucking of the quicksand beneath her feet.

## vi

Daniel saw the blue of Rohan's shirt from out at sea, and immediately altered his course to head inland. As he drew closer he strained his eyes to see what was happening on the beach but beyond the fact that Quist and Rachel were by the water's edge and Rachel appeared to be on her knees he had no idea what they were doing.

And then Quist started to run. Almost at the same moment Daniel realized that Rachel, who was still motionless, was on the edge of Cluny Sands.

Pulling out the throttle he revved the engine into a higher speed and headed straight for the beach.

## *vii*

Rohan saw the boat coming and stopped in his tracks. It came on without faltering, and then just as he thought it must surely come aground, the engines were cut and Daniel, emerging from the wheelhouse, stooped to the deck to pick up the anchor and fling it overboard. Then he stooped again and this time when he straightened his back he had a coil of rope in his hands.

Rohan thought for a moment, his brain suddenly cool, sharp, and detached. If he was lucky he could easily deal with Daniel who would be much too preoccupied with the rescue to notice Rohan's movements. And Rachel . . . Rachel was stuck in the quicksand. He could always say afterward that he had been unable to reach her. Two victims for the quicksands. He could almost see the newspaper headlines. Dual tragedy on remote Scottish coast, heroism of lone survivor. . . .

He stood his ground, waiting.

On the boat Daniel had slung the rope over his shoulder and was lowering himself into the shallows. As he moved swiftly through the water to the shore he made no attempt to speak and Rohan found his silence curiously unnerving.

"I was going back to the house," he heard himself say rapidly as Daniel came abreast of him. "There's a ladder there. I thought if I could crawl along the ladder I could reach her. I wasn't running away."

Daniel pushed past him without a word, and broke into a run.

"Daniel—" Rohan stared after him blankly for a moment, and then, pulling himself together, he ran back along the beach to where Rachel had left his empty gun.

## *viii*

"Wait," said Daniel to Rachel. "Don't move. The more you struggle the further in you'll sink." He was uncoiling the rope as he spoke, his fingers working to tie the last yard into a noose.

"Rohan was going to get a ladder," she said, and her voice was shaking in spite of all her efforts to keep calm. "He said there was a ladder in the gardening shed."

"He told me." The knot was tied, the rope firm beneath his fingers. "Now listen," he said. "Listen. I'm going to throw this to you. Slip the noose around your body and hold on to the rest of the rope as hard as you can. Can you manage that?"

"Yes."

Another wave broke. She felt the sands sucking at her legs, pulling them sickeningly downward, and suddenly the horror of it all was in every part of her and she hardly knew how to stifle her screams.

"Ready?"

"Yes."

And even as he threw the rope toward her she saw Rohan moving up behind with the butt of the gun glinting in his hand.

"Daniel—"

But he was much too quick for her to complete the sentence. As soon as he saw her expression change he had whirled around, dropping the rope on the sands, and had caught Rohan's upraised arm before the blow could fall.

They struggled. The tide swirled forward over their naked feet, and suddenly Rachel's mind was a mere camera incapable of any emotional reaction as it recorded the scene like a strip of film before her eyes.

The gun spun out of Rohan's hand into the quicksand and was gone a second later. Rohan took a step backward. Then another. And as his feet began to sink he lurched forward toward firmer ground and the blow from Daniel's fist caught him so cleanly on the jaw that unconsciousness must have come immediately. He keeled backward, his feet staggering from the weight of the blow, and even as Rachel opened her mouth to scream, he fell full length into the quicksand and the waves surged forward greedily over his body.

The world spun dizzily. She would have fallen, but the sand was up to her waist so that falling was impossible, and then just as she hovered on the brink of consciousness she felt the rope tighten around her body and Daniel's voice was ringing in her ears.

"Hold the rope!" he was shouting. "Pull as hard as you've ever pulled in your life! Pull, for God's sake!"

The rope was rough and seared her palms. Another wave disturbed the sands and suddenly her hips were free. She clung on, trying to move her feet, and again another wave helped her and shifted the sand. She pulled until she felt she could pull no longer, and suddenly her ankles were free and she was half skidding, half floating along the shifting sands.

She felt tears blur her eyes, her limbs lock in a paralysis of exhaustion, and then his hand was reaching for hers, pulling her back out of the long nightmare which had begun five years ago to the peace of another, saner, world beyond.

# *Epilogue*

Three days later, Rebecca Carey received a letter from her brother.

"It seems as if I shall be delayed in Scotland for longer than I thought," he had written. "The whole story is much too complicated to put in a letter so I shall have to explain the situation more fully when I see you. However, to put it as briefly as possible, I reached Roshven to find Rachel trapped on Cluny Sands by a rising tide, and managed to pull her to safety by a rope from the boat I'd rented. Quist wasn't so lucky. I'm sorry to tell you this, as I know you were seeing a great deal of him recently, but in trying to rescue Rachel he himself was trapped and died despite our efforts to reach him. I hope you won't be too upset by this. Perhaps when you feel ready to do so you could telephone his family, whom the authorities have already notified, and say that he died trying to save Rachel's life.

"Now perhaps you can guess one of the reasons for the delay, if not the other. When we got back to Kyle of Lochalsh we told the police what had happened and they have asked us to stay for the inquest, which will be held on the day you receive this letter. Then after the inquest is closed and the matter ended, I shall be driving Rachel back to Inverness (where I rented a car) and traveling from there by train to Edinburgh where we shall be staying for a further seventeen days. You will, of course, be utterly astonished to know that I shall be staying with Rachel in Edinburgh for an apparently arbitrary choice of seventeen days, so I had better explain that one is permitted to be married in Scotland if one has been resident in that country for three weeks. We have so far been resident four days so that leaves seventeen days unaccounted for.

"I do realize that this news will be something of a surprise to you, but I know you're far too intelligent not to realize how fine a person Rachel is and how fortunate I am to be able to marry her. Let me know when you'll be arriving for the wedding, won't you? We'll be staying at the North Briton Hotel near Princes Street, and you can contact us there.

"Rachel asks rather shyly (I wonder why?) to be remembered to you. I send my love as always, of course, and look forward to seeing you again as soon as possible. Your brother, Daniel."

# The Devil
## on Lammas Night

# Chapter One

## i

Nicola was dreaming. She was alone by the sea and before her stretched miles of empty sands. There was no sound. Even the waves made no noise as they rolled across the sands toward her, and because there was no sound she was acutely aware of the emptiness of the sands and the brilliance of the light. She walked and walked until suddenly she realized that she was no longer alone.

Evan was ahead of her.

He had his back to her and was a long way off, but she knew it was Evan because she could see his dark red hair and recognize the set of his shoulders. She called his name but when he did not turn to face her she ran across the sands toward him. She had to run for some minutes and after a while she could hear her sobbing gasps for breath, the only sound in that silent landscape, but no matter how far she ran she came no closer to him. Finally she stopped, and as she stared ahead of her Evan faded away into nothingness to leave her alone once more on that wild lonely stretch of shore. She tried to shout to him; the breath stuck in her throat but making one last effort she managed to scream his name at the top of her voice.

She awoke, still screaming, a second later.

"Oh, for heaven's sake, Nicola," said her roommate crossly. "I wish you'd never met that wretched man! Can't you dream about someone else for a change?"

It was five o'clock. When Nicola wandered into the living room a minute later the sun was rising across Hampstead Heath, and London was emerging from the night into a pale April morning.

Nicola sighed. She knew she would not sleep again before her alarm sounded at seven-thirty, so presently she resigned herself to her wakefulness, lit a cigarette, and went into the kitchen to make herself some coffee. In the bedroom Judy was already asleep again. Judy had no worries. If she dreamed at all she would dream of her fiancé or the job she enjoyed or the entrancing potential of her future. For Judy life was turning out exactly as it should and luck was inevitably, tediously, on her side.

"I'm not surprised," Judy had said complacently the previous evening. "These things go in cycles and I'm in a good cycle at the moment. Maris told me that this would be a marvelous year for Capricorn subjects because Jupiter would be coming into the ascendant, and . . ."

But Nicola did not believe in astrology.

"Oh, but Nicki, how silly! I mean, it's like saying you don't believe the earth is round! Now if you went to see Maris—yes, I know she's peculiar but she's a genuine Hungarian gypsy, and gypsies are so clever about all those sort of things— No, don't be insular, Nicki. Just because she's not English—"

But Nicola was skeptical of all fortune-tellers, even the English ones, and saw no reason why she should have any special faith in Maris whom Judy had met at some bohemian party in Pimlico. Maris owned a Hungarian restaurant off the Fulham Road and was a small mysterious woman of uncertain age with a carefully preserved accent and a wardrobe of eccentric clothes. She was reputed to do nothing, even selecting the menus for her restaurant, without first consulting the stars and making the appropriate astrological calculations.

"Well, if you ever do go to Maris," Judy had said with maddening confidence, "and if she predicts your future and if she turns out to be dead right, don't say I didn't tell you so."

But Nicola had no intention of consulting the stars. She knew exactly what the stars would say.

"You are passing through a difficult and unhappy phase but—courage! Venus will soon be entering your House and Venus in conjunction with such-and-such means that Love and Happiness are without doubt on the way . . . Five guineas, please."

The trouble with me, Nicola thought as she sipped her coffee and watched the sun rise over London on that April morning, is that I'm a cynic.

But she had not always been a cynic. Less than two years ago she had been as carefree as Judy; the company for which she worked had just promoted her to be secretary to the managing director, she was still savoring the independence of having her own home in London, and at long last Evan was showing signs of taking more than a friendly interest in her.

But there was no point in thinking of Evan now. Evan was no longer part of her present. The present now consisted of a job that bored her, a city that had grown jaded with familiarity and a roommate who was getting married and would have to be replaced. Nicola hated the dreary task of finding a roommate, and had recently been toying with the idea of living alone, but it was too easy to be lonely in a big city, particularly when one's social life was going through a bad phase, and irritating though Judy was in many ways, she did at least stave off the loneliness and oil the rusty wheels of Nicola's social life from time to time.

"Nicki, you just can't sit at home night after night! It's so—so wasteful! You can't give up just because one beastly man walked out on you—heavens, he's not the only man in the world! Listen, we'll give a party. You must be launched back into circulation."

Judy had tried very hard to help her roommate recover from

Evan Colwyn. Nicola could only wish she had been more interested in recovering.

Six o'clock came. Then seven. London was wide awake now,
and from her position by the living-room window Nicola could
see the postman progressing slowly down the street while the milk-
man trundled along behind him in his electric cart. It was time to
get up. After drinking some orange juice she returned to the bedroom and began the dreary task of dressing for what she already
knew would be another dreary day.

On her way to work she bought a paper at the tube station and
glanced at it as the train careened south from Hampstead into
Central London. She was about to skip the society gossip page
when she saw the picture of Lisa.

"Mrs. Matthew Morrison, wife of the millionaire industrialist,
at the charity ball held last night for the benefit of the starving
children in Africa. . . ."

Lisa's diamonds, thought Nicola, could have paid for a year's
supply of food for at least a dozen of the starving children. But
Lisa wouldn't have thought of that.

Nicola checked herself with an effort. She supposed it was natural for her to resent her father's recent marriage to a young and
glamorous socialite, but while acknowledging the resentment, she
must take care to keep it in control. Lisa could have been much
worse. Well, perhaps not much worse, but worse anyway. Nicola
smiled wryly to herself. Perhaps the plain truth of the matter was
simply that she was jealous of her stepmother. Lisa was only five
years her senior and yet she had been married twice, had indulged
herself in numerous romances between marriages, and had lived
in half a dozen different countries before settling down near
London with Nicola's father, who happened, by a most providen-
tial stroke of good fortune, to be a millionaire. Nicola could not
even pity her for being childless, for Lisa had two attractive children by her first marriage. Lisa had everything, and the most maddening part of all was that she was still only twenty-nine.

Nicola wondered how much would happen to her in the five
years that separated her from her twenty-ninth birthday. Very lit-

tle, probably. She had a sudden picture of herself still working at the same job, still her boss's faithful Miss Morrison who reminded him when to send flowers to his wife, still looking on while the latest roommate left the flat to get married.

Somebody bumped into her as she left the train and stepped onto the platform.

"I'm so sorry!" someone said in a throaty voice which Nicola realized dimly that she had heard before, and then the someone exclaimed, "It's Judy's friend! Nicki! It *is* Nicki, isn't it?"

It was Maris. Maris of the astrology and the palmistry and the zodiac signs and the Hungarian restaurant off the Fulham Road.

"Darling," said Maris, clutching Nicola's arm in the middle of the platform of Holborn-Kingsway station and sounding like a bad imitation of one of the Gabor sisters, "how strange I should meet you like this! I had a dream about you—"

Oh dear, thought Nicola.

"—a very strange dream—I had seen Judy, you see, and she had mentioned you, and my mind—all subconscious, of course—"

"Yes, of course," said Nicola. "How are you, Maris? What a surprise to bump into you like this."

"Well, darling, obviously it was destiny, wouldn't you think? Listen, have lunch with me today. I'll tell you about my dream. It was a very strange dream—"

"Maris, I don't think I—"

"Darling, do you know a man with red hair—dark red hair—and blue eyes, a very strong, masculine sort of man—"

The train was drawing out of the station. The crowds and the noise and the dust were intolerable.

Nicola thought: Judy's put her up to this.

But supposing Judy hadn't?

"Yes," she heard herself say. "That sounds like someone I used to know."

"*Most* interesting." Maris patted her dyed coiled hair in satisfaction and allowed her eyes to assume a dark inward expression. "Darling, we have to have lunch. Twelve o'clock at La Belle Époque—you know? Please—as my guest! You'll come?"

"I . . . yes, all right . . . thank you, Maris—"

"Lovely, darling," said Maris serenely and the next moment she had vanished into the crowds and Nicola was left wondering if the entire interview had been a hallucination.


## ii


"You were at the seaside," said Maris three hours later in a private corner of the little French restaurant east of Russell Square. "It was a very pretty seaside, sandy with big waves. Perhaps there were cliffs. I don't remember. But there was no one there. That I remember clearly. Just you and the young man with red hair."

The waiter arrived with the entrées. As Nicola automatically picked up her knife and fork, half her mind was telling her she was without doubt going mad while the other half was trying to remember all she had ever read about extrasensory preception.

"Darling," said Maris sympathetically, "don't, please, be cross. Judy, being your friend and being worried about you, did, it's true, tell me a tiny bit about your troubles, but—"

So that was it. Judy had described Evan and recounted every detail of Nicola's relationship with him before asking Maris naively for advice from the stars. But that still didn't explain the coincidence of the seashore.

"Did you really dream this bit about the seashore, Maris?" she asked curiously.

Maris at once became mysterious. "It was—in a sense—a dream. Yes. In another sense, no, it wasn't."

Nicola felt too confused to be irritated. She cut a piece from the escalloped veal on her plate and tried to sort out her thoughts.

"Never mind," said Maris grandly, "what kind of a dream it was. It was a dream. You and your young man were on this sand by the sea—"

"—and when I walked toward him he disappeared?" suggested Nicola in a crisp practical voice.

"Not at all," said Maris severely. "Quite wrong, darling. You walked toward him, yes. But he stood still, calling your name and you didn't answer. You walked right past him. He begged you to notice him but you didn't even hear. You walked past and eventually disappeared."

Around them the restaurant hummed with conversation and the discreet clatter of plates. Nicola found she was still staring at the piece of veal speared on the prongs of her fork.

"Of course," said Maris, sampling her ragoût de boeuf, "the meaning is perfectly obvious."

There was a pause. "Yes?" said Nicola at last.

"But yes! Of course! You mean you don't see what it means?"

"Well, I—"

"Obviously, darling, you are going to recover from your—your—"

"Infatuation," said Nicola dryly.

"—involvement," said Maris, "with this young man. You are within reach of a time when you walk past him without even noticing he exists. He may plead with you, but he will plead in vain. It will be over. Finished. You will be free," said Maris, very European suddenly, "to love again."

"I don't believe it," said Nicola before she could stop herself, and then, embarrassed by her own rudeness, added in a rush: "I'd like to believe it, but Evan's been away in Africa for a year now and I find I'm still thinking about him as much as ever. I just can't believe a time would ever come when I'd be completely indifferent to him."

"I am very seldom wrong about these things," said Maris.

"What are the odds on the prediction coming true? Surely there must be times when you're mistaken."

"May I see your palm for a moment?"

"Palm?"

"You wanted to know the odds, darling! I must have some sort of guideline!"

"Oh, I see—which palm?"

"I'll look at the left first."

Feeling absurdly self-conscious, Nicola laid down her fork and extended her left hand across the table.

"I am not an expert on palmistry," said Maris. "Never have I pretended to be an expert in a scientific sense. But sometimes there are nuances—impressions—you understand? I am very sensitive to nuances." She took Nicola's palm in both hands and examined it for a moment. Presently she released it. There was a silence.

"Yes?" said Nicola, suddenly nervous.

"Let me see the right palm now."

There was another pause. Maris' face was expressionless. Nicola wondered in panic if her lifeline were severed at an early point in time.

"Hm," said Maris. "Your left palm, as you probably know, shows your potential. Your right shows what you have made of it."

"I suppose I haven't made very much of it yet," said Nicola, trying to speak lightly.

"You haven't yet fulfilled your potential." Maris returned absentmindedly to the ragoût de boeuf. "You are a passionate person," she said at last. "You are emotional although you try to hide it. Your Evan may have been the strongest love of your life so far, but he won't be the last. No. Definitely not the last. So that persuades me that my dream is an accurate prediction—you will forget Evan and love again."

Nicola was acutely aware of Maris' impassive expression. "Is that such bad news?" she inquired uneasily.

"No, no," said Maris with a careless shrug of the shoulders. "Not necessarily. But perhaps yes. Who can tell? It depends on many things. But tell me one thing, Nicki. You're not attracted to dark men, are you?"

"Dark?"

"Dark hair, dark eyes."

"Not usually, no." She found herself remembering Evan's red hair with a pang.

"Lovely, darling," said Maris, relaxing with a smile. "In that case you have nothing to worry about. Now, how is your escallope de veau? The cooking here is usually good, not like so many French restaurants who think they can disguise a poor cut of meat by saturating it with a fourth-class wine . . . You must come to my restaurant one day! You like Hungarian food? Good! When you fall in love with this new exciting man, I want you to bring him to my restaurant and I'll give you both the best dinner our kitchens can provide."

"I'd love to—if I ever meet him. Thank you, Maris."

"Of course you'll meet him! Haven't I just told you so? Soon you'll have forgotten your Evan ever existed and you'll be content for him to spend the rest of his life in Africa."

All Nicola's skepticism came flooding back. After the meal was over and she had parted from Maris, she found herself wondering with that familiar bitter longing where Evan was at that moment and whether he ever thought of her.

*iii*

Evan Colwyn was working in a remote strip of Africa administered by the French and largely unmarked by twentieth-century progress. On the day that Nicola lunched with Maris in London he was holding his mobile clinic in one of the primitive villages and administering the injections and medications which the World Health Organization made available among the disadvantaged peoples of the underdeveloped countries. The villagers were not obliged to offer any form of payment to Evan for his services but he usually returned to his house in the capital with several chickens which his patients had offered in gratitude for the help he had given them. The nurse who assisted him on these expeditions, a strong silent Frenchwoman called Genevieve, disapproved of the chickens and regarded them as a source of infection, but

Evan did not want to insult his patients by refusing their gifts and he overrode Genevieve's disapproval.

On that particular day a woman whose child he had treated for one of the eye diseases prevalent in that part of Africa gave him a different kind of present, an intricately carved necklace, and told him in the strange French which even Genevieve had difficulty understanding that it was a gift for his wife.

"But I have no wife," said Evan in his Parisian French with the English accent, and Genevieve had to translate his words again because the woman could not understand.

The woman said that in that case it must be for his future wife since obviously one day he would consider marriage.

"Thank you very much," said Evan, trying not to think of Nicola. "It's a beautiful necklace. I'll take good care of it."

The next patient walked up for attention. And the next. And the next. It was very hot. Evan felt his shirt sticking to his back and the sweat darkening his hair, and his thoughts turned longingly to sea breezes blowing through the grounds of his father's house far away, to light rain falling from pale northern skies, to the frost and sleet and snow of a climate far from the Equator.

It was time to go home, he knew that now. His year with the World Health Organization would soon be completed and he would have the option of either signing on for a second year or returning to Britain to make the long-postponed decision about his future. His year of exile had at least enabled him to decide that he did not want to remain an exile for the rest of his life; on his return to England he thought he might join the staff of one of the big London hospitals or try private practice. Before his visit to Africa the current lack of incentive for doctors in Britain had made the idea of emigration to America attractive to him, but while his father was still alive and his sister was an invalid he had felt himself obligated to resist the temptation to emigrate. However, the temptation had been strong, and Africa had been his way of compromising between his duty to his family and his urge to go abroad. A year in Africa was a different proposition from a lifetime in the States. He had been able to say truthfully that the job would give him some valuable experience in tropical medicine, and despite his obligations at home he knew his family would tolerate his departure in the knowledge that his absence would be only a temporary state of affairs. Meanwhile Africa would prove to him how well he could settle in a strange environment and give him the necessary perspective to make the right decision about his future. He had been in a muddle before he had left England.

"I don't know what I want," he had said to Nicola. "I've got to get away and think about it."

Nicola would have married him, he realized that now. But he had been muddled about her, just as he had been muddled about everything else. If he had married Nicola he would have had to make a decision about his future and he had felt incapable of making a decision at that time. His father had wanted him to marry Nicola and, illogically and unfairly, his father's very approval had made him shy away from her. It was principally because of his father that he felt himself tied to Britain. Of course his father wanted him to marry Nicola! Marry, settle down, sink roots, forget all notion of emigration . . .

"I do love you," he had said to Nicola, "but I can't marry you. I've got to take this job in Africa."

"If you loved me," Nicola had said, "you wouldn't even be considering going to Africa."

"That's just a woman's way of looking at things."

"Romantic nonsense, you mean."

"Oh, for God's sake, Nicki . . ."

Evan winced. Better not to think of Nicola. It was all right to think of England and his home in Wales because he would soon have the opportunity to assuage his homesickness, but it was no use thinking of Nicola. She'd probably found some other man by that time anyway. It was all over with Nicola and it was no use thinking of her any more.

"The witch doctor wants to see you," said Genevieve, returning to the tent with some fresh vials of penicillin.

"Oh God . . . I suppose I'd better see him now. Is he outside?"

"Yes, but shouldn't you attend to the rest of the patients first? Why do you have to drop everything to see him?"

"Because he's a big man in the village and he's always been friendly and I want him to stay friendly." Evan's voice was abrupt. He disliked it when Genevieve tried to tell him what to do. "Show him in, would you, please?"

"Very well, doctor." Genevieve assumed her habitual expression of disapproval and departed.

The witch doctor was a powerfully built man in the prime of life with the superiority of a natural autocrat. He had hooded bloodshot eyes, a calculating smile, and an unexpected knowledge of intelligible French.

"Good-day, M. le docteur," he was saying grandly to Evan. "What a pleasure to see you again."

"It's a pleasure to be here."

The formal politenesses, Evan knew, would seem unending but his months among the people of this remote French possession had taught him not to give in to his usual impulse to speak abruptly and plunge into the heart of the matter before the proper preliminaries were concluded. The unreal phrases, enriched by the formality of the French language, were patiently recited, the insincere compliments meticulously exchanged. Evan did not like the witch doctor, whose psychological influence over the community he deplored, and the witch doctor did not like Evan, whose medical miracles threatened to reduce his hold on the village, but each respected the other's power and was intelligent enough to stave off an open confrontation. The witch doctor had long been spreading the rumor that he was responsible for Evan's visits and that each cure Evan achieved was by benign permission of the witch doctor himself; it seemed the wisest way of dealing with the threat Evan presented to him, and none of the villagers had so far given him any serious trouble.

"When may we expect you again, M. le docteur?" he inquired politely, watching Evan's blue eyes. He had long wondered if blue eyes saw colors differently, but he knew it would be a tactical mistake to ask point-blank; he did not want to mar his reputation of knowing everything. "Next month as usual?"

"I expect so, but I may not see you the month after that. In June I'm returning home to my own country."

The witch doctor knew this, since news traveled fast and he had an excellent information network, and he had been worried about it for some time. A new doctor might not be so easy to get on with. There might be a confrontation and he might suffer a loss of face with the result that his entire power over the people would be irrevocably weakened. Ever since he had heard the news of Evan's pending departure the witch doctor had been praying for a revelation which would encourage Evan to reverse his plans.

The revelation had taken some time coming, but it had been presented to him the previous evening during a perfect trance and afterward he had been highly pleased.

"I have news for you, M. le docteur," he announced sonorously. "News which may make you decide to stay with us."

"Really?" said Evan, scrupulously polite. "What news is that, sir?"

"Do not return to your homeland. The devil waits for you there. If you return, the devil will harm you and bring you close to death. Perhaps you will even die."

After a moment Evan said gravely: "And if I do return—how may I recognize the devil when I meet him?"

"He will be white."

Evan had suspected this; he knew the black races visualized the devil as white, just as the white races believed him to be black.

"He will be white," repeated the witch doctor, "but he will manifest himself from time to time as an animal. He will be at his most dangerous when he manifests himself as a black horse."

Evan suppressed a sigh and carefully avoided asking himself whether some of the world's more primitive peoples would ever emerge into the twentieth century.

"I understand," he said courteously to the witch doctor. "It was most gracious of you to advise me on this matter, sir, and you can be sure I'll give your advice every consideration."

The witch doctor was pleased. "It is always a pleasure to help a valued friend," he said, preparing to leave. "Au revoir, M. le docteur. I look forward to your visits to this village for many years to come."

*iv*

When Evan returned to his small house on the outskirts of the capital two days later after visiting several other villages in the interior, he found two letters waiting for him, one from his father, Walter Colwyn, the other from Evan's sister, Gwyneth. After telling his servant to unpack his luggage and his cook to go ahead with preparing dinner, Evan returned to the living room with a glass of beer, switched the air-conditioner to high, and settled down to absorb his weekly glimpse of home.

He opened his father's letter first. The main item of news was that Gwyneth had been ill again with a mystery ailment—news which made Evan snort in disgust and reach for his glass of beer. He knew perfectly well that his sister was a hypochondriac who made use of a genuine history of minor heart trouble to become ill if and when she thought it was necessary. He had never had much patience with Gwyneth, but she was the apple of their father's eye and Walter took every fluctuation in her health very seriously.

". . . so when Gwyneth became ill again," Walter had written to Evan in his delicate handwriting, "we asked this herbalist to try to help her. Mr. Poole is the most charming young man, a little older than you perhaps, who has been staying in Swansea while looking around for a house which he can use as the headquarters of his organization, and we happened to meet him by chance one weekend . . ."

Herbalist! Evan snorted again, finished his beer and slammed the glass irritably down on the table. Why was it that old men and impulsive young women were always so eager to put their faith in quacks?

". . . and he absolutely cured Gwyneth," Walter had written. "Wasn't that wonderful?"

Psychological mumbo-jumbo, thought Evan. Psychosomatic illness. Given the right circumstances, even the witch doctor could have cured her.

". . . so I invited him to stay at Colwyn Court while he tries to find his headquarters for the Society for the Propagation of Nature Foods . . ."

"Good God!" cried Evan and leaped to his feet to get another beer. When he returned to the living room he pushed his father's letter aside and turned to the envelope addressed to him in Gwyneth's willowy handwriting.

Gwyneth seldom wrote to him; as he unfolded her letter he wondered if he could guess why she had become excited enough to pick up a pen.

"Dearest Evan," he read, "What do you think! At last a little excitement has come to Colwyn! I know Daddy has written to tell you about Mr. Poole and how ill I was, but don't worry because I'm *miraculously better!* Mr. Poole is an expert on herbs, and I know you'll say it's just a lot of old wives' tales and worthless folklore, but all I can say is that I haven't felt so well for years. Mr. Poole makes up the medicine himself and I take one tablespoonful three times a day. I've asked him several times what's in the recipe, but he won't tell me. However, he's promised to teach me a little about herbs when he has some spare time. As you can gather, he's rather a super sort of person, and—"

Evan flung down the letter, hurled himself out of his chair, and grabbed his writing paper from his desk. As his second beer stood untasted on the table behind him he filled two pages with respectful admiration for the unknown Mr. Poole's healing powers tempered with tactful warnings that it might be best to leave Mr. Poole well alone.

At least his months in Africa had taught him self-restraint. Evan, surveying the skillfully diplomatic tone of his letter, wondered what they would have thought at Colwyn Court if he had simply written: "This man is probably a fraud, no matter how charming he is. Some herbalists may do good but the genuine ones recognize their limitations and would not expect to work miraculous cures. Don't trust him too much, don't rely on him too heavily, and whatever you do, don't give him any money for the Society for the Propagation of Nature Foods . . ."

## V

Evan's letter reached the village in South Wales four days later and was carried from the post office at Colwyn to its final destination at Colwyn Court by the local postman on an elderly red bicycle. The mail for Colwyn Court that day was substantial; as well as Evan's letter and several bills from nearby tradesmen there was an envelope with a Cambridge postmark, and then, quite apart from the letters to Walter Colwyn, there were the letters addressed to Mr. Tristan Poole, Managing Director of the Society for the Propagation of Nature Foods.

Colwyn village was intrigued by Mr. Poole and his society. One rumor, inspired by the word "nature" in the society's title, hinted darkly that Colwyn Court was about to be turned into a nudist camp. A counter-rumor protested that although Walter Colwyn was now well over sixty he was by no means senile enough to abandon all sense of decency, especially while his young unmarried daughter lived at home, and insisted that the society was nothing more than a collection of amateur botanists whom Walter, himself a keen botanist, naturally found congenial. Another rumor suggested that Mr. Poole and Walter's daughter, Gwyneth, had fallen in love with one another and that this explained why Walter should have invited Mr. Poole to stay for a few days at Colwyn Court. On the whole this was the rumor which found most favor among the female population of the village, and everyone was waiting with bated breath for the engagement to be announced.

Meanwhile the possibility of his daughter's and his guest's falling in love had never occurred to Walter. It was not simply that he was getting older and more absentminded and less interested in the people around him than in the flowers and shrubs and trees on his estate; it was not even that he had so many worries—the nagging anxiety that Evan might choose not to return to England, for example, or the secret dread of a twilight future or the more imminent fear that he might have to mortgage his family home to pay his bills. Walter had not imagined a romance could exist between Gwyneth and his guest because there had been no signs of such an entanglement to spark his imagination. Mr. Poole had been friendly and pleasant to Gwyneth but nothing more, and Gwyneth herself, although enthusiastic about Poole's powers as a herbalist, had shown no sign of looking lovelorn. Walter had a vague idea that young women in love wandered around sighing, reading poetry, and evincing a general lack of interest in food and all practical matters. But since her recovery from her mysterious illness Gwyneth had been eating voraciously, answering her letters from pen friends in ten different countries, and devoting herself as usual to her enormous record collection, her files of trivia on pop music, and her library of pop art posters. Gwyneth, in short, was exactly as she had always been. If she were in love with Poole she was savoring the fact in secret, and why would she want to do that? It did not occur to Walter that for Gwyneth the world of imagination had long been more rewarding than the world of reality; in reality, Mr. Poole might show a mere platonic interest in her welfare, but in dreams he could speak to her in the voice from the record player and promise her unbelievable delights, and with the door locked and the curtains drawn she could live exactly as she wished in the brilliantly colored world of her own creation.

But Walter knew nothing of this. To Walter, Gwyneth was still his little motherless daughter, nineteen now but still a child with her naively enchanting interest in all those alien, absurd modern art forms. The very idea of her falling in love would have seemed incongruous to him, so strong was this image in his mind that Gwyneth was too young to play a leading role in the romance which the villagers of Colwyn busied themselves in inventing over interminable cups of tea.

Walter had never understood either of his children. He had loved them and marveled at their existence, but he had always thought of them as stereotypes acting out their lives in cliché-ridden situations. He still thought of Evan as the "son and heir," all set to become a "brilliant surgeon" one day, and of Gwyneth as the "delicate daughter" who would one day make a "perfect match" to a young man from one of the local county families. This two-dimensional vision of his had even extended to his dead wife; he had married late in life when he had inherited the estate with a view to "settling down" after years of travel on botanical expeditions, and had chosen a "society girl" ten years his junior to be his wife because she was bright and pretty and filled his concept of the sort of wife he ought to have. She had left him a year after Gwyneth had been born and had died two years later in the south of France. The odd part was that he had always been convinced she would be the "dutiful wife" and return to him in the end, and for a long while he could not reconcile himself to the fact that she was dead. He had gone on his way, becoming a little more absentminded each day, a little more devoted to botany, a little more absorbed in the book he was writing on the wild flowers of the Gower Peninsula until one day he was able to look back on his marriage, realize that it had been unhappy, and make a mental resolution to remain a widower till the end of his days.

"You never like to look at the truth, do you, Father?" Evan had said once. "You're always so much happier playing the ostrich and burying your head in the sand."

It had been a terrible shock when Evan had gone abroad. It had been an even bigger shock when Evan had flung out defiant hints of America and implied that as far as he was concerned the sun didn't rise and set entirely either on a small village along the south coast of Wales or on an estate which had been in Colwyn hands for six hundred years. Every time Walter received a letter from Evan he was frightened to open it for fear it would contain news that Evan had decided not to come home.

The letter which arrived that morning in April was no exception. Walter picked it up and looked at it and turned it over and felt so nervous he could not begin to eat his breakfast. But as usual his fright was all for nothing. Of course the tenor of the letter was a little severe—all those warnings about Mr. Poole were quite unnecessary—but the boy meant well and that was the important thing. There was even a sentence at the end of the letter saying Evan expected to be home in June and would soon be booking his flight. Walter put down the letter with a sigh of relief and attacked his eggs and bacon so heartily that it was some minutes before he remembered he had another letter to read that morning.

It was the letter with the Cambridge postmark, a note from Walter's cousin Benedict Shaw who was a professor in classics at the University.

"My dear Walter," said Benedict's handwriting with its cross-scratchy strokes of the pen. "How are you after all this time? No doubt you will be surprised to hear from me out of the blue like this but I was hoping you might be in a position to give me some advice. I'm planning to write a thesis this summer after the commencement of the Long Vacation, and very much fancy the idea of retiring somewhere far from the madding crowd for two or three months. Do you know of any places for rent around Colwyn? Jane and I wouldn't want more than a small cottage, and I thought you might know of someone who rents such a place to summer tourists. Any ideas? If you know of anywhere quiet, comfortable, and secluded I'd be most anxious to hear of it. I hope Gwyneth is well. When does Evan return from Africa? Jane sends her love and says she hopes to see you soon—a hope which I, of course, share. Yours, Benedict."

Walter finished his eggs and bacon slowly and read the letter again. He could not make up his mind if Benedict were angling for an invitation to stay. The letter gave no hint that Benedict expected an invitation but surely in the circumstances he would think an invitation would be forthcoming. The words "if you know of anywhere quiet, comfortable, and secluded" at once suggested Colwyn Court to Walter, and he began to feel guilty. It was not that he disliked his cousin; although they seldom met nowadays and had little in common, they had always been on good terms. But if Mr. Poole decided to relieve Walter of his current financial worries by hiring both wings of Colwyn Court for the society there would hardly be much room left for Benedict and his wife.

"Dear, oh dear," said Walter aloud and gazed with unseeing eyes at his half-finished toast and marmalade. "Dear me, how very awkward."

The door of the dining room clicked softly. Smooth shoes sank noiselessly into the carpet and a faint draft from the hall made the curtains shiver by the open window.

"Awkward?" said Walter's guest in his warm, flexible voice. "Tell me about it, Mr. Colwyn! Perhaps I'll be able to help you."

## vi

He was a tall man with a face which people found hard to remember because it was capable of so many different expressions. His eyes were deep-set above high, broad cheekbones and a wide, mobile mouth, and his hair, though thick, was short and neat and parted in a conventional style. He wore a conventional dark suit, a conventional white shirt, and a conventional conservative tie, but the impression of the conventional English businessman, so meticulously created, was blurred by his hands and his voice. He had beautiful hands, the fingers long and tapered, and, contrary to the habits of many conventional Englishmen, he wore a ring on the third finger of his right hand, an intricate un-English ring inscribed with odd patterns and cast in some dull, silverish metal of uncertain origin. When he spoke his voice was so easy on the ears that at first it was hard to decide why it too should fall short of conventional English standards, but after a time, when the ear became attuned, a listener could detect the inflections of a foreigner in the occasional ambiguous vowel sound or choice of words. Mr. Poole seldom used any of the more obvious Americanisms, but with an occasional short "a" in the wrong place and a rare un-English use of a preposition it became clear he had in the past spent some time on the other side of the Atlantic. It was hard to say how old he was; Walter thought of him as the same age as Evan, who was thirty, but to Gwyneth he was closer to forty, cosmopolitan, experienced, and immeasurably sophisticated.

"Perhaps I can help you," said Tristan Poole to his host. His glance noted the pile of unopened bills beside the letters from Evan and Benedict, and he wondered how severe the financial troubles were. It was probable that they were a mere temporary inconvenience. The house was well kept and filled with valuable possessions; the estate was large; if Walter Colwyn were at present hard pressed for ready cash he would still be a long way from bankruptcy. "What's the trouble? Nothing too serious, I hope."

"Oh no, no, no," said Walter, turning to his guest in relief. Really, it was amazing how soothing it was to talk to Poole . . . "Help yourself to eggs and bacon, my dear fellow . . . No, the trouble is simply that—" And in his rambling way he explained the contents of Benedict's letter and all the complications inherent in Benedict's request.

Poole poured himself some tea and made a mental resolution that as soon as he was living at Colwyn Court on a more permanent basis he would insist that coffee—real coffee—was served at breakfast as well as the inevitable pot of tea.

". . . so anyway I thought—can I pass you something, my dear fellow? Salt?"

"No, thank you," said Poole.

". . . yes, well, I don't know *what* I thought, except it's all most awkward. You see, I would indeed like you and your society to come here, but . . . well, Benedict . . . very tricky . . . I ought to issue an invitation—"

"But surely," said Poole, "there's a very simple solution, Mr. Colwyn? Don't you have that cottage down by the beach which you've been renting to summer visitors for the last two years? Why don't you simply rent the cottage to your cousin this summer— or offer it to him rent-free? That should satisfy Professor Shaw since he'll be living in your grounds even if not in your house, and I think he'll find it quiet enough to suit his tastes. Besides, couldn't you be mistaken in thinking his letter is a hint for an invitation to Colwyn Court? It would seem to me he had the cottage in mind, not the house."

"Oh, Benedict doesn't know I've been renting the cottage these last two summers," said Walter vaguely. "My old chauffeur used to live there, you know—I let him have it for a nominal rent when he got too old to drive—and then when he died—"

Poole was thinking of the cottage. It would be better for it to be rented to a professor absorbed in his work than to a series of families on holiday with a stream of inquisitive children. "Have you rented the cottage yet?" he inquired when Walter paused to recollect his original train of thought. "Is it still available?"

"No, I rented it in January to this very nice family—"

"Ah, but surely your cousin must come first!"

"Yes, but I don't quite see how I can—"

"Surely," said Poole, "your cousin must come first."

"But what shall I say to—"

"Leave it all to me. I'll handle the matter for you. If you'll give me the address of these people I'll write to them and explain the circumstances."

"Well, I . . . hardly like to trouble you—"

"It's no trouble at all," said Poole with his wide, charming smile. "I'd be delighted to be of assistance." He took a sip from his cup, forgetting that it contained tea, and grimaced as the strong flavor dragged at his sense of taste. "Tell me about your cousin. He's a contemporary of yours, I take it."

"Benedict? Well, no, actually he's only about forty-six. My mother had a very much younger sister who married . . ."

Poole listened patiently and buttered a slice of toast. The toast was cold. Why did the British always have cold toast? When he was at Colwyn Court on a more permanent basis . . .

". . . married a girl of twenty-seven," said Walter. "We were all absolutely dumbfounded, of course. Let's see, how old is Jane now? I forget how long they've been married. About five or six years, I think . . . no children, unfortunately . . . she's rather a nice girl, quite pretty, very pleasant—can't think what she saw in dear old Benedict who was one of those crusty sort of bachelors . . ."

One professor absorbed in his work, thought Poole, one woman probably absorbed in her husband, neither a threat.

"How very nice," he said to Walter in his warmest, most interested voice. "They both sound delightful. I'll be looking forward very much to meeting them . . ."

## vii

"Of course," said Benedict Shaw crossly to his wife at breakfast two days later, "Walter must be either mad or on the verge of destitution or both. Imagine letting some crackpot society have the free run of one's own home! And imagine charging me rent for that nasty little cottage where his chauffeur used to live! How dare he charge me rent! Me! His own cousin! It would be an insult if it weren't so patently absurd. He must be on the verge of bankruptcy, that's all I can say. Maybe when Evan comes home in June I ought to have a word with him about it."

Jane Shaw said vaguely: "Is Evan definitely coming home then?" She was trying to work out how many calories there were in one slice of toast liberally covered with butter and marmalade.

"According to Walter's letter, yes, he is." Benedict was polishing his glasses furiously. "God knows what Evan will make of the situation! Society for the Propagation of Nature Foods—my God! Ridiculous!"

Two hundred and twenty calories, thought Jane, I really mustn't. She tried to think of something else. "I expect Walter does find Colwyn Court very expensive to run," she said reasonably. "I know you always think of Walter as being rich, Benedict, but what with taxation and the rising cost of living nowadays—"

"My dear," said Benedict, "you don't have to remind *me* about the monstrous iniquities of taxation and the rising cost of living."

"I suppose not," said Jane and almost reached for the forbidden slice of toast. How hard it was to be strong-minded sometimes. "I know you know much more about that sort of thing than I do, darling."

Benedict smiled. He had a sudden smile which smoothed away the irascible lines about his face and made his eyes twinkle behind his thick glasses. When Jane leaned forward and kissed him impulsively he took her hand in his and squeezed it before rising to his feet. "One of the best things about you, my dear," he said, "is that you always say all the right things."

"But that sounds as if I never mean what I say, and I do!"

"I know you do. Far be it from me to accuse you of sycophancy."

"What a funny word," said Jane, not sure what it meant. "Benedict, are you going to accept Walter's offer of the cottage? I know it *is* rather strange that he's charging you rent, but—"

"Most unlike him," said Benedict, cross again. "Not at all the done thing in the circumstances. And as for this crackpot society at Colwyn Court—"

"—but the cottage is in a lovely position, isn't it, and of course it would be so quiet and peaceful for your writing—"

"Quiet and peaceful? Surrounded by a bunch of nincompoops eating nature foods?"

"I don't suppose you'd see anything of them at all. I'm sure they wouldn't bother you at the cottage."

"You want me to go there," said Benedict, very fierce, "don't you."

"Not unless you want to, darling, but I think it might turn out quite well if you did."

"And to think I was half-hoping for an invitation to Colwyn Court itself!"

"You wouldn't have liked that really," said Jane. "Walter would have got on your nerves and Gwyneth's never-ending pop music wouldn't have given you a moment's peace."

"But to pay Walter rent for this miserable hovel—"

"You'd have had to pay rent anyway if we'd taken a cottage elsewhere," said Jane practically, "and the 'hovel' is actually rather nice. I went inside it once with Gwyneth when she was taking the old chauffeur a present for Christmas. And think how soothing the sea is, Benedict! You know how well you work by the sea."

"Hm," said Benedict. "I see I have no choice in the matter." He roamed moodily over to the window and gazed at the tiny garden which Jane tended so carefully behind the house. "Maybe I should go down to Colwyn, if only to find out how senile Walter is. Maybe this wretched society's swindling him." He turned, flung himself down in his chair at the table again and toyed with his empty cup. "Is there any more coffee?"

Jane poured him another cup. "You don't really think Walter's in financial difficulty, do you?"

"Wouldn't surprise me. Walter always was a complete fool about money. And of course a big house like Colwyn Court is an absolute white elephant these days. He ought to sell it or turn it into flats or something."

"But Benedict, he couldn't! His ancestral home!"

"Such sentimentality," said Benedict, "is out of place in the latter half of the twentieth century."

A thought struck Jane. "Maybe Walter's planning to sell Colwyn Court to this society!"

"Good God!" cried Benedict. "He couldn't do that! He wouldn't be such a fool!"

"But if he's desperate for money—"

"Money," said Benedict. "I hate all this talk about money. Money, money, money. Money's so depressing."

"Yes, dear. But useful."

"Take that brother-in-law of yours, for instance. Whenever he's mentioned in the papers it's always: 'Matthew Morrison, the millionaire industrialist'—why don't they simply say: 'Matthew Morrison, the industrialist?' Why do they have to drag in the 'millionaire' label all the time? Does the word 'millionaire' make Morrison a different breed of homo sapiens?"

"Well, it does make a little difference," said Jane. "I mean, if you're a millionaire you don't live in quite the same way as the local butcher."

"Naturally!" said Benedict. "We all know your sister would hardly have married Morrison if he'd been a mere butcher!"

"Darling, isn't that a little bit unfair to Lisa?"

Benedict had the grace to look sheepish as well as defiant. "Can you see Lisa marrying a butcher?"

Jane couldn't but would not allow herself to say so. For one long moment she thought of her sister. Lisa. Twenty-nine years old. Poised, glamorous, effortlessly smart. Lisa who had everything from a selection of mink coats to two beautiful children . . .

Jane reached for the last slice of toast and had buttered it before she realized what she was doing. "Lisa's very romantic," she heard herself say levelly. "She probably would marry a butcher if she fell in love with him."

"Fiddlesticks," said Benedict. Instinct told him to veer away from the subject. "What's Morrison's daughter doing nowadays? Is she still working in London?"

"Yes, she's still living in Hampstead and doesn't go home too often. Lisa said she hadn't seen Nicola for ages."

"Hm," said Benedict, and wondered if he could guess why Nicola no longer found her father's house appealing.

"It was such a pity Nicola's romance with Evan didn't work out," Jane said, taking a bite of toast. Two hundred and twenty calories. Maybe she could skip lunch. "It would have been so awfully suitable if they'd got married."

"Suitable strikes me as being a very apt word," said Benedict dryly. "The way things are probably going with Walter, Evan would need to marry an heiress."

"Oh darling, I'm sure Evan wouldn't marry anyone just for their money!"

"Money," said Benedict. "That dreadful word again."

"But Benedict—" Jane stopped. Better not to remind him that he had introduced the subject. On an impulse she pulled one of the morning papers toward her and began to thumb through it. "Heavens, I almost forgot to read my horoscope! Maybe there'll be some hint about whether we should take Walter's cottage or not."

"I've already made up my mind to take it," said Benedict. "I'm not the slightest bit interested in what some syndicated fraud invents daily for a gullible public." He stood up, stooped to give her a kiss, and made for the door. "I must be off. Don't expect me for lunch, will you, my dear, because I'm lunching in town today."

"All right, darling . . . have a good day." She saw him to the front door as usual and waved him good-bye as he walked into the street to their white Austin. They had a small house in a quiet tree-lined road barely a mile from the heart of the city, and Benedict had only a short drive to his college. When he had gone, Jane wandered back into the dining room and resumed her search for her horoscope before stacking the dirty dishes.

"Your Fate Today," ran the heading at the top of the column, and then under Jane's zodiac sign were the words: "Think carefully before making any decision today. Now is the time to dream of travel, but be wary of the unexpected invitation."

## viii

"What's his horoscope today?" said Jane's small niece Lucy a day later at Matthew Morrison's home in Surrey. "What does it say?"

"'Your luck is in,'" read her brother Timothy laboriously.

" 'Take advantage of an unexpected opportunity. Be bold.' " He looked up in triumph. "That means he'll get a chance to escape from China!"

"Tibet," said Lucy. "Daddy was in Tibet. He crossed the Himalayas with a solitary guide and went down one of those rivers on a raft like that film we saw, and finally he got into a helicopter—"

"Well, well, well," said Lisa Morrison, sweeping into the drawing room where the twins were closeted with the daily horoscopes. "Who's this you're talking about, darlings? The hero of one of those awful comic strips?"

The twins looked guilty and for once seemed at a loss to know what to say. She saw them glance furtively at each other before giving her careful smiles.

"We were just imagining, Mummy," said Lucy. "Just picturing things."

"Just picturing how Daddy would get home if he hadn't been drowned in the boat after all," said Timothy impulsively. "If he'd swum to safety, you see, he would have been on the mainland of China and nobody gets out of China easily so he might have been imprisoned there for some years before he escaped."

"But darling," said Lisa, not knowing what to say but aware that something should be said. "Daddy's dead. He's been dead for a long while now. Do you think I could have married Uncle Matt if I'd thought Daddy was still alive?"

They watched her. Both their faces looked blank. There was a silence.

"Well, of course," said Timothy, "it was only a story. We were only imagining."

"Only imagining," said Lucy.

Lisa felt a wave of relief. "That's all right, then, isn't it?" she said, drawing on her gloves as she spoke. "Now darlings, I'm just off to London with Uncle Matt, so have a lovely day and I'll see you this evening. Where's Costanza?"

Costanza was the Spanish *au pair* girl who was supposed to supervise the twins and leave Lisa free to enjoy an uninterrupted social life. The twins prided themselves on the fact that it was they who supervised Costanza. After three months they had her tightly in control.

"Upstairs," said Lucy.

"All right. Now be good, darlings, won't you?" She kissed both of them, smiled, and swept back toward the door. "I mustn't keep Uncle Matt waiting . . . 'Bye, darlings. Have a lovely time."

They chorused good-bye politely and wandered over to the window to watch her depart. Their stepfather was already striding up and down beside his new Rolls Royce.

"She's kept him waiting," said Timothy.

"As usual," said Lucy. "He looks cross."

"He was awfully cross last night."

"Was he? When?"

"About twelve o'clock. I woke up and heard them. They were being pretty noisy, I thought, considering how late it was."

"What did they say?"

"I couldn't hear properly."

"Didn't you go and listen?"

"Well, I considered it," said Timothy, "but I couldn't be bothered. It didn't sound very interesting anyway."

"Was it actually a row?"

"Oh, definitely."

"Who was crosser, Uncle Matt or Mummy?"

"Uncle Matt. It was all about taxes and money. He wants to live in the Channel Islands or something because he'll save money. Mummy said: 'The Channel Islands?' she said, 'Darling, you have to be crazy,' she said. 'Why would I want to live in a dump like that?' Then Uncle Matt got really angry and said he wasn't going to retire to the Bahamas just to please her. So Mummy said—"

"Timmy, you did listen!"

"Well, just for a minute or two. I was starving hungry and on my way downstairs to the kitchen . . . So Mummy said: 'At least in the Bahamas I might have a bit of fun.' And Uncle Matt said: 'That's all you think about, isn't it?' he said. 'Well, I'll have my fun in the Channel Islands,' he said—he sounded very cross. 'Take it or leave it,' he said."

"What happened then?"

"I had to run because Mummy came out of the room and I only just managed to get away in time."

"Where did she go?"

"Oh, only to the spare room. Nowhere special."

"Married people aren't supposed to spread themselves over two different bedrooms," said Lucy. "I heard Cook say to Mrs. Pierce that that's how you can tell if a marriage is a success or not."

"I expect Mrs. Pierce was grumbling because she had to make two beds instead of one . . . Look, here comes Mummy. Uncle Matt still looks cross."

They watched from the window in silence. Then:

"Timmy, do you suppose—"

"Yes?"

"If Mummy and Uncle Matt got divorced . . . I mean, just supposing—"

"And Daddy came back from China—"

"Tibet."

"—it would be sort of nice . . . although I like Uncle Matt—"

"Yes, he's okay."

"Maybe we could still see him sometimes after the divorce."

"Maybe we could." They smiled at one another. "I'm sure," said Timothy firmly, "that it'll all work out pretty well in the end."

"Yes, but how much longer do we have to wait for Daddy to come home?" said Lucy disconsolately. "Sometimes I feel as if we'll have to wait forever and ever."

Timothy did not answer. They were still standing in silence by the window when the Rolls Royce moved away from the house and purred down the winding drive on its eighteen-mile journey to London.

## ix

After a while Matthew Morrison said: "I'm sorry about last night."

It cost him a big effort to say that. Matt was proud enough to hate having to apologize and to hate it even more when he felt that such an initial apology should not have come from him at all.

"Oh?" said Lisa, very cool. She was looking at her best that morning, he noted; the April weather was uncertain but she wore a smart spring dress with a matching coat as if there could be no doubt that winter was over and summer only just around the corner. Her skirt was short; from his position beside her he had a perfect view of her long, elegant legs.

"You're an awful driver, Matt," said Lisa. "You never keep your eyes on the road. I wish you'd hire a chauffeur."

But Matt didn't believe in chauffeurs. He was fifty-five years old and was by now used to the conveniences which money could buy, but he hated the thought of being a passenger in his own car. He also had a secret dread of what he called "giving himself airs and graces" and "trying to be what he wasn't." The result was an inverted snobbism, a desire to maintain the simple habits he had acquired long ago before he had worked his way up from office boy to chairman of the board of an enormous industrial empire. Now he owned a big house in which he always felt faintly uncomfortable, employed a first-class cook who despised the plain English cooking he loved, and possessed a beautiful and well-bred wife whose tastes he could not bring himself to share. Privately he deprecated the house ("that rambling old barn," was how he described it to himself in irritable moments), the cook's prowess ("damned French nonsense"), and even his wife, who he knew was spoiled and willful, but at the same time he was well aware how reluctant he would have been to give any of them up. He might want to believe he was still at heart just a simple fellow whom success had not changed, but he was honest enough to know that he had indeed changed and that, distasteful as it was to have to admit it to himself, he had a sneaking fondness for the glamorous assets his wealth and position had brought him. But this fondness he was careful to keep to himself. He knew what was said about self-made men who openly enjoyed their wealth, and he had a horror of the sneering lable "nouveau riche."

"I don't believe in chauffeurs," he said abruptly to his wife. "They're nothing but ostentation nowadays, and you know I don't believe in being ostentatious."

"Oh no," said Lisa, "you just believe in being the 'Simple Man' and hiding yourself away in some deadly corner of the Channel Islands after an early retirement."

"Now Lisa—"

"What's the point of saving money on taxes if there's nothing to spend it on?"

"We needn't be in the Channel Islands all the year round."

"I can't see what you've got against the Bahamas. You could swim and fish and lead your Simple Life just as well there, and the climate's such heaven—"

"It's too far from England."

"Oh Matt, how insular! Anyway nothing's far from anywhere nowadays!"

"Well, if you think I'm about to become a member of the jet set—"

"What's wrong with the jet set if you can afford it? Too 'ostentatious,' I suppose! What a hypocrite you are, Matt!"

"You don't understand," said Matt, and set his mouth in a stubborn line.

"Well, after you retire in June we might at least have a decent holiday before you decide where to settle down! Why don't we go to Spain again?"

"Spain in June's too bloody hot and I can't stand all that silly food they eat. I'd rather stay by the sea somewhere in England."

"My God," said Lisa, "you'll be telling me next you want to join Jane and Benedict at Colwyn."

Matt looked surprised. "Are they down there?"

"Not yet, but Benedict's renting a cottage on the estate for the Long Vacation. Didn't I tell you about the conversation I had with Jane yesterday?"

"You were too busy telling me how you wanted to live in the Bahamas. Maybe we could visit them at the cottage for a couple of weeks in June."

"You're joking, of course."

"How big is the cottage?"

"Oh, it's a horrible little place, very pokey. Matt, you can't be serious!"

"I like that part of the Welsh coast," said Matt. "Walter Colwyn's lucky having an estate in the Gower Peninsula."

"No wonder you were so disappointed when Evan Colwyn jilted Nicola and went off to Africa!"

"He didn't jilt her," said Matt, thinking of his daughter with a painful nostalgia. "There was no engagement."

"Nicola played it too cool," said Lisa. "Of course she has absolutely no idea how to handle men."

"At least she's a decent girl who wouldn't play fast and loose with a man to get him to marry her!"

"How do you know?" said Lisa. "You hardly ever see her."

"Whose fault is that?" yelled Matt, forgetting to watch the road ahead. The car swerved as he swung around on her in a rage and Lisa gave a sharp scream.

"For God's sake, be careful! Matt, if you can't drive properly, I'd rather get out and continue by taxi—my nerves just won't stand it."

Matt said nothing. He gripped the wheel a shade more tightly and stared at the road ahead and after that there was a silence between them until they reached the salon in Knightsbridge where Lisa had a hair appointment.

"Have a good day," was all he said as she got out of the car. "See you this evening."

"Thanks." She was gone. As he watched her walk into the salon he thought of his first wife, Nicola's mother, who had died ten years before, and in a flash of despair he asked himself how after such a successful first marriage he had ever managed to make such a bad mistake with his second.

### x

At Colwyn Court, Gwyneth was taking her first exercise since the onset of her mysterious illness by walking with Tristan Poole along the path which wound up to the cliffs where the ruins of Colwyn Castle stood facing the sea. When they reached the castle walls Gwyneth sank down to rest on the grassy turf and listened with interest to the rhythm of her heartbeat.

"I hope the walk wasn't too much for me," she said after a moment.

Poole did not answer. He was standing a few feet from the edge of the cliffs, and his black jacket was flapping in the breeze.

"Tristan."

He turned with a smile. "I'm sorry, what did you say?"

"You don't suppose the walk up here was too much of a strain, do you? My heart seems to be beating awfully fast."

"You'll be all right. Just rest there for a while."

Gwyneth leaned back on the grass, put her hands behind her head and replayed the scene in her imagination. After she had said how fast her heart was beating Tristan would have knelt beside her and felt her heartbeat with his long fingers and then . . .

"You've got a very vivid imagination, Gwyneth," said Tristan Poole.

She sat bolt upright. Her cheeks were burning. For a moment she could not speak.

But he wasn't laughing at her. He was still standing watching the sea, still detached and remote from her.

"Why did you say that?" she demanded unsteadily.

"Why not?" he said, turning to face her. "Isn't it true?"

She was nonplussed. In her confusion she searched around for some way of changing the subject but her ingenuity deserted her.

"Imagination," said Poole, "is seldom so satisfying as reality. Have you ever considered that, Gwyneth?"

Gwyneth's thoughts were whirling in a million jumbled pieces. She opened her mouth to speak but no words came.

"Why are you afraid of reality, Gwyneth?"

"I'm not," said Gwyneth loudly, but she was trembling. She had to fight against an impulse to rush back to the house and imprison herself in the comforting security of her room.

"But you prefer the world of the imagination." Poole sighed. He supposed he had known from the beginning that the girl was too neurotic to be of interest to him. It was such a pity, such a waste. But it was no use working with damaged material. The anxieties in Gwyneth would all work against him with the result that she would be unreceptive to what he had to offer. She could accept him only in the guise of doctor; in any other role her fears would chase her back into the world of her imagination and away from any world he might attempt to present to her.

Gwyneth, gazing around frantically and seeing the chauffeur's cottage far away above the beach, said in a rush: "Daddy's cousin Benedict is definitely going to come here in June—did Daddy tell you?—he's terribly academic and untrendy, not a bit switched on, you know, not a clue Where It's At or anything, he's at least thirty years behind the times, but *she's* rather sweet, his wife, Jane, I mean, although she's old-fashioned too, but she's quite pretty, not as pretty as Lisa though, Lisa's her sister and she's really pretty, gosh, I wish I was Lisa, she's so glamorous and she's even married to a millionaire—have you heard of Matthew Morrison the industrialist?"

Poole was watching the sea crashing on the beach far below. "I believe I have." He glanced sharply back at Gwyneth. "So Mrs. Benedict Shaw has a millionaire for a brother-in-law."

"Yes, because Jane's sister—"

"What did you say her name was?"

"Lisa."

"Lisa," said Poole. "Lisa Morrison. What a charming name."

"Oh, she's as charming as her name," said Gwyneth glibly, relieved to have diverted attention from herself. "She's an awfully attractive person."

"She is?" said Tristan Poole, turning again to watch the sea, and added more to himself than to Gwyneth: "How very interesting . . ."

# Chapter Two

*i*

It was June. In Cambridge the river wound limpidly along the "backs" past the colleges, and the lawns of the quadrangles were a weedless green. The students were gone and the city had already begun to shrink in their absence, becoming quieter, more deserted, more overshadowed by the silence of ancient buildings and an even more ancient past. In the little house on the outskirts of the town Jane was packing haphazardly and trying not to panic.

"I'm sure I shan't remember everything," she said to Benedict. "Did I cancel the milk and newspapers? I honestly can't remember what I've done and what I haven't done. If only we were at Colwyn and all this awful packing was over!"

"Since the papers didn't arrive this morning," said Benedict, "and since we seem to have run out of milk, I presume you canceled both orders. What have you done about the cat?"

"Oh, Marble's coming too! I couldn't possibly leave him!"

"My dear Jane, he'll leave *you* if you cart him off to Wales!

You know what cats are like! They find their way back to their home by instinct if you try to remove them to a new environment."

"Marble's not like other cats," said Jane.

"Well, if you think I'm going to drive all the way to Wales with that wretched animal caterwauling every mile of the way on the back seat—"

"He'll be in his basket on my lap," said Jane firmly. "He'll be as good as gold."

"I'll believe that when I see it," said Benedict, but he made no effort to argue the point further. He had himself given the cat to Jane a year ago after she had seen the white kitten in the window of the local pet shop, and the cat had been dotingly cared for ever since. It was now fourteen months old, a large elegant creature with thick fluffy white fur, malevolent pink eyes, and pale, destructive claws. Benedict, who though not a cat lover had admired the animal at first, now regarded its presence in the house with mixed feelings. He felt there was an element of sadness about Jane's affection for it; it seemed such a waste to him that Jane, who had such an abundant supply of maternal affection, should have to expend it all on a bad-tempered albino feline.

"Come along, Marble," said Jane, picking the cat up and placing him in his basket. "We're going on a lovely holiday."

Marble looked at her in disgust. Once in the car he started to protest and the air vibrated with angry noises.

"I told you so," said Benedict.

"He'll settle down," said Jane defensively.

"Hm . . . Have we got everything?"

"I think so . . . oh my goodness, I didn't throw out the bread! Just a minute—"

"I'll do it," said Benedict. "You'd better stay with the animal. I'd rather not be responsible for him."

They eventually managed to leave, Benedict driving in his usual erratic fashion out of the city and setting a westward course across the middle of England toward South Wales. The cat settled down,

Jane heaved a sigh of relief, and Benedict began to hum a phrase from Beethoven's "Pastoral Symphony."

"I never thought we'd finally get away," said Jane to him. "Why am I always so disorganized? How marvelous it must be to be one of those dynamic, practical, efficient women who never get in a muddle."

"I detest dynamic, practical, efficient women," said Benedict. "If you hadn't been exactly the way you are I wouldn't have dreamed of marrying you."

Jane sighed happily. For a second she could remember overhearing Lisa say to a friend at a party: "I can't think what Jane sees in him!" Lisa had never understood. Neither had their mother, who had died a year ago. Jane, her thoughts drifting further into the past, could hear her mother saying to her with polite exasperation: "Jane, dear, don't you think it's time you changed your hairstyle? . . . not quite up to date, is it, and your hair gets so untidy . . . dear, I don't think that dress really suits you. . . . Jane, you're really quite pretty—if you made a little more effort you could be so attractive . . . just a question of being smart . . . Lisa, for instance—"

"But I'm not Lisa," Jane had said. "I'm me."

She could remember the boys at parties long ago. "You're not Lisa's sister, are you? Are you really? Oh . . ." Then there were the teachers at school. "Jane tries hard, but . . ." Lisa hadn't done well at school either but that, everyone agreed, was because Lisa hadn't tried. And finally there arose the awful problem of being overweight. "It's such bad luck you're not like Lisa, dear—Lisa eats twice as much as you yet never seems to put on an ounce . . ."

Lisa. Always, always Lisa.

"You can't possibly be in love with me," she had blurted out to Benedict. "I'm fat and very stupid and I usually look a mess and I always get in a muddle, and compared to Lisa—"

"I despise women like Lisa," Benedict had said.

"But—"

"I like you exactly the way you are," Benedict had said. "If you ever try to change I shall be extremely cross."

He had repeated this several times during the six years since they had first met, but even now Jane hardly dared to believe he meant what he said. As the car droned steadily west toward Wales on that long day in June, she stroked Marble's thick fur and found herself thinking that the cat's sleepy purrs echoed her own overwhelming feeling of contentment and peace.

It was evening by the time they reached the big industrial port of Swansea, and the sun had set by the time they had skirted all the man-made ugliness and emerged into the wild country of the Gower Peninsula. Colwyn village lay a mile from the sea on the peninsula's southern side; as they approached the village, the wooded part of the countryside faded behind them until they were surrounded by open country, fields enclosed by stone walls, remote farms with acres reaching up to the heathland on top of the cliffs or stretching toward the rocky shore. It might have been two hundred instead of merely twenty miles from Swansea.

"How anxious Evan must be to get home!" Jane said, gazing dreamily at the darkening sea beyond the fields. "It's not long now till his return, is it? How excited he must be."

They drove through the village and down the lane to the gates of Colwyn Court. The drive wound through borders of flowering shrubs until finally it twisted around to end before the front of the house. It was an old house, Elizabethan in origin, which had been remodeled in the eighteenth century by a Colwyn who had wanted to keep abreast of the latest trends in architecture. The facade was Georgian, white, grave and symmetrical, but behind it, invisible from the drive, stretched the two wings of the Elizabethan E and the formal precision of an Elizabethan garden.

"The place looks as quiet as a morgue," said Benedict. "Perhaps everyone's gone to bed. What time is it, my dear?"

"Nine o'clock."

"It must be more than that!"

"Well . . . yes, my watch has stopped. I must have forgotten to wind it—how silly of me! What shall we do?"

"I'd better just see if Walter's still up—or at least leave a message to say that we've arrived safely—and then we can drive on to the cottage."

"All right." Jane carefully put the lid on Marble's basket and followed Benedict out of the car. Her legs felt stiff after the long journey, and she had a sudden longing to relax in a hot bath.

There was a pause after Benedict had rung the doorbell. Above them the stars shone and a bat swooped blindly through the dusk.

"It looks as if everyone's gone to bed." He rang the doorbell again. "We should have made an earlier start from Cambridge," he added as he turned away, "but never mind—we can walk up from the cottage after breakfast tomorrow. I hope Walter had the presence of mind to leave the place unlocked for us."

A light went on in the hall. As Benedict swung around again and Jane hesitated by the car, the door opened to reveal a plump middle-aged woman with softly waving gray hair and a serene smile.

"Good evening," she said warmly. "Professor and Mrs. Shaw? Allow me to introduce myself: I'm Agnes Miller, secretary of the Colwyn branch of the Society for the Propagation of Nature Foods. Do come in!"

*ii*

Marble peered through the chinks of his basket on the front seat of the car and pawed fretfully at the wickerwork. On hearing Benedict's voice some way off and Jane's murmur from closer at hand he was aware of being abandoned and yet not abandoned. Rage overcame him. He hated his wicker basket. He hated cars. It had been a long hard day.

Taking a deep breath he yowled, arched his back, and flayed out with all four paws.

The lid of his basket burst open. Marble blinked in the bright light from the porch and then sprang triumphantly through the open window of the car to the freedom of the gravel drive below.

"What a lovely cat!" exclaimed an unknown feminine voice, and an alien hand stooped to caress him delicately on the back of his neck.

"Careful, Miss Miller," said Benedict nervously. "He's not at all friendly to strangers."

Marble quivered. His spine was tingling so hard that his fur stood out in a huge white ruff around his neck. He felt bemused and overwhelmed and quite unlike himself.

"Here, Marble," said Jane suddenly, and picked him up. The alien caressing stopped. Marble blinked, remembered he was free, and bounded out of Jane's arms and up the steps into the house.

"Marble!" exclaimed Jane.

Marble took no notice. There was an elderly man coming down the stairs and saying: "Benedict, how nice to see you again! I do apologize for being so slow to greet you—I was in my study and . . ."

"Marble!" called Jane, distressed.

Marble felt deliciously wicked. It had been a long hard day and now that it was over he had every intention of celebrating. He found a passage leading off the hall and darted down it. Halfway along he paused, nostrils flaring, but there was no enticing smell, only his unerring instinct that he was heading in the right direction.

"Marble!" cried Jane desperately from a long way off. "You naughty cat! Come here at once."

Marble skipped smartly round a corner and found himself in another corridor. On his left a beam of light streamed into the passage from a door left ajar. Marble shot forward, stood up on his hind legs, and brought both front paws to bear against the door. To his gratification the door swung wide and the next moment he was padding into an enormous kitchen.

A strange smell from the stove assailed his nostrils. He paused. Somebody noticed him.

"What a beautiful cat!" another strange feminine voice said. "Look, Harriet, look at that cat!"

"Here, pussy!"

Marble backed away.

"Give him some milk."

"Where did he come from?"

Someone opened a refrigerator and took out a milk bottle. Someone else stooped to touch him but Marble arched his back and hissed. He wasn't at all sure where he was and he didn't like the strange smell from the stove. Instinctively he looked around for Jane but Jane seemed to have given up the chase. He was alone.

"Here, kitty!" said one of the strange women.

They were all women. Every one of them.

"Isn't he sweet?"

"Put the milk in a saucer for him."

Marble tried to find the door and bumped into a table leg. He began to panic. He was about to make an undignified bolt for the nearest corner where he could ward off anyone who approached him when a soft draft ruffled his fur and he saw a door open nearby, a door leading outside into the freedom of the night.

Marble shot across the room so fast that he did not even see the man's black trousers until he cannoned into them. The collision gave him the shock of his life; yelping, he sprang backward in fright and clawed at the air as he toppled over onto his back.

"I see we have an unexpected guest," said a dark, quiet voice from the doorway.

Marble was breathing very hard. The door was still open and he could see a yard beyond and could feel the fresh sea air from the night outside, but he found it curiously hard to move. And then a man stooped over him and touched the nape of his neck with long delicate fingers, and Marble forgot about the car journey and the smell from the stove and the promise of freedom inches away outside the back door.

"What's your name?" said the stranger in that quiet, dark voice. "Or have you always been nameless, waiting for me?"

Marble put out a weak paw and fastened his claws around a black shoelace.

"I name you Zequiel," said the quiet voice, "and claim you for my own."

And suddenly strong hands were lifting him through the air and there was the smell of a clean white shirt and the soothing silk of a man's tie and a feeling of immeasurable peace.

"Marble!" called Jane's voice from the passage outside the kitchen door. "Marble, where are you?"

But Marble did not hear her. He had closed his eyes and relaxed every limb and was purring in a trance of shivering ecstasy.

*iii*

"Don't worry, Mrs. Shaw," said Agnes Miller, catching Jane just outside the kitchen. "We'll find him. Please don't worry about it. He's bound to turn up soon."

Jane was distraught. She knew her distress was irrational and knew that Miss Miller's advice contained nothing but common-sense, but she was still upset. She tried to tell herself that her uncharacteristic behavior was the result of the long journey but she knew it was not. Her distress seemed to spring from some strange atmosphere in the house; perhaps it even sprang from the presence of this unknown woman who had befriended Marble so easily or from the bat which had flickered through the dusk after Benedict had rung the doorbell. Maybe her distress even had some connection with the alien but fragrant odor which was wafting toward her from the half-open kitchen door. But whatever the source of her anxiety was, Jane was conscious of unreasoning panic. With horror she realized she was on the verge of tears.

"I've got to find him," she said, turning blindly toward the door. "I must."

Miss Miller stepped neatly in front of her and poked her head around the door of the kitchen. "Has anyone seen—" she began brightly, and then exclaimed in delight. "Why, there he is! It's all right, Mrs. Shaw, he's safe and sound! He's among friends and having a lovely time!"

Marble has no friends, thought Jane fiercely, only me and Benedict. Her eyes were blurring with the ridiculous tears again, and then as she stood there, not trusting herself to speak, a shadow fell between her and the light and a man's voice said politely: "Your cat, Mrs. Shaw."

Jane blinked away her tears, but even before she could see properly she could hear Marble's purrs. He was lying limpidly in his captor's arms, his fur very white against the man's black jacket.

"You naughty cat, Marble," said Jane in an unsteady voice, and picking him up crushed him tightly against her breast. "You naughty disobedient cat."

Marble spat and began to struggle.

"Quiet." The stranger laid his index finger on the cat's head. "Behave yourself."

The cat was still.

Jane looked up for the first time at the man facing her.

"Mrs. Shaw," said Agnes Miller, "this is Mr. Poole, the managing director of our society. Perhaps Mr. Colwyn has mentioned him to you."

"I don't think he . . . at least, I'm not sure—I don't remember . . . How do you do, Mr. Poole."

"How do you do, Mrs. Shaw." He smiled at her.

Jane looked away. "Thank you so much for capturing Marble . . . I'm afraid I was rather silly . . . panicky . . . he's not used to strange places, and I was afraid he might run away and get lost."

"Of course," said Poole. "I quite understand."

"Such a lovely cat," said Miss Miller warmly. "Such a very beautiful cat."

Poole said nothing. Jane was suddenly aware of his lack of sentimentality toward Marble. There was no effeminate gushing about how handsome the cat was, no fatuous remarks, forgivable in a woman, about how naughty the animal had been, no uneasy insincerities about how glad he was to have been of service. Instead there had been the competent handling of the cat, the kind

of handling a veterinarian might have shown, and the short ad-
monition when the cat had become hostile. Jane had an impression of controlled power, economical movements, and a cool, spare
masculinity which seemed incongruous in a man who had a way
with cats and who made his living by directing what Benedict had
called a crackpot society.

"I wish you a pleasant stay at the cottage, Mrs. Shaw," the man
was saying. "I trust we'll be seeing you from time to time during
your visit."

"Yes . . . thank you," said Jane, not sure what she was saying. "If you'll excuse me—"

"Of course. Good night, Mrs. Shaw."

"I'll come back to the hall with you," said Agnes Miller, leading
the way down the corridor. "Now I do hope you have everything
you want at the cottage. I hold myself responsible for the arrangements because Mr. Colwyn's housekeeper gave notice a week or
two ago and really, it's so difficult to get staff nowadays, and so
the girls and I have been running the house ourselves—"

"The girls?"

"Yes, there are twelve of us," said Miss Miller sociably. "All
ages from all walks of life, so stimulating! My sister Harriet and I
are 'in charge,' so to speak, and organize the different duties
among us. We attend to all the mundane details so that Mr.
Poole is free to plan and direct the more important activities."

"I see," said Jane blankly. "So all twelve of you—"

"Thirteen," said Miss Miller, "with Mr. Poole."

"Yes . . . I see, but what do you actually do?"

"We are engaged," said Miss Miller in a brisk, sensible voice,
"in a sociological study of the benefits, physical and psychological,
of a diet unadulterated by the vagaries of mankind. It is our con-
tention that through eating foods unpolluted by chemicals, foods
that spring directly from nature, we may be at one with nature
and may move closer to the natural forces which dominate all our
destinies."

Heavens, thought Jane. "I see," she said again. It seemed the
safest thing to say.

"We are only the newest of several little groups scattered all over the country," said Miss Miller brightly. "We consider ourselves very privileged that Mr. Poole has donated so much of his valuable time to help us get established in our own headquarters. Mr. Poole is—how shall I say?—the Guiding Light. He's in touch with all the groups and directs policy on a national scale. Once we're established on a stable footing he'll move on elsewhere but for the moment we're fortunate enough to have him here directing operations in person."

"Ah," said Jane. "Yes. Of course."

"Dear me, you must be wondering about the cottage and here I am talking nonstop about the society! I *do* apologize. Now, here's the key to the cottage—there's milk in the refrigerator and I put a few things in the larder to tide you over until you can get to the shops . . . The stove is electric; I prefer gas myself, but still, electric cooking is very clean and most efficient once you get used to it. The kitchen is fully stocked with cutlery, pots and pans, dishes, and so on, and all the linen is in the airing cupboard just outside the bathroom. The laundry calls here every Wednesday, so if you bring the dirty linen up to the house on Wednesday morning I'll see that it gets sent away to the wash. I think that's more or less everything, but if you need anything else please don't hesitate to let me know . . . ah, here's your husband and Mr. Colwyn—and Gwyneth in her dressing gown! Gwyneth, dear, I thought Tristan advised you to go to bed early tonight?"

"I've been asleep," said Gwyneth, "but I couldn't help waking up when everyone started shouting for the cat. Hello, Jane! So this is the cat! Is he real? He looks like a toy."

"Unfortunately he's all too real," said Benedict. "Jane, I think we should be on our way."

"Yes," said Jane. "Definitely."

"Come over tomorrow as soon as you're settled in," said Walter. "Meanwhile I hope you sleep well. Jane looks very tired."

"You look tired yourself, Walter," said Benedict crisply. "I think we'd all feel better for a night's rest."

"I'm all right," said Walter vaguely and wandered with them to the door. "You know the way? Just take the lane past the stables toward the sea."

"Fine. How about the key?"

"I've got that somewhere," said Jane. "Good night, Miss Miller. Thank you again. Good night, Gwyneth . . . Walter . . . see you tomorrow."

They escaped. Marble, too sleepy to protest, was put in his basket again, Benedict switched on the headlights, and the car began to bump forward away from the house down the dark lane which led to the coast.

"Benedict," said Jane, "there's something very peculiar going on in that house. Those people have completely taken it over. Did you notice how awful Gwyneth and Walter looked? What on earth do you think is happening?"

"My dear, don't make a mystery out of it," said Benedict, trying to concentrate on avoiding the potholes in the rough road. "Gwyneth always looks like a Victorian heroine in the last throes of consumption and Walter's aged a bit since we last saw him, that's all. Of course he must be on the verge of bankruptcy to have allowed those people to take over part of his house, but—"

"All his house, Benedict! Miss Miller's running the entire place!"

"Well, if that's so, at least he's saved himself the expense of engaging a housekeeper. But anyway I intend to have a talk with him at the earliest opportunity to see if I can give him any financial advice. I know Walter! He'll muddle into almost anything unless someone takes him firmly by the hand and leads him out of it. The whole trouble probably began when Evan went abroad last year and there was no one to keep an eye on what happened at Colwyn Court. Thank God Evan will be home before the end of the month! Between the two of us we should manage to sort matters out, I should think."

"But Benedict, that society—"

"Just a bunch of harmless middle-aged women, my dear, who like to dabble in herbalism. As a matter of fact, it was a relief to meet Miss Miller and see what a nice woman she is. I'm sure the society poses no threat in itself; they've merely managed to take a legitimate advantage of Walter's unfortunate economic situation."

"You didn't meet Mr. Poole," said Jane.

"Who's Mr. Poole?"

"The 'Guiding Light,' Miss Miller called him."

"That's funny, Walter said they were all women . . . Well, what's wrong with Mr. Poole? I suppose a man who works with a dozen middle-aged women cultivating nature foods is probably some sort of elderly pansy, but—"

"Mr. Poole isn't like that at all," said Jane. "He's about thirty-five, tall, good-looking, well-educated, well-dressed, very polite, and—"

"And?" said Benedict, too astonished to feel even the smallest pang of jealousy.

"—and rather frightening," said Jane, and shivered so violently that Marble's basket nearly slid off her lap onto the floor.

## iv

Three days passed. Benedict had begun to settle down to a routine of working all morning, reading in the afternoon, and working again in the evening, a routine which Jane had become accustomed to during the years of her marriage but which still managed to make her feel lonely unless she kept herself fully occupied. The day after they had arrived they had lunched with Walter and Gwyneth, but Colwyn Court had seemed less formidable in daylight and the members of the society had remained out of sight in their own sections of the house so that it had been hard to remember that the Colwyns did not have their home to themselves. Mr. Poole, Walter had announced, had gone to London for some reason and would be away for a day or two. Jane was conscious first of relief when she heard this news and then of regret that

Benedict would still not have the chance to meet Miss Miller's Guiding Light.

But perhaps Benedict would have found Mr. Poole as pleasantly ordinary as he had found Miss Miller.

After lunch Jane had suggested to Gwyneth that they leave the men on their own and walk through the grounds to the beach, but Gwyneth had received the suggestion without enthusiasm. It was time for her afternoon rest, she had objected, and anyway it was too hot to consider trekking all the way down to the cove; her health had improved but she had had a small relapse lately and "Tristan" had advised her to be careful for a few days.

"Is Tristan Poole his real name?" Jane had asked suddenly.

Gwyneth had stared at her in astonishment. "Why ever shouldn't it be?"

"Oh . . . I don't know. I suppose it seems rather an unlikely sort of name, that's all."

"I can't imagine why you should say that," Gwyneth had said disapprovingly. "Poole is a very ordinary sort of surname and Tristan . . . well, people *are* called Tristan, aren't they? I don't think it's any more unusual than Benedict."

Jane, not wanting to argue, had abandoned the subject and strolled off to the beach on her own. Colwyn Cove, which was private property and part of Walter's estate, had a small sandy beach sprinkled with rocks and framed by tall cliffs. The cottage where Benedict and Jane were staying was perched above the beach at the point where the cliffs were at their lowest, rising no more than twenty feet above the sands, and was set about two hundred yards from the cliff's edge. It was a perfect position, and from the picture window of the living room it was possible to see not only the surf in the cove but north to the ruined castle and chapel on top of the furthest cliff and south to the windswept bracken and heather of the cliff nearby. The sunsets were superb. After their first dinner at the cottage Jane and Benedict had lingered a long time by the window to watch the sun sink into the darkening sea.

"You were right as usual," Benedict had said, taking her hand

and smiling at her. "You knew this would be the best place for me to work." And the very next morning he had unfastened the trunk which contained his books, littered his papers over the table, and begun to hammer away at his elderly typewriter amid a sea of dirty coffee cups and overflowing ashtrays. Walter's problems were forgotten; Benedict had found out from his cousin that Walter was "a little hard pressed for ready cash," as Walter himself had put it, but by no means insolvent, and the discovery, together with the fact that the society seemed so unobtrusive, had convinced Benedict that he had been worrying unnecessarily.

"Of course if it were me," he had said to Jane, "I wouldn't care to let part of my home to a group of strangers, even if they were as orderly and well behaved as these people seem to be, but if it helps Walter financially and he doesn't mind their presence, I don't see why the arrangement shouldn't work out satisfactorily for all concerned. It'll do Gwyneth good to see a few more people. The life she leads here is much too isolated, in my opinion."

Jane spent some time pondering on the subject of Gwyneth. Despite the fact that she was Gwyneth's senior by more than thirteen years, Jane was always aware of a sense of inferiority on the rare occasions when they met. Gwyneth had received a poor education at home from a governess, but this made no difference to the fact that her intelligence was sharp; she had spent most of her life in indifferent health, but this had not affected her looks, which were striking. Jane had long admired her slender figure, curling red hair, and wide-set blue eyes, and in Gwyneth's presence she inevitably felt large and clumsy and not a little stupid. Moreover, Gwyneth's obsession with the modern subculture, her psychedelic posters of pop artists, her records of the fashionable white American blues, her literature on such nineteen-sixties noteworthies as Che Guevara, Andy Warhol, and Stokely Carmichael all contrived to make Jane feel hopelessly out of touch with such an aggressive and mysterious generation.

So even when Benedict had settled down to his work and Jane found she had too much time to herself, she avoided a routine of daily visits to Colwyn Court. Her excuse to herself was that she did not want to bore Gwyneth by turning up every day for a chat and that if Gwyneth wanted to be sociable she would manage to walk the three-quarters of a mile from the main house to the cottage. But Gwyneth evidently had no wish to be sociable. She paid no visits to the cottage, and although Jane was secretly relieved by this she was regretful as well. Apart from her morning visits to the village stores for food she saw no one but Benedict, and it would have been pleasant to have another woman to talk to now and then.

She contented herself by going for long walks. She walked up to the ruined castle on the cliffs and beyond, around the headland past a dozen deserted rocky coves toward the furthest tip of the Gower Peninsula, the rocky arm of the Worm's Head. She walked the other way too, walked east of Colwyn around a dozen more coves toward Port Eynon, and each time she walked she met no one. In June the holiday season was not yet in full swing and the weather was still too uncertain to attract the day-trippers. After her walks she felt increasingly aware of the cottage's isolation.

On the fourth day after their arrival the weather improved; the last two days had been showery but that morning the sun was shining and Jane decided to take advantage of the better weather by spending the morning sunbathing on the beach. After she had finished washing up the breakfast dishes she left Benedict among his cigarette smoke and intellectual thoughts and went down to the sands with her bathing wrap and the latest issue of her favorite women's magazine.

The cat followed her when she left. She had hardly seen him since they had arrived, for every morning he had disappeared on his own expeditions and not returned till nightfall, but this morning he stayed with her, padding down the path to the beach behind her, and scrambling over the rocks onto the sand. He was restless. Once a gull landed only a few feet away from them and he chased it fretfully toward the sea, but the menace of the incoming tide made him nervous and he could not settle down and sun himself in peace.

After a while his restlessness communicated itself to Jane and she looked up but there was nothing to see, no living thing in sight except for the gulls, and up on the cliff by the ruined castle, the wild horses grazing placidly on the short grass. She returned to her magazine but presently realized she had no memory of what she had been reading. When she looked up again she saw that Marble had gone.

He was pattering across the sand toward the path which led up from the beach, his tail waving gently, his ears very erect, and as Jane watched, wondering what had attracted him, she saw a figure reach the top of the path and pause before making the descent to the beach.

It was Tristan Poole.

v

He raised his hand when he saw her, and after a second she waved back and reached for her wrap. Why she felt the need to put on her wrap she had no idea. Her swimsuit was respectable and even flattering to her figure, and she was certainly not ashamed of her legs which had always, even during the fattest stages of her life, been good. But she put on the wrap all the same. It was not until she tried to fasten it that she realized how nervous she was. Her fingers were trembling and her palms were damp against the rough toweling.

Marble had reached Poole and was trying to attract his attention by rubbing himself around the man's ankles. Poole said something—Jane heard his voice but not what he said—and the cat dropped back a pace obediently.

No man should have such control over a strange cat, thought Jane suddenly. It's unnatural.

And she had to use all her willpower to stop herself shivering again as he came toward her.

"Hello," he said, sounding so normal that in a second she had forgotten her nervousness. "How are you? By the way, your cat seems to have taken a fancy to me, I can't imagine why. What did you say his name was?"

"Marble. You must have a way with cats. He's usually very hostile to strangers."

"Hostility is usually only a manifestation of fear. Your cat, like many people, is afraid of a great many things. Eliminate the fear and you eliminate the hostility—and you have a docile cat." He stooped, patted Marble's head absentmindedly, and glanced down with a smile at Jane. "May I join you for a moment?"

"Yes, of course," said Jane, anxious not to manifest her fear by a display of hostility. "When did you get back to Colwyn?"

"Late last night. I had business in London . . . Do you know London at all?"

"Not really. My family came from Hampshire and since my marriage I've lived in Cambridge. My sister lived in London for some time, but I never followed her example."

"You have a sister?"

"Just the one sister, yes. No brothers. She's younger than me."

"Does she still live in London?"

"No, she and her husband live about twenty miles away in Surrey, but I think Lisa would like a flat in town as well as the house in the country if she had the chance. However, Matt—my brother-in-law—isn't too keen on that idea. He's just about to retire early and he's anxious to get right away from London for a while." Heavens, she thought to herself, amazed, why am I telling him all this? She tried to ask him a question about himself, but he spoke before she could think of anything to say.

"If any man wants to escape from city life for a while," said Poole, "he should come down here. I don't know if your brother-in-law likes the sea, but this stretch of the coast is as good as a hundred light-years from London in my opinion."

"Yes, that's just what Matt says—he came down here after he married Lisa three years ago, and when they were staying at Colwyn Court I know he was very impressed by the countryside. You see, he's really a very straightforward person with very simple tastes . . ." And she found herself telling him all about Matthew Morrison, all about his whirlwind romance with Lisa, all about Lisa's first husband who had been a television producer specializing in documentaries on current affairs. She even told him how Lisa's first husband had met his death when he had been in the Far East filming an essay on the Chinese infiltration of Hong Kong and had drowned at sea during a foolhardy reconnaissance up the coast of Red China. From the subject of Lisa's first husband the conversation veered into a discussion of Lisa's children, and the subject of children led Jane to talk about Nicola who was Matt's only child. She was on the point of launching into the saga of Nicola's ill-fated romance with Evan Colwyn when she suddenly realized how much she was talking. "I'm sorry," she said, embarrassed. "Of course you can't be interested in all that. How silly of me."

He smiled. He had a very attractive smile. His teeth were not quite even, she noticed, but somehow this only made his smile more attractive than ever. Now that she had the chance to observe him more closely she saw that in fact he was not as good-looking as he had seemed at first glance; his mouth was too wide, his cheekbones too broad, his chin a fraction too square. But he was attractive. Not handsome in the classical sense, but very attractive. Too attractive, she thought, and glanced away quickly for fear that her unwilling interest in his face should be misinterpreted.

"You're wrong," he was saying idly. "I was most intrigued by what you were saying. People—especially people like your brother-in-law—always do intrigue me. I admire anyone who starts off in life as an office boy and ends as chairman of the board. I suppose there's no chance of your sister and brother-in-law visiting you while you're at the cottage?"

"Matt would like to, I'm sure," said Jane, "and so would the twins." She began to picture herself taking the twins for walks and playing with them on the sands.

"Why don't you give your sister a call and suggest it?"

"Well, the cottage is a bit small—"

"There are four bedrooms, aren't there? Wouldn't that be sufficient?"

"Yes . . . yes, I suppose so. Yes, it would be nice. But you see, my husband is working—a thesis—it would be a bit difficult—"

"He'd be on his own during the day. Everyone would be out enjoying themselves."

"Yes, that's true."

"When does your brother-in-law retire?"

"It's this month—I'm not sure of the exact date. It's soon, I know."

"Wouldn't it be fun for you to have some visitors? It must be dull for you here on your own."

"Well . . ."

"It must be lonely," said Poole. "Admit it. It's isolated here."

"It's isolated," said Jane.

"There's plenty of room at the cottage."

"Yes, plenty of room."

"I'm sure your husband wouldn't mind."

"No, I'm sure he wouldn't."

"Of course, they may have made other plans, but—"

"I'll phone Lisa," said Jane, "and find out."

"Good!" He smiled at her again and stood up, dusting the sand off his dark slacks. "Well, I must be on my way. No doubt I'll see you again soon, Mrs. Shaw. Give my regards to your husband, won't you? I hope I'll have the chance to meet him before long."

The cat stirred but made no effort to follow him.

"I'm sure you will," said Jane. "Good-bye, Mr. Poole."

He was gone. She watched him walk off up the cliff path, and when he had disappeared from sight she lay back limply on the sand and thought about him.

After a while she thought: I won't do it. I won't phone Lisa. I won't.

This made her feel better. She sat up, tossed back her hair, and flung off her wrap in a gesture of liberation. But then she thought: It would be nice if the twins were here. Perhaps they could come down on their own.

But the twins would be at school. How could she have forgotten that? They were at their separate boarding schools, and their terms would not end until the third week of July.

All desire to phone Lisa vanished. Jane put on her sunglasses again, dragged her magazine toward her and spent the rest of the morning trying not to remember the curious interview with Tristan Poole. But she remembered it just the same. Even when she returned to the house to prepare lunch she found she was still thinking of the odd effect his presence had had on her.

The telephone was ringing as she walked into the living room. Normally there was no phone at the cottage in order to protect Walter from any whim of his summer tenants to make long-distance calls, but a portable phone had originally been installed there for the retired chauffeur and had been reinstated a week ago for the Shaws' benefit.

Jane crossed the living room and picked up the receiver. "Hello?"

"Darling," said Lisa, "it's me. Listen, the twins are in quarantine for mumps, Matt's on the verge of flying to the Channel Islands, and everything's a perfect nightmare. Jane, you *must* help me, I'm desperate. I've got to play for time and stop Matt buying property in Guernsey, and the only way to stop him now, as far as I can see, is for me to wangle an invitation to Colwyn Cottage from you and Benedict. Darling, I hate to ask you, but do you think you could possibly—"

"Did you say the twins were at home?" said Jane.

"Yes, it's such a nuisance for them, poor things. Their half-terms fell on the same weekend so we took them out and went to see a friend of Matt's who has some grandchildren about the same age. Then one of the grandchildren came down with mumps the day afterward, so Matt said: 'Good, that gives us an excuse to take the twins away from school before the end of term and make an early start for Guernsey before the worst of the holiday crowds arrive.' Well, I . . . hello, are you still there?"

"Yes," said Jane.

"You're not saying very much," said Lisa accusingly. "Are you in the middle of lunch or something?"

"No. Lisa—"

"The point is that Matt's dead set on this Channel Islands scheme, and I'm equally dead set against it. But I'm sure I could still talk him out of it if only I had the tiniest bit more time, so if we could come down for a visit—"

"Benedict's working, Lisa."

"Well, we wouldn't interfere! After all, Matt would be out all day leading his wretched Simple-Life-Away-from-It-All, and the twins would be on the beach and—well, I can't imagine what *I'll* do, but I'm sure I won't disturb Benedict. I could leave the *au pair* in Surrey if that would help out with the accommodation. The twins are really quite sensible on their own nowadays and in an isolated spot like Colwyn I'm sure they wouldn't get up to too much mischief."

"I could look after the twins," said Jane.

"Oh darling, you know I wouldn't expect you to be an unpaid *au pair* girl, but you *are* so marvelous with children and the twins so enjoy seeing you—"

"When will you come?" said Jane.

"Perhaps at the end of the week—would that be all right? Oh Jane, you're wonderful! Honestly, I sometimes wonder what I would ever do without you to fall back upon whenever I get into one of these awful jams! Listen, I mustn't hold you up any longer —I expect you're busy cooking, and I want to find Matt straight away to tell him you've invited us all to stay for a couple of weeks. I'll phone you again later and let you know what time we'll be arriving."

"Yes . . . all right, Lisa. Fine."

"'Bye, darling. Love to Benedict and thanks a million."

"'Bye," said Jane, and began to wonder how she would ever summon the courage to tell Benedict such unwelcome news.

Benedict was furious.

"That woman!" he yelled, pounding the table so hard with his fist that the typewriter leaped half an inch into the air. "How dare she use us in an effort to stave off her marital troubles! How dare she!"

"Well, it's not quite as bad as that, Benedict. I mean—"

"It's not only as bad as that," cried Benedict, "it's worse. How on earth am I supposed to have any peace and quiet once the house is bursting at the seams with visitors? How am I supposed to do any serious writing when the Morrisons are airing their incompatability and the children are running around playing games—"

"I'll see the children don't disturb you," said Jane.

"I've no doubt you will! Lisa thought of that! She used those two children as bait!"

"No, she didn't," said Jane.

"Of course she did! And then in addition to everyone else there's that wretched *au pair* girl—"

"She won't be coming. Benedict, it'll only be for two weeks."

"I don't think I could be in the same house as Lisa for two weeks! I don't think I could do so without suffering a nervous breakdown!"

Jane turned without a word, went back to the phone, and started to dial the operator for Lisa's number.

"For God's sake," growled Benedict, ripping the paper out of his typewriter, throwing it on the floor, and stamping on it to relieve his feelings, "what are you up to now?" He stormed over to the phone, grabbed the receiver from Jane's hand, and hurled it back into its cradle. "You weren't phoning her to cancel the visit, were you?"

Jane was on the verge of tears. "What else can I do?"

"There, there," said Benedict guiltily. "There, there. You mustn't take me so seriously. You know I often say things I don't mean in the heat of the moment. Let the invitation stand."

"But—"

"I like Morrison and the only reason I resent Lisa so much is because I think she takes advantage of you most of the time, that's all. I resent her for your sake, not for my own."

"But your work—it was wrong of me to invite them—"

"Well, it's only for two weeks and if they're not tactful enough to leave me alone most of the time I shall have no compunction about asking them to do so."

"I don't know why I agreed to it," said Jane in despair. "I just don't know why I agreed to it."

The children, thought Benedict, and felt a quick stab of pain. Aloud he said, "Well, you'll enjoy entertaining the twins."

"It wasn't just because of the twins," said Jane stubbornly. "It really wasn't, Benedict."

"Oh." He thought: we ought to talk about adoption again. I was too rigid before, saying I couldn't care enough about a child unless it were my own flesh and blood. It was unfair to her. "Well—"

"I mean, perhaps it was partly because of the twins, but . . . Benedict, I met Mr. Poole on the beach this morning. We talked about Lisa and Matt and he—he told me to invite them down, and . . . well, when Lisa suggested the invitation I found I simply couldn't refuse. I hadn't the will to refuse. It was as if . . . oh, I don't know! But it's all Mr. Poole's fault somehow, I know it is. I just know it."

"There, there," said Benedict soothingly again. He took her in his arms and kissed her. "It doesn't matter. I'm sorry I lost my temper like that."

"Benedict, you weren't listening to what I was saying. Mr. Poole—"

"This man Poole obviously has you spellbound," said Benedict. "I can see I shall have to meet him as soon as possible to discover why you find him so irresistible."

"Benedict, I know you're not taking me seriously, but it really was as if I was spellbound—or hypnotized—or something—"

"Fiddlesticks," said Benedict placidly. "You love a mystery, my dear, that's your trouble, and if one doesn't exist you'll invent one. It's your romantic and feminine nature. The truth of the matter is that Poole, seeing you were on your own on the beach, suggested you should invite the rest of your family down for a visit. Then by coincidence Lisa rang up and suggested the same thing.

You were tempted by the prospect of seeing the twins and agreed to the visit. I can't think why you should want to blame everything on poor Poole who was probably only doing his best to be friendly and sociable."

"Yes," said Jane. "Yes, you're right. Of course you're right. It's just that—"

"Yes?" said Benedict curiously.

"—I don't like Mr. Poole," said Jane. "I can't help it, I just don't like him at all."

## vi

When Poole returned to Colwyn Court after his talk with Jane he found Agnes Miller in the small sitting room which had once belonged to the housekeeper. Agnes was adding up a column of figures in the ledger before her and looking perplexed.

"Don't say anything," she said as Poole entered the room. "I'm at a crucial stage. Four from nine is five, six from thirteen is seven, seven from two . . . seven from two? Oh yes, I see." She wrote down a figure and sat looking at it doubtfully.

"I'll have to buy you an adding machine," said Poole amused.

"My dear, we hardly have enough money left to buy a loaf of bread, let alone an adding machine! What on earth are we going to do?"

"How women enjoy a crisis," said Poole, sitting down on the nearby sofa and putting his feet up on the coffee table. "How women love to worry."

"You're quite wrong," said Agnes. "I absolutely hate it." She closed the ledger with a bang. "How sordid money is!"

"Not at all," said Poole. "It's the lack of money that's sordid. Money itself is highly enjoyable."

"Don't split hairs!" said Agnes crossly.

He laughed. She looked at him and in spite of herself smiled.

"Well, I must say," she said, "it's hard to be depressed when you're always so confident. I only wish I could be as confident as you are."

"Agnes," he said, "you're a woman of very little faith sometimes."

Agnes became unexpectedly serious. "It's not that," she protested. "Of course I have faith! When I think of all you've done for us, getting us settled in this ideal environment, handling the Colwyns, coping with everything—"

"Then don't worry about the money."

"All right," said Agnes. "But how do you plan to—"

"Never ask me my plans. It's a waste of time. If I want you to know them I'll tell them to you."

"Yes . . . well, let me tell you how we're placed at the moment. So far we've been existing well enough on the legacy from our last benefactor, but the way things are going the money will be running out some time in the middle of August, and if we have the usual Lammas expenses . . . Don't look like that, Tristan! After all, one must be practical, mustn't one? These things do cost money! One can't entertain more than fifty people and only expect to spend a shilling."

"Indeed not," said Poole without expression.

"Besides," said Agnes, warming to her subject, "I don't think it's disrespectful to be practical about such matters. Think of the Other Church. They've always been very money-conscious. The Other Church is very good at raising money and being practical in that respect."

He was silent. Agnes saw she had gone too far.

"I'm sorry," she said quickly. "I shouldn't have said that. I meant no disrespect."

There was another pause, and then suddenly he was smiling at her and she was able to relax again.

"There's no harm in being reminded of a rival from time to time," said Poole lightly. "One could almost say it spurs one to greater effort."

"Well, exactly!" said Agnes pleased. She glanced at the ledger again and wished, despite all he had said, that he would give her one small word of reassurance. "Tristan—"

"You've no faith at all, have you, Agnes!" he said, laughing at her. "None whatsoever!"

"I have," pleaded Agnes, "but . . . Tristan, how long do you plan to stay here?"

"My dear Agnes, you know the answer to that question so well I can't think why you bother to ask it. I shall leave when my work here is done, when you and the others are established here with enough money to live on in comfort. Walter Colwyn's an old man and won't live forever. His son has an urge to emigrate to America. Gwyneth will either get married or end up in a home for the mentally disturbed or possibly, depending on what she wants, both. One day before very long Colwyn Court will be up for sale, everyone will point out what an economic liability large houses are these days, and you'll be able to buy it for a song with the fund I shall provide for the purpose. I'm not worried about your future here—I'm fully convinced that I've provided you with a stable environment. By Lammas you'll have a stable bank balance as well, and after Lammas I shall probably move on. There! Is that what you wanted to hear?"

"I hope you're not relying on the Colwyn family for the money," said Agnes. "I'm absolutely sure Mr. Colwyn has a mortgage on the house, and Harriet's convinced he has. I think he'll die penniless."

"Probably."

"Well," said Agnes, "I just wanted to reassure myself that you weren't relying on any Colwyn inheritance."

Poole did not answer. After a moment he stood up and wandered over to the window. "Where is everyone?"

"Working in the herb garden. We're having trouble with the coriander and henbane—so tiresome . . . Oh, and Margaret and Jackie are in the kitchen preparing lunch. Tristan, I'm a little worried about Jackie—I've a suspicion that the weekly meetings in your room no longer satisfy her, especially now that we're all being so ascetic to prepare for Lammas, and I think she's hankering for a few bright lights and a good time. You know how young she is, and how immature in some ways. Anyway, this morning she said she wanted to borrow the car to go into Swansea next Saturday night, and I couldn't help wondering if—"

"Let her go."

"But supposing—"

"Agnes, sometimes you talk as if you were the Mother Superior of a convent!"

"Well, it's not *that*," said Agnes. "It's just that I suppose it's a little dull for her here at the moment, and if she dissipates her energies before August the first, she won't find the rites nearly such a rewarding experience. I do wish you'd have a word with her about it."

"She'll do as she's been told, don't worry. Since this is her first experience of Lammas she won't want to risk not getting the most out of it. That's basic psychology."

"It's her basic sexuality I worry about," muttered Agnes. "Not her basic psychology." She put the ledger away in the drawer and locked it. "What were you up to this morning?"

"Oh, I went for a walk. To the beach. The cat was there with Mrs. Shaw."

"She seemed a nice woman," said Agnes vaguely. "Intuitive too. She doesn't like us very much because of all your fun and games with the cat."

"Fun and games! Agnes, what an extraordinary word choice you have sometimes!" He fingered the edge of the curtain idly. "Mrs. Shaw could be an attractive woman if she wanted to be," he said after a moment. "The strange part is that for some reason she doesn't want to be. A subconscious opting-out of sibling rivalry, perhaps. Gwyneth tells me Mrs. Shaw's sister, Lisa, is very attractive indeed."

Agnes began to get the drift of the conversation. Her mind, always nimble, began to leap from one possibility to another. "You can't be interested in Mrs. Shaw," she said. "Too much basic hostility."

"But very intuitive," said Poole, "and most susceptible to suggestion."

"But—"

"No, I'm not particularly interested in Mrs. Shaw. Since when have professors been millionaires? But Mrs. Shaw has a beautiful sister and the beautiful sister has a husband who even in these overtaxed days has managed to become excessively rich."

Agnes' heart began to flutter excitedly in her breast. "How on earth did you find that out?"

"It didn't need a Sherlock Holmes to discover that one. The man's name is Matthew Morrison."

"*The* Matthew Morrison?"

"Uh-huh. And Agnes, you want to know something else?"

He's getting excited too, thought Agnes. He's forgetting his English accent. "Tell me," she invited with a smile.

"Professor and Mrs. Shaw are going to have visitors in the very near future. And you want to know who those visitors are going to be?"

"Matthew Morrison, the millionaire industrialist," said Agnes promptly, her faith restored in full, "and his very beautiful, very attractive, very desirable wife, Lisa."

# Chapter Three

*i*

Four days later in the back of Matt's Rolls Royce the twins were studying the road map. The car was traveling through orchard country on the way west to the Welsh border, and the boughs of the trees near the roadside were drooping with the burden of ripening fruit. It was raining, a steady drizzle, and the grass was lush and thick beneath the hedgerows.

"Wonderful weather for a holiday," said Lisa dryly, flicking a speck of ash off her belted white raincoat. "That's the trouble with England. Unless you're in love with the rain you might just as well spend your holiday abroad."

"Too many people knock England nowadays," said Matt. "Self-criticism can be healthy but constant self-abuse is a mistake."

"Patriotism's out of fashion nowadays, darling," said Lisa. "Everyone says so, even the Americans."

"Mum," said Timothy from the back seat. "Wales isn't England. You said we're going on holiday in England but we're not. We're going to Wales."

"Oh well, it's all the same thing really," said Lisa.

"You'd get lynched if you said that to a crowd of Welshmen," said Matt.

"Uncle Walter says the Gower Peninsula isn't really either Welsh or English," said Lucy, attempting one-upmanship. "He says there are a lot of English names in Gower as well as the Welsh ones and hardly anyone speaks Welsh there as they do in the rest of Wales."

"It's officially Welsh," argued Timothy. "Look at the map."

"I'm bored with the map," said Lucy. She twisted restlessly and pressed her face to the window.

"For heaven's sake, Lucy," said Lisa, "can't you sit still for more than five minutes at a time?"

"Why should I?" said Lucy, tired with the journey and annoyed by what she thought was an unjust criticism. "There's plenty of room in the back here and Timmy doesn't mind."

"Well, I do," said Lisa, "and don't answer back like that. It's rude."

"I'm not the only one in this family that likes to talk back," said Lucy rashly.

"Lucy!"

"That's enough," said Matt shortly in a tone of voice which reduced everyone to silence. "The journey's long enough without everyone trying to make it longer."

"I wish we were there already," said Timothy at last to no one in particular.

So do I, thought Matt.

If only we were on our way to the airport, thought Lisa, en route to Nassau or Bermuda or Jamaica.

"I wish it would stop raining," said Lucy, blowing on the windowpane and drawing a picture on the misted glass. "Surely it'll stop raining soon."

It did. By the time they reached the bleak landscape of the Rhondda Valley the clouds were higher, the rain had stopped, and the sky was clear toward the west. In Swansea the sun was shining, and by the time they reached Colwyn the evening light was already casting a golden glow over the fields which stretched to the sea.

"We can walk up to the castle," said Timothy. It was three years since they had all visited Colwyn Court after Matt's marriage to Lisa and the twins had only been six at the time, but Timothy remembered the ruined castle on top of the cliffs and the sea pounding against the rocks below.

"And the horses," said Lucy. "Don't forget the wild horses by the castle."

"And the caves on the beach!"

"And the rock pools—"

"—and shells—"

"And the silly sheep all along the top of the cliffs—the other cliffs, the cliffs opposite the castle—"

"Maybe Aunt Jane's made some biscuits for us."

"Cakes, I expect."

"Or fudge! Remember Aunt Jane's fudge!"

"Yummy!"

The twins' spirits had revived. They were bouncing around in the back of the Rolls Royce in anticipation.

"I wish we could stay at Colwyn Court," said Lisa, not for the first time. "Can this weird society have taken up *all* the available space? It does seem a shame."

"I'd rather stay with Jane," said Matt. "I'll bet she cooks much better than any housekeeper Walter employs."

"That's Jane's whole problem," said Lisa. "She's too good at cooking. All those calories!"

"Not all men like women who look like lampposts, you know."

"Thanks, darling," said Lisa.

They reached Colwyn Court and Matt took the rough road which led down to the cottage. The Rolls, enormous on the narrow track, purred gently in and out of the potholes with swaying distaste.

"There's Aunt Jane!" squealed Lucy and wound down the window. "Aunt Jane! Hey, have you made fudge for us?"

"Lucy!" exclaimed Lisa. "Haven't you got any manners at all?"

Timothy pushed Lucy out of the way and stuck his own head out of the window. "Have you made a cake?"

Jane was laughing as Matt halted the Rolls behind Benedict's small Austin. "I've made one chocolate cake," she called, "one tray of fudge, and one chocolate trifle."

The twins howled with delight and tumbled out of the car into her arms.

Matt was just opening the door for his wife when Benedict emerged, his scanty hair standing on end, his glasses on the tip of his nose. "God, what a noise!" he said mildly.

"I'm terribly sorry," said Lisa, feeling guilty. "Lucy—Timothy— stop it! That's enough!"

"It's all right," said Jane. "Benedict doesn't really mind . . . How are you all? It's so nice to see you . . ."

There followed several confused moments during which Benedict and Matt coped with the luggage, the twins raced off to sample the chocolate cake, and Lisa sank into an armchair in the living room and requested a drink.

"Yes, of course," said Jane, and hunted around for the bottle of gin which she had bought that morning. It seemed to have disappeared.

"Here it is," said Lisa. "Do you usually keep the drink in the coal scuttle?"

"Oh . . . I must have left it there for some reason . . ." Jane was aware of a growing feeling of helpless disorganization.

"Give it to me," said Lisa competently. "I'll do it. Matt! Do you want a drink?"

"I did buy whiskey as well," said Jane. "It's here somewhere."

Lisa had the drinks mixed in less than three minutes. The men were still upstairs with the luggage, and the twins' voices were receding as they abandoned the cake and wandered out of the back door.

"I can't tell you how awful the journey was," said Lisa. "Thank God it's over. Jane, it's so good to see you—listen, you simply must give me some advice. If your husband decided to go off and live at the North Pole, what on earth would you do?"

"Go with him, I suppose," said Jane, "but I can't see why Benedict would want to go and live at the North Pole."

"Oh Jane, don't be so dim! You see, the point is—"

The two husbands came clattering down the stairs and the conversation was brought to an abrupt end.

"Here's your drink, Matt," said Lisa.

"In a minute," said Matt. "I want to get the case of wine out of the car."

"Case of wine!" ejaculated Benedict, and followed his guest out of the front door to see if he had heard correctly.

"Of course there's always divorce," said Lisa in a low voice. "But . . . well, I don't really want that. I mean, I know I'd get alimony and that sort of thing, but it wouldn't be the same, and you know how it is, Jane, one gets used to all the little luxuries, and besides, the twins . . . I mean, for their sakes I should try to stick it out, shouldn't I? Matt's very good to them, and it's because of him that I can send them to the best schools . . . And I do love Matt. I really do. It's just that lately he hasn't been very understanding—you know how men are sometimes—"

"I suppose so," said Jane. "Well, yes, perhaps. No, I don't think I do. Lisa—"

The men returned with the case of wine between them and set it down on the dining-room table.

"This is very good of you, Matt," said Benedict, examining the label with interest.

"It's very good of you," said Matt, "to have us descend on you like this. Where's that drink, Lisa?"

"Here, darling."

"How's your daughter, Matt?" said Benedict, reaching for his own whiskey and soda.

"Yes, how's Nicola?" said Jane, seizing the chance to avoid thinking about Lisa's marital problems. "I wish she'd come and see us in Cambridge sometimes."

"Well, you know Nicola," said Matt. "She has to be pushed a bit before she does anything. But I'm sure she'd like to visit you."

"Nicola's in such a rut," said Lisa. "Same old job, same old flat in Hampstead. It's such a pity."

"If she's contented I don't see why it's a pity," said Matt sharply. "She's lucky if she's satisfied with the way things are."

"Don't be naive, Matt," said Lisa. "No unmarried unattached girl in her mid-twenties is ever satisfied with the way things are."

"I was," said Jane. "It was one of the happiest times in my life. I was looking after those children in Scotland and having a lovely time. The whole family was so nice."

The conversation drifted into a discussion of Scotland, and Matt, who was a keen fisherman, began to describe the prize salmon he had caught there the previous summer.

Jane suddenly remembered the casserole she had in the oven and set down her glass of sherry. "Heavens, I'd forgotten all about dinner! Excuse me, everyone."

Lisa slipped after her into the kitchen.

"I wonder where the twins are," said Jane, hoping to stave off a further discussion of Lisa's marital situation. "Dinner will be ready in about twenty minutes. Do you think that perhaps you should see if you can find them?"

"Perhaps I should," said Lisa disconsolately. "Can I do anything to help you in here?"

"No, no—it's all right. It looks a muddle, I know, but I think I've got everything under control . . ." She opened the oven door and peered inside.

"Well, maybe we can have a talk later," said Lisa. "Just you and me. I feel I *must* pour out my heart to someone or I'll burst, and you're always so understanding, Jane."

"Hm," said Jane, poking a carrot to see if it was done.

"Maybe tomorrow sometime?"

"All right." To her relief she saw Lisa move over to the back door in search of the twins. "Twenty minutes, Lisa," she called after her.

"Fine, darling. I hope those little monsters haven't gone too far." Lisa wandered away from the house and took the path which led down to the beach. The twins were nowhere in sight. Fortunately she was wearing her new narrow suede walking shoes designed specifically for weekends in the country so she had no difficulty in reaching the beach and setting off toward the caves which she knew the twins had found irresistible on their previous visit to Colwyn.

"Lucy!" called Lisa. "Timothy!" But there was no reply.

She walked on. It had been raining shortly before their arrival, she realized, because the sands were now steaming in the strong light from the sun. The rising steam created a ghostly effect, and Lisa began to have a strange feeling of unreality as if she were moving through the landscape of a fantasy. She could no longer see the caves clearly.

"Lucy!" she called. "Lucy, are you there?"

There was still no answer. Reluctantly she moved forward toward the caves at the foot of the cliff, and as she moved she thought she saw someone drifting toward her through the wraith-like columns of the mist.

Lisa stopped. Like many people at home in a metropolis she had the secret fear of rural isolation and the city nervousness of meeting a stranger when she was alone in a deserted place.

"Who's that?" she called sharply.

It was a man. She still could not see him clearly, but she knew he was tall and wore a dark sweater and dark slacks.

Damn the twins, thought Lisa, bringing me down here like this. She didn't know whether to turn and run or whether to stay and pretend she hadn't a care in the world. Instinct told her to run, but he was too close now and she had a sudden horror of making a fool of herself by bolting for safety like a startled rabbit. She took another look at him and was reassured by what she saw. He looked eminently sane, not in the least like a homicidal maniac on the loose.

"Excuse me," she called, acting on an impulse. "Have you by any chance seen two children, a boy and a girl, about nine years old, fair-haired and blue-eyed?"

"I'm afraid not." He smiled at her. "You must be Mrs. Morrison—am I right?"

Now that he was closer to her and the sinister mist was no longer separating them, she found her fears ebbing and was glad she had not been so foolish as to run away. He looked rather nice. She liked his smile and found herself smiling back.

"How did you know that?" she said, surprised.

"I'm from Colwyn Court and I knew the Shaws were expecting you and your family today."

"Oh," said Lisa, understanding, "you must be one of the Society for—I'm sorry I forget its title, but—"

"Yes, I'm the managing director."

"Oh, I see! Well, how do you do, Mr.—"

"Poole. Tristan Poole. How do you do, Mrs. Morrison." He held out his hand.

Lisa held out her own hand automatically and felt his fingers close on hers. There was a pause. Beyond them the tide was going out and the gulls were wheeling over the wet beach and the steam was still rising from the sands, but Lisa did not notice. All she saw was the line of Poole's jaw and his windblown hair and the bright luminous quality of his eyes.

"Well, well," said Poole. "Things are looking up on the Colwyn estate." And he smiled again.

God, thought Lisa, what an attractive man. "What are you doing down here?" she said, saying the first thing that came into her head. "You look the sort of person who ought to be in London —or Paris or New York."

"And so do you, Mrs. Morrison. Maybe we can help each other adjust to the rigors of country living."

"The Simple Life," said Lisa, thinking of Matt.

"There's no simple life," said Poole. "Just simple people. And some people are more simple than others."

"You can say *that* again," said Lisa, and then checked herself. What was she doing talking to a stranger like this? The unfamiliar country air must be going to her head. "Well," she said, "I really must try to find my children—my sister's going to dish up dinner in ten minutes, and—"

"Let me help you search for them. Are you sure they came down to the beach?"

"No, I—"

"Perhaps they went up to the ruined castle and chapel. That would be the kind of place to appeal to children, I should think."

"Of course!" exclaimed Lisa, remembering that the twins had mentioned the castle earlier in the car. "How silly of me! Why didn't I think of that?"

"It was natural for you to think of the beach first," he said easily and offered her his hand again. "Be careful of the rocks here," he said. "They're very slippery."

Lisa took his hand without a word. Her heart was beginning to thump against her ribs and she knew it wasn't solely due to the scramble up the rocky path from the beach. When she paused for breath at the top, she found her self-restraint was slipping away and her tongue had a will of its own.

"Are you married?" she heard herself say abruptly.

"Not at the moment."

"You mean you've been married?"

"In a certain sense."

Lisa's mind flickered over her vocabulary of sophisticated euphemisms. "You mean you lived with someone," she said, "without the blessing of the church."

He smiled but said nothing.

"I've been married twice," said Lisa. "My first marriage was just about finished when my husband got himself killed. The second isn't doing much better. Sometimes I feel very anti-marriage and think it's the most idiotic social institution."

"You can always opt out."

"No, I can't. I've got too much to lose. There's no question of me getting a divorce."

"Who said anything about a divorce?"

"But . . . well, because either I stay married all the way or else I finish it off completely. Matt wouldn't let me compromise. There's no question of him letting me have some sort of arrangement—I mean, I couldn't possibly consider being unfaithful to him—"

"Who are you trying to fool? Not me, I hope."

"But—"

"All you've lacked so far is the perfect opportunity. Once that comes you won't even hesitate."

"That's not true!" cried Lisa.

"Liar," said Poole, and she felt his long fingers slipping around her waist.

Afterward Lisa could not remember clearly what happened next. She had the incredulous feeling she had actually turned to him and offered her mouth to be kissed, but this couldn't have been true. She had done some wild things in her time but she had never considered herself promiscuous, and what could be more promiscuous than offering oneself to a strange man one had known for only five minutes? But whether her role had been passive or not there could be no doubt that Poole had kissed her on the mouth and that she had clung to him until he had gently disentangled himself.

"We mustn't let your husband see us," he said with a smile, and glanced over his shoulder at the cottage.

Lisa felt herself incapable of speech. She was trembling in every limb. Even movement was impossible.

"It's all right," said Poole. "We were just out of sight of the cottage windows, thanks to this large and very opportune boulder." He gave the boulder a friendly slap with the palm of his hand and turned away from her. "Why don't you come up to the main house tomorrow?"

"All right," said Lisa. Then: "No, I'd better not."

He shrugged, amused by her ineffectual struggles with her conscience and commonsense.

"I have to go now," said Lisa, not moving. "I must go."

"Well, if you must," said Poole, "I suppose you must."

They stood still, facing each other. Poole suddenly made an odd gesture with his hand. "Go ahead."

Strength and coordination seeped back into Lisa's limbs. She began to run. The path led uphill and her breath was soon sobbing in her throat but she went on running. She ran until she reached the back door of the cottage and stood panting on the threshold of the empty kitchen.

Jane came in a second later. "Lisa! What's the matter? What's happened?"

"Nothing," said Lisa fiercely. "Nothing."

"But—"

"Don't talk to me."

"All right," said Jane. "The twins came back, by the way, and I sent them upstairs to wash their hands. Dinner'll be in about five minutes. The vegetables took a bit longer than I thought they would, so—"

Lisa went into the living room. Matt was telling Benedict about the characteristics of the salmon which were found in the River Wye.

Lisa ran upstairs, and through the open door of the bathroom she saw the twins pause to look at her guiltily as they washed their hands in the basin.

"I'm sorry if you went searching for us, Mum," said Timothy at last. The twins had long since decided that Timothy was the best at apologizing. "We didn't mean to make you upset."

"It's all right, darlings," said Lisa. "I'm not upset." And seeing one of her suitcases in a nearby bedroom she plunged across the threshold, slammed the door behind her, and collapsed in a heap upon the bed.

*ii*

"Maybe we ought to walk up to the main house this morning," Matt said to Lisa as they dressed before breakfast the next day. "We ought to see Walter and Gwyneth."

"I don't think I want to do that," said Lisa in a rush, and as

Matt looked at her in astonishment she added, confused: "I mean, I want to see Walter and Gwyneth but I don't want to go up to Colwyn Court just yet. Maybe they'll come down here to visit us instead."

"Why the devil don't you want to go up to Colwyn Court?"

"Oh . . ." Lisa looked listless. "I don't feel like walking anywhere today. I don't feel too well."

It was a weak excuse but to her relief Matt seemed to accept it without an argument.

"All right," he said. "I'll take the twins up there this morning for a few minutes to be polite, and while we're there I'll suggest to Walter that he and Gwyneth come down to the cottage some time this afternoon. I'm sorry you're not feeling good—why don't you stay in bed this morning and rest?"

"Well, I might, I suppose," said Lisa, but she did not. As soon as Matt and the twins had left after breakfast she put on her blue and white pantsuit, applied her makeup to give her a casual country-style complexion, and tied back her thick blond hair with a scarf which matched the blue of her outfit.

"I'm going down to the beach, Jane," she said, finding her sister in the kitchen. "I think the sea air might do me some good . . . can I give you a hand with that washing up?"

"Of course not!" said Jane, fearing a forthcoming discussion of Lisa's problems. "You're on holiday! I'm glad you're feeling better."

"It was just that I felt tired after the journey," said Lisa vaguely. "I feel more rested now." She wandered through the open back door and Jane's cat followed her, his pink tongue licking furtively around the corners of his mouth as if he expected her to give him something delicious to eat.

"Shoo!" said Lisa, afraid of Marble's dirty paws on the pastel shades of her pantsuit. "Scram!"

But he followed her all the way to the top of the beach and only turned back when she began to scramble down over the rocks to the sand. She saw him dart away in the direction of Colwyn Court, his fluffy tail waving behind him, his legs moving so fast that they were a mere white blur against the brown of the path.

Lisa wandered across the beach and watched the incoming tide. The sun shone fitfully; the air was cool but Lisa was warm enough in her jacket and sweater and did not notice. She stood watching the sea for a long time, watching the white foam bite into the sand as the surf thudded on the beach, and when she turned at last and found herself no longer alone she was aware only of a surprise that she should be so unsurprised. The next moment her heart was beating very fast and her mouth was dry and her spine was tingling with anticipation.

"Hello, Lisa," said Tristan Poole as he strolled across the sands toward her. "How very nice to see you again."

### iii

"Uncle Matt," said Lucy, taking her stepfather's hand. "Let's go up to the castle."

The social politenesses had been exchanged at Colwyn Court. The twins had drunk lemonade and eaten ginger biscuits while Walter had shown them the latest additions to his collection of rare wild flowers and Gwyneth had graciously allowed them to hear the tangled notes of the latest single to reach the top of the hit parade.

"I like Gwyneth," Timothy had said to Lucy. "She's not really like a grown-up at all."

After the interlude with Gwyneth they had met Miss Agnes Miller of the Society for the Propagation of Nature Foods, and had played their "twins" role beautifully for her, gazing at her with wide innocent eyes and smiling sweetly as she had exclaimed what fun it must be to be twins and how they looked just like two little angels.

"Looks can be deceiving, Miss Miller!" Matt had retorted, and all the grown-ups had laughed—very fatuously, the twins had thought. "You're little devils really, aren't you, twins?"

"Fiends incarnate," Lucy had said sedately, and Miss Miller had given her a very odd look indeed.

"I didn't like that Miss Miller," Timothy had said afterward.

"Why not? She was just another silly old woman. You know how stupid they get at that age."

Finally after several glasses of lemonade and innumerable ginger biscuits, the social obligations had been completed and Matt had led the twins through the garden and down the path to the cottage.

"Were we all right, Uncle Matt?" Lucy had demanded, knowing they had been on their best behavior but anxious for a compliment. "Were we good?"

"Perfect!" Matt had smiled broadly at her as she bounced up and down at his side. "You both were."

It had been then that Lucy, flushed with triumph, had suggested that they all walk up to the castle.

"You don't want an old man like me tagging along, do you?" said Matt, thinking he ought to return to the cottage to see how Lisa was.

"Yes, yes, yes!" cried Lucy, and grabbed his hand to imprison him.

"Triple-yes!" yelled Timothy and grabbed the other hand so that the prisoner had no chance to escape.

"Okay!" Matt laughed. "Whoa!" It wouldn't matter about Lisa. She'd probably be still lying in bed and sulking about the Bahamas. "All right, we'll go up to the castle."

The castle had been built some six hundred years ago after Edward I had subjugated the Welsh, but had already been abandoned by the time the Tudors came to power at the end of the fifteenth century, and was now a mere weathered ruin astride the cliffs on the west side of Colwyn Cove. There was part of a keep, the shell of a tower and an assortment of scattered walls, while through the Norman windows one could still look out across the headland to the sea, the surf, and the sands.

"Isn't it a super place?" said Timothy with shining eyes.

Adjoining the castle was a chapel, roofless but better preserved than the castle itself. An archeologist had told Walter the chapel had been built later with bricks from the castle that had already begun to fall into disrepair, but the chapel had not been used since the time of the Reformation and its active life must have been short. Walter had applied for a grant from the Ministry of Works to keep the ruins safe and prevent them from deteriorating further, and in return he was obliged to open the grounds of Colwyn Court to the public once a month so that the taxpayers could see the castle and chapel on which their money had been spent. But few people came. There were no printed guidebooks available for them, no postcards, no snack bars or souvenir shops, and most of the tourists who visited the area could not be bothered to investigate what many would have considered to be "just another heap of old ruins."

Around the castle were about twenty of the wild horses from the family which had existed on the Colwyn estate since time out of mind. They were lean graceful animals with long necks, soft eyes, and tails which streamed in the wind whenever they galloped down the hill to the shore. They began to gallop now as Matt and the twins approached the castle, and a minute later the entire herd was thundering down the path which led into the next cove where a stream flowing into the sea provided the horses with a supply of fresh water.

"I'd like to live here," said Timothy. "Forever. In the castle with my own horse." When he saw that Matt was a few paces away and gazing down into Colwyn Cove he whispered to Lucy: "If Daddy got out of China—"

"Timmy, we'd agreed it was Tibet!"

"Maybe he's in India by now. Is India next to Tibet? But when he finally gets home—"

"With all his riches," said Lucy, "his jewels from the Taj Mahal, he could restore the castle and we could all live in it—"

"—forever," said Timothy, and added suddenly: "What's Uncle Matt looking at?"

"I don't know . . . Uncle Matt! What are you looking at?"

Matt did not answer so the twins wandered over to him to see for themselves.

"Why, it's Mummy!" said Lucy surprised. "On the beach! Who's that man?"

"Let's go and find out," said Matt, and set off abruptly down the hill from the castle.

"Hey, wait for us!" cried Lucy.

"Wait, Uncle Matt!" called Timothy, but Matt barely slackened his pace and they were obliged to run to keep up with him.

"They're leaving the beach," panted Timothy after a minute. "They'll just be at the top of the rocks by the time we get there."

"Let's race them," said Lucy, inspired by Matt's long strides. "Come on, Timmy, let's run!"

They ran, rushing downhill to the top of the beach, and presently arrived gasping for breath at the path which led from the beach to the cottage.

"Ooooh!" panted Lucy, clutching her side. "I've got a stitch!"

"Me too!" Timothy flopped down in the heather.

"Where's Mummy? Oh, here she comes. Gosh, the man with her looks like the man in that TV series."

"Which series?"

"*You* know, stupid . . . oh, he's not so like him after all. But he looks nice anyway. Nicer than the man in the TV series."

Timothy did not answer. He stood up slowly, watching his mother and thinking how pretty she looked. Her cheeks were pink from the sea breeze and her eyes were sparkling and her hair shimmered in the pale sunlight.

"Darlings!" said Lisa. "What a lovely surprise! Have you been to Colwyn Court already?"

"And up to the castle." Lucy looked at Poole. "Who's this?"

"This is Mr. Poole, who's the managing director of the society at Colwyn Court. Tristan, this is—"

"How do you do," said Lucy, jumping at the chance to demonstrate yet again how exquisitely she could behave if the occasion demanded it. She gave her sweetest, most innocent smile, the one that never failed, and said with her best diction: "We met Miss Miller at Colwyn Court just now. She mentioned you and told us all about your wonderful society. We thought she was such a nice lady, didn't we, Timothy?"

For some reason which he did not understand, Timothy was acutely embarrassed. He could feel himself blushing and turned away to hide his confusion.

Poole was smiling. He saw Timothy's discomfort and noted it. He saw Lucy's long, straight, fair hair, her wide, black-lashed, violet eyes and her rose-colored mouth, and noted that she was an exceptionally pretty child. He saw the innocence in her eyes and the angelic expression on her face and noted that she was lying about Agnes Miller. But he went on smiling.

"Hello, Lucy," he said pleasantly.

The child hesitated, but after a second smiled back willingly enough.

"Timothy, say how do you do to Mr. Poole," said Lisa sharply, but Timothy was rescued from having to respond by Matt's arrival on the scene. Lisa was at once diverted. "Matt," she began, "this is Mr. Tristan Poole, the managing director of the society at Colwyn Court . . . Tristan, this is my husband."

The two men looked at one another. There was a small pause before Poole held out his hand and murmured a conventional phrase.

Matt took the hand, shook it once and dropped it without a word. "Do you feel better?" he said without expression to his wife.

"Marvelous!" said Lisa rashly and added, making matters worse: "The sea air cured me completely!"

There was another pause.

"Tristan's invited us up to Colwyn Court for lunch," said Lisa in a rush. "All of us, I mean. I was just on my way up to the cottage to tell Jane not to bother to cook anything for us."

"I've made other plans," said Matt.

"Oh, but—"

Matt looked at her with an expression he had perfected in a thousand board meetings and she was silent.

"Some other time perhaps," said Poole carelessly. "There's no reason why it should have to be today. And now, if you'll excuse me . . ." He moved away, casual and unconcerned, and as he took the path up to Colwyn Court they could hear him whistling to himself before he disappeared from sight.

"Darlings," said Lisa to the twins, "run on ahead to the cottage for me, would you, and tell Aunt Jane I shan't be in for lunch."

The twins looked at Matt but Matt said nothing.

"Run along," said Lisa with a smile.

The twins turned and walked away toward the cottage without a word. After a moment they joined hands and began to walk two abreast on the narrow path, but they made no attempt to look back.

"All right," said Matt in a low voice. "Talk and talk fast. Just what the bloody hell's going on?"

"Matt, I—"

"And don't start lying or you'll be sorry! I saw what you were doing on the beach!"

"But Matt, we weren't doing anything—"

He slapped her across the mouth and she stepped backward with a gasp.

"Why, you—"

"I told you you'd be sorry," he said, "if you started lying."

"How dare you strike me like that! If you were a gentleman instead of someone who'd dragged himself out of a Birmingham backstreet—"

"Don't give me that kind of rubbish. If you were a lady instead of the selfish little bitch you are I wouldn't have laid a finger on you. Now look here, Lisa. I don't know who that man is and I don't know how long you've known him, but I know this: You're not seeing him again. If you're flirting with him to pay me back for not giving in to you about the Bahamas—"

"I wasn't flirting with him! Just because I choose to sit on the beach with an attractive man my own age—"

"You were lying full length on the sand and he was kissing you until he became aware that he was being watched. Don't be a damned fool, Lisa! You can't get out of this by lying, so why waste breath trying to? If the twins hadn't been here I'd have taken that man by the scruff of his neck and thrown him back onto the beach. You're not seeing him again and you're not going up to Colwyn Court for lunch."

"Oh, don't be so absurd, Matt! Walter will be there, and Gwyneth, and Tristan's assistant, Miss Miller—"

"Look," said Matt. "Do I really have to spell it out to you? I may be old-fashioned, but I have certain views and I've no intention of changing them. You're my wife, and as long as you're my wife you don't play around with other men. If I catch you so much as batting an eyelid at that bastard again, I'll—"

"Oh Matt!" Lisa burst into tears. The tears happened to be entirely genuine, but it was the cleverest move she could have made; like most men given to flexing the dominant side of their personalities, Matt was softhearted beneath the steel of his boardroom manner.

"Now Lisa . . ." He could feel himself weakening.

"You just don't understand me!" sobbed Lisa, twisting away from his outstretched arms, and stumbled off, still sobbing wildly, up the path to the shelter of the cottage.

But Matt was afraid he understood all too well.

### iv

In the afternoon Jane took the twins down to the beach, Benedict returned to his work and Lisa remained in her bedroom to which she had retired before lunch. Matt was on his own. After considering several ways of passing the afternoon he rejected all of them and drove his car out of the Gower Peninsula toward Swansea. In the suburbs he stopped at a cluster of shops, found a telephone kiosk, and began to count his change for a London call.

"I want a person-to-person call," he told the operator. "To Miss Nicola Morrison. Hampstead 59611."

But Nicola was out. It was a Saturday and she had gone off on some expedition of her own.

"Sorry," he heard the roommate's cheerful voice say to the operator, "but I'll tell her who phoned as soon as she gets in." The operator had disclosed Matt's identity at the start of the call.

Matt sighed. He did not know why he had had such a strong urge to talk to his daughter but he felt alone and unhappy and Nicola was all the family he had in the world.

The telephone was ringing just as he walked through the front door of the cottage. Benedict, taking a nap upstairs, had not heard the bell, and no one else seemed to be about.

Matt picked up the receiver. "Hello?"

"Daddy? I've just got in. Judy said you'd phoned but I had an awful job getting through to the cottage—the operator said first of all that it wasn't on the phone. How's everything at Colwyn?"

"Well . . ." He glanced up the stairs to see if the door of Lisa's room was shut, but found he could not see the door from where he was standing. "Not too good. Walter's leased half the place to some crazy health-food group and I think Lisa's about to join."

"Oh Lord! Daddy, you're not serious, are you?"

He ignored that one. "Why don't you come down for a few days? Walter and Gwyneth were both asking after you when I saw them this morning."

"Oh, I couldn't possibly."

"Why not?"

"Well . . . my holiday doesn't crop up till September."

"Take it earlier."

"It would be too much of an inconvenience to my boss."

"Rubbish," said Matt. "No one's indispensable. That boss of yours would appreciate you more if you didn't fall in with his wishes just for once."

"Well . . ."

"Evan isn't here, you know. He's not due back till next week."

"It's got nothing to do with that," said Nicola, knowing perfectly well that her reluctance to visit Colwyn was because it was so full of memories of Evan and the good times they had had there together. "Nothing at all."

"Well, think about it. There's not much room here at the cottage but Gwyneth said there was still one spare room at Colwyn

Court in spite of the damned society." He heard the door of Lisa's room open with a small creak. "How's life in Hampstead?"

"Fine. No news really."

"All right, well, look after yourself and try to get down here if you can. I hardly see anything of you nowadays."

Nicola felt guilty. After they had said good-bye and she had replaced the receiver she spent some time wishing that Lisa did not make visits home such a trial. And what had Matt meant about the society and Lisa's interest in it? Nicola frowned and wandered into the kitchen to make herself some coffee. For the first time she began to wonder if her father were as happily married as she had always assumed he was; her brief, uneasy visits home had given her no obvious hints that Matt and Lisa's relationship was not all it should have been.

She was still thinking of them ten minutes later when the phone rang. Judy was out by this time and Nicola was alone in the apartment. Tilting back her chair she reached for the receiver.

"Hello?"

There was a stream of pips from an STD phone before the coin dropped and the line cleared. She heard some assorted background sounds which suggested that the call was being made in a transport terminal; there was the distant drone of a loudspeaker announcement, the dull murmur of footsteps and voices.

"Hello?" repeated Nicola.

"Hello," said the voice she had told herself a thousand times she would never hear again. "So you're still at the same flat. How are you?"

The shock was so great that she could not speak. It was a hallucination, she thought. She was going mad.

"Nicki, are you there?"

He sounded just the same, terse and friendly, and suddenly she could see him, his red hair short and tousled, the freckled nose broken long ago at rugger, the blue, humorous eyes.

"It can't be," she said aloud. "You're not here till next week. It's a hoax."

"Some hoax!" He spoke lightly but she knew he was having trouble choosing his words. "I've been worried about my father and I managed to get away early from Africa. My plane arrived half an hour ago, and at the moment you're the only person in the entire country who knows I'm here."

"Is that a cue to swoon with delight?" She could have kicked herself as soon as the words were spoken; she had had no wish to sound so sarcastic.

"No, I don't expect that." She knew he was rebuffed and her heart ached. She wanted to say: "I'm so glad you're back! I'm so glad you phoned! Oh, how I'd love to see you again!" but all she found herself saying was: "When are you going down to Colwyn?"

"Tomorrow. But I thought I'd rest tonight in London to recover from the long journey. Look, Nicki—"

"Yes?" she said, her mouth dry.

"—you won't tell anyone I'm here, will you? I want to take them by surprise at Colwyn."

"All right."

There was a silence. I must say something, thought Nicola desperately, or he'll go away. "How was Africa?" she asked, saying the first thing that came into her head, and her words sounded horribly bright and false to her. "It must have been a wonderful experience."

"Yes."

Oh God, thought Nicola. She was clenching the phone so tightly her fingers hurt. Say something, she prayed silently. Please. Say something. Don't hang up. Please.

"Nicki," said Evan.

"Yes?"

"I had a lot of time to think in Africa."

"Oh."

"I would have written, but—"

"No, I told you not to."

"Yes, I know but . . . well, I almost wrote many times."

"Did you?" Tears filled her eyes. She had to struggle to keep her voice level.

"Yes, I . . . well, it seemed so unnecessary in retrospect. The way things ended . . . you understand? Although maybe you were justified in taking the line you did, but—"

"You were justified too," said Nicola. "I should have realized that going to Africa was something you had to do."

"Yes. Well . . ." She heard him take a deep breath. "I suppose you've got someone else by this time," said Evan, "but perhaps we could meet just for old time's sake. What do you think?"

"Why not?" said Nicola. Her blandness amazed and appalled her. How could she possibly sound so indifferent? She began to panic again. "Yes," she said, trying to sound enthusiastic but only managing to recapture that awful false brightness. "That would be nice."

"How about a drink tonight? As it's Saturday I suppose you'll have already made arrangements for dinner, but—"

"Not this Saturday," said Nicola.

"No? Well, how about dinner as well?"

She realized to her astonishment that she was crying. Huge tears were rolling silently down her cheeks. "Yes," she said. "I'd like that."

"Good. I'll hire a car and pick you up at six-thirty."

"Fine."

"Marvelous! See you soon, Nicki," he said, pleased, and was so excited he even forgot to say good-bye. Bursting out of the phone booth he grabbed his suitcases, collared a taxi, and sang out the address of the hotel in Central London where he had reserved a room for the night. He was home, he was within hours of seeing Nicola again, and as the cab swept him toward the city he forgot all his worries about his family and thought only of the evening to come.

v

After everyone else at the cottage had gone to bed that night Matt stayed up to write to his daughter. It was quiet. A few hundred yards away the sea was breaking on the sands but apart from the murmur of the surf and the tick of the grandfather clock by the stairs the house was silent. The twins were long since asleep; Lisa had gone upstairs complaining of a headache directly after dinner, and Benedict had stubbed out his last cigarette an hour ago to follow Jane upstairs to their room. Matt was alone.

". . . so that's how the land lies at the moment," he was writing to Nicola as he tried to unburden himself of his pain by spelling it out on paper. "By the way, have you ever heard of this man Tristan Poole? He's a youngish bloke about Lisa's age . . ."

That hurt, he thought looking at the words wryly and remembering that he was now nearer sixty than fifty. But it served him right for marrying a girl young enough to be his daughter.

". . . ordinary looking, nothing obviously special about him, casual sort of manner, polite and well spoken—I wondered if you might have bumped into him at one of your London parties, but maybe that would be too much of a long shot. However, I'm sure Lisa's met him before—can't believe she's only met him twice and both times just for a few minutes, though she swears that's the truth. She's been making a real fool of herself so far, but I think I've straightened things out a bit now . . ."

He wished Nicola were with him in the room. Nicola was the only person he could talk to when he was very depressed. He remembered the hours they had spent together after her mother had died years ago. He had always felt very close to Nicola after that. Until he had married Lisa.

". . . yet I wish there were a hundred miles between Lisa and this so-and-so Poole," he wrote, his pen digging into the white paper so that the words glared boldly back at him. "I wouldn't be surprised if he was something of a crook. Walter Colwyn's one of the most gullible men under the sun and you know how things are with Gwyneth . . ."

The door creaked. He looked up sharply but it was only the cat coming in from the kitchen.

". . . I think Evan will have something to say about affairs at Colwyn Court once he gets back from Africa. I hope he doesn't find that Poole's conned Walter out of his home and fortune . . ."

Marble sat on the hearth and began to wash his paws.

". . . sorry this is all about Poole but the blighter happens to have upset me. I can tell you, if I find Lisa messing around with him again there'll be all hell to pay because I'm too proud to stomach that sort of thing, and that's a fact. I'd rather be divorced than made a fool of—and the truth is I don't think Lisa would mind a divorce if it weren't for the money. Well, she'll get my money when I'm alive but that's it. If there's any more fuss I'll see she doesn't get a penny after I'm dead . . ."

He stopped. He suddenly realized that the cat had sprung onto the dresser behind him and was breathing down his neck.

"Off!" said Matt sternly, and when the cat did not move he gave it a shove onto the floor.

Marble yelped. His pink eyes narrowed to hostile slits.

Matt added a sentence to finish the letter, addressed an envelope, and put the letter inside. It was time to go to bed. Leaving the sealed letter on the table he went slowly upstairs to his room where Lisa was pretending to be asleep, and the living room was plunged into darkness as he switched off the light.

Marble waited for several minutes. Then, when even the light beneath Matt's bedroom door had vanished, he sprang onto the table, picked the letter up between his sharp white teeth, and disappeared silently into the night.

## vi

"That's odd," said Matt. "Jane, did you move the letter I left on the table last night?"

"Letter? No, I didn't. I don't think I even noticed it. Benedict, did you see a letter which Matt left on the table in the living room?"

"There wasn't one," said Benedict. "I was downstairs at seven and there was nothing on the living-room table. I particularly noticed because I put my foot on the chair there to retie a shoelace."

"Twins," said Jane, "did you see a letter Uncle Matt left on the living-room table last night?"

"No," said Timothy. "What's for breakfast, Aunt Jane?"

"Sausages and eggs. Lucy, did you—"

"No," said Lucy yawning. "Can I have my egg poached, please?"

"Not today, it's too complicated. I'm scrambling them all," said Jane, and added to Matt, "Are you sure you left it there?"

"It's all right," said Matt. "I think I can guess what happened." And he went swiftly upstairs to his room.

Lisa was dressed and sitting at the dressing table examining her mascara brush. She looked up as he came in.

"Okay," said Matt. "Where is it?"

"Where's what?" said Lisa astonished.

"The letter I wrote to Nicola last night."

"My dear Matt! Why on earth should I take a letter you wrote to Nicola?"

"Because I said a few uncomplimentary things to Nicola about your precious Mr. Poole!"

Lisa did not know whether to feel bewildered, angry, or indignant. In the end anger won. "How dare you tell Nicola about what happened between me and Tristan!"

"So you did take it," said Matt.

"I didn't!"

"Then how did you know I'd told Nicola you'd made a fool of yourself with that man!"

"You said—"

"I said I told her about Poole. I didn't tell you what it was I said."

"But I thought—"

"Where is it, Lisa?"

"But I didn't take it!" said Lisa desperately. "I didn't!"

"You got up in the night, went downstairs—"

"I never moved from this room!" Anger blazed through her again. "How dare you tell that daughter of yours about our private and personal troubles!"

"You think everyone doesn't know about them already?" He turned, made sure the door was tightly shut, and swung back to face her. "All right," he said shortly. "Let's sit down and consider this quietly for a moment. I think it's time you and I had a very serious talk together."

## vii

An hour later a disheveled and breathless Lisa arrived at Colwyn Court and asked to speak to Tristan Poole.

"I'll fetch him," said Agnes when the message was brought to her in the kitchens. "Show her into the sitting room." She had just finished delegating the morning's chores and was herself helping to dry the breakfast dishes.

Poole was in his room. When she knocked he came to the door. "Yes?"

"Lisa's here to see you."

"Trouble?"

"I've no idea—I haven't seen her."

He turned back into his room without a word. She saw one of his books was lying open on the bedside table, and in the dressing room beyond the black box was unlocked and the lid thrown back.

"Was there some complication, Tristan?"

"Morrison's hard to control. He's a tough customer." He shut the book with a bang and went into the dressing room to replace it in the black box. When he returned all he said was a casual: "Where is she?"

"Downstairs in the sitting room."

"All right, I'll see her." He gave Agnes a folded sheet of notepaper as he passed her in the doorway. "Read that and burn it."

"Yes, Tristan." She glanced down and began to read Matt's letter to Nicola.

She was still in his room, still looking at the letter, when he rejoined her ten minutes later. He found her sitting on the edge of the bed and looking thoughtful; as he entered the room she looked up with a start.

"Has she gone already?"

"She's still there. I had to have a quick word with you. Listen, Agnes, this marriage is disintegrating much too fast for my liking. I hoped we'd find him the doting husband anxious to shower his young wife with everything he possessed but as you can see from the letter, it isn't like that at all—quite the reverse, in fact. They had a bad quarrel this morning when he blamed her for the lost letter, and one thing led to another until the word divorce was being bandied around like a ping-pong ball. It was a pity about the letter, of course, but it might have had unfortunate repercussions if it had been sent and anyway the marriage is so rocky that if the letter hadn't started the latest quarrel something else would have done. So we've got to act and act fast. She says Morrison took the car and drove off to Swansea in a rage—the situation's highly inflammable, but I reckon we've still got twenty-four hours before he makes any definite move which would be adverse to us. Now this is what I want you to do: drive down to the village, go to the public phone box there, and call me here at Colwyn Court. I'll take the call in the sitting room in Lisa's presence and tell her I've had an urgent summons to Swansea. That'll get her out of the way. Then, when you come back, make sure no one disturbs me. How are we off for sacrifices?"

"We've got four black cocks and six hares at the moment."

"Good. Bring one of the cocks to my room. After the sacrifice I'll give you the bloodstained knife and you can cut the hazel rod for the wand while I take a bath and get into my robes. Oh, and purify my room, please. You'd better do that first. Use juice from laurel leaves, camphor, white resin, and sulfur—and don't omit the salt. I know salt is anathema to us all, but it does represent purity and I want to run no risk of the room not being purified. We're running enough risks as it is by not cutting the hazel rod at dawn and taking all the other routine precautions, but time's running against us so we have no choice."

"Yes, Tristan. And when you're ready—shall I help you draw the circle? Would you like me to be in attendance?"

"Did you eat breakfast this morning?"

Agnes' face fell.

"I'm sorry, Agnes, but I'd better have someone who's at least gone through the motions of fasting. Who's dieting hard enough at present to have skipped breakfast?"

"There's Jackie. But—"

"She'll do. I'll need a clairvoyant anyway."

"Try Sandra," suggested Agnes. "Her powers are so much better developed in that direction, and she never has more than a glass of orange juice for breakfast."

"No, it's time Jackie earned her keep, and besides it'll alleviate her boredom with country life for a few hours. Oh, and Agnes—"

"Yes, Tristan?"

"Summon the cat."

## viii

Matt was a man accustomed to summing up evidence and making a quick decision under pressure. He had been conducting his business affairs in that manner for over thirty years and when the opportunity presented itself to him he had no hesitation in handling his private affairs in exactly the same way. The latest bitter quarrel with Lisa had presented him with what he considered was irrefutable evidence: his wife did not love him, had secretly wanted a divorce for some time, and had only hesitated because of his money and material possessions. All right, he thought furiously, all right. Perhaps it was his fault for losing his head in a middle-aged infatuation with a girl such as Lisa. Perhaps he shouldn't have married her in the first place. But they had married and the marriage had failed and now he wanted to recognize the fact by severing his marital ties to Lisa as soon as possible. Matt preferred to be honest. He preferred to face the truth, accept it, and learn to live with it. It was part of the strength on which he had always prided himself. So now he faced the end of his marriage, and in facing it he faced it in his own hardheaded practical way and immediately began to think about his money.

As soon as he reached Swansea that morning he went to one of the largest hotels, used their writing room for ten minutes, and then made a long-distance call from the public phone in the lobby.

A string of rules, learned long ago when he had been making his way in the world, kept flickering back and forth in his mind. Never put off till tomorrow what you can do today. Examine the evidence, make the decision, and stick to it. Indecision and hesitation lost both time and money. Indecision and hesitation were signs of weakness.

Just before he made the phone call he thought: men of my age drop dead with coronaries every day. Leave nothing to chance. Nothing.

His conversation on the phone lasted some time because the man on the other end of the wire was so doubtful and disapproving, but at last it was over and Matt was able to complete the necessary formalities of the task he had set himself. His next step was to consider what he should do next. After some consideration he decided to return to the cottage to see what had happened in his absence; if Lisa had gone he would stay on to complete his holiday as planned, but if she were still there he would have to forgo the holiday and leave the cottage himself. He found himself wondering what would happen to the twins. Would Lisa take them with her when she left the cottage or would she leave them with Jane while she saw her lawyers and tried to reorganize her private life? He did not know, but his mouth twisted in bitter regret as he thought of them.

The drive out of Swansea was uneventful, but as he entered the Gower Peninsula he increased the speed of the car until he was cutting corners on the empty road and ignoring the signs posting the speed limit. A light rain began to fall as he approached Colwyn; the open landscape looked bleak as it stretched to the gray blur of the sea. By this time he was in farming country, and on either side of the road stood the stone walls which bordered the fields.

He did not see the cat until too late. He swung around a corner and there it was, sitting in the middle of the road and washing its damnable white paws as if it had every right in the world to sit there.

Shouting a curse, Matt slammed on the brakes and wrenched the wheel. The last thing he saw before the car slewed out of control was the cat leaping for safety, its white fur flying and its skin drawn back in a sneer from its sharp malevolent teeth.

Myrtle Pilcher

# Chapter Four

*i*

Evan was confused. He had been looking forward to seeing Nicola again so much that when the time had come and they were finally face to face he had been conscious only of a sense of anticlimax. He had raced to her apartment that Saturday evening in a fever of anticipation—his hand had even been shaking when he had rung the doorbell—but once she had opened the door he had found it hard to know what to say.

Even now, at the end of the evening, he could not understand what had happened. Why, he asked himself in bewilderment, should he feel so disappointed? It was not that she did not look her best. Her shining dark hair curled softly upward at the ends, just as it always had; her gray eyes were just as wide, just as steady and just as beautiful as he remembered. But the spontaneity he had liked so much had ebbed; she seemed more serious, more withdrawn, and much harder to approach. Finally he decided it was the formality of her manner which grated on him the most.

"Would you like to come in and have a drink before we leave?" she had asked him politely when he had arrived at the apartment at six-thirty, and he had been unable to tell whether she had wanted him to accept the invitation or not.

"Well . . . I don't want to disturb your roommate—"

"She went home for the weekend this afternoon."

"Oh. Well, perhaps later . . ."

But later he wasn't asked.

"Can I come up?" he said at last after that baffling evening during which he had sustained a seemingly endless conversation about Africa. The taxi had halted outside the house where Nicola had her flat, and he had helped her out of the car before paying off the driver.

"Yes, all right," she said without much interest and turned away as he told the driver not to wait.

They went into the house, through the hall and up the stairs to the landing without saying a word. Evan wondered why he had invited himself in. After such a stilted evening his first impulse should have been to escape as soon as possible, but some stubborn instinct made him insist on extending the evening until he had made contact with Nicola on a more intimate level. He felt he had invested so much time thinking about her while he was in Africa that it would be too humiliating now to turn his back on her without a struggle to understand what had happened.

"Coffee?" she said in that polite voice he had come to detest.

"Please." He began to roam around the living room while she went into the kitchen. After a minute he could feel the frustration welling inside him till he could bear it no longer. "Nicki."

"Yes?"

"What happened?"

She looked up with a start. "Nothing! What do you mean?"

"There's someone else, isn't there?"

"No." She thrust the kettle onto the stove and turned on the gas. "It's instant coffee—I hope you don't mind."

"Would you rather I left?"

She shook her head violently and began to drag the cups and saucers from the cabinet.

"Who is he?"

No answer. Anger began to mingle with Evan's frustration. "Why didn't you tell me to get lost if you didn't want to see me again? Why lead me on? What was the point?"

"I did want to see you again. I'm sorry the evening was a failure." She had her back to him and was shoveling the coffee jerkily into the cups.

"Oh, for God's sake!" He tried to clamp down on his rage. "Let's stop playing around, shall we? Why don't we get right down to the truth? You've found someone else, you saw me merely as a friendly gesture for old times' sake, and I've made a complete fool of myself. That's the way it is, isn't it?"

No answer.

"Are you sleeping with him?"

That got to her. He saw her back stiffen with pride and her head jerk up.

"No."

"So there *is* someone else!"

"No."

"Then why—"

"No, no, no!" She whirled to face him, her composure gone, her eyes bright with tears. "There's no one else—no one, no one, no one! Now go away and leave me alone!"

"Nicki . . ." When he took her in his arms she made no effort to push him away. He began to kiss her. On the stove the kettle began to boil but neither of them noticed.

"Evan, I—"

He kissed her on the mouth, and suddenly everything was as he remembered and her body was soft and yielding against his own.

"Oh, how I've missed you!" he heard her say when her mouth was free again. "Oh, how I've longed for you to be here . . ."

He was hazily aware of steam from a boiling kettle and the harsh glare from the overhead light, but he had forgotten where he was. The world was reduced to shining dark hair and smooth, silky skin and his own aching longing.

"Here . . ." He kept one arm tightly around her waist and groped for the door.

"Evan—"

He picked her up to avoid argument. It was so easy to swing her off her feet and edge out of the kitchen toward the closed door of the bedroom.

"Open the door," he said to her as he held her in his arms, and waited for her to reach out with her free hand, but she did not. "Go on, open it."

"Evan, I—"

He set her down, flung open the door so violently that it shuddered on its hinges, and turned to pull her into the bedroom with him, but she had moved away.

"Nicki," he said. "Nicki."

She stood there looking at him, and there was a silence. At last she said: "You must think I'm an awful fool."

"Look, I love you. I'm crazy about you. I—"

"So you said fifteen months ago. Those were your exact words."

"Things are different now—"

"They'd damned well better be," she said, "or I want no part of it."

"Listen, I—"

"No!" she said, suddenly as spontaneous and honest as he remembered her to be. "No, you listen to me for a change! For three whole years, ever since my father remarried and I happened to meet you and your family through Lisa and Jane, I've been mooning around over you like some teen-ager with a crush on the current teen idol. After the first eighteen months—during which you barely noticed my existence—you finally looked down from your high and mighty cloud and noticed me. Marvelous! No wonder I lost my head and acted like a crazy schoolgirl without an ounce of sense! All right, so you went away. Served me right. It was no more than I deserved. I then had a whole year to recover. Fine! Just what I needed! And yet now—*now* you have the insufferable nerve to wander back from Africa, glance down from your high cloud again, and think you can carry on exactly where you left off! How dare you think that! If you knew what I've been going through all these months while you've been flexing your noble soul in the wilds of Africa—"

"I'm sorry. I didn't mean it to seem that way."

"Well, it did!"

"But Nicki—"

She backed away from him into the kitchen. "Don't ask me to do what you want now," she said, "because I won't. I'm too scared of getting hurt again."

"But Nicki, I promise—"

"Yes?" she said fiercely, turning off the kettle. "What do you promise?"

But Evan wasn't sure. It seemed to be the wrong moment for a proposal, and besides he wasn't at all certain he ought to propose until he had settled down again in England, straightened out his family problems, and decided what to do next. "All right," he said at last, turning away automatically toward the front door. "If that's the way you want it."

"Evan—"

"Yes?" He was aware of swinging around much too quickly, betraying how much he wanted her to change her mind.

"Don't you want your coffee?"

"Oh . . ." He ran his hand impatiently through his hair. "No, perhaps another time . . . Listen, Nicki, I'll phone you next week from Wales when I feel more settled—maybe you could come down to Colwyn for a long weekend—"

"All right," she said. "I'll expect to hear from you." She moved toward him as he opened the front door. "Thanks for the dinner. I'm sorry if you think I'm stupid—it's not that I don't care—"

"I know," he said, and the longing for her swept over him again so violently that he hardly dared risk even the quickest of kisses. "Take care of yourself," he mumbled. "Nice seeing you. 'Bye." And the next moment he was running downstairs two at a time and racing up the road as if he could dissolve the violence of his emotions in a burst of physical energy.

There was a train to Swansea at three o'clock the following afternoon. After a morning which he spent walking feverishly around the park and absorbing the sights and sounds of London again he returned to his hotel room to find the telephone ringing by his bedside.

Nicola was the only person who knew he was in England. He grabbed the receiver so fast he nearly dropped it. "Hello?"

"Evan . . ." Her voice was muffled and far away. He hardly recognized it.

"Nicki?" he said doubtfully.

"Oh, Evan, I—" He heard her choke back a sob.

"What's happened?" he demanded at once. "What is it? What's the matter?"

"I've just heard from Wales . . . Jane phoned . . . about my father, he—had an accident—driving . . . oh Evan, he's dead, I can't believe it, it was a car accident—an open road, no other car involved—he skidded into one of those stone walls and was killed instantly—"

"I'm on my way over," said Evan, the words tumbling out of his mouth in his desire to be with her when she needed him. "Give me ten minutes. I'll be with you just as soon as I possibly can."

## ii

"Millionaire Industrialist Killed in Car Smash," intoned the Monday editions of the popular press, giving Benedict yet another chance to deplore the vulgarity of the word millionaire. "Mystery Death on Lonely Welsh Road."

"Morrison Inquest Rules Accidental Death," said the Thursday editions. "Coroner Cautions Against Fast Driving."

None of the papers mentioned when or where the funeral was to be held for the simple reason that none of them knew. Matt's secretaries and aides had descended on Colwyn after his death, consulted Nicola who had arrived at Colwyn Court with Evan on Sunday night, and, in between issuing statements to the press, had made the arrangements for a quiet funeral at the village in Surrey where Matt had lived since his second marriage. The secretaries and aides had tried to consult Lisa about the funeral arrangements, but Lisa had been too incoherent to do more than advise them to talk to Nicola instead.

"Poor Lisa's quite prostrate with grief," said Walter, worried, to Agnes Miller. "I feel so sorry for her."

"Poor soul," said Agnes sympathetically. "What a terrible tragedy for a young girl."

"That just shows," said Gwyneth, who had always admired Lisa's glamour, "all those people who said cattily that Lisa married Matt for his money were wrong as could be. She really did love him."

If only I had loved him a little more, thought Lisa in an agony of guilt. If only I could feel grief instead of this awful secret relief that it's all over without the sordidness of a divorce. If only I could talk to someone about how I really feel. If only . . .

If only Tristan Poole had not been summoned away to London for a week on one of his mysterious visits.

She had not dared attempt to see him for the first two days after Matt's death, but at the inquest she had spoken to Agnes Miller, who had told her of Poole's absence from Colwyn. Lisa had wanted to ask her for a phone number where he could be reached, but her nerve failed her. She had not even dared ask when Poole would be returning, although Agnes eventually told her that he was expected back within the week. She was trying very hard not to think of Poole, but the more she longed for someone to confide in the more she longed to see him. At last, unable to bear the isolation of her guilt any longer, she turned to her sister.

"I feel so awful, Jane," she said on the evening after the inquest. They were in the kitchen; Jane was preparing dinner in her haphazard way and Lisa was not sure Jane was concentrating on what she was saying; however, so desperate was her longing to confide in someone that she took no notice of Jane's air of abstraction. "If only Matt and I hadn't quarreled so badly just before he died—"

"Yes, I know," said Jane. "It must be awful, darling. But we all know how much you loved each other despite your troubles. Don't think we don't understand."

"But I didn't love him!" said Lisa wildly. "I'm glad he's dead!"

"Oh, Lisa, darling, you're just upset—you don't know what you're saying . . ."

It was hopeless. Lisa gave up. The next morning, Thursday, they all left the cottage and drove to Surrey for the funeral, which was to be held on Friday afternoon.

Matt's battered Rolls Royce was still in the hands of one of the large Swansea garages, so Benedict drove Lisa and Walter to Surrey in his Austin while Evan followed in Walter's more spacious Bentley with Nicola, Jane, and the twins. Nicola had spent a blurred, confused five days at Colwyn Court, vaguely aware of Walter's kindness, Jane's concern, and Evan's grave attentiveness. She had barely noticed the society's existence. Evan had said to her once or twice that he intended to have a heart-to-heart talk with his father when events had returned to normal, but she had not understood what he meant. She had hardly spoken to Lisa. Lisa had burst into tears as soon as they had met and after that Nicola had avoided her for fear that such noisy grief would be so contagious that she would break down and be unable to pull herself together.

"You ought to cry," said Evan. "It's the natural thing to do. Although I do realize," he added quickly, remembering a book he had once read on psychology, "that grief takes people different ways." It would never do to make her feel guilty because for some reason she felt unable to shed any tears.

"I have cried," said Nicola, "but I don't want to follow Lisa's example and be constantly weeping on the nearest available shoulder."

"Lisa can't help herself, I dare say."

"She can't help being a hypocrite. She only married Daddy for his money."

"I don't think Lisa's as bad as all that," said Evan before he could stop himself, and realized too late that he had said the wrong thing.

"All men say that," said Nicola, and went off for a walk without him.

Evan's immediate reaction was to feel exasperated with her, but he managed to summon his patience and check his irritation. He told himself it was no use expecting her to respond to him in a more normal way until the funeral was over and her shock was on the wane, so in an effort to divert his thoughts from her he turned his attentions to the others. But there was little he could do. Jane and Benedict were shocked but calm; Lisa was tearful but recovering; the twins were unexpectedly phlegmatic.

"All people die when they get old," said Lucy plainly. "What was sad was that this was an accident. That was what was sad."

"The accident was the worst part," echoed Timothy.

"Much the worst. Poor Uncle Matt."

"It's too bad for Mum," said Timothy, "but it's good too."

"Why's that?" said Evan.

"Because . . . just because."

"She's free now," said Lucy.

"Yes, she can get married again one day."

Evan saw them exchange private knowing glances.

"It'll all come right in the end," said Lucy mysteriously, "won't it, Timmy?"

"Of course," said Timothy.

Evan wondered what was going on but made no further effort to discover why the twins should be thinking of their mother's possible remarriage. He had already decided that it would be no surprise to him if Lisa had a lover; after talking to her he had had the suspicion that although her distress was sincere the source of her distress was more obscure than anyone had guessed.

But Lisa did not know that of all the people at Colwyn Court

Evan came closest to understanding her. She made no effort to confide in him more fully, and on the day of her return to Surrey she was so busy nerving herself for the funeral that even her guilt was pushed to one side. At last when all the guests were settled in their rooms she was about to retire to bed for an early night when the maid told her that someone wished to speak to her on the telephone.

"If it's the press," said Lisa, "I don't want to talk to them."

"He said he wasn't the press, madam," said the maid. "I asked to make sure. He said he was the director of some society about nature foods—"

"I'll speak to him," said Lisa and flew upstairs to her room.

The receiver slipped in her moist palm. Her heart was banging against her ribs. "Hullo?" she said in a low voice. "Tristan?"

"How are you?"

"Oh . . ." She paused to get her breath. Various conventional phrases slithered around in her mind but she could not decide which one to choose.

"My condolences about the accident."

She tried to say "thank you" but he spoke again before she could frame the words with her lips.

"Are you all right?"

"No, I'm not," she said in a rush. "I feel terrible. I must talk to you. Please. It's so urgent."

"When's the funeral?"

"Tomorrow afternoon. Three o'clock."

"At Wickerfield Church?"

"Yes. It's going to be very quiet. Just the family and one or two of Matt's oldest friends."

"All right," he said. "I'll be in touch with you afterward."

"When?" she said. "Where? Is there some number where I can—"

"I'll be in touch with you," he said in a quiet voice which made her close her eyes weakly in relief. "Good night, Lisa."

And before she could say another word she found herself listening to the hum of an empty line.

*iii*

Near the end of the service she glanced up and saw him. The mourners were outside, grouped around the open grave as the clergyman read the last part of the service, and overhead the sky was overcast with dark clouds. Poole was standing by the lych-gate, and for a moment she thought he was going to enter the church-yard to join them but he did not. He wore a black suit and a black tie and stood watching silently from his position outside the boundaries of the consecrated ground.

As soon as the service was over and the clergyman had closed his book Lisa turned, oblivious of the arm Benedict offered her, and walked quickly toward the lych-gate.

"Who the devil's that?" muttered Evan to Benedict.

"God knows," said Benedict.

Lightning flashed far away beyond the hills; thunder rumbled menacingly in the distance.

"Never saw him before in my life," said Benedict, after polishing his glasses to make sure.

"Benedict," whispered Jane, catching his sleeve. "That's Mr. Poole."

"I think it's going to rain," said the clergyman kindly to Nicola. "It's just as well we held the service when we did."

"Yes," said Nicola. She felt numb and lost. She didn't want to talk to anyone.

"Maybe I can come back to the house with you for a few min-utes, Nicola," said a familiar voice. "There's something I think I should speak to you about."

She turned. It was one of her father's oldest friends, the solici-tor Peter Marshall who was the senior partner of the firm of Tate, Marshall, Marshall and Tate.

"Oh." She tried to collect herself. "Yes, of course." For the first time she noticed that Lisa had gone on ahead and was talking to some unknown man by the lych-gate.

"Are you all right, Nicki?" said Evan's voice at her side.

She nodded, unable to speak and suddenly terrified of breaking down, but to her relief Walter came to her rescue by diverting Evan's attention.

"Evan," he called. "Let me introduce you to Mr. Poole."

Evan tried not to look annoyed and moved reluctantly toward the stranger who stood in the shadow of the lych-gate.

He saw a man of his own age who looked as though he might be a useful tennis player. The stranger had that silky kind of athletic slimness which would look more at home on a tennis court than on a rugger field or a cricket pitch. A bit soft, thought Evan who had always privately considered tennis a woman's game, and then remembered that the man had bulldozed himself and twelve strangers into Colwyn Court. The hackles rose on the back of Evan's neck. Dislike washed through his body in a huge, silent tide.

"How do you do," said Poole, very courteous.

"How do you do," said Evan shortly and was silent.

"And this is Nicola Morrison," said Walter, feeling it necessary to gloss over any further conversation between his son and his guest. "Nicola, my dear, this is Mr. Tristan Poole, the director of our society at Colwyn Court."

"How do you do, Miss Morrison," said Poole. "Please accept my sympathy."

"Thank you . . ." She was hardly aware of him. She had a vague picture of a man who was shorter and narrower than Evan, a man with nondescript features and some brownish hair. She did not even notice the color of his eyes.

". . . my cousin Benedict Shaw," Walter was saying. "I don't think the two of you have ever met."

"No, we haven't," said Poole. "How do you do, Professor Shaw. I've spoken to your wife a couple of times but you were always too elusive for me."

"It's a pity we have to meet on such a sad occasion," Benedict murmured. He was wondering why Jane had found the fellow so sinister. He seemed rather a nice young chap, a little like one of his assistant lecturers up at Cambridge.

"Good afternoon, Mrs. Shaw," said Poole to Jane, and smiled at her. "The twins aren't here, I see."

"We thought it would be too upsetting for them," said Jane awkwardly.

"I don't believe in children going to funerals," said Lisa. "Tristan, let's go."

They all looked at her in surprise.

"Go where?" said Benedict sharply, and took a second look at Poole.

"I've offered Lisa a lift back to her house in my car," said Poole. "I hope that doesn't upset any arrangements. All right, Lisa, I'm sure you want to get home—my car's over there under the oak tree."

"Oh dear," murmured Jane in the silence which followed. "Oh dear, oh dear." She knew her sister had done the wrong thing and was embarrassed for her.

"Poole meant well, I'm sure," said Walter innocently.

So that's how the land lies, thought Evan. Aloud he said: "How long has she known him?"

"Does it matter?" said Nicola. She turned blindly toward the waiting cars. "Let's follow their example and go back to the house before it begins to rain."

The thunder rumbled again in the distance as if on cue; large drops of rain spattered from the darkening skies.

"Nicola's right," said Evan. "Let's go."

Nobody said much on the way back to Wickerfield Manor. When they arrived at Matt's home Nicola was about to dash away to the comforting solitude of her room when she remembered that her father's solicitor was probably on the point of arriving to talk to her.

"When Mr. Marshall arrives," she said hastily to the maid, "show him into my father's study. I'll be waiting for him there."

"Can I do anything?" said Evan, appearing suddenly at her elbow.

"What? Oh, no thanks . . . it's all right. Daddy's solicitor is arriving soon to see me. I suppose it's about the will or something horrible like that."

It was. Mr. Marshall arrived two minutes later and suggested to Nicola that Lisa should be present.

"It won't take long," he said. "But now the funeral's over, I feel I really must speak to you both about one or two things."

"Of course," said Nicola mechanically and went in search of Lisa. After hunting for several minutes she braved the rain, which was now falling heavily, and ran across the lawn to the summer house. They were there. They must have watched her run across the lawn, for neither of them looked surprised to see her when she reached them. She noticed Lisa's defensive expression but ignored it.

"Lisa, could I interrupt you for a few minutes, please? Peter Marshall's here and he wants to talk to us both. Excuse us, Mr. Poole."

"Of course," said the man. "Would you like me to go back to the house and bring an umbrella for you both? It seems to be raining much harder now."

"Please don't bother," said Nicola. "It only takes a minute to run across the lawn. But thank you all the same."

Lightning flared unexpectedly. Lisa jumped, covering her ears as the thunder crashed overhead.

"I'm so afraid of storms!"

"I'll come with you to the house," said Poole. He slipped off his jacket and draped it around her shoulders. "That'll save you from getting too wet."

She flashed him a grateful smile.

Nicola stopped, suddenly aware of the potential of their relationship. Could Lisa possibly . . . on the day of her husband's funeral . . . no, surely not even Lisa would have the nerve to do such a thing! She heard herself say sharply: "Are you staying here, Mr. Poole?"

"No," he said. "I leave for London tonight."

So he at least had some decency, even if Lisa had none. She was so angry she did not trust herself to say anything else. Lightning blazed again as she left the summer house and tore across the lawn through the rain to the French windows of the living room. When Lisa and Poole joined her seconds later she still said nothing but merely led the way across the hall to Matt's study where Mr. Marshall was waiting.

Mr. Marshall seemed to find it difficult to know where to begin. He started by saying how shocked he had been by the tragedy and how deeply he sympathized with both Lisa and Nicola. He said he had long considered Matt one of his closest friends and how sad it was to be called upon to execute his will. He then said what a difficult and painful task it was for him to tell them what was in the will. He even admitted he was not altogether sure how to put the contents into words.

"Please, Peter," said Nicola, beginning to feel desperate and well aware that Lisa was on the verge of one of her contagious crying bouts, "don't worry about upsetting us. We couldn't be more upset than we are already and I for one don't care much about what was in Daddy's will anyway. I suppose most of it goes in taxes."

"This is true," said Mr. Marshall, secretly relieved by this plain talking. "However, he had to some extent made arrangements to avoid death duties. Eight years ago he disposed of a large portion of his money in your favor, Nicola, and I'm happy to tell you that you are now in possession of a fund of some half a million pounds which is not subject to death duties."

"Oh," said Nicola blankly.

My God, thought Lisa, half a million pounds outright. My God. She had to grip the sides of her chair tightly for self-control.

"Don't tell me all my share goes to support the Welfare State, Peter," she said with a light little laugh. "But I suppose it does since Matt and I hadn't been married long enough to enable him to avoid death duties where I was concerned."

"This is true," said Mr. Marshall again, and opened his mouth to say something else but nothing came out.

"How much did Matt leave?" said Lisa. "I suppose you can't count this previous arrangement for Nicola as that sum wasn't officially part of the estate."

"This is true," said Mr. Marshall. He cleared his throat. "The exact dimensions of the estate are not known at present but it seems likely that it will be in the nature of at least three million pounds . . ."

That means twenty percent of three million for me, thought Lisa. Six hundred thousand pounds. Or are death duties higher than eighty percent? But I'll get at least three hundred thousand and probably more. Perhaps five hundred thousand. Half a million pounds.

"Originally," said Mr. Marshall, clearing his throat again, "the money was left to you outright, Lisa, since Nicola was already well provided for, and there were certain legacies, of course—one thousand pounds to each of your children—"

"How terribly generous of him," said Lisa, tears springing to her eyes. "They were so fond of him."

"—and various other bequests," Mr. Marshall was saying. "However—" He took a deep breath—"shortly before he died Matt did a very . . . well, it was a very strange thing. I tried to talk him out of it—tried to tell him to wait for a while—"

"What do you mean?" said Lisa. "What did he do?"

"He executed a codicil to his will. He actually telephoned me on the morning he died to check that he had the wording right. In the codicil he said—"

"It's not legal, of course," said Lisa.

"Well, actually," said Mr. Marshall, going to bright pink, "I'm very much afraid that it is, Lisa. He wrote that the words 'National Society for the Prevention of Cruelty to Children' should be substituted for your name whenever it appeared in the will."

There was a silence. Lisa had turned a greenish shade of white.

"As a matter of fact," said Mr. Marshall, "you'd probably find a judge more than sympathetic to your case. Of course the purpose of the law in construing a will is to follow the testator's wishes and decide what he meant by what he said, but . . . well, a wife is usually entitled to something . . . mitigating circumstances . . . if I were you I'd—"

"I'll contest it," said Lisa.

"Well, take counsel's opinion anyway. I can't act for you, naturally, but I can recommend an excellent solicitor, a friend of mine—"

"Thank you," said Lisa. "Please leave his name and address and I'll get in touch with him on Monday. Excuse me." And rising awkwardly to her feet she stumbled across the room, wrenched open the door, and ran sobbing down the corridor in search of Tristan Poole.

## iv

When Poole returned to his unobtrusive London hotel that night he immediately placed a call to Colwyn Court.

Agnes' sister Harriet Miller answered the phone.

"Get Agnes," was all Poole said.

"Yes, Tristan." He could hear the shock in her voice and knew his brusqueness had startled her. There was a pause. Then:

"What happened?" said Agnes.

"Agnes, why the hell did you let me use Jackie as an acolyte instead of Sandra?"

"But I thought Jackie did so well! She told you exactly when Morrison was leaving Swansea, exactly when he reached Colwyn— she provided such a complete monitoring service for you, I thought! After all, I know the demon you summoned to the circle to possess the cat was anxious to do your bidding, but the demon had to be guided and if Jackie had been inaccurate with her forecast—" She stopped abruptly, aware of the silence at the other end of the wire.

"Have you quite finished?" said Poole politely.

"Yes, Tristan. I'm sorry. How did Jackie fail?"

"I asked her what he was doing in Swansea and she told me he was having a talk with an old friend."

"And wasn't he?"

"You bet he was! His goddamned lawyer on the goddamned phone! Sandra could have told me that! But Jackie makes it seem as if Morrison's dropping in at a garden party and chatting about the latest fish he'd caught! You can tell Jackie that if she ever wants to achieve any real credibility in that field of work she'd better learn to concentrate on the job instead of letting part of her mind get lost somewhere along the astral line!"

"Oh dear," said Agnes nervously. "I'm so sorry, Tristan. You're right—I shouldn't have let you use her. I must say, I did have my doubts, but—"

"Yes, you did. All right, Agnes, it was really more my fault than yours. I should have taken her limitations more fully into consideration."

"But what did Morrison say to his lawyer? You're not trying to tell me he—"

"He executed a codicil to his will."

"Oh no!"

"Of course I don't have to tell you what was in the codicil."

"He left little Lisa penniless," said Agnes with a sinking heart.

"She may not be penniless in the long run but after the government has taken eighty percent of the estate and after Lisa's paid her lawyers she's not going to have more than peanuts to play around with. Morrison left the money—or what's left of it after taxes—to the N.S.P.C.C., and from what I hear it seems as if most of it's likely to stay with them. If Lisa's lucky some softhearted judge will give her a cut which may keep her in hats for a few years, but that's all. So forget the idea of Lisa as a rich widow. In fact forget Lisa. We're back at square one."

"Oh *dear*," said Agnes, almost in tears. "After all our hard work! It does seem a shame."

"Cheer up, Agnes," said Poole, and although she could not see him she thought she could sense his smile. "Perhaps we're not quite back at square one after all. Let's say we're at square two instead of square three."

Agnes felt her spirits rise. "You've got another plan?" she said in excitement.

"Well, I suppose you could call it that," said Poole casually. "But for the moment let's just call it an interesting possibility."

# Chapter Five

*i*

When Nicola awoke the next morning the sky was clear after the thunderstorm and the air felt fresh and cool after a night of rain. It was late. Her exhaustion had caught up with her at last, and by the time she arrived downstairs for breakfast it was ten o'clock and the dining room was empty. She was just drinking her second cup of coffee and trying to eat a slice of toast when Evan entered the room.

"Hello," he said, and stooped to give her a kiss. "How are you this morning?"

"I'm not sure," said Nicola. "Better, I think, thanks. I had a splitting headache yesterday but that's gone now."

"The storm cleared the air." He pulled over a chair and sat down next to her. "What are your plans?"

"I don't know that I have any. I'll probably go back to London this afternoon and try to get back to normal. I don't want to stay here longer because I know without a doubt I'd end up by having a row with Lisa. You heard what happened yesterday, of course."

"Lisa broadcast the news from the rooftops."

"Isn't it awful? I do feel sorry for her being cut off without a shilling when I'm so embarrassingly well provided for, but I know Daddy wouldn't have changed his will like that if he hadn't had a very good reason."

"It's my bet she was fooling around with that fellow Poole."

"Mine too." Nicola recalled the scene in the summer house with distaste. "Although I can't imagine what she sees in him. He seemed so ordinary to me."

"He didn't seem ordinary to me," said Evan. "He looked like a remarkably smooth operator with a crooked streak, and as soon as I get back to Colwyn Court I'm going to see he and his friends are evicted at the earliest opportunity . . . Talking of Colwyn, Nicki, why don't you take next week off from work and come down to stay with us? It would do you good to get away from all this for a few extra days, and I don't like to think of you going back to London on your own."

"It's . . . very kind of you, Evan, but I really can't take a second week off from work at the moment—it's so inconvenient to my boss, and besides . . . well, you may not understand but I *want* to go back to work. Work represents continuity for me at the moment, something stable and unchanging . . . If I went to Colwyn I'd probably sit around and get introspective, but if I go back to work I won't have time to think about anything . . . Will you be coming back to London soon, do you think?"

"I'm not sure. I have to straighten out affairs at home." He leaned forward on an impulse. "Nicki, won't you think over the invitation to Colwyn? I've been thinking about this all last week, and I've come to the conclusion—"

The door opened, interrupting him. Jane peeped anxiously into the room.

"Oh," she said, embarrassed, "I'm so sorry, I was looking for Benedict. You haven't seen him, have you, by any chance?"

"He wandered off somewhere with my father," said Evan.

"Knowing my father's hobbies I suggest you try the greenhouses first. How's Lisa, Jane? I haven't seen her this morning."

"Well," said Jane, and hesitated uncomfortably. "She's still awfully upset. In fact—" Jane took a deep breath—"I've insisted that she return to stay at the cottage with us until she's feeling better. Well, actually she asked if she could come and I hadn't the heart to refuse. I do hope Benedict will understand. I mean, I know he'll understand but—"

"I'm sure he will," said Evan, "but doesn't the cottage have sad memories for her?"

"Yes, but Matt wasn't actually killed at the cottage . . ." Jane's voice trailed off uncertainly. She blushed in confusion. "I'm sorry, Nicola."

"Well, he wasn't," said Nicola. "That's all right, Jane."

Jane looked relieved. "Well, I really must find Benedict . . . excuse me . . ." She backed awkwardly out of the room and closed the door again.

There was a pause before Nicola said, pouring herself a third cup of coffee: "That settles it. I'm not going to Colwyn if Lisa's going."

"Oh Nicki, for God's sake—"

"I can't help it," said Nicola. "I just can't stand her. I can't be hypocritical about it. Sorry, Evan."

"Nicki, Lisa'll be at the cottage—you'll be with me at Colwyn Court—"

"I think I'm afraid of that too," said Nicola.

"Look," said Evan, "if you want to give me a hard time, no doubt I deserve it, but why give yourself a hard time too? Don't be so damned proud!"

"I can't help being proud," said Nicola. "It's just the way I am."

"But Nicki, I love you! As soon as I've got things straightened out at home—"

"I'm always waiting for you to straighten things out," said Nicola. "You went to Africa to straighten yourself out. Now you're going to Wales to straighten your family out. There's always something which has to be straightened out before you get to me."

"I'm trying to get to you, aren't I? Why do you think I've invited you to Colwyn?"

"Because you want to have your cake and eat it," said Nicola.

"Oh Christ!" yelled Evan and stormed out of the room in a rage.

The maid, coming in to clear the table, collided with him and gave him a look of astonished reproof as he strode past her without an apology. When she had collected herself she said to Nicola: "Excuse me, miss, but have you finished?"

"Yes," said Nicola. "Sorry I was so late this morning." She set down her coffee cup and wandered out into the hall. The house seemed oppressively large. On an impulse she pulled open the front door and stepped out into the morning sunlight. It was then, before she had even had time to recall the unfortunate scene with Evan and give way to her regrets and depression, that she saw the black Jaguar purr smoothly up the drive toward the steps where she was standing.

Lisa's lover, thought Nicola, how dare he come back to my father's house like this! Anger choked in her throat but she conquered it and ran lightly down the steps as he emerged from the car.

"Good morning, Miss Morrison," he said pleasantly, and smiled at her.

He looked different. Nicola hesitated, and as she hesitated she forgot what she was going to say. She found herself staring at him. He wore an expensively cut sports shirt of a smoky red, and the material clung to his body so that she could see the muscles in his chest and the strong set of his shoulders. His slacks were black, as perfectly pressed as they were perfectly tailored, and his shoes were as black as his slacks. Nicola thought she had never seen a casually dressed man look so elegant.

"Good morning," she heard herself say as if from a long way away.

He held out his hand politely and after a moment she held out hers and felt his long fingers close upon her skin. She saw for the first time that he was dark. He had dark eyes, deep-set and brilliant, and dark hair, and his skin was tanned from hours in the summer sun of the Gower Peninsula.

"You look different," she said suddenly.

"No," he said. "You're just more observant today, that's all."

He was still holding her hand and she was suddenly very aware of his long fingers next to her flesh. She withdrew her hand and took a pace away from him.

"Won't you come in?" she said abruptly, and led the way into the hall.

"Thank you," he said and followed her out of the sunlight into the shadows of the house.

"I suppose you want to see Lisa. I think she's still in bed, but if you like I'll go and tell her you're here."

"Well, as a matter of fact," he said from just behind her shoulder, "it was you I came to see, not Lisa."

She swung round in surprise. "Me?" she said, astonished, and felt the hot color suffuse her face as if she were a schoolgirl again. "Why me?"

"Is there a room where we can talk in private?"

"Oh . . . yes, of course . . . Come into the living room."

He opened the door for her.

"Can I offer you some coffee?" said Nicola uneasily, still not sure how to react to his presence.

"Only if it's percolated," said Poole, "and made without that appalling hot milk the English love so much."

Nicola found herself laughing. "Cook would have hysterics! She only keeps instant coffee in the kitchen anyway. How about some tea?"

"I don't think I could face it," said Poole. "Don't think I'm unappreciative of your hospitality, Miss Morrison; it's just that in this particular matter I'm very hard to please. Shall we sit down?"

"Oh . . . yes, of course." She sat down awkwardly on one end of the sofa and after she was seated he sank into the armchair opposite her and interlaced his long sinuous fingers.

"I owe you an apology," he said at last.

"Do you?" said Nicola surprised.

"Yes, a large one, unfortunately."

"What on earth for?"

"My intrusion yesterday on a very private family affair."

"Oh." Nicola felt confused.

"I'm surprised you're being so polite to me this morning. I had a most unpleasant suspicion when I saw you watching my arrival just now that you were about to summon every servant in the house to throw me out in the best nineteenth-century tradition. Wasn't that the way they used to deal with rogues, vagabonds, and unwanted suitors?"

"I suppose it was," said Nicola amused. "But which category of undesirable visitor do you fall into?"

"All of them, of course," said Poole with his wide charming smile. "Haven't you heard about me? According to popular rumor I've tricked Walter Colwyn out of his family home, established a nudist camp and worse at Colwyn Court, and played fast and loose with your stepmother. Surely you can't be unaware of my extreme notoriety!"

Nicola laughed. "You make the gossip all sound very foolish!"

"Gossip often is. Nobody thinks of checking to see if Walter Colwyn gave me a lease; nobody wants to believe that the word 'nature' in the society's title refers to food and not to a lack of decent clothing. Everyone always likes to believe the worst because the worst is usually so much more exciting than the best, isn't it? And the human race loves to be excited and titillated. If there's no excitement they invent it. Even foolish gossip is better than no gossip at all in those circumstances."

After a moment Nicola said: "And Lisa?"

"I'm not responsible for Lisa," said Poole. "She was your father's problem, not mine."

"I don't think he believed that Lisa was faithful to him at the end."

"Of course he didn't," said Poole. "Husbands can never believe that their wives are resistible. To believe such a thing would be an insult to their egos."

"Hm," said Nicola, digesting this with a frown.

"Look," said Poole, leaning forward suddenly, "I really must apologize, Miss Morrison. I know you think I intruded yesterday in order to see Lisa, but in fact it was Lisa who demanded to see me. She sounded so close to hysteria that I gave in, much against my better judgment, and spent some time with her here after the funeral in an attempt to calm her down." He paused. "I have some experience in clinical psychology. I thought I could help her."

"I see," said Nicola slowly.

"I knew when I met her a few days ago that she was troubled and on an impulse I made the mistake of trying to help her. She developed a dependence on me very rapidly—much more rapidly than I'd anticipated—and things got out of control. When I tried to extricate myself she became hysterical and . . . well, you can imagine how it was. I won't go into further details. Suffice it to say that yesterday I tried to persuade her to consult a London specialist about her emotional troubles, and I hope I managed to make her see reason."

"I don't think you did," said Nicola. "She's decided to return to Colwyn Cottage to recuperate with Jane and Benedict."

His eyes were suddenly so dark that they seemed black. His mobile mouth was straight and still. "Oh?" he said at last. "That's unfortunate. But I think she'll soon be obliged to realize that whatever tenuous relationship existed between us is now at an end. There's nothing further I can do for her."

"I'm glad about that," said Nicola before she could stop herself.

He smiled at her. His eyes lightened, sparkled, crinkled at the corners. He had the most extraordinarily expressive eyes. "What about you?" he said. "You're not going to stay on alone in this enormous house, are you?"

"No, I . . . have to get back to work on Monday. I don't live here anyway. I have a flat in Hampstead."

"If you'll forgive me saying so," said Poole, "I don't think you should go back to work so soon."

"But I want to," said Nicola, repeating what she had said to Evan. "If I don't I'll get introspective and maudlin. I want to be so busy that I won't have time to think about myself."

"Exactly," said Poole. "Sometimes that sort of sublimation can be most unwise. Far better to let the shock and grief work itself naturally out of your system."

"Oh," said Nicola. She felt confused again. On an impulse she said quickly: "Are you really a psychologist? Or just an amateur one?"

"I have a degree in psychology. I've had clinical experience. I don't think you could call me an amateur."

"What university did you go to?"

"I was at college in California."

"So that explains it!"

"Explains what?"

"Your accent. It's a bit off-key sometimes. Are you an American?"

"No, I'm a British subject. But I spent my formative years in the States. You haven't been to California, have you, by any chance?"

"No. I'd love to go there one day, though."

"You should," said Poole. "It's the most extraordinary place, a latter-day Garden of Eden . . . After the Fall, of course." He smiled at her. "But never mind California for the moment. I was thinking of places nearer home. Colwyn, for instance. If I were advising you—which I realize I have no business to do at all—I'd recommend you take at least another week off from work and come down to Colwyn Court for some rest and sea air. My society has taken over the east and west wings, but there's still one small spare room in the main part of the house and you'd be more than welcome to stay there for a few days. I can say that with authority because I spoke to Walter Colwyn after the funeral yesterday and he suggested more or less the same thing himself."

"Well . . ."

"If you're worried about Lisa, don't be. There's no reason why you should meet."

"How did you know I—"

"My dear Miss Morrison, one doesn't have to be a psychologist to guess your attitude toward your stepmother after her recent behavior."

"I—" Nicola felt dazed.

"I'll look after you if you visit Colwyn. If you're afraid of introspection or simply afraid of being afraid I think I might be able to help you."

"I'll be all right," said Nicola at once.

"So you'll come?"

"Well, I—"

"You will come, won't you."

"I . . ."

"You will come."

"Well, why not?" said Nicola unexpectedly. "It's a bit feeble to be afraid of introspection, isn't it? Why shouldn't I spend a few days by the sea?"

"Good!" said Poole. "That's a much healthier attitude to take." He stood up before adding casually: "Perhaps I can give you a lift down to Wales? I'm leaving on Monday morning and it'd be very easy for me to stop here at Wickerfield to pick you up."

"But I'll be in London too," said Nicola. "I planned to go back after everyone leaves for Wales tomorrow morning."

"Better still! Give me your address and I'll stop by at your apartment."

"You mean you'll call in at my flat," said Nicola, and they laughed together.

"When I'm excited I forget which side of the Atlantic I'm on," said Poole disarmingly.

Nicola was aware of the most extraordinary sense of elation. "Would you like to stay to lunch?" she offered on the spur of the moment.

"I would, but unfortunately I have to get back to town. Now before I forget, what's your address in Hampstead?"

She gave him her address and phone number and asked him where he was staying.

"The Salisbury Hotel by the British Museum. I'll call for you at nine-thirty on Monday morning—or will that be too early?"

"No, that'll be fine."

They were in the hall. No one was about.

"I wouldn't tell Lisa I called, if I were you," said Poole, opening the front door. "Best to avoid unnecessary complications in that direction. I'm sure you understand."

"Of course," said Nicola.

He held out his hand again, and Nicola reached automatically to touch him.

"Till Monday," said Poole, turning away from her. The strong sunlight gave his dark hair a reddish tinge.

"Till Monday," said Nicola, and stood watching him as he got into his black Jaguar and drove away out of sight of her mesmerized eyes.

## ii

"I've changed my mind about coming to Colwyn Court," said Nicola to Evan as they met by chance before lunch. "I'm going to drive down on Monday and stay for a week."

"How do you know the invitation still stands?" said Evan, still smarting from their unfortunate conversation at the breakfast table. "Anyway, what made you change your mind? Did you decide to let me have my cake and eat it?"

"What? Oh . . . Evan, I'm sorry! I was just upset and didn't know what I was saying . . . Would you really prefer me not to come?"

"Don't be such a little ass," he said clumsily, and tried to kiss her but she turned her face away from him.

"I suppose I did get het up about nothing," she said vaguely. "You had every right to be cross."

"Let's forget it. Nicki, let me drive you down to Wales on Monday—Benedict and Jane can take Father home tomorrow as planned, and I can stay on here—"

"No, you don't have to do that, Evan. It's nice of you to suggest it but I've made other plans."

"You mean you've decided to go by train?"

"No, by car. It's all arranged."

"But don't be silly, it would be no trouble for me to—"

"Mr. Poole's traveling back to Colwyn on Monday and he offered to give me a lift."

"Poole!" Evan stared at her. "Are you trying to tell me you're going to shut yourself up in a car for God knows how many hours with that—that—"

"Shhh!" said Nicola. "Don't yell it out to all the world! I don't want Lisa to know or she'll kick up some kind of embarrassing scene."

"When did you talk to Poole, for God's sake?"

"This morning. He confirmed your advice and said I'd be better off if I spent next week quietly at Colwyn instead of returning to work, so that made me feel I'd be stupid to ignore the advice of two doctors—"

"He's no doctor!" shouted Evan.

"Well, he's a psychologist—"

"He's a quack! Nicki, don't believe half of what that man says. In fact, don't believe any of it."

"But my dear Evan, he only gave me exactly the same advice as you did!"

"But—"

"Why do you dislike him so much?"

"He's bogus," said Evan. "He's a fraud. He's wormed his way into my home."

"He says he has a lease from your father."

"I don't believe it!"

"And he has a degree in psychology from a college in California—"

"California!" scoffed Evan.

"—and he's had clinical experience—"

"Did he mention the name of the college where he got his degree?"

"No, he didn't say, but—"

"I don't believe a word of it," said Evan. "He's a fake."

"He's not," said Nicola annoyed. "I think you're being most un-reasonable, Evan."

"You're the one who's being unreasonable in believing all that nonsense he told you! Look, Nicki, phone Poole, cancel Monday's drive, and come down with us all to Colwyn tomorrow."

"I can't," said Nicola mulishly. "I must go back to the flat first to do some washing and ironing and repacking."

"Then let me drive you down on Monday. Just the two of us."

"It's not necessary, Evan. Mr. Poole—"

"Damn Mr. Poole!" yelled Evan.

"Oh, for heaven's sake, Evan!" said Nicola, exasperated. "What on earth's the matter with you?"

And they parted once more in anger.

## iii

"Father," said Evan, finding Walter on his own admiring a rare species of orchid in one of Matt's greenhouses. "I want to talk to you."

"Ah," said Walter, trying not to sound nervous and wondering if this was to be the scene he had tried to postpone for so long. "Of course . . . have you seen these orchids in here before, by the way? They're truly exceptional. Such color—texture—"

"Father," said Evan sternly, "I want to know just where we stand with Tristan Poole and his society."

"Ah," said Walter. "Yes. Exactly."

"I suggest we go outside and sit on that seat over on the far side of the lawn. It's too hot in here to conduct a serious conver-sation."

"It's very hot, isn't it? Marvelous for orchids, of course." He wandered on to the next species.

"Father—"

"You mustn't worry about it, Evan. It's entirely my responsibility."

"That's not true," said Evan. "It's my responsibility to look after you."

"My dear boy, I'm perfectly capable of fending for myself! I appreciate your solicitude, but you're worrying yourself unnecessarily."

"What's all this about Poole having a lease?"

"Just a gentlemen's agreement," said Walter, wishing the orchids would march forward and swallow him up. "I've leased the east and west wings to Poole for a year. We weren't using the rooms anyway and I thought a bit of extra money might come in useful."

"How much is he paying you?"

"Well," said Walter, frantically playing for time. "That's a good question. I'm very glad you asked that. You see—" He stopped.

"Yes?" said Evan.

"Let's go and sit over on the bench as you suggested," said Walter on an inspiration, and earned himself another two minutes to try to think of a satisfactory answer. But when they were both sitting on the wooden seat facing the lawn and the rose garden, he found he still had not invented a plausible reply.

"Yes, Father?" said his inquisitor relentlessly.

"The fact is," said Walter, "there's no money involved at the moment. The society have the accommodation in exchange for Miss Miller acting as housekeeper and for Poole looking after Gwyneth."

There was a pause. Walter, every limb tense, waited in dread for an explosion which never came.

"I was afraid of that," said Evan at last. "Well, perhaps it's a good thing. If there's no money involved your so-called lease to Poole may not be valid."

"Well, actually—"

"Did he give you any money?"

"Just a shilling as a nominal rent—"

"Oh, my God," said Evan. "Father, I don't wish to seem disrespectful, but how did you get mixed up with this man? How did you meet him?"

"Well, you know how I have to open Colwyn Court to the public once a month in return for the Ministry of Works maintaining the castle and chapel ruins? Poole came in March. He said he was a tourist with an interest in old buildings, and Gwyneth, who was feeling well that day, showed him around the garden and took him up to the castle. Poole was tremendously interested and asked such intelligent questions that I invited him to lunch. He then offered to lease the entire estate for a year, but of course I couldn't agree to that and he went away again. The next day Gwyneth was ill—one of her attacks—and I was getting rather worried about her and the doctor was considering the hospital when Poole turned up again to ask if I'd had second thoughts about the lease. On hearing Gwyneth was ill he said he was a herbalist and asked if he could prescribe a remedy. Of course I said yes—I didn't see it could do any harm since the doctor wasn't doing much good, and anyway I'm rather a believer in the power of herbs myself. After all, in the old days—"

"So Poole mixed the potion and Gwyneth was instantly cured," said Evan. "That wasn't the herbs, Father. That was the power of suggestion."

"Perhaps," said Walter, not daring to argue. "Anyway, I was grateful to Poole, as you can imagine, and when he suggested a compromise over the lease—just the two wings instead of the whole house—I found myself agreeing—"

"I see."

"He seemed such a nice young man," said Walter defensively, "and after all, I am saving money on a housekeeper, and the society does do all the cleaning, and Gwyneth really has been much better—"

"Who pays the bills?"

"Bills?" said Walter, hoping he had misheard the question.

"Bills," said Evan. "Who shoulders the expense of feeding and maintaining thirteen extra people at Colwyn Court?"

"Well, as a matter of fact," said Walter, "I've been paying them, but Poole is going to repay me after August the first. Apparently the society is a little low in funds at the moment, but as soon as August comes—"

"I understand," said Evan in a quiet level voice that frightened Walter much more than an open display of temper would have done. "Now, Father, how are your financial affairs standing up to this? If you considered renting any part of Colwyn Court you must have been in difficult financial straits, and yet from what you tell me you must be leasing at a loss so far. Are you overdrawn at the bank? Have you had to sell some shares?"

"Well, I do have a little money," said Walter. "Your mother's money—which is in trust for you and Gwyneth to inherit when I die—gives me a small but steady income. I've had to sell one or two stocks and shares, but—"

"How much?"

"Well . . . rather a lot, I suppose, but then I took out a small mortgage on the house—"

"I see," said Evan.

"It's not too bad really," said Walter hopefully.

"Father, I don't want to contradict you, but with all due respect I hardly think matters could be much worse. However, one thing at least seems crystal clear. You're in no position financially to afford to keep thirteen people at your own expense at Colwyn Court. The society will have to go."

"But the lease—Gwyneth's health—I told Poole—"

"I'd be surprised if the lease is valid," said Evan, "but if it is maybe I can buy him out. That would probably be cheaper in the long run. As for Gwyneth, what she needs is a damned good psychiatrist. I don't like the thought of my sister being used as a guinea pig by a quack herbalist—in fact I refuse to sanction it once we're back at Colwyn Court. I admit Gwyneth has her troubles, but she needs professional help, not amateur folklore."

"Gwyneth's just a delicate girl," said Walter timidly.

"Father, this is the twentieth century. She doesn't have to be."

"I know you don't really believe that Gwyneth's genuinely ill, but—"

"Yes, I do. The fact that an illness is psychosomatic in origin doesn't make the physical symptoms of that illness any the less real. But the cause of her illness is mental, not physical."

"But she's so intelligent," said Walter doubtfully. "There's nothing wrong with her mind."

"This has nothing to do with intelligence, Father."

"But . . . well, Gwyneth will want Poole to stay. I know she will. Evan, wouldn't it be easier—less trouble all around—if he stayed?"

"You can't afford it, Father. And you can't afford to let Gwyneth use him as a crutch either. He won't cure her and in the long run she may be worse off than she was before she met him."

"I shan't know how to tell him to go," said Walter heavily. "I shan't know what to say to him. He's been such a nice young fellow—so kind—considerate—"

"I'll deal with him," said Evan. "Let me sort it out for you, Father."

"Well, I don't like to impose my troubles on you like this or you'll start to wish you'd never come home and then you'll think about going away again—"

"Not this time, Father," said Evan.

There was a silence. I must have misheard, thought Walter, not daring to believe his ears. He must have said something else.

"Of course there's so much opportunity for doctors in America," he said. "I know that."

"There are different kinds of opportunity," said Evan, "and money isn't everything. I came to realize while I was in Africa that I wasn't prepared to leave Wales—or England—on a permanent basis."

Walter said nothing but took Evan's hand in his and held it. Presently when he could speak again he said: "That rose garden's a lovely sight at the moment. It's been a very good year for roses."

They sat there for a time and watched the roses beyond the

smooth lawn. At last Evan stood up and ran a hand absentmindedly through his hair.

"So I have your permission to speak to Poole about this business?"

"Do whatever you think is best," said Walter, conscious only of
relief that the long-dreaded scene was over and of gratitude that
his dearest wish had been granted. "I leave it entirely up to you."

"I'll speak to him on Monday as soon as I have the chance to
see him in person," said Evan, and against his better judgment
began to picture Poole inviting Nicola to Wales as if he, not
Walter, were the master of Colwyn Court.

*iv*

It was late on Sunday when Evan and Walter reached Colwyn
Court and Benedict, Jane, Lisa and the twins arrived back at
Colwyn Cottage. Evan had decided there was nothing more he
could do about the society until Poole returned, but on Monday
morning he summoned all his patience and went to see his sister.
As he glanced into her room he found her designing an enormous
poster with a series of felt-tip pens.

"Can I see you for a moment, please, Gwyneth?" he said politely, raising his voice to be heard above the thunderous noises
from the record player. He glanced at the poster again. Gwyneth
had drawn a series of circles above a bold black pentagram which
stood on one point with two of the other points rising toward
the top of the paper.

"What's that?" said Evan, trying to remember what he had read
about occupational therapy.

"My concept of the fifth dimension," said Gwyneth, and
switched off the record player.

"I see," said Evan. Various Rorschach tests flickered hazily across
his mind. "Gwyneth, I want to talk to you about Father."

"If it's going to lead on to something nasty about Tristan," said Gwyneth, sharp as a needle, "you can go and talk to someone else."

"I'm mainly concerned with Father at the moment." He sat down on the rug beside her in an attempt to establish some sort of intimacy. "Gwyneth, Father's in a bad way financially. It seems that the society is living off him at the moment, and the expense is certainly much more than he can afford."

"I'm sure Tristan will pay him back eventually," said Gwyneth, unconcerned, and drew a circle around the entire pentagram.

"Possibly," said Evan, "but meanwhile I don't think Father's in a position to support the society at Colwyn Court. In fact he's hardly in a position to support himself, let alone the society."

"Well, what am I supposed to do about it?" said Gwyneth aggressively. "It's no good expecting me to go out and get a job."

"No, I know you're not fit enough for that at the moment. But medicine's so advanced nowadays, and I really think one of the top men in Harley Street might—"

"I'll never be fit enough to earn my living," said Gwyneth.

"Maybe not, but wouldn't you at least like to live without the fear that one of your attacks might be just around the corner?"

"I'm incurable," said Gwyneth. "Daddy understands, even if you don't."

"Supposing I were to tell you that Father's anxious for you to take my advice and see a Harley Street specialist to see what—if anything—can be done to help you?"

"Daddy would do anything you told him," said Gwyneth. "That doesn't mean anything."

"But—"

"Oh, why don't you go away to America and leave us alone!" burst out Gwyneth. "It was so peaceful when you were in Africa! Daddy and I are quite happy here without you barging in and messing everything up! Why do you always have to interfere and spoil everything?"

Phrases from a dozen textbooks on Freud flashed through Evan's memory.

"I'm only trying to help," he said at last.

"No, you're not," said Gwyneth. "You're trying to drive a wedge between me and Daddy."

There was a silence.

"And between me and Daddy and Tristan," added Gwyneth as an afterthought.

"Gwyneth, the society isn't going to stay here forever, you know. Poole's going to leave one day."

"I'll be ill if he goes," said Gwyneth, and drew another circle with a violet marker.

"If you're ill perhaps you'll think differently about seeing someone in Harley Street."

"If I'm ill perhaps I'll die."

"Possibly," said Evan, "but I doubt it." And he stood up and walked abruptly out of the room.

The record player started blaring seconds after he had left.

On an impulse he entered the east wing where half the society had their rooms, and after knocking on the doors opened them and looked inside. All the rooms were littered with feminine possessions but none of the occupants responded to his knock for admittance. The rooms were empty. Retracing his steps Evan moved across to the west wing where the other half of the society was quartered and swiftly followed the same procedure.

The last door was locked.

Evan did not hesitate. Two minutes later he was opening the door of the housekeeper's cupboard off the scullery, and when he did not find what he wanted he immediately sought out Agnes Miller.

"Miss Miller, where is the duplicate key of that very large bedroom at the extreme end of the west wing—the bedroom with the dressing room attached to it?"

"Duplicate key?" said Agnes, very plump and benign.

"Yes, it seems to be missing from the housekeeper's cupboard where all the duplicate keys are kept."

"Ah," said Agnes, "that's because the room belongs to Mr. Poole and he keeps both the key and the duplicate key. Mr. Poole has very strong views on privacy, living as he does in the midst of twelve women. I'm sure you understand."

"I think there should always be a duplicate key available," said Evan, "in case of fire."

"How sensible!" exclaimed Agnes admiringly. "I hadn't thought of that. I'll speak to Mr. Poole about it just as soon as he arrives back this afternoon, and I'm sure he'll be able to suggest a suitable compromise."

"Thank you," said Evan abruptly, and turned aside.

"Is there something you want from Mr. Poole's room, Dr. Colwyn?"

"It's not important. I thought I had some things stored in that big cupboard in the dressing room, and to get to the dressing room one has to go through the bedroom."

"Yes, I see. Have you tried the attics? I know that everything in that particular cupboard at the moment belongs to Mr. Poole, so if you had anything stored there it must have been moved to another part of the house."

"In that case I'll try the attics. Thank you, Miss Miller."

But he made no effort to search the attics. Instead he took the car and spent the afternoon savoring the familiar scenery of the Gower Peninsula and planning his coming interview with Poole. He went to the church by the beach at Oxwich, and drove beyond Oxwich to Port Eynon along the twisting country roads. From Port Eynon he headed for Rhossili and sat for a while on the cliffs while the sheep grazed peacefully nearby and the waves broke on the empty beach which stretched to the sand dunes of Llangenith. By the time he arrived back at Colwyn it was after six and Poole and Nicola had still not arrived from London.

At that point Evan had to take a tight grip on himself. He could feel the rage begin to boil within him and knew he was on the verge of losing his temper before he had even seen the man. Why had Nicola accepted the lift from Poole? How had Poole managed to persuade her to come to Colwyn when Evan himself had failed? Poole . . . Who was Poole anyway?

Evan's patience snapped; recklessness overcame him. Slipping into the potting shed near the greenhouses he found a strip of wire and pocketed a screwdriver. Then, making sure that no one saw him, he returned to the west wing and checked each room again to be certain that no one was about.

No one was. The members of the society were either helping in the preparation of the evening meal or else congregated in their sitting room downstairs, and he was alone on the second floor. Evan made up his mind, bent the wire into the most accommodating shape and inserted it carefully in the keyhole of Poole's locked door.

But the lock was so old and stiff that it was hard to spring. Evan tried the cover of his driving license after he had abandoned the wire, but when this too failed he turned to the screwdriver and resorted to the extreme measure of dismantling the panel which surrounded the handle.

Seconds passed. A succession of small sounds kept him glancing repeatedly over his shoulder, but they all came from the sitting room downstairs and the corridor remained deserted. The front of the lock came off; the unmasked mechanism confronted him. Using the screwdriver Evan flicked the lock aside, pressed the catch back, and walked into the room.

The first noticeable characteristic of the room was its neatness. Everything was in place; no knickknacks littered the room, no discarded clothes, no framed photographs. Above the bed was the only picture in the room, a crude modern painting of a black pentagram on a violent red background. The pentagram, which stood on one of its five points with two other points stretching upward, reminded Evan with a jolt of Gwyneth's drawing. Perhaps, he thought, Poole had brought her to this room. Perhaps he had even . . .

Evan had to grab his self-control again as it threatened to slip away from him. With a great effort he managed to pull himself together. Perhaps Gwyneth had painted the picture and given it to Poole as a token of appreciation. In which case it would be perfectly natural for Poole to hang the picture in his room.

The bedroom was large, but the furniture had been arranged in such a way that the center of the room was empty. The slim single bed was pushed against one wall; the chest of drawers hugged the wall opposite, and the table and chair had been placed beneath one of the windows. A gray, black-flecked carpet yawned emptily across the uncluttered floor. Evan was reminded of a room which had been cleared to allow people to dance. Perplexed, he wandered across to the dressing room beyond and opened the door of the large built-in closet which stretched along one wall, but all he found there were ten suits, either black or gray, and an assortment of black shoes. He was about to leave the dressing room when he saw the dark stain on the bedroom floor where the black-flecked carpet did not quite reach the wall.

The stain looked like blood. Evan pulled back the carpet and saw that the wooden floorboards had been marked by chalk pentagrams and, beyond, the curve of an enormous circle. Rolling back the carpet further he became aware of an odd odor, unpleasant and hard to identify. After a moment he replaced the carpet, straightened his back, and strode back into the dressing room to see if any of the suits in the closets were bloodstained, but he found no mark of any kind on the clothes. He was about to turn away from the closet again when he saw the box.

The closet was deep and the box was at the back of it so Evan was not surprised that he had missed it during his first inspection. He tried to drag the box forward into the light and was surprised how heavy it was. Grabbing the handle he tilted the box on its side, and heard a clink and a thud as the contents fell against one another. His fingers worked at the hasps without success. The box was locked and Poole obviously had the key.

Evan stepped back and surveyed his discovery thoughtfully. One locked black wooden box. Several floorboards defaced with childish drawings and covered by a brand-new carpet. One stain which might or might not be blood and which someone had carelessly left only partially concealed by this same brand-new carpet. One very odd smell of uncertain origin, and a remarkable preponderance of pentagrams.

Mr. Poole, thought Evan, without doubt has a most curious taste in interior decoration.

He was still considering Poole's tastes a second later when without any warning there was a small cough behind him and the sound of someone clearing his throat.

"May I help you, Dr. Colwyn?" inquired Tristan Poole from the doorway.

# Chapter Six

*i*

Poole was wearing yet another of his dark suits, white shirts, and conservative ties. He looked like a city executive accustomed to daily board meetings in the conference room of some massively influential corporation. Apart from the fact that there was faint creases across the front of his trousers there was no hint that he had just spent several hours sitting at the wheel of a car.

"May I help you?" he repeated politely. His dark eyes were watchful, his face expressionless. "Were you looking for something?"

"Yes, I was," said Evan, keeping his voice cool and controlled. "I had some papers stored in this cupboard and I was wondering where they'd gone."

"They're in the attics, the room where the old upright piano is. The boxes containing your papers are on the floor next to a defunct sewing machine."

"Thank you," said Evan.

"You're entirely welcome," said Poole. "I'm only sorry your need for the papers was so great that you had to dismantle the lock on the door and break into my room."

"Wasn't that a pity?" said Evan blandly. "I'll just put the lock back into place again before I leave."

"Thank you so much. Incidentally, may I, as Miss Miller's friend, inquire—purely as a matter of interest, of course—why you chose to regard her as a liar?"

"I beg your pardon?" said Evan.

"I understand Miss Miller told you the papers were in the attic some hours ago."

"She didn't tell me which attic," said Evan. "I couldn't find the papers and thought she was mistaken. Excuse me, please." And he walked past Poole through the bedroom and proceeded to re-assemble the mutilated lock.

"I'm sure you're unaware of this," said Poole's voice behind him, "but the lease your father granted me gave you no right to enter either the east or west wing which are now the private property of the society."

"The landlord usually has an implied right to enter his property to make repairs," said Evan, twisting the screws deftly into place.

"But not to break down doors and commit acts of trespass."

Evan said nothing but continued reassembling the lock.

"Maybe you'd like to see the lease," said Poole.

"I'd be delighted," said Evan, fastening the last screw. "As a matter of fact, that was one of the things I was anxious to talk to you about."

"Oh?" Poole was opening the drawer of the table by the window. When he turned Evan could see a legal document in his hands. "Well, you're welcome to inspect the lease," he said, and held out the document to Evan.

Evan straightened his back, tried the door to make sure the catch was working, and pocketed his screwdriver again. Finally he accepted the document and glanced at it casually.

"Does my father have a copy of this?"

"I'm sure his solicitor gave him a copy, yes."

"His solicitor?"

"His solicitor drew up the lease. Didn't your father tell you?"

"I see." Evan stared at the lease, unable to grasp a word of the fine print confronting him, and clung grimly to the calm manner he had adopted.

"I think you'll find it's all perfectly legal," said Poole serenely.

"Thank you." Evan handed the lease back to him.

"Was there something else you wanted to talk to me about?"

"Yes, I understand you owe my father a considerable amount of money."

"I have nothing to do with household expenses," said Poole. "Miss Miller handles those sort of trivial details for me, I'm glad to say. But I can assure you that all debts will be settled in August. If you like I can ask Miss Miller to itemize the expenses your father has had recently in connection with the society, and present you with a copy so that you can see how minimal the debt really is. Your phrase 'a considerable amount' strikes me, if you'll forgive me saying so, as exaggerated. However, if the situation is troubling you I'd be happy to give you an I.O.U. for the amount in question."

"There's no exaggeration," said Evan. "In relation to my father's current financial situation I still say that you owe him too much money. I'm afraid it's not an economic possibility for him to continue to support your society here at Colwyn Court."

"August is less than four weeks away."

"I'm afraid that makes no difference. He can't afford to lease his home rent-free."

"He's saving money on a housekeeper."

"His expenses are greater than his savings. And talking of a housekeeper, that reminds me of something else I wanted to say. I don't like the cooking this society of yours specializes in. Why should we be obliged to eat nature foods if we don't want to?"

"Your meals are ordinary meals prepared especially for you."

"Well, I don't like the cooking. Doesn't your cook ever use salt? The food is bland, tasteless, and almost inedible."

"Too much salt in a diet, Dr. Colwyn," said Poole, "can have an adverse effect on those who suffer from high blood pressure."

"And no salt at all," said Evan, "can cause painful cramps in certain groups of muscles. Are you trying to teach me my profession, Mr. Poole?"

"Are you trying to tell me to get out of Colwyn Court, Dr. Colwyn?"

"I'm sorry, but all things considered, I think it would be best if the society found somewhere else for its headquarters. If the lease is valid I could of course offer you compensation—"

"The lease is valid," said Poole. "I reject your offer of compensation."

There was a pause. They stood looking at each other, Evan big and untidy with his red hair standing up in tousled, angry tufts, Poole slim and controlled, his appearance immaculate, his eyes dark with a polite detached interest.

Damn him, thought Evan furiously, he's getting the better of me.

"Dr. Colwyn," said Poole, "let's be rational about this. There's no sense in losing our tempers. I appreciate the fact that you're worried about the money we owe your father; I'll have Miss Miller work out exactly what we owe him and then I'll write you a promissory note which I shall be able to honor within the next two months. I appreciate the fact that you're dissatisfied with the cooking; I'll pass on your complaints to Miss Miller and no doubt she'll make the necessary alterations when your meals are prepared in future. But don't, please, expect us to move from Colwyn Court before our lease is up. We have every right to be here and, distasteful though it may be to you, we have every intention of staying."

"I see," said Evan. "Well, at least you've made your intentions clear."

"I'm sorry you should feel so much hostility toward us. If you were to accept our presence I see no reason why we shouldn't co-exist peacefully enough."

"Since we're being so frank with one another," said Evan, "I may as well tell you that I have every intention of seeking legal advice on that lease. And while you're at Colwyn Court I'd be obliged if you would have nothing further to do with my sister. I'm aware that she's ill, but I think any amateur help could do more harm than good at this stage."

"I'm not an amateur," said Poole.

"I understand you were educated in America. Are you entitled to put the letters M.D. after your name?"

"Dr. Colwyn, if you'll forgive my saying so, I think your judgment is clouded by the conventional Englishman's dislike of America and all things American."

"You couldn't be more wrong," said Evan. "Are you entitled to the letters M.D. or aren't you?"

"Do I call myself Dr. Poole?"

"Is that an answer?"

"It tells you I don't believe in the conventional worship of initials bestowed by an ignorant establishment."

"So you're not a qualified doctor. Thank you. Now would you kindly leave my sister to the attentions of those who are qualified?"

"The attentions of those who are qualified," said Poole, "were hardly helping your sister before I came on the scene."

"Nevertheless—"

"I have a degree in psychology, Dr. Colwyn. In fact I know a hell of a lot more about Gwyneth's trouble than either the inefficient family doctor who was attending her before I came here or, with respect, you yourself with your admirable—and in this case utterly irrelevant—background of tropical medicine."

"I—"

"Tropical illness," said Poole, "is not what Gwyneth is suffering from."

"Why, you—"

"Would you like a clinical diagnosis about what's wrong with your sister?"

"I'm not interested in a few psychological terms flung together by some fraudulent quack!" yelled Evan. "You stay away from my sister or I'll—"

"My dear Dr. Colwyn, anyone would think I was sleeping with

her, judging from all the fuss you're making about the relationship!"

"I wouldn't be surprised if you were!" shouted Evan, beside
himself with rage. "I wouldn't be surprised if you were sleeping
with all twelve of those women you've got here! I wouldn't be
surprised if—"

"What a tribute to my sexual capacity," said Poole. "Thank you
very much."

"And another thing I want to talk to you about is Nicola Morrison!" Evan burst out, hardly hearing what the other man said.
"You stay away from her, do you understand? You keep your
hands off my girl! If you think you can—"

"Your girl?" said Poole. "Congratulations! I didn't know you
were engaged."

"We weren't engaged!" growled Evan. "But we're engaged now
so just you stay away from her."

"All right," said Poole. "But I'd check with Nicola first, if I were
you. I had the distinct impression on the journey down here today that she didn't consider herself engaged to anyone. Now if
you'll excuse me, I really must have a bath and change my clothes
before dinner. Good night, Dr. Colwyn, and—" He paused for a
smile—"try to feel more confidence in your self-image. Then you
won't feel so threatened by any unfamiliar element in your surroundings."

And before Evan could begin to swing his fist the bedroom
door was shut in his face and Poole was deftly turning the key in
the lock.

*

## ii

"Nicki?" said Evan, knocking on the door of the tiny spare room
in the main part of the building. "Nicki, can I talk to you for a
minute?"

"Wait." There was a pause before she opened the door an inch. She was wearing a white bathrobe, which he guessed she had dragged on in a hurry, and was barefoot. "Hello," she said. "I'm just changing. Can it wait for half an hour?"

"No, I don't think it can." He wondered if she was wearing anything beneath the bathrobe. A stream of muddled thoughts began to clamor in his mind and seep deliciously through his body. "Can I come in?"

"Well, I suppose so," said Nicola warily, and hugged her bathrobe closer to her as if it were a life belt. "What's the matter?"

"Nicki—" He stepped into the room and closed the door. "—Nicki, I've been an absolute fool, thinking I didn't know my own mind about all this, putting off any major involvement, wallowing in my indecisiveness the whole damned time. Nicki, I'm sorry about all the mess in the past. I love you and I want to marry you and let's go into Swansea first thing tomorrow morning to see if they've got a decent ring for me to give you to celebrate the engagement."

There was a pause. He was breathing unevenly but felt as if a huge burden had been lifted from his back, and the blood was starting to sing through his veins.

"Engagement?" said Nicola blankly.

"Engagement!" He smiled at her and moved to take her in his arms but she stepped away from him before he could reach her.

All she said was: "Isn't this rather sudden?"

"Sudden! After all these months?" He burst out laughing. "Darling, I've been as slow as a caterpillar and you know it! How can you call it sudden?"

The bathrobe slipped a little; he felt himself moving forward again before he could stop himself. "We can get married as soon as possible," he heard himself say. "This month, next month—any month you like." By this time she had her back to the dressing table and could retreat no further, so he took her in his arms and started to kiss her. So exhilarated was he that it took him a full minute to realize she was making no effort to respond to him.

He stopped. "Nicki?"

Her gray eyes were dark with some expression he did not understand. At last she said, "I've got to think about this. I can't
give you an answer straight away. I'm sorry, Evan, but you've got
to give me time to think about it."

He heard her words but his mind refused to accept them. "But
you've had months and months to think about it!"

"Please," was all she said. "Please, Evan."

"All right," he said, baffled. "If you want to play it that way,
what does it matter? Every girl's entitled to time to consider a
proposal, no matter how obvious the outcome is! But meanwhile
. . . . Nicki, I want you so much! Can I—let me—"

"Please don't touch me," she said sharply.

He stopped. A chill began to inch through the heat in his body.
He looked at her uncertainly.

"I want to marry you," he said at last. "I'm going to marry you.
Surely you're not going to tell me that you—"

"I don't want that at the moment. I don't want to go to bed
with you now."

"Isn't that a bit hypocritical? It's not as if nothing's ever happened between us. And since we love each other and we're going
to be married—"

"Are we?" said Nicola. "I'm not sure. I've got to think about
it. Let's leave it for now, Evan. Please."

Every muscle in his body went taut. He could feel the hurt and
anger lock together in his throat so that it was hard for him to
breathe.

"Is it Poole?" he said suddenly. "It's Poole, isn't it."

"Don't be ridiculous," said Nicola. "I hardly know the man.
Please, Evan, please leave me alone. I don't want to talk about it
any more tonight."

He hesitated, then moved awkwardly toward the door. She saw
his fingers slip unsteadily on the handle as he wrenched the door
open and stumbled into the passage.

She was alone.

For ten long bewildered minutes she sat on the edge of the bed
and tried to make sense of her thoughts. What she was most con-

scious of was that she felt nothing at all. No relief, no joy, no sadness, no anxiety. She felt as if she were in a state of limbo where
all emotions were suspended.

"But I'm crazy about Evan," she said aloud. "Crazy about him."

The words echoed hollowly around the empty room. She got
up, walked over to the window, leaned her arms upon the sill.

"I've spent fifteen months aching to marry him," she reminded
herself incredulously. "Fifteen months of crying at odd moments,
fighting off depressions, and turning down dates because no man
ever measured up to Evan."

She waited. Nothing happened. She felt surprised but nothing
else. Perhaps it was good to feel surprised. To feel something was
better than to feel nothing at all.

"Perhaps I've gone mad," she said to herself and sat down on
the edge of the bed again to consider the idea with interest. "Or
perhaps I'm drunk. Or perhaps I'm dead and don't know it."

She was still considering this intriguing possibility when there
was another knock on her door.

"Come in!" called Nicola, too fascinated by her emotional
numbness to care who it was.

The door opened. She looked up.

And suddenly her emotions blazed into life. It was as if they
were switches on a huge board and someone was flicking them all
into action with a gigantic sweep of his hand. She felt lights
streaming down on her, the warmth of a thousand flames, the
whirl of brilliant colors cascading through her mind.

"Tristan!" she exclaimed. She jumped up and ran over to him.
"Tristan, I feel so peculiar I can't even begin to explain it to you!"

He smiled at her. His clothes were black and white but all she
could see was color, and color was something she could touch and
taste and drink until the well ran dry.

"I'm going to faint," said Nicola.

"No, you're not."

Time was displaced. She could see him grasping it in his hands
and turning back the clock. One month. Two months. Three . . .

four . . . And time was something one could twist and bend, a slave in the hands of eternity. One year. Two. Three—

And suddenly she was back in the days when she had never known Evan Colwyn and she was free and young and it was good to be alive.

"I'm drugged," said Nicola.

"No, you're just seeing things as they really are."

"I'm going crazy."

"You're sane for the first time in three years."

"Oh my God," whispered Nicola, "I really believe I am."

He touched her and everything seemed to steady down. When she clung to him instinctively the tiny room looked the same again and Poole's suit was black and his shirt was white and his dark eyes were inches from her own.

He kissed her. At first it was just like any other kiss a man might have given her but then it changed and it was like nothing she had ever experienced before. Senses which she had not even known existed flared to life until she saw the world expanding into an unknown and mystical dimension which existed without beginning and without end in a wilderness of time.

He stopped kissing her. The world tilted back to normality and the room spun around to meet her. The evening light was streaming through the window to slant across the panels of the closed door.

"Take me back," said Nicola. "Where we were before. Take me back." And she reached up and pulled his face down to hers so that she could touch his mouth again with her own.

She felt his fingers sliding over her skin and realized for the first time that her bathrobe was on the floor and she was naked. But then his mouth closed on hers and all the conventions of a petty decaying world were lost amid the velvet darkness of a hundred solar systems and the heat was blazing down upon her from a vast and invisible powerhouse.

"Oh God," said Nicola, "I'm in heaven."

He laughed. Opening her eyes she saw him above her, his face so close to her own that she could glimpse only the wide curve of his mouth and the whiteness of his uneven teeth.

"Why are you laughing?" she whispered.

"Because you've just said something which amused me," he said, and his voice was the voice of darkness welcoming her to the brilliance of a fierce and fiery night.

## iii

The sun had set by the time Poole left Nicola's room and padded downstairs in search of Agnes. He found her in the society's dining room where a place was still set for him at the table, and as soon as he walked in she jumped to her feet with an exclamation of relief.

"At last!" she said as if she had given up all hope of seeing him again that night. "I knew I couldn't interrupt you so I spent the last half hour willing you to make yourself accessible as soon as possible! Listen, Tristan, Lisa's here. She's been waiting in the sitting room and she absolutely refuses to go without seeing you. What on earth are we going to do about her?"

"Agnes," said Poole. "You're an incurable worrier. Where's my dinner?"

"But what about—"

"I'm damned hungry, Agnes. If there's any dinner left I'd like some at once, please."

Agnes sighed. "Yes, Tristan. Just a minute—I'll get it for you."

"Thanks." He sank down in the high-backed chair at the head of the table and traced a pentagram on the tablecloth with his fork as he thought of Nicola.

When Agnes returned with a plate of steaming food all she said was: "Satisfactory?"

Poole took a mouthful of stuffed aubergine. "Delicious."

"I didn't mean the food," said Agnes.

"Neither did I," said Poole.

They were still smiling at each other when Agnes' sister popped her head around the door of the dining room.

"Lisa's back again, Agnes—bothering us in the kitchen, I mean. She says she refuses to wait in the sitting room any longer and that she absolutely insists on seeing Tristan without delay. What shall I do?"

"Oh, bother the woman!" said Agnes irritably. "I'll go and fend her off again."

"Don't waste your time," said Poole. "Show her in, Harriet."

"Oh, by the way," said Agnes as her sister vanished obediently, "before I forget—Evan's talking of going to London again tomorrow, something about finding a doctor for Gwyneth and consulting some private detectives. You've made an enemy there, Tristan."

"Agnes," said Poole tolerantly, "will you kindly stop worrying? You'll give yourself an ulcer and it's really quite unnecessary."

"All right," said Agnes. "Well, I'll leave you alone with your ladyfriend and try to think about something else."

"You can make an itemized list of how much we owe Walter Colwyn. I promised Evan an I.O.U."

"You brute," said Agnes. "If anything's going to give me an ulcer it's those wretched accounts. Very well, I'll do my best. Good luck with Lisa."

"Good luck with the adding and subtraction." He took another mouthful of aubergine and was still chewing it thoughtfully when Lisa swept into the room. "Hello," he said. "How are you?" He made no effort to stand up but merely motioned her to sit down next to him at the table. "Have a seat."

"Thanks for the five-star welcome," said Lisa. "Where the hell have you been?"

"In London."

"You said you'd phone on Saturday! I waited all day—"

"I'm sorry about that," said Poole.

"Well . . ." She hesitated. She was nervous, he noticed, and there was a stubborn look in her eyes. "I think you might have kept your promise," she said unevenly.

"I'm sorry," said Poole.

There was a pause. Poole kept on eating.

"What's the matter?" demanded Lisa, mystified. "What is it?"

"Nothing."

Another pause.

"Tristan, I must talk to you!"

"Go ahead."

"Well, I . . . I'm in an awful mess, and—well, it's not entirely my fault, is it? I mean, if Matt hadn't seen us together on the beach—"

"My dear, you can't blame me just because your husband changed his will in a fit of temper and drove into a wall before he could calm down enough to change the will back again!"

"Of course I can blame you!" stormed Lisa. "If I hadn't met you Matt wouldn't have changed his will like that!"

"If it hadn't been me it would have been someone else."

"How dare you!" She sprang to her feet in a rage.

"Oh, let's be honest, Lisa! You were bored to tears with that husband of yours and were more than ready to offer yourself to the first man that was willing!"

She tried to hit him but he dropped his knife quickly enough to lunge forward and catch her wrist. There was a silence. Lisa tried to back away but he only tightened the grip of his fingers so that her effort to escape was useless. She began to panic.

"Tristan, I'm sorry—I—I didn't mean it, I—"

"Lisa," said Poole in a quiet, level voice, "you didn't love me. You don't love me. You never will love me. I apologize if I seem undeservedly brutal, but at this stage I think it's important that we both face this basic truth. We met, there were unfortunate repercussions that left a nasty taste in my mouth—and in yours too, I've no doubt—and I think it would be best for both of us now if we decided to go our separate ways. I say that for your sake, just as much as for my own. If word gets around about what we

were doing before your husband died I think you might find even
a sympathetic judge unfriendly when you start to contest the will."

"Well . . ."

He waited.

"Yes," said Lisa at last, "I suppose that's so. But—"

"Yes?"

"I do love you, Tristan. I can't help it—"

"You don't love me, Lisa."

"But—"

"You don't love me."

She was silent.

"I'm right, you know. It's much better to part now before any
further harm's done."

"I . . . suppose so."

"It is."

"Yes." She turned away, but he still held her wrist.

"Lisa."

"Yes?"

"One last kiss for old times' sake?"

She smiled shakily and raised her mouth to his but he kissed
her on the forehead. His hands stroked her hair softly and began
to untie the scarf that tied her hair back from her face. "Will you
give me a keepsake?" he said softly. "Something to remember you
by?"

She nodded and her gesture shook her hair loose as he pulled
the scarf away. He noticed again with a vague pang of regret how
pretty she was.

"Good luck, Lisa. I'm sorry, but I know this is for the best."

"Yes." She was groping for the door. "You're right. But it seems
pretty damn hard." And then she was gone, her shoes echoing
dully in the corridor, and as he listened he thought he heard her
crying.

Agnes slipped into the dining room thirty seconds later. "I can't
help it," she said, "I couldn't resist coming to find out—what
happened?"

Poole had returned to his dinner. "This meal's very good, Agnes. First-class."

"But what about Lisa? Is everything all right?"

"I'm not sure. Sit down, Agnes." He waited until she was seated in Lisa's chair before adding casually: "I want you to do something for me. Do you think you could reverse an induced infatuation?"

"I don't see why not," said Agnes, glancing at Lisa's scarf which lay limply on the table. "Does the scarf have any of her hairs on it?"

"Possibly. But it's her scarf. That's all that matters."

"I'd rather have the hairs. More personal."

"True. Are you sure of the precise preparations needed?"

"I could look them up," said Agnes, "just to make sure."

"Would you? Agnes, I do appreciate the way you take all these trivial matters off my shoulders . . . Use my room first thing tomorrow morning and choose whichever acolyte you feel would be most suitable. I'd do the job myself but I don't want to spend all tomorrow morning playing the magician when Nicola will expect me to spend it playing a very different role . . . I'm sure you understand."

"Of course," said Agnes sympathetically. "Don't worry about Lisa—I'll take care of her for you. But can't you simply hypnotize her? Wouldn't that be equally effective?"

"Perhaps. And perhaps not. Hypnosis is an uncertain tool in some ways, and in Lisa's case I don't want to rely on hypnosis when I have a more reliable way of dealing with her. I'm using some hypnosis at present but I'd prefer you to summon a more permanent force to solve the problem for us."

"Yes, Tristan."

"Oh, and Agnes—"

"Yes, Tristan?"

"Try not to kill her, please. It might cause unfortunate comment so soon after her husband's death."

"Yes, Tristan," said Agnes obediently, and began to dwell with pleasurable anticipation on the powers she would summon to subjugate Lisa's unruly passion . . .

*iv*

A week passed.

In London, Evan, still smarting from the lack of enthusiasm which had greeted his long-delayed proposal of marriage, had talked to a well-known psychiatrist about his sister, taken counsel's opinion on the ill-fated lease, and had hired a firm of private detectives to make inquiries into Poole's past. After four days of brooding the counsel had reported that the lease was legal; the psychiatrist had told Evan he would be willing to see Gwyneth if she could be coaxed to London for treatment; and the detectives had announced that if there was anything unsavory about Mr. Tristan Poole it would certainly be revealed by their unflagging efforts to excavate the details of his background. For the time being Evan had done all that he could, and he decided to return to Colwyn Court to see if Nicola were in a more reasonable frame of mind.

He felt most annoyed with Nicola. As each day passed he became more convinced than ever that she was treating him badly, and he found it hard to restrain himself from phoning Colwyn Court to talk to her. But he did not phone. He had decided to give her exactly what she wanted—time to think over his proposal—so that when he saw her again she could not accuse him of pestering her into a rushed decision.

Meanwhile at Colwyn Cottage Benedict was making good progress with his thesis and Jane was enjoying every minute of her time with the twins. After a while she realized she was seeing more of the twins than Lisa was. Lisa was silent and withdrawn and spent most of the time in her room. After worrying about her Jane decided Lisa was still suffering from the shock of Matt's death, and resolved to make an even greater effort to be kind and sympathetic toward her.

Lisa herself felt indifferent to everything; she had never suffered from such lassitude before but when Jane suggested it was the aftermath of shock Lisa accepted the explanation and ceased to worry about it. She would have liked to have seen Poole again, but she was too tired even to walk up to Colwyn Court. Lying in bed she would think of Poole for hours on end, but gradually her memory of him became dulled and the violent excitement his presence had roused in her was replaced by that same baffling indifference which Jane had attributed to shock. But after a week of lassitude she began to feel better, and on the day Evan left London again for Colwyn she decided to get up after lunch and take a stroll on the beach.

It was a fine afternoon. As Lisa dressed slowly in her room Jane was mixing a batch of scones in the kitchen and the twins were sprawled full-length on the turf inside the walls of Colwyn Castle. The mythical saga of their long-lost father had reached a crucial and absorbing stage.

"So there he was," said Timothy. "Face to face with the Bengal tiger."

"And the Star of India glittering evilly in his hip pocket."

"Do rubies glitter?"

"The Star of India's not a ruby, stupid! It's a—" Lucy stopped.

"Yes?" said Timothy.

"I hear something." Lucy was listening intently. "Voices."

"Just like Joan of Arc!"

"Shhh! Can't you hear them?"

Timothy could. "Let's hide."

"Okay."

They jumped up, flattened themselves against the castle walls, and peered through one of the slits which served as windows.

"It's that Miss Miller," said Timothy.

"It's both the Miss Millers. The other one's her sister. I wonder if they're coming into the castle."

"No, they're going to the chapel."

"When they're inside let's—"

"—sneak up on them and see what they're doing. Yes, let's,"

said Timothy, annoyed that Lucy had thought of the idea before he had.

Agnes and her sister Harriet disappeared slowly behind the walls of the chapel and the sound of their voices abruptly vanished.

"Let's go," said Timothy.

"Okay."

They sped along, bent double across the yards of turf which separated the castle from the chapel. Two of the wild horses grazing nearby lifted their heads in astonishment and further down the hillside one of the flock of grazing sheep lifted his head and bleated disapprovingly at the sky.

"Silly sheep," muttered Lucy.

"Shhh!"

They crawled to a gap in the weather-beaten masonry and peered through into the chapel ruins. The voices reached them clearly now; they could hear every word that was said.

"Such a lovely place," said Agnes. "Tristan was so right about it. It's got the most wonderful nuances."

"What a treat for Lammas! I shall feel so proud to be one of the hostesses in a setting like this!"

"Won't we all," said Agnes comfortably. She was examining the stone slab which was all that remained of the altar.

"I suppose there's no doubt about the chapel being deconsecrated?" said Harriet.

"None at all. That was the first thing Tristan confirmed with Walter Colwyn."

"Lovely!" said Harriet. After a pause she asked: "Have you any idea yet what form the rites will take?"

"I haven't discussed it thoroughly with Tristan yet, but there'll be a ceremony of homage as usual, of course, followed by the mass—"

"What's Tristan going to do about the problem of getting a virgin?"

"He's thought of a way out of that one. There's going to be a christening. The virginity will be offered to the powers in the form of a christening instead of in the form of the mass."

"How nice! I don't think I've ever been present at a christening before. Will the mass take a nuptial form?"

"Yes, we must start thinking about making the dress. Black satin, I thought, with lots of black lace . . . Perhaps we can go to Swansea next week and pick out a pattern."

"Lovely!" said Harriet. Then: "What will the sacrifice be?"

"Oh, a lamb, of course. The heroic symbol of the Other Church."

"What about the heroic symbol of *Our* Church? Will there be a goat?"

"You mean for the self-indulgence after the mass and the christening? I don't think so. Not since Tristan will be there in person. Why bother with a substitute in those circumstances?"

"Why indeed?" agreed Harriet as they left the chapel and wandered away leisurely together down the hillside, their black skirts flapping in the breeze.

Far below the surf crashed against the cliffs and flung spray high into the air. A sheep bleated again in the distance and the horses browsed quietly among the short grass.

The twins looked at one another.

"Did you understand any of that?" said Lucy frankly at last. "I thought they were talking English but after a while I wasn't so sure."

"'Course I understood," said Timothy loftily, making the most of one of Lucy's rare confessions of inadequacy. "The society have their own special religion which is sort of like Roman Catholics but a bit different and there's going to be a wedding and a christening."

"Maybe they *are* Catholics."

"They can't be because of the chapel not being consecrated. Consecrated means holy, and if the chapel's not holy any more, Catholics can't use it. Protestants couldn't either probably."

"Well, if they're not Catholics and not Protestants, what are they? And what was all that about a lamb and a goat?"

"That must be part of the religion. Like the Romans. The Romans were always sacrificing goats and lambs and things."

"They weren't going to sacrifice the goat," said Lucy. "The goat was for self-indulgence. What did that mean, do you think?"

"It must be like the Catholics. They have things called indulgences."

"What are they?"

"Just part of the religion," said Timothy, who had no idea.

"Well, if you ask me," said Lucy dissatisfied, "it's all very peculiar."

"The society *is* peculiar," said Timothy with a yawn. "Everyone knows that."

"Do we tell anyone?"

"Well . . . maybe we could tell Aunt Jane. She's the only person I can think of who might be interested."

"That's a good idea," said Lucy. "Let's tell Aunt Jane."

"Okay."

They set off down the hill and quarter of an hour later were at the back door of the cottage.

"Hello, twins," said Jane. "You're just in time for some scones fresh from the oven! That was good timing."

"Aunt Jane," said Lucy, "guess what. There's going to be a wedding at the chapel on the cliffs. The society is organizing it and—"

"—people are coming from miles around to be there," said Timothy, "because the society is going to be the hosts, just like a party. And there's going to be a christening too."

"But they're not going to have a goat," said Lucy, who somehow felt the goat was important, "only a lamb."

"And they're going to sacrifice the lamb," added Timothy. "Just like the Romans."

"Well!" said Jane, laughing. "Whatever will you two think of next? By the way, did your father manage to escape from the sultan with the saber at the Taj Mahal?"

"Yes, thank you," said Timothy politely. "May I have jam on my scone, please?"

"All right, but run along and wash your hands first."

In the privacy of the bathroom the twins exchanged long looks. "Aunt Jane's one of the nicest people in the world," said Lucy slowly at last, "but sometimes even the nicest people fall short of what one expects of them. It's not her fault. She can't help it."

"What does it matter," muttered Timothy. "I might have known not even Aunt Jane would believe us this time. Let's forget all about it."

"Okay," said Lucy willingly enough, and reached for the cake of soap as if to wash her hands of the incident.

## v

Lisa left the cottage ten minutes before the twins arrived at the back door and walked briskly to the beach. It was most remarkable, she thought, how her lethargy had vanished. Her apathy had been transformed into a sharp interest in her surroundings; as she scrambled over the rocks to the sands she felt exceptionally full of vitality.

She saw them five minutes later. They were sunning themselves beneath the cliffs on a patch of sand enclosed by a semicircle of rocks. Nicola was lying face downward, her bikini top discarded so that her back would tan evenly, and Poole was lying on his back, his hands behind his head and his long limbs stretched leisurely toward the sea. As Lisa watched he rolled over on his side and ran a finger down Nicola's bare spine.

"Well, well!" drawled Lisa in contempt. "What an intimate little picture!"

Poole spun around. She saw all expression die from his dark eyes and suddenly the floodgates of her self-control burst apart and the rage swept through her in a fierce noisy tide.

"You bastard!" she said, trembling. "You rotten, treacherous, lying, deceitful—"

He was on his feet in a flash. "Lisa," he said in a steady soothing voice. "Lisa, be quiet."

"No, I won't!" cried Lisa passionately. "Not until I've told you how much I hate you! Not until I've told Nicola what a fool she is to get mixed up with a man like you!"

"Nicki, darling," said Poole to Nicola, who was still fumbling, confused, with the top half of her bikini, "there's no need for you to hear this. Wait for me up at the house."

"All right, Tristan." She struggled into her wrap and stooped to pick up the straw bag which contained her possessions.

"You wait!" screamed Lisa to her. "You'll see! I could tell you things about this man which you wouldn't believe! I could tell you—"

Nicola began to run away across the sands.

"Be quiet, Lisa," said Poole, and gripped her shoulders with his strong fingers. "Be quiet, do you hear? Be quiet."

"I hate you!" cried Lisa, unable to control herself, oblivious to everything, even the power in Poole's eyes. She was delirious with the ecstasy of venting such a strong passion. "I hate you, I hate you, I hate you—"

Poole tried an incantation. It was a traditional French method of bringing a woman into submission. "Lisa—" He caught her wrist so that his power could merge with the words more effectively—"Lisa, Bestarbeto corrumpit viscera ejus mulieris."

No use. She was beyond the power of a simple incantation. He made another effort to project his mind around hers and strangle it into submission, but Lisa was making so much noise that he couldn't concentrate. At last in desperation he slapped her.

She slapped him right back.

"Murderer!" she shouted at him. "Do you think I'm so stupid I can't see what's happened? You seduced me to get at Matt's money and when Matt left all his money to Nicola—"

Poole resorted to an invocation. It was humiliating to have to call on the lesser powers for help but the virulence in Lisa had to be controlled at once; the circumstances were too dangerous for him to afford the luxury of pride.

In the name of Baal, he thought, bending his entire will to the signal for assistance, in the name of Astaroth, in the name of Lucifer, help me control this woman and make her obedient to whatever I may suggest.

"—you dropped me and turned to Nicola without a second thought!" sobbed Lisa, and sat down abruptly on a nearby rock.

"Lisa," said Poole, seizing his chance, "you're much too upset to discuss this properly now. Why don't we meet here early tomorrow morning and talk about it in a more level-headed way?"

"And have you kill me as you killed Matt?" scoffed Lisa, not so loud now but still very far from placid. "No, thank you!"

"My dear Lisa, when Matt was killed I was at Colwyn Court among the members of the society! Talk sense, please. However, if you're really afraid for your safety I'll meet you at the point where the beach path reaches the rocks—then you'll be in full view of the cottage and you can tell your sister to watch from the window. Satisfied? Good, I'll see you there at eight o'clock tomorrow morning."

"I'll be there!" said Lisa dangerously. "And don't think it'll be a friendly discussion because it won't be."

"Do I have your word not to discuss this with anyone till after we've met tomorrow?"

"All right, but—"

"Thank you. Eight o'clock tomorrow, Lisa," said Poole and escaped.

He ran all the way back to the house. The kitchens were empty but four members of the society were playing a friendly game of bridge on the terrace outside the sitting room.

"Where's Agnes?" he yelled at them.

"In her room," someone called. "Resting." They were all staring at him with open mouths.

Poole raced upstairs and burst into Agnes' room without even the formality of a knock. Agnes, who was painting her nails and listening to "Woman's Hour" on her transistor radio, was so startled that she knocked over her bottle of nail polish.

"Tristan! What's the matter?"

"What the hell happened to that spell?"

"Spell?" said Agnes, very nervous.

"Spell! I know I told you to stop Lisa being in love with me, but—"

"Oh dear!" said Agnes, flustered. "You mean it didn't work? I was so sure I'd been successful—"

"You've been successful all right! You've been so damned successful that now she hates my guts! Agnes, listen to me, we're in deep water and we've got to act and act fast . . ."

## vi

Evan had arrived back at Colwyn after an early start from London ten minutes before Lisa had embarked on her stormy scene on the beach, and on hearing that Nicola and Poole had gone sunbathing he left the house and headed swiftly down the path to the cove.

He was on the sands by the time he saw Nicola. She was running toward him, her wrap flying back from her shoulders, her bikini two strips of pale yellow against the tan of her skin.

"Nicki!" he called.

Perhaps Poole had upset her. She looked upset about something. If Poole had done anything to upset her, Evan thought grimly, he'd soon live to regret it.

"Nicki!" he called again.

It was as if she didn't see him. She kept running toward him until presently she was near enough for him to see her parted lips and windswept hair and the dark abstracted look in her eyes.

"Nicki," he said, reaching out to her, "what's the matter?"

But Nicola was in the landscape of her dream, a silent world where she was running across the sands of a deserted shore. She didn't hear him. As he watched, hardly able to believe his eyes, she ran past him without a word and scrambled up the rocks to the path without looking back.

"Nicki!" shouted Evan in a haze of anger and bewilderment. "Nicki, where are you going?"

But Nicola was fulfilling Maris' prophecy. At that moment, as far as she was concerned, Evan had ceased to exist.

## *vii*

The night passed. Nicola ate dinner in the society's dining room and Evan did not see her; when he knocked on the door of her room later there was no reply and when he tried the door he found it was locked. Evan went to bed in a fever of painful confusion and injured pride, and tossed and turned continually throughout a sleepless night.

Poole also spent a sleepless night. Agnes had slipped a mild drug into Nicola's coffee to make sure that Poole would be unhampered by her presence, and as soon as Nicola was in bed asleep Poole locked the door of her bedroom and returned to the west wing to begin his preparations. He consulted his books, meditated, and made his plans, but shortly before dawn he prepared himself for action. He had eaten no dinner in order to fulfill the need for fasting, and now he took a bath to meet the requirement of cleanliness before dressing in the black linen robe which Agnes brought him. The third requirement, continence, could not be observed, but since it was useless to regret the time he had recently spent with Nicola he merely shrugged his shoulders and asked Agnes if everything else was ready. It was. As soon as the sun had risen they walked up to the castle together and Agnes lit the small brazier amid the castle ruins in order to burn the laurel juice, camphor, white resin, sulfur, and salt and purify the area in preparation for the circle. Poole drew the circle as soon as the purification was complete. He drew it while he moved in counterclockwise direction, and used vermilion paint which contained mercury and sulfur. After it was finished he drew a second circle eight feet in diameter inside the first, and as with the first circle he was careful to leave a gap in the line so that he and Agnes could enter and leave both circles freely until everything was ready. Then, leaving Agnes tracing the appropriate names and symbols in the space between the two circles, he took his fresh hazel rod which served as a wand and walked out of the castle toward the wild horses grazing nearby.

Poole was not unfamiliar with horses but it was some years since he had handled one and he found it hard to suppress a flicker of uneasiness when he approached the large black stallion on the edge of the herd. He had to pause to eliminate the human weakness, but once that was done everything proved to be absurdly easy. He raised his wand; the horse pricked up its ears. Even when the other horses edged away the stallion stayed motionless, waiting for him, and presently he touched the animal with the wand, murmured some words beneath his breath, and slipped the noose of a rope over the horse's head. When he returned to the castle ruins the horse was walking docilely behind him.

"Are we ready, Agnes?"

"Yes, I think so."

"Good." Keeping the animal outside the circle, Poole tied the rope to a corner of fallen masonry in case the horse should try to bolt for freedom, but the horse itself made no protest and only gazed at him trustingly with dark intelligent eyes.

"Light the fire again, Agnes," said Poole.

Agnes lit the charcoal in the brazier. After a moment Poole joined her in the middle of the inner circle and stood watching her.

"Feed the fire," he said at last.

Agnes added camphor and brandy to the inky smoke.

"All right," said Poole quietly. "Close the circle."

Agnes picked up the paintbrush and the can of vermilion paint and quickly completed both the inner and the outer circles.

"Very well, Agnes. Now for the fragrance beloved of the powers of darkness. When I call the name of the herb, feed it to the flames. Ready?"

"Yes, Master."

"Coriander," said Poole, and paused. Then: "Hemlock . . . parsley . . . black poppy liquor . . . fennel . . . sandalwood . . . henbane."

Agnes flung the last ingredient into the flames and for a while they stood watching the fire. A rich dark odor began to envelop them. Poole stooped to the covered basket which Agnes had brought with them into the circle and dragged out the black cock inside.

"To my comrades," called Poole in a loud voice, "to my subjects, to my cohorts, to my legions I offer this sacrifice."

The fumes from the brazier were growing stronger; his voice had thickened and his hand as Agnes gave him the knife was unsteady.

The cock died a bloody death.

Agnes fell to her knees to bow before the unleashed force, but Poole stood his ground and let the force take possession of him. After three seconds of rigid immobility his frame shook with violence; as Agnes watched with worshiping eyes, he stretched his bloodstained hands to the dark morning sky and in a hoarse and vibrant voice summoned his demons to meet him at the circle's edge.

*viii*

When her alarm clock went off at seven o'clock that morning Lisa was still sound asleep, exhausted by the exhilaration of her hatred for Poole. She had a hard time dragging herself out of bed, but presently the thought of the rendezvous with him was too tempting to be resisted and she was wide awake when she went downstairs.

Jane was already in the kitchen brewing Benedict's early morning tea. "My goodness!" she said in surprise when she saw her sister. "You're up early!"

"I'm meeting Tristan."

"Oh, Lisa!"

"No, it's not what you think. That's all finished. I'm just going to drive home to him how much I despise him . . . Jane, watch what happens, will you? I'm meeting him above the beach and if he knows someone's watching he won't dare harm me."

"Lisa, wouldn't it be more sensible to—"

"I must go," said Lisa, "or I'll be late." And she slipped out of the back door.

Jane made the tea, took it up to Benedict, and then returned downstairs with a worried frown to the living room windows which faced the sea.

Lisa was waiting at the point where the path reached the rocks about twenty feet above the sands. It was a pale, clear morning and the sea was a dark, calm blue beyond the cliffs. Kneeling on the window seat Jane glanced at her watch. Five minutes past eight. Lisa was pacing up and down in a fever of impatience. Ten minutes past eight. No sign of Poole.

He's not going to come, thought Jane. She went to the front door and opened it.

"Lisa!" she called at the top of her voice. "Come back! Please!"

She saw Lisa turn her head at the same time as she saw the horse out of the corner of her eye. She glanced up sharply toward the castle. The largest of the black wild horses seemed to be in the midst of a lone stampede. She saw him gallop down from the castle cliffs, and the flock of sheep in his path took fright and fled before the thunder of his flying hooves.

Jane stared mesmerized. The sheep, bunched together in fright, were pounding blindly across the hillside toward the cottage, but as she watched she saw the horse veer and drive them toward the place where Lisa was standing above the cliffs.

"Lisa!" shouted Jane in terror. "Lisa, look out!"

But Lisa moved too late. The sheep swept down upon her before she could escape them, and the next moment she was jostled over the jagged rocks by their close-packed bodies to meet her death on the beach below.

# Chapter Seven

## *i*

"I'm going to marry Tristan," said Nicola to Evan. "We're getting married on August the second."

They were in Matt's house in Surrey on the evening after Lisa's funeral. A week had passed since Lisa's death, a week filled with newspaper reporters, police, another inquest, and yet another verdict of accidental death. Everything had been disrupted. Benedict was thinking of abandoning the cottage and returning to Cambridge; Jane was suppressing a hundred doubts and a thousand nameless fears by devoting herself to the twins; and the twins were waiting with more dogged patience than ever for their father to return from his travels and make everything right again. Poole had driven Nicola to Surrey for the funeral but had not been present at the service. Afterward, while Poole was still absent, Evan had his first chance for several days to speak to Nicola alone and demand to know what her feelings for Poole were.

"I love him," said Nicola, her gray eyes defiant. "He's proposed and I've accepted. We're going to be married just as soon as possible."

"You're crazy," said Evan. "You must be crazy. You're out of your mind."

"Oh, for God's sake, leave me alone and go away!" cried Nicola and tried to escape, but he wouldn't let her go.

"How can I go away when you're planning to return to Colwyn Court?"

"I'll stay in the west wing with Tristan! You can't stop me staying there!"

And Evan knew he could not. He felt so sick at heart that he wanted to walk onto the next plane to America, but that too was out of the question. Not only was it impossible for him to abandon his family but he found it impossible to abandon Nicola. As the hours passed he became more convinced than ever that she was somehow not responsible for her actions.

"It's wonderful news about Nicola's engagement," said Jane to him doubtfully on the morning after Lisa's funeral. "But I do hope she knows what she's doing. She hardly knows Tristan at all, and . . . oh, Evan, I can't help feeling it's all wrong! I'm sorry —perhaps I shouldn't be saying this, but—"

An ally. In spite of his despair Evan felt his spirits lift a little. He began to talk, pouring out all his doubts and fears to her, and Jane in turn confessed her uneasiness and her intuitive conviction that Poole was the cause of all the recent troubles at Colwyn Court.

They talked for over an hour together.

"Have your private detectives found out anything worthwhile yet?" asked Jane at last.

"Not so far. I'm going up to London this afternoon to see how far they've got with the investigations."

"I'm sure they won't find anything incriminating," said Jane. "Tristan's much too clever—inhumanly clever, Evan, you'll laugh at me I know, but sometimes I've even wondered if Tristan is human at all. The way he attracted Lisa—and now Nicola . . . it's as if he bewitched them. I know it sounds ridiculous to talk about bewitching and black magic nowadays, but—"

"Poole's human all right," said Evan. His mind flickered quickly over the memory of the strangeness of Poole's room before he dismissed the strangeness as eccentricity. "He's just a slick operator with a fair degree of psychological know-how and a sizable gift for hypnosis. I agree with you that Nicola's bewitched, but I don't think anyone's been weaving spells. Poole's simply managed to subject her mind to his so completely that she's a different person."

"That must be witchcraft," said Jane.

"No," said Evan, "just a form of hypnotic control inspired by a very human desire to get his hands on half a million pounds. No, he's human and he's crooked and I'm going to do my damndest to expose him before he marries Nicola, ruins her life, and makes off with her money . . . Jane, I'm going to ask you a big favor. I know you don't want to go back to the cottage after what happened to Lisa, but it would be a great relief to me if I knew you were there—if I knew there was someone at hand who understood the situation and whom I could turn to for help if the need arose. You've no idea what a help it's been to have found someone who can sympathize with me about all this."

"It's been a help to me, too," confessed Jane. "I was beginning to feel neurotic about Tristan. I thought I was the only one who disliked him."

"So will you come back to Colwyn?"

"Well . . . I don't want to go back, but on the other hand I couldn't possibly return to Cambridge now and abandon Nicola—and you—without lifting a finger to help. If I can help you by being at Colwyn, and if you can help Nicola—"

"I'm going to get Nicola away from that man if it's the last thing I ever do!"

"Oh Evan, don't say things like that!" exclaimed Jane, touching wood in superstitious panic. "Not after all these sudden deaths!"

"They were accidents."

"I wonder," said Jane.

"You're not seriously suggesting—"

"No," said Jane, "just wondering . . . Evan, if you're going up to London today to see the detectives, would you do something for me there?"

"Of course. What is it?"

"Go to Foyles and buy me a really good book on witchcraft."

## ii

On returning to Matt's house the next morning to collect Nicola and drive her back to Wales, Poole met the twins. They had just said good-bye to their *au pair* girl who had departed for her home in Spain to escape from the atmosphere of sudden death which was apparently hovering over the household, and were relaxing in their newfound freedom; although they had liked Costanza they had become tired of looking after her and teaching her English. As Poole drove up to the house in his black Jaguar he found them sitting on the front doorstep and watching his arrival with interest.

"Good morning," said Lucy with impressive formality as he stepped out of the car. "We would like to congratulate you on your engagement."

"Thanks!" He smiled at her and glanced at the boy, but Timothy was looking at his toes.

"Where's the wedding going to be?" said Lucy brightly, abandoning the gravity of the formal welcome. "In the chapel?"

Poole looked at her. Lucy felt a thrill of pleasure tiptoe down her spine. Poole made her feel important and clever when he looked at her like that.

"We heard Agnes talking about it," she said, explaining. "But we didn't tell anyone because we thought it was a secret."

Poole smiled at her. "It was a secret," he said. "In a way it still is. The society is giving a party in the chapel on the evening of August the first, and we're going to stage a pageant in the chapel to fulfill a tradition of the society's history. Since Nicola and I are getting married the pageant will take the form of a wedding this time, but it won't be a proper wedding because the chapel isn't consecrated. The legal wedding is to take place the next morning at the registry office in Swansea."

"Can we come to the pageant?" said Lucy promptly.

"I thought you were both going to Cambridge to stay with your Aunt Jane."

"Oh, Aunt Jane's changed her mind," said Lucy. "We're all going back to the cottage. We're glad, aren't we, Timmy? It's nicer by the sea than in the middle of a big town."

"I wish we were going to Cambridge," said Timothy. "I wouldn't think of Mum so much there."

"Yes, you would," said Lucy roughly, and to divert herself as well as Timothy she turned to Poole. "Can we come to the pageant?"

Poole was giving her that special look again. She jumped up, ran over to him, and slipped her hand in his. "Please!" she begged, opening her blue eyes very wide and assuming her most appealing expression. "Please, Tristan! Can I call you Tristan now that you're going to be my step-brother-in-law?"

"Why not?" said Poole, and thought again what an exceptionally pretty child she was. A perfect offering . . . He began to picture the christening robes. "Would you like to be a bridesmaid in the pageant?" he suggested with a smile.

"Ooooh!" Lucy squealed. "May I?"

"Of course you can, but keep it a secret, will you, Lucy? The pageant is a private affair held by the society for their friends and we don't want a crowd of outsiders standing by and gaping at us."

"I won't tell a soul," promised Lucy fervently. "Can Timmy be a page?"

This was awkward. Poole looked at Timothy, at his straw-colored hair and downcast eyes and hostile mouth, and decided that the boy was totally unsuitable for his purposes. "You don't want to be a page, do you, Tim?" he said lightly. "You're too old for that sort of stuff, aren't you? I know how boys of your age feel about that kind of thing."

Timothy was smitten with an irresistible urge to be difficult. He was not at ease with Poole and privately thought Lucy was making a fool of herself. "If Lucy's going to be a bridesmaid," he said, staring at the ground by Poole's black shoes, "I want to be a page."

Poole knew when a subject left him no room to maneuver. "All right," he said, well aware that he had no intention of admitting Timothy to the rites. "We'll talk about it later when we're all back at Colwyn, and remember—not a word to anyone meanwhile. Okay?"

"Our lips are sealed," said Lucy grandly.

Timothy said nothing.

"Tim?" said Poole.

"Okay," said Timothy, "if you like. And my name's Timothy, not Tim. Lucy's the only person who doesn't have to call me by my full name."

"Honestly, Timmy!" exclaimed Lucy, annoyed after Poole had disappeared into the house. "How could you be so rude when he was so nice to you?"

"I didn't like the way you jumped all over him as if you were a puppy who wanted to be taken for a walk."

"I've never been so insulted in all my life!" said Lucy furiously and walked off in a huff to leave Timothy still sitting unhappily on the front doorstep.

A quarrel was rare for the twins; Timothy was aware of his distrust of Poole turning to an active dislike . . .

*iii*

When Evan arrived at Colwyn Court a day later, he left the house at the first available opportunity and hurried down to the cottage above the beach. He found Jane alone in the kitchen; the twins were exploring the caves and Benedict had gone into Swansea for more stationery supplies.

"Oh, good!" said Jane, abandoning the cream she was whipping and leading the way into the living room. "I was just thinking about you. Is there any news?"

"Yes, there is." Evan looked better. His eyes were less bloodshot and his face had lost its drawn, tired look. "By the way, here's your book on witchcraft—it seemed both readable and comprehensive, so I hope you'll find I chose the right one."

"Did you read it?"

"I read the parts about witchcraft in Africa and they seemed reliable enough. I didn't bother with all the mumbo jumbo about witches and black cats and the orgies on Halloween." He flung himself down in an armchair and pulled some folded sheets of paper out of the inside pocket of his jacket. "Jane, I've got some data on Poole and the detectives are still working on the investigation so I hope they'll discover even more than they've discovered already. Meanwhile, listen to this. Poole's thirty-five years old, born Tristan Robert Poole in Cheltenham, Gloucestershire—"

"How respectable," said Jane.

"—only child, father an engineer, attended kindergarten in Cheltenham and later Wyndham Hall prep school near Salisbury—"

"More respectable than ever."

"—emigrated to America with parents at age twelve and attended high school in San Francisco, graduated high school and attended courses in psychology and anthropology at Berkeley—"

"There must be a catch somewhere," said Jane. "I don't believe it."

"—dropped out of Berkeley after one year, and went to a smaller college at Las Corridas, a town near Sacramento, where he majored in psychology. After getting his degree he went on to study for his master's, and the subject of his master's thesis was—" Evan took a deep breath: " 'The Role of Psychology in the Modern Practice of the Occult.' "

"What did I tell you!" exclaimed Jane in triumph.

"Wait! Listen to this. At this stage 'subject', as the detectives' report calls him, became involved with several groups loosely classifiable as eccentric religious sects. Subject has no police record, but he was present at a witchcraft ceremony held twelve years ago on August the first, in an orange grove some miles northwest of Los Angeles. Apparently the first of August is one of the four big days of the year for those who practice witchcraft—they still call it Lammas, the name given by the early English church to the harvest festival which was celebrated on that date, and it seems to be on a par with the more famous date of Halloween. On this particular occasion the ceremony was interrupted by the police who made several arrests for disorderly conduct, lewd behavior, and so on, but Poole wasn't one of the ones arrested. He was found unconscious and taken to the hospital. For ten days he remained unconscious while the doctors tried to decide what was wrong with him, but eventually he recovered and settled down to an elusive but legal life, traveling all over America and establishing chapter houses of this damned society. So great was his success that he decided to expand his operations to England, and during the past three years he's set up various other groups, of which this Colwyn Court bunch happen to be the latest. He seems to have a private income, although the detectives are still trying to find out where it comes from—I would suspect a Swiss bank. The various chapter houses of the society seem to be financed by a mixture of subscriptions and bequests, but everything appears to be legal and above suspicion." Evan paused. "'Subject's parents are now dead, he has no known relatives, and he's unmarried.'" He looked up at her. "What do you make of all that?"

"I don't think he's the real Tristan Poole at all," said Jane promptly. "I think they succeeded in summoning the devil in that orange grove twelve years ago during the Lammas rites, and the devil took possession of one of his most promising followers."

"Seriously, Jane!"

"I *am* serious!"

"Well . . ." Evan gave an awkward laugh. "I agree that you were right when you suspected Poole of witchcraft. I think myself that this society of his is a cover for a phony religion—for dabbling in the occult—and if this is true it should give me some sort of lever to use against him. If they're practicing witchcraft in between harvesting their nature foods, they'll be tempted to celebrate Lammas, and if the celebration they have in mind is the one I suspect they have in mind, I can call the police and catch them all redhanded in the middle of the orgy. As soon as I leave you now I'm going to confront Poole, warn him that I know what kind of game he's playing, and advise him that unless he wants trouble on his hands he'd better give up Nicola pretty damn quickly. Thanks to the detectives I believe I have enough evidence to shake him out of his complacency and prise him away from Colwyn Court—and from Nicola too."

"Oh Evan, do be careful!"

"Poole's the one who's going to have to be careful! Don't worry, Jane, 'subject' is going to have second thoughts about marrying Nicola and staying at Colwyn Court! I think I've got him exactly where I want him . . ."

*iv*

Poole was working out some astral positions from his charts and scanning the forces to be at his disposal on the first of August. He was so absorbed in his work that when Evan knocked on the door of his room he did not even bother to inquire who it was.

"Come in!" he called.

The door opened. "I'd like to talk to you, Poole," said Evan's voice abruptly from behind him.

Poole swung around. His left hand moved automatically to close his book and when he stood up his body blocked Evan's view of his calculations. "Shall we go downstairs?" he suggested evenly.

"No, we can talk here. I merely wanted to tell you that the game's up as far as Colwyn Court's concerned. I know exactly what your society does in its spare time, and unless all of you clear out of here as soon as possible you'll regret it. Oh, and when you go you can leave Nicola behind because she's not going to marry you. I'll see that the police make this part of Wales too hot to hold you before I'll see you hypnotize her to the nearest registry office. I trust I make myself quite clear."

There was a pause. Poole put his hands in his pockets so that his clenched fists would be out of sight.

"Dr. Colwyn, I think there must be some mistake. I've done nothing legally wrong. I have no criminal record. The behavior of the society has been exemplary, as I'm sure the police would be the first to admit. And please let's not talk about my fiancée because I can't believe you and I could ever have a profitable discussion on the subject."

"Profitable must be a very favorite word of yours," said Evan. "Especially in relation to Nicola."

"I refuse to discuss Nicola with you."

"How about discussing the occult?"

"A fascinating subject," said Poole, "but not one which I would have thought appealed to you."

"Look, Poole, you're walking on thin ice. I've only got to catch you using your hobby as an excuse for sexual aberration—"

Poole made up his mind. "Dr. Colwyn, why is it that you're always dragging up the subject of my sexuality? As a psychologist I must say I find your obsession with my relationships with women unhealthy, to say the least. Are you so unsure of your own sexuality that you have to be constantly jeering at a man who's sexually confident?"

He achieved the exact result he wanted.

"Why you—" spluttered Evan, and swung his fist wildly in Poole's direction.

Sidestepping the expected blow, Poole moved so deliberately that he might have been parodying a slow-motion film. As Evan lunged off balance Poole hit him on the jaw, flung him back against the wall, and watched as the other man sank unconscious to the floor.

"Agnes!" called Poole sharply, but Agnes did not fail him. She was in the doorway.

"Scissors."

"Here." She handed them to him as if she were a nurse in an operating theater.

Poole knelt, snipped off a lock of Evan's hair and said without looking up: "Envelope."

Agnes held the envelope open for him. He slipped the red hairs inside and gave the scissors back to her.

"Do we act straight away?" said Agnes.

"No, he can't do a damn thing before Lammas unless he wants to make a fool of himself."

"And on Lammas Evening?"

"Agnes," said Poole, "how you love to worry!"

She smiled at him. On the floor Evan stirred and groaned.

"He's coming around. Get a glass of water." He knelt down by Evan's body as Evan shook his head and raised himself gingerly on one elbow. "Dr. Colwyn, are you all right?"

"Leave me alone, you bastard," growled Evan, and tried without success to stand up.

"Here, Dr. Colwyn," said Agnes, offering him a glass of water. "Drink this."

"I must warn you, Dr. Colwyn," said Poole politely, "that Miss Miller witnessed the entire incident and should you wish to charge me with assault she won't hesitate to tell the police that you struck the first blow."

Evan did not answer. He drank the water, levered himself to his feet, and turned to the door. "I'll get you in the end," he said between his teeth. "You'll see. You'll regret this."

"Dr. Colwyn, your hostility does you no credit, if you'll forgive me saying so. In fact it may even rebound with unfortunate results on those you love. If you try to make trouble for me you can rest assured that I'll have no hesitation whatsoever about making trouble for you."

Evan whirled around. "What do you mean?"

Poole was very still. Agnes stood silent and grave behind him.

"Dr. Colwyn," said Poole at last, "you have a very delicate sister. Perhaps you may have underestimated how delicate she is."

Evan groped for words. "Are you trying to—"

"I'm merely making statements, Dr. Colwyn. That's all. Just statements."

"You're not qualified to make statements like that about my sister," said Evan.

Poole said nothing.

"If you threaten me like that again—"

"I'm not threatening you, Dr. Colwyn, just making statements. By the way, when you were in Africa did you hear how the witch doctors there have been known to put a man to death simply by use of the power of suggestion? A most macabre achievement, I've always thought." He paused. "Some people are very susceptible to the power of suggestion, Dr. Colwyn."

Evan swallowed. Words deserted him. For the first time in his meetings with Poole he felt totally unnerved.

"I ask just one thing," said Poole at last. "Leave us alone. Make trouble for us and we'll make trouble for you, but if you leave us alone no one will get hurt. Do you understand what I'm saying?"

Evan nodded. There was another pause. Then:

"You can go now," said Poole.

Evan went without a word. His head ached. His eyes smarted with childish tears. He felt as if every nerve in his body had been battered by an unseen force until all his defenses were in ruins. Automatically, without stopping to think, he left the house and stumbled blindly down the path which led to the cottage and to Jane.

*v*

Jane made him feel better at once. There was something very comforting about her soft, untidy femininity with its sympathy, warmth, and responsiveness. He even recovered himself sufficiently to feel envious of Benedict having such a woman to look after him; after the way he had been treated by first Nicola and then Poole, Evan decided he was much in need of some feminine attention and that Jane's society might in its own platonic way do much to restore his flagging self-esteem.

"I'm not at all surprised Tristan threatened you like that," she said frankly. "It was frightfully brave of you to face him. I should have fainted instantly in sheer terror."

It had not occurred to Evan that he might have acted bravely, but it was nevertheless very pleasant to have a woman regard his foolhardy behavior with such admiration. He smiled at her. "You talk as if he's the devil incarnate!"

"I think he is," said Jane seriously, and reached for her book on witchcraft.

"You don't really believe that, Jane!"

"Yes, I do. Honestly. Listen to this: 'Witches and warlocks form groups called covens, consisting of thirteen people or, according to one authority, twelve people plus a person representing the devil or even the devil himself—' "

"Oh, I don't doubt they're dabbling in witchcraft," said Evan, "but you can't take it seriously, Jane!"

"You took it seriously when Tristan threatened Gwyneth, didn't you? And just listen to this! 'One of the well-known characteristics of a witch or warlock is the presence of the animal familiar, an attendant demon taking the form of a cat, dog, mole, hare, toad . . .'" Jane skipped several species of animals before continuing: "'The black cat is a famous symbol of witchcraft, but in fact cats of all kinds were used by witches as a physical home for their attendant demons, and a white cat was not unknown—'"

"They haven't got any cats at Colwyn Court at the moment," said Evan, and added as a fascinated afterthought: "But they do keep several hares in hutches."

"Never mind the hares!" exclaimed Jane, too agitated to allow him to finish. "What about my poor Marble? He's lost weight and hardly seems to know who I am and every morning he pads away up to Colwyn Court and stays there all day—"

Evan, who privately thought Jane tended to be somewhat fool-ish where her cat was concerned, decided that it would be wiser to turn the conversation into other channels. "The tradition of the animal familiar is probably little more than folklore," he said shortly. "I wouldn't worry about Marble if I were you, Jane—take him to the vet if he keeps on losing weight. Now, what does the book say about Lammas—or haven't you got that far yet?"

"Lammas," muttered Jane, turning her distracted gaze back to the book and flicking over several pages. "Oh yes, here we are. 'Each coven holds a sabbath at regular intervals throughout the year, but on the four great days of the occult calendar, namely February 2nd (Candlemas), the eve of May 1st (Walpurgisnacht), August 1st (Lammas), and October 31st, the eve of All Hallows (Halloween), several covens may join together to celebrate the full rites of the Devil's Church—'"

"They're going to celebrate Lammas," said Evan. "I'm sure of it. If I didn't feel so hamstrung by Poole's threats to Gwyneth I'd go this very minute to Swansea and tip off the police."

" 'The Devil's Church is in many ways a direct parallel to God's Church,'" Jane read, barely listening to him. " 'But everything in the Devil's Church is the exact opposite of everything in God's Church. Thus virtue becomes sin and sin becomes virtue—'"

"I'll summon the police somehow," muttered Evan. "I'll catch them all redhanded."

" 'The Christian act of communion is paralleled by the black mass, the christening is paralleled by an act of bestowing the Devil's Mark to welcome the child into the Devil's flock, the mar-riage with the bride wearing white is reflected by a contrary serv-ice in which the bride wears black—' Evan, I've been thinking of this all morning and I'm sure I'm right—before Lisa died the twins told me that the society was going to have a wedding in the ruined chapel on the cliffs, and I took no notice because I thought they were making it up. But now I'm sure they weren't. I think they overheard something Miss Miller or even Tristan himself said. Before Tristan marries Nicola at the registry office on August the second, I'm sure they're going to be married according to the rites of the Devil's Church when the Lammas ceremonies begin after sundown on August the first."

"I won't let them!" shouted Evan. "My God, if Poole tries something like that—"

But Jane had returned to her book again. "'The nature of the sabbaths vary and there seems to be no set form,'" she read. "'However, one or two features appear constantly. Among them is the act of homage wherein each member of the coven pays individual homage to the devil or his representative by the obscene kiss . . .' —Perhaps I'd better skip that bit before I start to blush—'. . . After the religious observances the witches rub themselves with aconite, a drug used in the old days to give the illusion of flying through the air—hence the time-honored picture of the witches flying on the phallic symbol of the broomstick—'"

"Damned perverts!" growled Evan. "Jane, we've got to think up a plan. We've got to stop them."

"'—and this is followed by dancing and mass copulation,'" Jane continued, unable to stop herself by this time. She looked puzzled. "But how can that be if the coven consists entirely of women?"

"No doubt they take the precaution," said Evan dryly, "of inviting a coven of men to share their celebrations. Jane, surely the best plan is to catch the group in the middle of their orgies and have the whole lot of them rounded up on some sort of indecency charge. We've somehow got to see the police and arrange some sort of trap without anyone in the society knowing about it."

"I'm sure Tristan would know," said Jane with a shiver. "He'd find out. I know he would."

"I could leave it until the very last minute—until the morning of the first of August."

"But what would you do then? If you rushed to Swansea and told the police you wanted them to break up some occult rites they simply wouldn't believe you!"

"Oh yes, they would! I'd tell them a bunch of hippies planned to hold an orgy! But perhaps I've got a better idea. My father knows the retired Chief Constable, and as you know, the Chief

Constable controls the police in his particular district. I'm sure any Chief Constable, even if he does happen to be retired, would still be able to pull some influential strings. I'll drive over to Milford Haven to see him on Lammas morning and bulldoze him into taking the necessary action. Even if Poole has me followed he won't see anything objectionable about my visiting an old friend of my father's."

"That sounds like a splendid idea. I—Marble! Marble, don't scratch the paint, naughty cat!" She jumped up. The cat was standing by the closed front door and pawing fretfully at the woodwork as he mewed for attention. "I wish Marble would get better," said Jane anxiously as she let him out. "I didn't like leaving him here when we were in Surrey for the funerals, but I was afraid he might run away if I took him to yet another strange environment and when Miss Miller volunteered to look after him . . . oh, Evan, do you think Miss Miller changed him into a familiar when we were away? He's been so odd lately, so tired and unlike himself—"

"My dear Jane," said Evan kindly, "I'm sure the very last thing Marble is suffering from is an attendant demon. Perhaps he has a slight chill on the stomach and feels a bit liverish. Why don't you take him around to the local vet tomorrow and set your mind at rest?"

Outside the front door Marble stood listening. Then, receiving a summons from a different direction he summoned his failing energy and wandered slowly away from the cottage toward the kitchens of Colwyn Court.

## vi

The rest of July passed lazily, the days trickling away into the past as effortlessly as leaves floating downstream on an unhurried river. But time meant little to Nicola now. Sometimes she felt she was in a dream and that her one contact with reality lay through Poole. He had helped her write letters to give notice of her intention to leave both her job and her apartment, and he had gone to London to collect her possessions and ensure her roommate had not been inconvenienced financially by Nicola's decision to leave at such short notice. At Poole's suggestion too she had written to several friends and relations to tell them she was planning to marry quietly in the near future, but she felt no distress at the thought that none of them would be at the wedding.

"I think a wedding should be small and private," Poole had said. "It should be a personal, intimate affair."

"But what about the pageant?" Nicola had asked after agreeing wholeheartedly with him. "Surely that will hardly be small and private."

"I think you'll be pleasantly surprised by the pageant," Poole had told her with a smile. "You'll be surprised how personal and intimate it'll turn out to be."

Nicola had spent some time pondering dreamily about the pageant. The idea fascinated her but her knowledge about the ceremony involved remained bewilderingly vague.

"Tristan," she said on the morning of the thirty-first of July, "tell me some more about the pageant. The more I think of it the more exciting it seems—it's such a romantic idea to have a wedding service in that chapel at sunset! You were so clever to think of it."

"You're sure you don't feel it's in bad taste?"

"No, as I told you when you first suggested the idea, I like the tradition of the wedding service but since I don't believe in anything much as far as religion goes I couldn't care less if the chapel is consecrated or not. And we'll be married properly in the registry office the next day, so what does it matter if the service in the pageant isn't strictly valid?" They were sunbathing on the beach again; Poole was drawing mysterious patterns in the sand as she spoke, and she propped herself up on one elbow to watch him. "I hope it doesn't rain," she said as an afterthought.

"It won't." He looked up at her seriously. "You really should believe in something, you know."

"I can't help it if I don't," said Nicola languidly, "and I'm not hypocritical enough to pretend to be religious when I'm not." She rolled over onto her back and reached for her sunglasses. "Tell me more about the order of ceremonies for tomorrow—you still haven't told me what actually happens. Oughtn't we to have a rehearsal or something?"

"There's no need for you to worry about that."

"Well, just tell me one thing," Nicola said with sleepy curiosity. "Why can't Timothy be a page? Lucy really means it, you know, when she says she won't be a bridesmaid unless Timothy takes part in the pageant too. The twins are very loyal to one another."

"Lucy will be a bridesmaid," said Poole. "You don't have to worry about that either . . . Nicki darling, I think we really should discuss your spiritual beliefs. I don't think I approve of my wife being an atheist."

"It's a bit late for disapproval now!" murmured Nicola, amused, thinking he was joking.

"I'm serious, Nicki. How can you visualize the world except as a continuous war between the forces of good and evil?"

"Oh Tristan!" She yawned indolently. "Isn't that sort of talk all rather old-fashioned?"

"You doubt that evil exists?"

"Well, I suppose in an abstract sense—"

"But you doubt the presence of evil as an all-powerful metaphysical force."

"I don't believe in the devil, if that's what you mean," said Nicola placidly.

The last thing she heard him say before her memory deserted her was:

"I want none of your pitiful ignorance in tomorrow's ceremony, my dear, and none of your pathetic skepticism either. Give me your disbelief and your will to disbelieve and your memory of disbelief, and let me cleanse your soul of all taint of heresy . . ."

And suddenly the sun was snuffed out and the stars faded one by one and she began her journey along the edge of a black and never-ending night.

## *vii*

Lammas dawned.

The cloudless sky was reflected in the brilliant blue of the sea. The earth glistened after a night of rain, but now that the sun was rising the world was bathed in shimmering light.

"March-hares-and-rabbits," said Lucy to herself as she woke up. Someone had once told her that this was a lucky thing to say when one awoke on the first day of a new month. She looked at the clock by her bedside. Only six! Lucy felt annoyed. She was so wide awake that the idea of returning to sleep was impossible. Slipping out of bed she padded to the window and peered out at the new day.

Nicola's wedding day, she thought, the secret wedding day. If only I could have been in the pageant! She found herself wondering for the hundredth time why Timothy was not allowed to be a page. Nobody had suggested that she should give up her cherished ambition to be a bridesmaid, but after an agony of indecision she knew she had no choice. It wouldn't have been fair to abandon Timothy, and Timothy had to come first.

"Bother Timmy," said Lucy aloud, leaning over the windowsill. It was then that she heard the cat.

He was mewing outside the back door below her, and sounded lost and forlorn.

"Just a moment, Marble," called Lucy and turned back into the room. It took less than a minute for her to pull on her shorts and slip a sweater over her head; after pushing her feet into her gym shoes she left her room and pattered downstairs to the back door.

But Marble did not want to come in. He mewed, looked at her, ran a little way down the path, stopped to look back, and mewed again.

"Silly cat," said Lucy. "What are you up to? Here!"

Marble edged away.

He's playing a game, thought Lucy with interest. He wants me to follow him. Perhaps he's got something to show me.

"Here, Marble!" she said, following him, and saw him dance out of her reach again as he bounded down the path.

Clever cat, thought Lucy, intrigued, and walked down the path after him.

He kept at a safe distance from her while he led her slowly up-hill to the castle. When she saw his white fur vanish amid the gray stone of the castle walls she felt satisfied. Now she'd catch him. She could edge him into a corner and—

Lucy stopped.

Marble was not alone in the castle. He was nestling in the arms of the one who owned him body and soul, and his purrs were so loud that Lucy could hear them as she stood twelve feet away in the gap in the castle walls. Later when she tried to look back at what had happened, the last thing she remembered with any degree of clarity was Tristan Poole giving her that special look and saying in his dark, quiet voice: "Hello, Lucy! I wonder if you realize what an important day this is going to be for you."

## viii

When Evan arrived at the cottage after breakfast he found a distracted Jane telling Timothy to search the beach.

"Hello," he said. "What's the matter?"

"Lucy seems to have disappeared," said Jane anxiously. "Bene-dict says she's probably gone off on some private expedition and that I shouldn't worry unless she misses lunch, but I can't help worrying a little. She didn't turn up for breakfast and that's so unlike her."

"She can't have gone far," said Evan soothingly. "Timothy will probably find her on the beach."

"That's what Benedict said . . . How are things at Colwyn Court?"

"Everything's fine. Father's well and in good spirits. Gwyneth's playing a new record which arrived in this morning's post. No problems on that score."

"Thank goodness for that! Are you off to see your Chief Constable?"

"Yes, here's his name, address, and phone number in case anything happens. If all goes well—and I don't see why it shouldn't—we'll have the chapel surrounded by police as soon as dusk falls tonight and the ceremonies begin."

"Wonderful," said Jane in relief. "Evan, if you get the chance, do phone me during the day and tell me how things are going. I'll be keeping my fingers crossed for you."

"Will that protect me from evil spells?" said Evan with a laugh, and suddenly winced in pain.

"What's the matter?" said Jane, alarmed.

He put a hand to his head. "I felt as if someone had hit me with a hammer." He swayed unsteadily on his feet. "I feel . . . God, what a headache! That came on suddenly! I feel as if . . . as if . . ."

"Evan!" said Jane, frightened. "Evan!"

". . . as if I'm going to faint," said Evan in a disbelieving voice, and Jane was just in time to break his fall as he slumped unconscious upon the carpet.

# Chapter Eight

*i*

At Colwyn Court Agnes was in conference with Poole in the dressing room next to his bedroom. The cupboard door was open; Poole's black box was unlocked and its contents set out on a long table.

"All right," said Poole. "Let's make a check. Vestments?"

"They're being pressed downstairs."

"Incense?"

"Rue, myrtle, dried nightshade, henbane, and thorn-apple. Yes, they're all assembled and ready for burning."

"Good. Now, we have the altar cloth here, and the crucifix—is the chalice being polished?"

"Yes, Tristan, and I've set aside the candles. We've made the bread, so as far as the mass goes I think I can safely say that everything's ready."

"What about Lucy's dress?"

"Harriet's finishing that off. Nicola's dress is ready. By the way,

Nicola and Lucy are asleep in my room—I locked the door as a precaution, but they won't wake up for hours yet."

"Excellent. What about the food and wine for the festivities after the service?"

"The wine's in the cellar, and the food will be ready by two o'clock. We're going to carry the food up to the cliffs at the last minute in two hampers and leave them in the castle ruins. The wine we plan to take up on two golf-trolleys at about seven. That's all under control. Tristan, is the sacrifice arranged? Did you manage to get hold of a lamb?"

"Ray's bringing one. I spoke to him on the phone."

"Ray? Oh, the farmer from Stockwood. How nice it'll be to see that coven again! Are you paying him by check for the lamb or should I send someone out to the bank?"

"I'll give him a check." He turned to the table and fingered the altar cloth. "We'll go up to the chapel this afternoon and set up the altar. I'll need a small dais too which we can place in front of the altar for the act of homage; perhaps we can use the black box here—it's about the right size . . . oh, and remind me to take the tape recorder to the chapel and check that the tapes are all in order and that the machine's working properly. You did buy the new batteries for it, didn't you?"

"Yes, Tristan. Is there anything else?"

Poole fingered his books, his amulets, and finally the sharp knife with the shining handle. The blade glittered as he caressed it with his fingers. "Bring one or two towels. There'll be a lot of blood."

"Yes, Tristan."

"Incidentally, there's still a bloodstain on the floorboards here from the time Jackie and I were working on the Morrison affair. I want it eliminated."

"Very well, Tristan. I'll arrange for it to be removed first thing tomorrow."

Poole put the knife back on the table. "Did you deal with Evan Colwyn?"

"Yes. Sandra finished the job about ten minutes ago."

"Where is it?"

"Where's—oh, I see. In her room, I suppose. That was where she went to work."

"Bring it here. And I want the door of this room locked. There must be no risk of any accidental meddling. What are you doing about Walter Colwyn and Gwyneth?"

"Walter's in his study and Gwyneth's in her room—both absorbed in their respective hobbies. Harriet has full instructions about drugging the afternoon tea."

"Good," said Poole. "Then we're all set."

There was a pause.

"Tristan," said Agnes tentatively at last, "I know you don't like me to question you about your future plans, but—"

"Aha!" said Poole with a smile. "I thought you wouldn't be able to resist asking me about them!"

"What happens after the registry office wedding tomorrow when you go away on your honeymoon?"

"We go to London for five days, long enough to make mutual wills in each other's favor and long enough for Nicola to write me a check for five hundred pounds which I shall immediately endorse in your favor so that you can settle all debts and pay running expenses until I return."

"And after that?" said Agnes, trying not to sound too excited.

"Nicola will make over her money to me and then have a most tragic nervous collapse which will necessitate her being placed in one of those tasteful nursing homes for wealthy psychiatric cases. She will remain there for just long enough to ensure I won't have to pay death duties on the money she handed over to me, and then she'll suffer a seizure and leave me a grieving widower. Meanwhile, of course, I shall have seen that you're well provided for and firmly established here at Colwyn Court."

"Delightful!" sighed Agnes and added with admiration: "You've been more than good to us, Tristan."

"I always like to take care of those who depend upon me," said Poole, and ran his long index finger lightly along the shining blade of the butcher's knife.

## ii

"Benedict!" said Jane desperately as the ambulance containing an unconscious Evan bumped away up the track from the cottage on its journey to the hospital at Swansea. "Benedict, please! You've got to believe me! Evan had discovered that the society practices witchcraft and that they're going to have an orgy tonight and Nicola's going to be in it and Evan was going to talk to the retired Chief Constable to call in the police but it all has to be done secretly because Tristan Poole might harm Gwyneth and now they've struck down Evan and we've just got to *do* something, Benedict, and you can't sit here and wonder how on earth you're going to tell Walter about Evan losing consciousness like that because Walter wouldn't believe you if you told him it was witchcraft—"

"And I wouldn't blame him in the least for not believing such a thing," said Benedict firmly. "My dearest, it's that wretched book that Evan brought you from London the other day. Ever since it came you've been seeing a witch behind every harmless broomstick in the kitchen cupboard."

"But it must be witchcraft! There's no other explanation. Tristan must have made a wax image of Evan and stuck a pin through its head—"

"Absolute nonsense," said Benedict severely. "Witchcraft was evolved by ignorant and superstitious minds to explain any deviation from the norm of recognized social behavior. Nowadays we call the deviates emotionally disturbed and send them to psychiatrists instead of burning them at the stake."

"Benedict," begged Jane, trying another approach, "you know you've always said the society is odd. Well, you were right. It's odd. It's so odd that they're using witchcraft as an excuse to hold an orgy tonight and practice all kinds of sexual—sexual—" Her vocabulary failed her.

"Personally I don't believe in censorship," said Benedict. "I take a very liberal view of all that sort of thing."

"But . . . but Nicola's involved—she's hypnotized—she's . . . Benedict, for my sake, please—please—" She groped for words and to her distress felt her eyes fill with tears. "Benedict, it's not an innocent undergraduate romp where no one gets hurt and everyone laughs afterward and says: 'What a lot of good clean fun!' This is different. This is—this is—"

"There, there!" said Benedict hurriedly. "There's no need to be upset! Don't cry. I had no idea you were taking all this so seriously! What do you want me to do?"

"Oh!" cried Jane, and burst into tears in sheer relief. After he had helped her to mop herself up she managed to say: "Please go to see this retired Chief Constable—here's his name and address which Evan gave me before he fainted—and tell him there's going to be an orgy up on the cliffs directly after sundown. Get him to arrange for the police to surround the chapel and catch everyone redhanded."

"Very well," said Benedict, beginning to be intrigued by the situation. "But perhaps I should see Walter first about Evan."

"I'll see Walter," said Jane, who knew exactly what she was going to do as soon as Benedict was on his way. "Just go, Benedict. You've got a forty-mile drive ahead of you so please, darling, please check the gauge to make sure you don't run out of gas in the middle of nowhere."

"Naturally," said Benedict dryly. As he opened the front door he stopped short on the threshold. "Talk of the devil!" he muttered. "Look who's just arrived."

"Oh my God," said Jane.

"Now my dear, don't panic. Don't worry. I'll—Jane, what on earth are you doing? What's all this?"

Jane was pulling off the gold cross she wore as a necklace and slipping it around Benedict's neck. "Wear this," was all she said, "and go. Quickly."

"But—"

"A cross protects you against—oh, never mind, Benedict! Just go! Please! Go!"

Benedict gave up. With a shrug of his shoulders he walked out to his Austin just as Poole came up the path toward the cottage.

"Good morning, Professor Shaw!" he called. "Off for a drive?"

"Yes," said Benedict, suddenly intoxicated by the cloak-and-dagger role to which he had so unexpectedly been assigned. "Just off to Milford Haven to see an old friend of Walter's who used to be Chief Constable of this area." That'll put the fear of God into him, he thought, satisfied, if he really is planning any monkey-business.

Jane felt the color drain from her face so fast that she thought she was going to faint.

"How nice," said Poole. "Have a good time." He stood watching as Benedict drove off. When the car was out of sight he turned with a smile to Jane. "Mrs. Shaw," he began pleasantly, "I wonder if you've seen Dr. Colwyn? I'm trying to find him but haven't had any success so far."

Checking up, thought Jane. Every muscle in her body ached with tension. Her throat was dry. "He was taken to the hospital at Swansea quarter of an hour ago," she managed to say. "He lost consciousness here at the cottage and I couldn't bring him around."

"Lost consciousness! But what a shock for you, Mrs. Shaw! Does Mr. Colwyn know about this yet?"

"No, I'm waiting for definite news from the hospital."

"Much the best idea. We don't want to worry Mr. Colwyn unnecessarily about his son . . . I wonder what the trouble is. I hope it's not serious."

"I don't think it is," said Jane. She was amazed by the calmness of her voice. "Evan's been missing sleep and meals lately and worrying too much about—well, about certain things, and I think this morning all the strain came to a head and caused a physical collapse. At least, that was what the local doctor thought when he summoned the ambulance."

"Ah," said Poole and looked rueful. "Yes, I knew he took the news of Nicola's engagement hard." He hesitated before adding:

"Mrs. Shaw, may I trouble you for a glass of water? It's a hot day and I'm very thirsty."

"Yes, of course," said Jane, fleeing to the kitchen. "Come in."

"Thanks." He walked swiftly into the living room as Jane disappeared at the back of the house. A discarded sports jacket of Benedict's lay tossed over an armchair. In a lightning search of the pockets Poole found a handkerchief and concealed it as Jane re-entered the room with his glass of water.

"Thanks," repeated Poole, accepting the glass and taking a long drink. Then: "That feels better. Well, if you'll excuse me, Mrs. Shaw—"

"Of course," said Jane thankfully and held her breath as he moved down the path away from the cottage. As soon as he had gone she grabbed her book on witchcraft and collapsed weakly into the nearest chair.

"A waxen image of the victim is made," she read from the passage on imitative magic, "usually incorporating either hairs or nail clippings from the victim's body. The image of the face should be as good a likeness as possible, and across the breast of the image the victim's name should be inscribed. A pin or wooden splinter is then inserted into that part of the anatomy where pain is desired; a black candle should be burned if possible and the one who casts the spell must focus all his hatred upon the intended victim. The effect of the insertion of the pin or splinter can range from sudden death (a clean piercing of the pectoral area around the heart) to a mild headache (a slight prick in the skull). Slow death may be achieved by dissolving the image over a flame. When reversing a spell by removing the splinter, great care must be taken or the spell may rebound on the one who cast it and fell him in exactly the same manner as the victim. One authority recommends that in these circumstances the magician should wear an iron cross and chant the Sator formula as he removes the splinter . . ."

Jane closed the book and stood up. She was certain now that somewhere at Colwyn Court was an image of Evan with a splinter embedded in its skull, and if Evan were to recover consciousness someone would first have to find the splinter and remove it. Taking a deep breath she left the cottage and began to walk as quickly as she could along the path to Colwyn Court.

## iii

In Colwyn village Benedict stopped the car and firmly removed the gold cross which Jane had draped around his neck. Superstition was all very well for gullible women, he thought crossly, but he had no intention of turning up at Milford Haven looking like a Christmas tree.

Before he started the engine again he paused and frowned. There was something Jane had told him to do before he embarked on his journey but he could not remember what it was. He stared in annoyance at the dashboard. What was it? He had a feeling it was something very obvious, but the memory still eluded him. When he turned the ignition key the needle of the gas gauge hovered near the "E" to indicate the tank was almost empty, but although Benedict noted this, some unseen force stopped the knowledge from reaching that part of his brain which enabled him to draw a conclusion from the fact and take appropriate action. Still feeling annoyed that his memory had so unaccountably failed him, he put the car into gear, raised his foot from the clutch, and drove off down the country road towards the west.

## iv

Timothy was still looking for Lucy. He had tried the beach, the castle and the chapel but there had been no sign of her. Finally he decided to try Colwyn Court. Perhaps Lucy had been unable to resist the lure of the pageant and was hiding at the house because she felt too guilty to face him.

Timothy's mouth turned down at the corners. It had been a bad summer. First Uncle Matt having the accident, then—Timothy's thoughts slid off the word "Mum" before his eyes could fill with tears—and now Lucy abandoning him in favor of Mr. Poole. Timothy knew Mr. Poole was no good. He was like the villains in the old-fashioned westerns that were shown on television. One knew they were villains because they always wore black. Black meant evil and Timothy knew, no matter what Lucy might think, that Mr. Poole was just as evil as any villain in a television western.

"I wish Daddy was here," said Timothy aloud to himself as he padded up the path to Colwyn Court. "Please, God, send Daddy home soon. Even if he did get drowned all those years ago, please raise him from the dead like in the Bible and send him home soon. Lucy and I are relying on You. Thank You. Amen."

He waited, listening in case God answered, but the only voice he heard was a voice from the darkest corner of his mind, the corner he always tried not to listen to, saying he would never see his father again.

It had been a bad summer.

When he reached Colwyn Court he slipped into the house through one of the side doors and pattered up to Gwyneth's room, but Gwyneth hadn't seen Lucy either. "Try the society," she suggested. "Maybe they've seen her."

But Timothy didn't trust the society. The society was the Enemy, the Tool of the Villain. Leaving Gwyneth he crept into the west wing and began peeping into each bedroom until a locked door brought him to an excited halt.

"Lucy!" he hissed into the keyhole, but there was no answer.

They've kidnapped her, thought Timothy, enraged, and turning the key which Agnes had left in the lock, he burst into the room.

She was there. She was lying on one half of a double bed and

Nicola was lying beside her. They were both so sound asleep that neither of them stirred when he rushed into the room.

"Lucy!" cried Timothy, and shook her shoulder.

But Lucy, breathing evenly, did not move.

"Lucy, Lucy, wake up, you stupid, silly twit!" Timothy felt frantic. He shook her again. "Lucy, what's the matter with you?"

A hand fell on his shoulder. Strong fingers bit into his flesh and made him yelp with shock as he was swung around to face his captor.

"I had a feeling you were going to make trouble, Tim my friend," said Tristan Poole leisurely. "I can see you and I are going to have to have a little talk together."

## v

Jane was also at Colwyn Court. She was pausing in the drawing room in the main part of the house as she tried to decide where Poole would conduct an experiment in black magic. The kitchen? Too public, surely. One of the bedrooms, perhaps. Or the cellar. Jane hesitated. The cellar would be an ideal place. Plenty of space and darkness and privacy . . .

She slipped off toward the kitchens, and after making sure that there was no one about she darted past the sinks in the scullery and opened the cellar door. Her hands scrabbled for the light switch without success; there was no electric light in the old-fashioned cellar of Colwyn Court. Turning back to the stove, Jane grabbed a box of matches and tiptoed hurriedly down the cellar steps, but although she lit a match as soon as she reached the bottom all she saw on the floor was a row of tall bottles containing homemade wine. She was just surveying them in disappointment when the door clicked shut behind her and the draft blew out the match.

Jane jumped. The darkness was suddenly intense. Fumbling

with the box she struck another match, ran back up the steps to the door, and reached for the handle.

It took her a full ten seconds to realize what had happened. There was no handle on her side of the door. She was trapped.

## vi

"Agnes," said Poole, "if you saw Mrs. Shaw giving her husband a gold cross on a chain, what conclusions would you draw?"

"The worst," said Agnes. "Mrs. Shaw has a lot of feminine intuition."

"She also has a book on witchcraft lying around in her living room. Agnes, I think something should be done about Mrs. Shaw. I'm not worried about the professor. He's not the kind of man who would wear a gold cross to please his wife once he was out of her sight, so I hardly think he constitutes a serious problem. But Mrs. Shaw bothers me. I find myself wondering what she'll be up to next."

"How do you think we should cope with her?"

Poole thought for a moment. "Nothing active," he said at last. "There's been too much of that already. But I think she should be watched. Send someone down to the cottage to keep an eye on her, would you?"

"Very well, Tristan."

They were up at the chapel when the message reached them two hours later. It was afternoon by that time, and they were setting up the long narrow table which was to serve as an altar.

"I watched the cottage for ages," gasped the messenger, "but when there was no sign of life I went inside and—well, she wasn't there. There was no sign of her."

"That's odd," said Agnes. "Where can she have gone?"

"She's probably looking for the twins." Poole decided he

did not want to bother himself with the triviality of Jane's where-abouts when there were other more important matters to attend to. "Never mind, forget her. She's basically harmless anyway and I don't think she'll cause us any trouble."

"True," agreed Agnes, "but I rather wish she was under observation . . . By the way, Tristan, what did you do with the boy? Did you hypnotize him?"

"No, he was a bad subject." Poole shrugged. "You find that happens sometimes with children. Their hostility is uncomplicated by adult guilt feelings and raises a powerful barrier against any attempt to control the mind . . . But you needn't worry about the boy. I'll deal with him later. At the moment he's under lock and key and not in a position to give us any trouble."

"But supposing Mrs. Shaw searches the west wing? If the boy's wide awake and waiting to be rescued they'll easily make contact with one another, and then there'd be trouble! Let me put someone on duty in the west wing, Tristan, just to keep an eye out for Mrs. Shaw."

"Whatever you think best," said Poole abruptly, and returned to the absorbing task of erecting the inverted crucifix behind the black altar.

*vii*

They came down to the cellar to fetch the wine at seven o'clock that evening.

Jane hid behind a packing case in one corner of the huge underground room and watched. Presently she realized that the two women who had been assigned to move the wine were working to a pattern; they would take four bottles at a time up the steps and would disappear for two minutes before returning. After they had disappeared for the third time, Jane dashed up the steps, raced through the wedged-open cellar door, and just had time to squeeze behind the door of the scullery to hide from the two women as they returned for the last of the wine.

Once they were back in the cellar Jane slipped outside and took refuge in the nearby woodshed. She felt dirty and sticky and close to tears. It took her some minutes to reestablish her self-control, but at last she glanced at her watch and tried to decide what she should do. It was evening. Sunset was less than two hours away, and with luck Benedict should have seen the Chief Constable and organized the police raid. Jane's first instinct was to rush home to the cottage to rejoin the twins who she felt sure were anxiously awaiting her, but then she thought of Nicola. Supposing Benedict had by some terrible chance been unsuccessful. Evan was no doubt still unconscious in the hospital, so if Benedict's expedition had gone awry there was no one but Jane herself to help Nicola once darkness fell.

She glanced at her watch again. She could dash back to the cottage to see the twins, but time was short and she knew she had to find a good hiding place in the ruins before everyone arrived for the start of the ceremonies. She reassured herself anxiously that the twins were sensible; when they found that both she and Benedict were missing they would walk up to the main house and Walter would look after them.

Stumbling out of the woodshed Jane began to hurry uphill to the chapel on the cliffs.

*viii*

Timothy was watching from the window of Poole's bedroom where he was locked up. The sun was setting and the party on the lawn seemed to be drifting toward an expectant silence, a mass tension Timothy found hard to understand. He had glimpsed parties given by his mother and stepfather, but these parties had usually become noisier, not quieter, as the evening progressed.

This was an odd party, he could tell that just by looking at the guests. They all wore black. The younger women wore cocktail dresses, the older women were more conventionally dressed in less sophisticated outfits, and the men wore dark suits. Counting heads to pass the time Timothy decided there were fifty-two people present in addition to the members of the society and that the majority of them by a narrow margin were women.

As he watched he saw the members of the society detach themselves from their friends and file back through the French windows into the house. It was then that he realized that Poole was nowhere to be seen. Timothy was just wondering where his archenemy was when Agnes emerged again onto the terrace and walked across the lawn to make an announcement.

All conversation instantly stopped.

As Agnes turned aside the guests formed four groups of thirteen and waited in silence, their gaze riveted hungrily on the house. Timothy craned his neck to see what they were staring at but could see nothing. He was just wondering if he could open the window and lean out for a better view when the members of the society walked out of the house two by two to join their friends on the lawn.

Poole was behind them.

He wore a long red robe with a red-horned miter and did not look like the Poole Timothy remembered at all but like some presence from another age when men lived in daily fear of heaven and hell and the world was racked by plague, famine, and war. By Poole's side walked Nicola, very erect, very beautiful in a flowing black gown. She was smiling radiantly. And behind Nicola walked Lucy, an angel in scarlet, her fair hair streaming down her back and her eyes wide with innocence.

"Lucy!" yelled Timothy, and beat his fists on the pane. No one heard him. Using all his strength he heaved up the window and leaned over the sill.

"Lucy!" he shouted at the top of his voice.

But no one heard him, least of all Lucy. He shouted again and again but it was as if there were a soundproofed screen between him and the group on the lawn for no one even glanced in his direction. At last when they had all disappeared from sight behind the rose garden he leaped onto the window seat in frustration and wondered if he could jump to the ground below.

But it was too far. He looked down, quailed, and withdrew. However, he noticed that the ledge outside the window was broad, broad enough for him to sit on, and he could see that the window of the locked dressing room next door was open an inch.

Maybe there's a way out into the corridor through the room next door, thought Timothy.

Ten seconds later he was sitting outside on the ledge, his legs dangling over the long drop, and trying not to feel sick. It was surprising how rapidly the broad ledge had dwindled into a narrow parapet.

Timothy shivered, squeezed his eyes shut and began to edge sideways toward the dressing room window. But when he arrived safely he was faced by the problem of heaving up the window far enough to enable him to crawl into the room, and it took him a long time to work himself into a position where he could tug at the window frame without fear of overbalancing. The window was stiff. He was just despairing of ever being able to move it when it shot upward and he was scrambling thankfully onto safer ground—only to discover with a sinking heart that there was no door offering him an easy escape into the corridor.

Timothy shed several tears of acute disappointment and even allowed himself the infantile gesture of stamping his foot. But presently he felt ashamed of this lapse of courage, wiped his eyes with the back of his hand, and began to survey his new surroundings.

The first thing he saw was the cardboard box on the table by the locked door.

Inside he found plasticine, a substance he had played with for hours as a toddler. He had made cars with it, he remembered, and Lucy had made dolls. Occasionally she had stamped on his cars and he had revenged himself by twisting the dolls out of shape until they looked like freaks.

Fancy Mr. Poole playing with plasticine at his age, thought Timothy.

He poked around inside the box again and picked up a small object wrapped in tissue paper. Once the paper was discarded he found himself holding a cleverly made doll about nine inches long, a doll with red hair and a loin cloth which might once have been part of a man's handkerchief, a doll with EVAN COLWYN inscribed across the chest and a slim splinter of wood inserted into the skull at an odd angle.

Timothy stared. Stories began to flicker across his memory, folklore handed down from one generation of schoolboys to another since time out of mind. This was how you won a fight with the school bully even though he was much bigger than you were. You stole a candle from the school pantry, melted it, molded it into the bully's image, pricked it in the groin with a pin, muttered "I hate you" three times, prayed for victory, and then buried the image in the kitchen garden after lights-out. The bully would lose all his strength and flunk the fight. Timothy had never tried the experiment himself but everyone at school was positive that it worked. His own best friend had had no doubts at all on the subject.

Timothy stared down at the little red-haired doll in his hands, and then using his thumb and forefinger he removed the splinter, set it down on the table and rewrapped the doll carefully in its tissue paper.

## *ix*

Jane was hiding in the chapel ruins and watching in mounting horror as the groups assembled for the rites. As soon as she had seen Lucy behind Nicola she had almost fainted; the world had tilted dizzily and she had been gripped by the urge to scream, but she had neither fainted nor cried out. She knew too well that if she interrupted the group before the rites had begun the police would fail to catch the participants in the midst of their obscenities and all Evan's plans would be ruined.

Jane tightened her grip on her self-control, fought her panic, and began to pray for help without even realizing that she was praying.

The next moment she felt better. Harriet Miller was leading Nicola and Lucy away to wait in the castle ruins until the appropriate part of the ceremony arrived, so for the time being at least they were both safe. Abandoning her frightened prayers Jane peered through the gap in the wall in front of her and watched as Poole walked to the altar and motioned Agnes to bring him a brand from the brazier which was already burning in the center of the chapel.

The six black candles surrounding the altar were lit; Jane had a clearer view of the inverted crucifix behind the altar and of the tapestry which had been hung on the wall behind the cross. The tapestry was woven in black and scarlet and showed a goat trampling on a crucifix. In front of the altar was a square black box eighteen inches high, and as Jane watched, Poole stepped in front of it and turned to face the assembled men and women awaiting him.

"Dearly beloved brethren," she heard him say in his dark, quiet voice. "You are gathered together today in Our Presence to celebrate the great festival of Lammas, to worship, to honor, and to obey those Powers of Darkness which have existed since the beginning of time and which will exist until the end of time, through the Grace of Beelzebuth, Astaroth, Adramelek, Baal, Lucifer, Chamos, Melchom, Behemoth, Dagon, Asmodeus, and all other Lords of Darkness in the Hierarchy of Hell—"

The sun had sunk into an opaque sea. The sky was a deep darkening blue shot with the aftermath of sunset, and far away the surf crashed in a burst of boiling foam at the foot of the black cliffs. It was eerily quiet.

"—and lastly," said the figure in the red robes in his measured voice, "through My Grace, which will be bestowed always among my Chosen, World Without End—"

"Hail Satan!" said sixty-four voices in unison. The expressions on the faces of the congregation were as united as their voices. The worshipers had an intense, yearning look, their lips parted as if they were waiting for some magic drink which would slake an unbearable thirst.

"My friends," said Poole, "I come to you as the One God, the administrator of great sins and greater vices, cordial of the vanquished, suzerain of resentment, treasurer of old hatreds, king of the disinherited—"

"Hail Satan!"

"—and I offer each one of you now the chance to demonstrate your loyalty by participating in the act of homage . . . My friends, let us begin our sacred rites in celebration of this sacred day."

The congregation forsook their enrapt immobility and began to strip off their clothes. They moved with quiet speed, the men leaving their clothes on one side of the chapel, the women leaving their clothes on the other, and when they were naked they mingled again and re-formed in front of the altar.

Jane, who was not prudish but thought that human beings usually looked better with clothes than without them, found herself riveted to the spot with an appalled fascination. But even before she could ask herself incredulously how the elderly, the obese, and the ugly could reveal themselves in such a way without a qualm, her attention was caught by Poole. He was tearing off his red robes, hurling them aside, and she saw that around his waist was a thin belt from which a plaited tail of animal hair swung toward the ground.

"Let the ceremony of homage begin!" he shouted, and as Jane watched he sprang onto the black box before the altar and turned his tanned back to the congregation.

Jane began to feel dizzy again. The most horrifying part of all, she realized, was that in spite of her revulsion she found herself unwillingly excited by Poole's strong supple body.

Agnes was the first to pay homage. Phrases from the book on witchcraft tumbled through Jane's mind and she felt the color rush to her face as she recalled her own voice reading about the obscene kiss of a millennium of witches' sabbaths.

"Master," said Agnes in a clear passionate voice, "I promise to love, worship, honor, and obey you, now and forever more."

The rest of the Colwyn Court coven followed her one by one. After that came the turn of each member of the four other covens.

The ceremony lasted some time.

At last when the final act of homage had been paid, Poole turned to face the congregation again and raised his hands toward the stars.

"My blessing be upon you all."

"Hail Satan!"

"May you all prosper."

"Hail Satan!"

"May you work tirelessly in my name."

"Hail Satan!"

"May all power be upon you now and forevermore."

"Hail Satan!"

Poole let his hands fall slowly to his sides. "My friends, let us prepare ourselves for one of our most sublime moments of spiritual communication. I call upon my chief acolyte here tonight to give a brief introduction to the ceremonies."

A light wind blew in from the sea and cooled the sweat on Jane's forehead. As she shivered from head to toe she saw Agnes Miller step forward to the altar to make an announcement to her colleagues.

"Beloved friends," Jane heard her say in a voice which vibrated with emotion, "in a moment the bride will be brought into the chapel for the wedding, and after the wedding will come the traditional offering to the Powers, a young virgin who will receive the Master's Mark and be admitted to Our Church and grow up, we trust, to become one of the Master's most devoted followers. You may wonder why the bride herself is ineligible for this role. There are three reasons: first she is not a virgin, second her intellect is spiritually barren, and third she can be of no use to the Master in this world since her time in it is to be short. She was chosen for the bridal ceremony for her looks—I think you will agree that she is beautiful—and for the size of her dowry . . . After the Wedding and the Marking will come the Festivities." She paused. "Are we all ready?"

There was a murmur of assent. Everyone's eyes turned toward Poole again.

"My friends," said Poole, "prepare yourselves for the Black Mass."

The congregation sucked in their breath greedily. At a sign from Poole two of the Colwyn Court coven began to feed the brazier with bunches of herbs, and when the smoke was rising from the crackling flames Poole shouted: "Let the bride be brought to the altar!"

The first fumes from the brazier reached Jane. She couldn't make up her mind whether it was the fumes which made her feel so sick or the knowledge that as far as she knew there was no policeman within miles of the chapel. She could feel the panic rise inside her as she tried to decide what she should do.

Nicola was brought into the chapel by Harriet Miller and led slowly to the altar where Poole was waiting. Jane noticed with relief that Lucy was still being kept out of sight.

"Let the sacrifice be brought to me!" cried Poole.

One of the men dragged forward a coal-black lamb and Agnes handed Poole the butcher's knife.

Poole began to speak. So unnerved was Jane by the pervasive fumes from the brazier, Nicola's presence at the altar and the prospect of a bloody slaughter, that it took her several seconds to realize that Poole was speaking in a language she did not understand.

He reached the end of his incantation and leaned forward to grab the lamb's halter. The knife flickered wickedly in the candlelight as the animal made a strangled noise and slumped to the ground in a heap. When Jane had finished being sick she saw that Poole had filled a chalice with the lamb's blood while two members of Agnes' coven were piling pieces of a substance which looked like black bread onto two large platters.

The congregation, stimulated by the fumes from the brazier,

were beginning to sway on their feet; their voices were droning a hypnotic chant which grew louder as the minutes passed and their excitement grew.

Poole did something unprintable to both the contents of the chalice and the plates of black bread. Several females in the congregation screamed in ecstasy.

I've got to act, thought Jane, I've got to stop this.

Agnes was helping Nicola out of her wedding dress and guiding her into her position on the altar. Nicola had a dreamy expression on her face and looked blissfully happy. The chant of the congregation grew louder as they saw Nicola's bare skin gleaming against the black altar cloth.

Jane stood up. Or tried to. To her horror she found that the fumes had affected her sense of balance and that something had gone wrong with her legs. When she tried to walk she fell to her knees, and it was then, as she made vain efforts to struggle to her feet again, that she realized what had happened. She had failed. Benedict had failed. Evan had failed.

And no one was going to come to Nicola's aid.

Poole was saying something, placing the chalice on Nicola's body, moving toward one end of the altar.

God help us, thought Jane, God help us all. Prayers tumbled through her mind, silent pleas to a God to succeed where ordinary men had failed. Please God, stop them. Our Father which art in heaven . . .

At one end of the altar Poole looked down at Nicola and then stooped to run his hands over her thighs.

Several women in the audience screamed again. Black smoke from the brazier was making the light uncertain and the black candles were flickering in the draft.

Hallowed be thy name, prayed Jane, thy kingdom come . . .

Poole stopped.

"Master?" whispered Agnes nervously, seeing the expression in his eyes.

He swung around on her. "There's a heretic among us!" He whirled to face the congregation and flung up his arms for silence. "There's heresy here!"

The chanting died abruptly. A sea of faces stared at him in shocked disbelief.

And then Poole turned his back on them. He turned very slowly until he was facing the place where Jane was hidden.

"She's there," was all he said.

The congregation howled like a pack of wolves and raced to drag Jane from her hiding place but Poole held them in check.

"Let her come to me of her own free will."

Jane found herself able to walk again. She walked to the altar to meet him because she had no power to do anything else, and when she reached him she knelt at his feet.

"Agnes, take this woman to the other side of the castle. Mrs. Shaw, look at me."

Jane looked at him.

"Go where Agnes takes you. Stay there until you're told you can leave."

Jane nodded.

"You'll remember nothing of what you have seen since sunset."

Jane nodded again. Agnes led her away.

The congregation began to chant and sway again, building up the tension afresh as Poole stood by Nicola's inert body and waited for Agnes to return.

She slipped back into the chapel a minute later and rejoined Poole at the altar.

"All's well, Master."

Poole smiled. As Agnes watched he returned to the end of the altar and stooped over Nicola's body.

"In the name of Satan and all the Lords of Darkness—"

A torch blazed from the doorway of the chapel. As everyone shouted in alarm and moved to close the ranks against the intruder, Evan's voice shouted: "In the name of God, STOP!" and the next moment there was an icy draft which blew out all the candles, an enormous thunderclap which shattered the torch in Evan's hand, and finally, a second later, the acrid reek of brimstone.

# Chapter Nine

## *i*

When Evan recovered consciousness some time later he could not at first remember where he was or what had happened. And then it all came back to him in a rush, how he had awoken earlier to find himself in the hospital, how he had discharged himself amid the protests of the staff and dashed outside to hitch a lift from Swansea to Colwyn; he could remember tearing up to the cliffs, bursting into the chapel, staring at the naked bodies illuminated by black candles, the glint of the chalice, Poole moving to possess Nicola's body on the black altar . . .

"In the name of God, STOP!" yelled Evan, reenacting the scene in confusion, and sat up with a start.

He was alone. It was pitch dark and a soft sea wind was moaning through the ruined walls of the deserted chapel.

After a moment he hauled himself shakily to his feet and stumbled through the chapel to the altar. His foot knocked against a small rattling object. Stooping he found an abandoned box of matches, and after striking a light he was able to see that the altar cloth, the desecrated crucifix, and the tapestry were all gone and that the only signs left to hint at what had taken place that evening were the table which had served as an altar and the pool of lamb's blood on the floor. But the lamb's corpse was gone and so was Nicola's inert body. Shaking out the match, Evan left the chapel and stumbled down the hillside to Colwyn Court.

Agnes was waiting for him. As he opened the back door he saw her sitting at the kitchen table, her face expressionless, her hands clasped in front of her as if in prayer.

She was alone.

"Where's Nicola?" demanded Evan roughly, and his voice was unsteady. "Where is she?"

"In her room asleep. You don't have to worry about her any more. She'll wake up tomorrow with no memory of the last thirty-six hours and an imperfect memory of the last month. I think you'll find her condition satisfactory." Agnes stood up. "Dr. Colwyn, I want to negotiate with you about what happened this evening and I'd be grateful if you would spare a few minutes to talk to me."

Evan stared at her blankly. "There's nothing to negotiate, Miss Miller. Where's Poole?"

There was a silence. He was just noticing that her eyes were red-rimmed from crying when she said in a flat voice, "He's dead."

"I don't believe it," said Evan. "Show me his body."

Agnes stood up without a word and led the way upstairs to Poole's room. "You won't recognize him," was all she said.

"Why not?"

"You'll see."

Poole was laid out on his bed, his body clad in pajamas. Evan walked up to him and looked down at the face he had hated so violently.

He saw a mild, easy-going man with a mouth capable of a cheerful smile and features which in life might have reflected a good-natured intelligence. The eyes were closed so that their secret was hidden forever, but Evan thought he could glimpse the recklessness in them which had led the man to the Lammas rites in the California orange grove where he had offered his body for his Master's use.

"You're right," said Evan to Agnes. "I don't recognize him."

"He will rise again," said Agnes, and with a shock he realized she was speaking not of Poole, but of her Master. "He will be reborn in someone else. The history of Tristan Poole is at an end. But the history of some other unknown man is just beginning." She turned to face Evan again. "I must talk to you, Dr. Colwyn."

"I'll see Nicola first," said Evan, checking Poole's pulse as a matter of routine before he left the room.

Nicola was sound asleep in her tiny bedroom in the main part of the house. He took her pulse, felt her forehead, and lifted an eyelid.

"She's drugged."

"She'll be all right tomorrow," said Agnes. "That's a promise, Dr. Colwyn. Unless you make trouble for us with the police, of course."

There was a pause.

"All right," said Evan abruptly. "Let's talk."

They returned to the kitchen and sat down facing each other across the table. "What are your terms?" said Evan at last.

"We'll tear up the lease, leave Colwyn Court, and never come near you again. Nicola will be completely cured of her infatuation for Tristan—his power over her will have ceased at his death—and she'll only have a blurred memory of the affair. Your father and sister will recover quickly enough from the drugged sleep induced several hours ago to keep them out of the way, and you'll find Tristan's influence over your sister will also be a thing of the past. The twins and Mrs. Shaw are asleep at the cottage. Much as she may want to help you I think you'll find Mrs. Shaw a most inadequate witness. Lucy won't remember anything of the ceremony either but you can rest assured she was quite unharmed. As for Timothy—" She bit her lip. "I could murder that child very easily," she said at last in a brisk voice, "but fortunately for those that depend on me I think commonsense will prevail and I shall

leave him alone. He won't be any use to you as a witness either—
he was locked up at Colwyn Court during the ceremony."

"In other words," said Evan, "what you're saying to me is this:
we'll leave you alone with everyone intact if you leave us alone
by fending off any inquiries from the police. However, if you *are*
so foolish as to complain to the police you'll find yourself with no
witnesses and no evidence which could not be explained away as
the aftermath of some wild, but not necessarily criminally obscene party. Am I right?"

"Exactly," said Agnes. "But I would prefer you not to complain
to the police. You're a doctor, a man of standing, and your word
would carry a certain weight behind it. That's why I'm prepared
to concede so much to avoid any trouble."

"When will you leave Colwyn Court?"

"Could you give us forty-eight hours? I think we could manage that."

"I wouldn't let you go before then. I want to make sure everyone makes a complete recovery."

"They will," said Agnes.

There was a silence.

"Very well," said Evan finally. "I agree to your terms. I'll say
nothing and you'll fulfill your promises."

"Thank you, Dr. Colwyn," said Agnes.

"All right. Now tell me something. You know, of course, that
I lost consciousness this morning and was taken to the hospital. I
suppose you claim credit for that."

"Naturally."

"Do you also claim credit for my dazzling recovery?"

"No, you can thank Timothy for that. The wretched child dis-
mantled the spell so recklessly that it rebounded on Sandra who
initiated it, and two of the girls are working hard this very minute
to try to bring her back to consciousness. She fainted during the
homage ceremony."

"I'm not sure I understand. Do you mean—"

"Oh, look it up in Jane Shaw's witchcraft book," said Agnes irritably. "Why should I bother to explain it to you?"

After a moment Evan said slowly: "Do you claim many other such . . . successes?"

Agnes shrugged. "We were responsible for Lisa's death, of course, and Matthew Morrison's. It's remarkable what the powers can do for you when properly applied. But then of course with the Master all things are possible."

"Except the ability to survive when someone yells 'In the name of God, stop!' " said Evan dryly.

"My dear young man," said Agnes, "you don't really think that was what killed Tristan, do you?"

"But then what the hell did kill him?"

"Well, I suppose to be strictly accurate, your invocation did help," admitted Agnes grudgingly. "You destroyed the powers inherent in our assembly and hurled an enormous counterforce at us. It was both very frightening and very overwhelming. I think we all lost consciousness for at least a minute."

"I remember a loud bang—"

"Did the noise surprise you? Your gesture had the same effect as someone who fires a cannonball through a glass window into a china shop. No wonder the result was audible!"

"But what killed Poole?"

"It was only the body that was killed," said Agnes. "Only his fragile mortality was destroyed. That was all."

"But—"

"Dr. Colwyn, you are by no means a believer in my Church although I admit that for a skeptic you're showing an unusual ability to accept the unacceptable. Don't ask too many questions. I've suffered a dreadful shock tonight and an appalling reverse of all my hopes for the future, and frankly I don't want to discuss this further with you. All I'll say in response to your question is that witchcraft can be fought by witchcraft. It's a dangerous thing to do and it can have lethal results. Now if you'll excuse me . . . was that the front doorbell?"

"Yes, it was. Who on earth can that be?"

"Oh, that must be Professor Shaw and the police at last," said Agnes wearily. "Tristan had impaired Professor Shaw's memory

but as soon as Tristan died no doubt Professor Shaw made a miraculous recovery from his partial amnesia . . . Could you cope
with them, please? I'm very tired and I want to be alone. I
couldn't face seeing any more people tonight."

"Very well," said Evan, thinking how strange it was that she
should look just like a middle-aged housewife suffering from over-
work. He even felt a pang of compassion for her. "I'll deal with
them. Good night, Miss Miller."

"Good night, Dr. Colwyn," said Agnes, and added, annihilat-
ing his compassion with a cold measured contempt: "Oh, Dr. Colwyn, make sure you hold to our agreement, won't you? Because
if you don't, I'll certainly kill your sister. Even without Tristan
that would be well within my powers."

The doorbell rang far away as Evan stood looking at her. Her
green eyes were as inhuman as a cat's. Her plump comfortable
frame was heavy with menace, and her mouth was thin and hard
as she stared back at him.

"The agreement stands," Evan heard himself say at last. "Good-
bye, Miss Miller." And turning abruptly he walked away from her
toward the hall, the front door and the police.

*ii*

"So there we were," said Benedict to Jane the next morning.
"I've never felt so foolish in all my life. There was Evan, fit as a
fiddle, saying there'd been a party on the cliffs but it was all over
and everyone was all right. The police poked around up there and
found nothing except for some peculiar marks on the ground in
the castle which might have been made by a child. Naturally when
they heard that the twins liked to play there they assumed—my
dear, what's the matter? You surely can't blame me for being
cross! All that mumbo jumbo about witchcraft! I knew it was a
false alarm."

"But Benedict darling," said Jane, "what happened to you? Why did you take such a long time to fetch the police? What happened on the way to Milford Haven?"

"Well, it was the most extraordinary thing," said Benedict, polishing his spectacles. "I ran out of gas on a wild road miles from anywhere—"

"Benedict, you took off my gold cross, didn't you?"

"—and then I didn't feel well and decided to have a nap, but after that it took hours to get a lift to the nearest gas station and when I got there I couldn't remember where I'd left the car—"

"Poor darling," said Jane, forgiving him because he looked so guilty and bemused. "Never mind. Everything worked out satisfactorily in the end. I've just been speaking to Evan and he says that the society are leaving Colwyn Court tomorrow because Mr. Poole died suddenly last night, so—"

"Good God!" exclaimed Benedict. "A healthy young fellow like that? What was the cause of death?"

"Evan called in the local doctor and they agreed it was a cardiac arrest."

"Well, I'll be damned," said Benedict, astonished, and was silent. Then: "What did happen in the chapel—if anything?" he inquired sardonically. "What were you doing while this orgy of yours was supposed to be going on?"

"You wouldn't even begin to believe me," said Jane and added regretfully: "Besides I don't remember much about it."

"Why not?"

"Oh . . . I think amnesia must be catching at the moment. Everyone seems to be suffering from it except Timothy and Evan . . ."

Outside the kitchen door Marble was roused from sleep by the sound of their voices and opened one cautious pink eye. Finding himself alone in a patch of sunlight he opened the other eye, unsheathed his claws, and stretched himself luxuriously. It was a long time since he had had the energy to give himself such a luxurious stretch, but for a long time he had felt as if an enormous weight had been strapped to his back. But now the weight was gone. Marble, whose brain was small and memory smaller, did not question the cause of his past malaise or link it with people already half-forgotten, but merely sat up, washed his paws and began to think of his stomach. He found he was exceedingly hungry. Jumping up, he bounded into the kitchen, rubbed himself with a cunning display of affection against Jane's ankles, and began to mew for her undivided attention.

"Marble's looking better today," Benedict commented. "In fact he's looking more like his old self again."

"That's because Tristan's dead."

"My dear, whatever will you think of next!"

Jane laughed. "All right, shall we forget last night and the society and Tristan Poole for a moment? There's something I've been worrying about for ages and I do so want to discuss it with you."

"By all means," said Benedict thankfully, "let's forget the fiasco of last night with all its attendant little mysteries. What is it that's worrying you?"

"Well, darling, it's the twins. You see, Lisa left no will and so they don't have an official guardian and I know they're feeling terribly lost and alone now that both Lisa and Matt are dead, and . . . oh, I'm so worried about what's going to happen to them! Do you think . . . perhaps . . . possibly—"

"Of course," said Benedict. "An excellent idea."

"I know our house in Cambridge will be much too small, but—"

"Well, I was getting tired of it anyway," said Benedict. "It would be nice to have a bigger house and I think we could afford it without too much scrimping and saving. I'll tell you what we'll do. As soon as we get home you can start house-hunting and I'll see our solicitor to find out how we can set about getting a court order of legal guardianship—if the twins are agreeable, of course! You're sure they approve of the idea?"

"I think they've already taken it for granted," said Jane, and smiled at him brilliantly through her tears.

*iii*

"The most peculiar thing of all," said Lucy that same morning as she and Timothy sat on the beach and watched the incoming tide, "is that I can't even remember what Tristan looked like exactly. I just remember thinking he was like Daddy."

"He wasn't a bit like Daddy!"

"Oh, let's face it, Timmy," said Lucy crossly, "we can't even remember what Daddy looked like anyway. If it wasn't for those photos of Mummy's we wouldn't know him from Adam. We'll never really know now what he was like."

"We might," said Timothy. "He might still come home."

"We don't truly believe that," said Lucy. "Not truly. That was just imagining."

Timothy swallowed and was silent.

"Well, it's all very sad, of course," said Lucy, "but it could be worse. You know what Cook always says back at home. 'Look on the bright side, dears, and count your blessings.'"

"I don't see how things could be worse," said Timothy mulishly.

"Don't be dim, Timmy. Supposing there was no Aunt Jane?" Lucy yawned and drew a pentagram on the sand with her toe. "Do you know what that is?" she said, gesturing toward the pattern. "It's an evil sign. At least it can be a good sign, but when it only stands on one point and has two points sticking upward it represents evil. Gwyneth told me. She heard it from Tristan."

Timothy swept the pentagram into oblivion with a circular motion of his heel. "I want to bury all that evil and forget about it. Let's hold the funeral and stop messing around."

"All right," Lucy agreed. "After all, that was why we came down to the beach, wasn't it? I'd almost forgotten."

"Here's your spade," said Timothy, feeling better. "Let's begin."

They began to dig a deep rectangular hole in the sand. "Phew!" gasped Lucy ten minutes later. "That's deep enough, isn't it?"

"I think so." Timothy opened the cardboard box which they had brought down to the beach and carefully lifted out a plasticine figure of a man. The image had the letters T. POOLE inscribed across his chest and was clad in a piece of material which Timothy had cut from one of the suits in the cupboard of Poole's dressing room. The wooden splinter which had once pierced the skull of Evan's image was driven through the left breast where the heart would have been.

"I still don't know how you thought of it," said Lucy admiringly. "How did you know what to do?"

"You poor thing," said Timothy pityingly. "Don't they teach you anything at that stupid girl's school of yours?"

Lucy for once was humbled. "What did you do exactly? Was it hard once you'd made the plasticine figure?"

"'Course not," said Timothy. "I got the splinter and said: 'Please God, arrange for Tristan Poole to be killed because he's wicked and evil and I don't think You'd like him if You met him.' Then I gave God a choice—just in case He thought Mr. Poole was okay after all and didn't want to kill him. I said: 'But if You want to save him that's okay by me because I know You'll have a good reason. Thank You. Amen.' And then I stuck the splinter through the heart and left it up to God. It seemed a pretty fair way of doing things."

"But does that mean God killed Tristan? I didn't think God ever murdered anyone."

"Maybe God borrowed an evil spirit from hell," said Timothy comfortably. "He must have some arrangement for those sort of circumstances."

"So evil killed evil," said Lucy satisfied. "That's nice." She glanced at Poole's image. "Shall we begin?"

"Okay." They laid the image gently in the deep hole in the sand and looked at it for a moment.

"Rest in peace," said Timothy, not sure what was said at a funeral service.

"Now and forevermore, Amen," said Lucy obligingly. She glanced at Timothy. "Will that do, do you think?"

"I expect so."

They shoveled the sand back over the image and stamped on it.

"Well, that's that," said Timothy satisfied. "What shall we do next?"

"Let's go back to the cottage," said Lucy. "Wasn't Aunt Jane going to make fudge again this morning?"

"Aunt Jane's a wonderful cook!"

"The best," said Lucy, and they smiled at one another in satisfaction as they walked off hand in hand over the beach.

*iv*

"How are you feeling?" said Evan to Nicola, sitting down on the edge of her bed and reaching tenderly for her pulse.

"Very weird," said Nicola frankly. "Did I go mad or something?"

"Or something," said Evan. Her pulse seemed normal. He produced a thermometer. "Let me take your temperature."

"Did I have a nervous breakdown?" said Nicola before putting the thermometer in her mouth.

"Let's call it a nervous suspension from reality."

Nicola took the thermometer out of her mouth again.

"What's the date today?" she demanded.

"August the second."

"It can't be!"

"Don't let it bother you. I'll explain everything later."

"Have I been in a mental home?"

"No, you've been walking around here and giving a rather distorted semblance of normality. Don't let it worry you, Nicki. It was all entirely natural in the circumstances."

"Was I drugged? Those colors . . . dreams . . . illusions . . . or were they illusions? My God, perhaps they were reality!"

"You were probably drugged some of the time."

"And the rest of the time?"

"Poole had you hypnotized."

"Evan—" Nicola broke off.

"Yes?"

"Did I dream it or did I really—" She stopped again.

"You did," said Evan, "and yet in a sense you didn't. You weren't responsible for your actions."

"Oh Evan, how could I!" cried Nicola, and burst into a flood of tears. After he had managed to calm her she said, distracted: "What can you think of me! Why are you being so nice to me? How can you even bear to talk to me after what I did to you?"

"It served me right for playing around with you for all those months," said Evan. "Don't feel too sorry for me. And as for why I'm acting as if nothing happened, I repeat—you weren't responsible for your actions . . . Nicki, what's the last thing you remember with any real degree of clarity?"

Nicola gulped. "You. Proposing to me. And me wondering why on earth I couldn't bring myself to say yes."

"All right," said Evan, "let's pick up where we left off. Nicki, will you marry me?"

Nicola gulped again. "Evan, you must be the most wonderful man in the whole world and I just don't deserve—"

"Spare me the martyred self-pity. Do you love me?"

"More than anyone else on earth, but—"

"Then you'll marry me?"

"Right now this very minute if I could," said Nicola without hesitation, and saw his taut frame relax in relief as she smiled radiantly into his eyes.